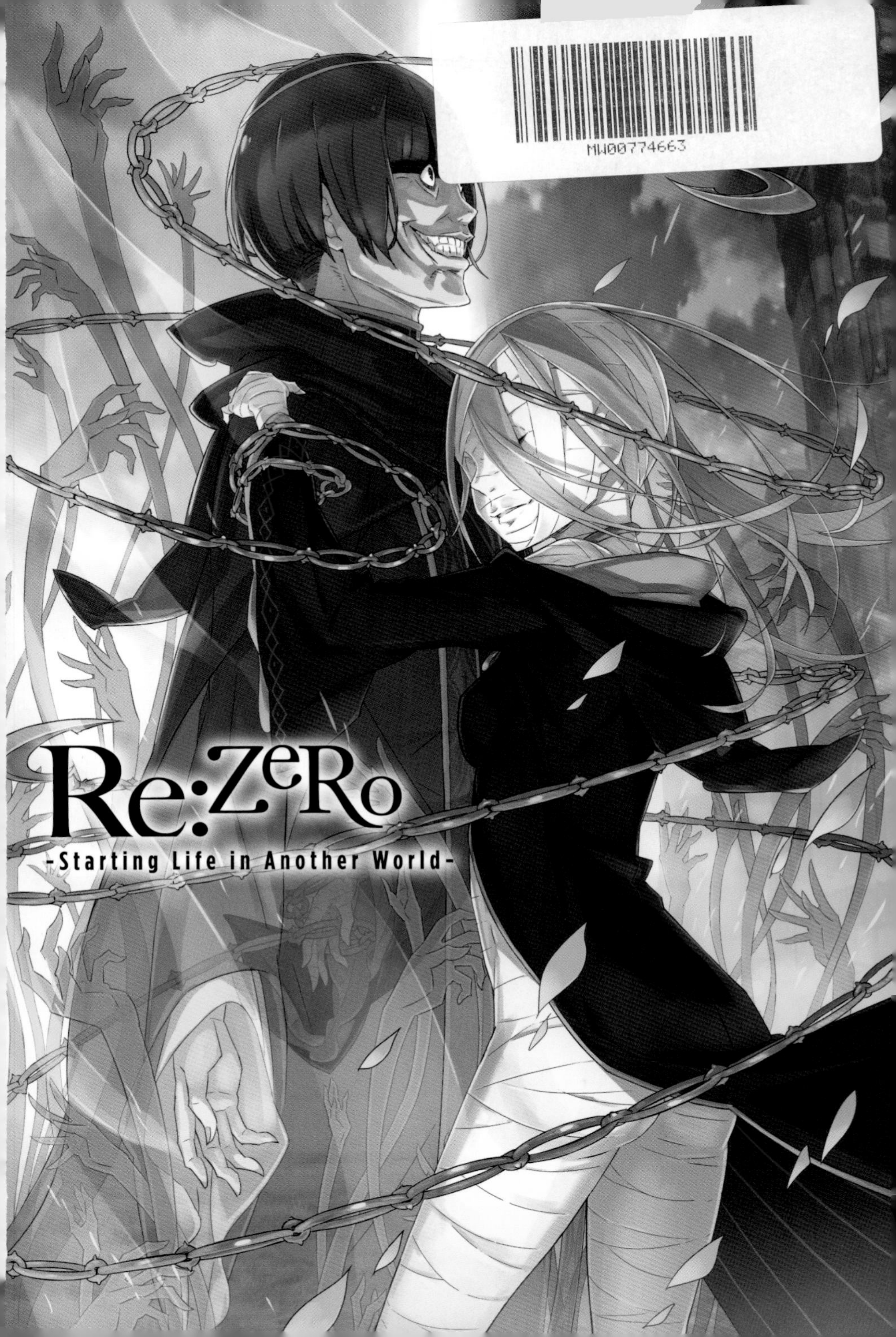

MW00774663
Re:ZeRo
-Starting Life in Another World-

Characters

Re:ZERO -Starting Life in Another World-

The only ability Subaru Natsuki gets when he's summoned to another world is time travel via his own death. But to save her, he'll die as many times as it takes.

The Songstress. Minstrel by trade and an old friend of Subaru and company.

Joshua

Julius's younger brother. Greatly adores his older brother.

Heinkel
Reinhard's father and Wilhelm's son. Vice-captain of the Kingdom of Lugunica's Knights of the Royal Guard.
Sirius
An eccentric whose entire body is bandaged and chained.

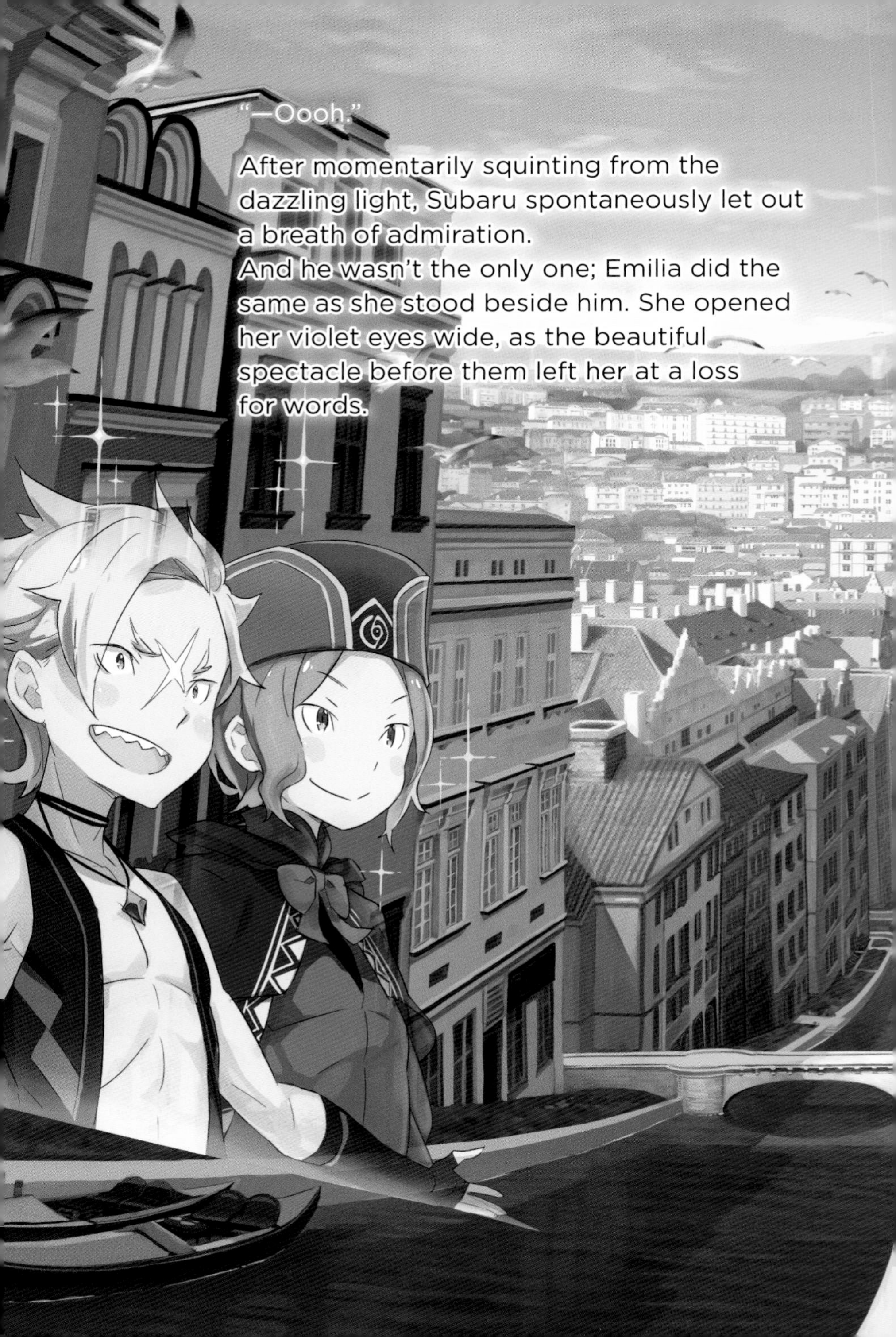
"—Oooh."
After momentarily squinting from the dazzling light, Subaru spontaneously let out a breath of admiration.
And he wasn't the only one; Emilia did the same as she stood beside him. She opened her violet eyes wide, as the beautiful spectacle before them left her at a loss for words.

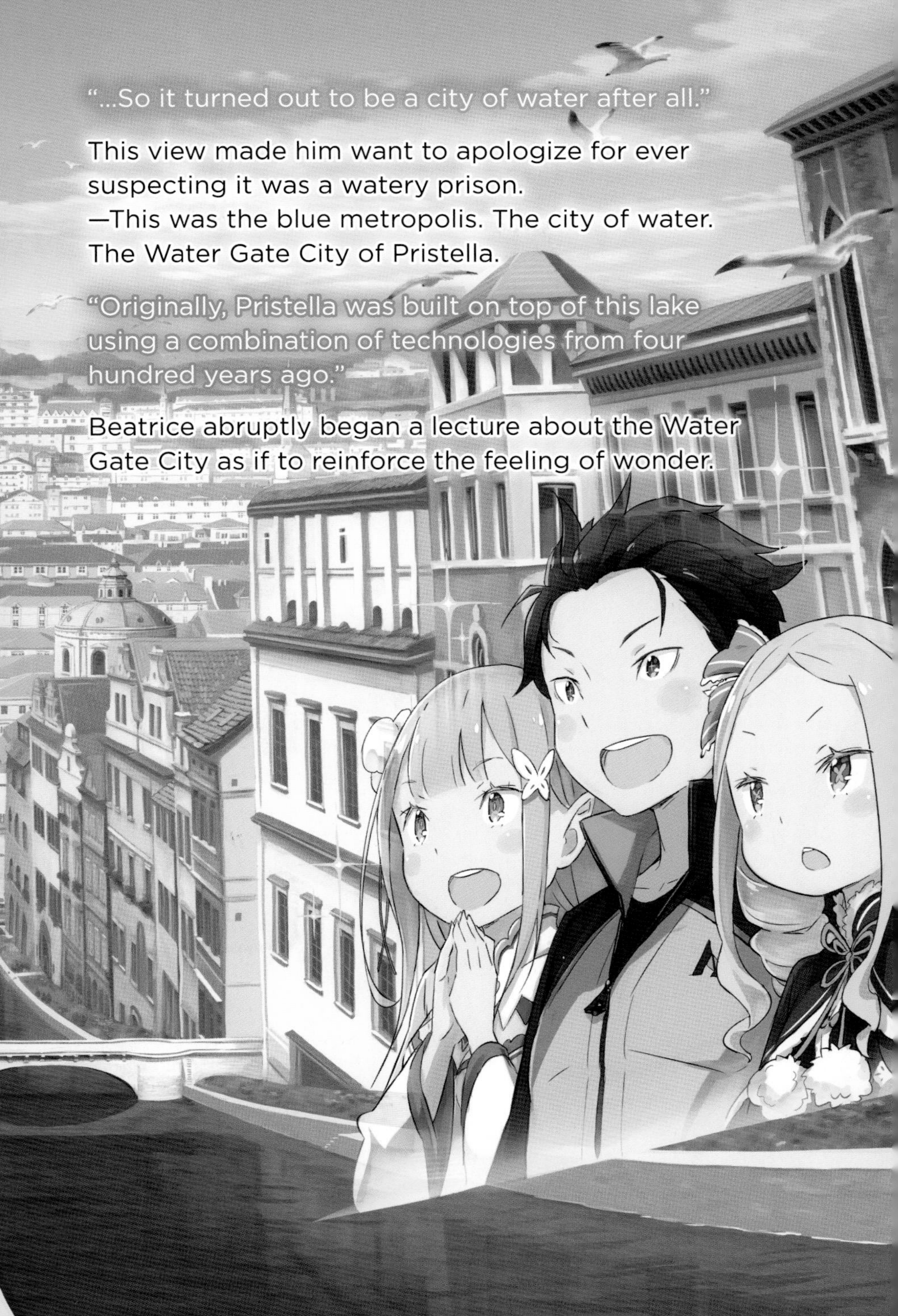
"...So it turned out to be a city of water after all."
This view made him want to apologize for ever suspecting it was a watery prison.
—This was the blue metropolis. The city of water. The Water Gate City of Pristella.
"Originally, Pristella was built on top of this lake using a combination of technologies from four hundred years ago."
Beatrice abruptly began a lecture about the Water Gate City as if to reinforce the feeling of wonder.

"—To all those whose conversations and busy schedules I've interrupted, I offer my apologies."
Near the top of the time tower, a lone figure emerged from an open window to stand precariously on the edge.
"Please lend me but a tiny instant of your time. Thank you."
—This person's head was covered in raggedly wrapped bandages that left one eye visible, gleaming mysteriously as it surveyed the world below.

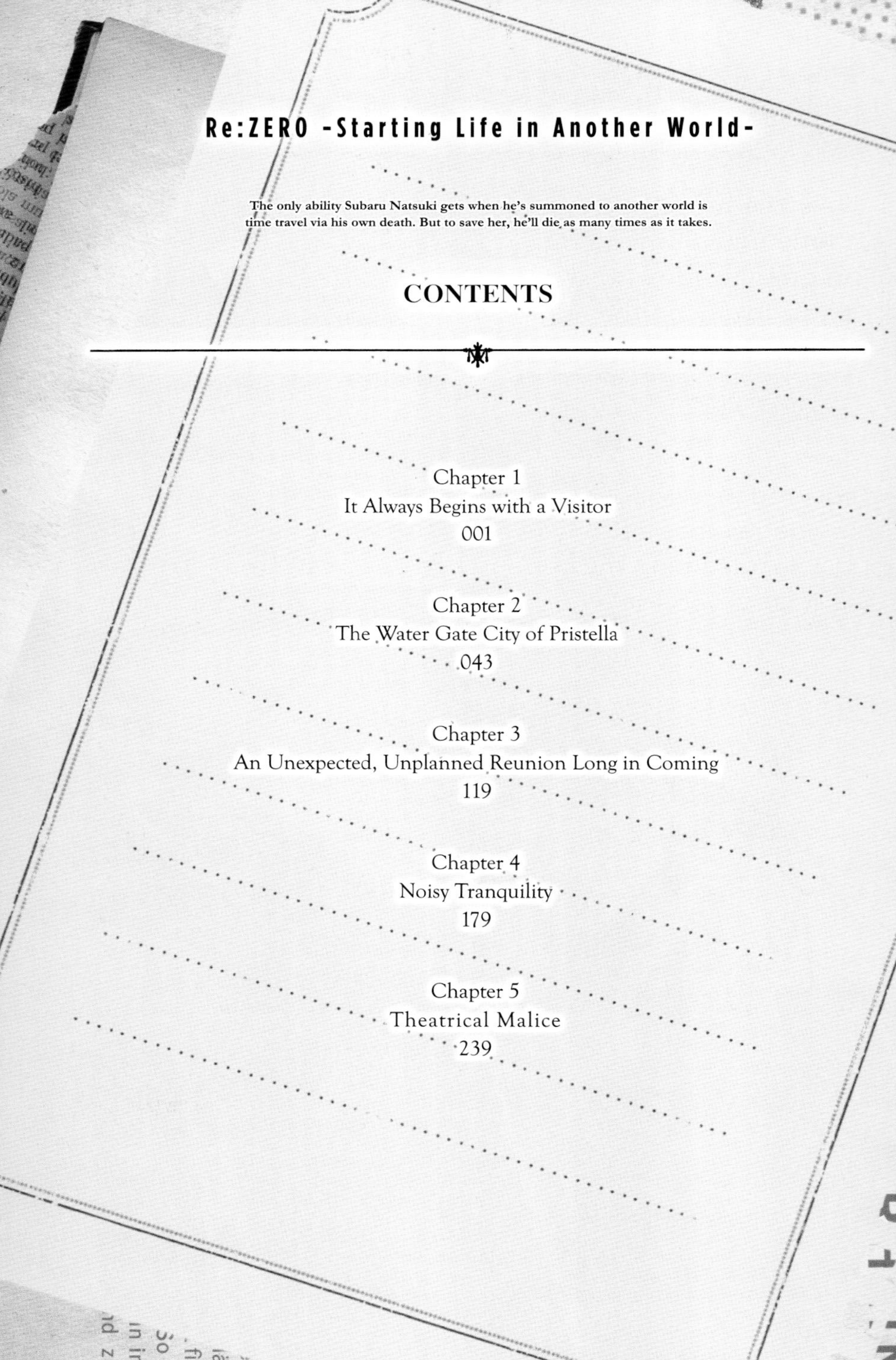

Re:ZERO -Starting Life in Another World-

The only ability Subaru Natsuki gets when he's summoned to another world is time travel via his own death. But to save her, he'll die as many times as it takes.

CONTENTS

-Starting Life in Another World-

VOLUME 16

TAPPEI NAGATSUKI
ILLUSTRATION: SHINICHIROU OTSUKA

NEW YORK

Re:ZERO Vol. 16
TAPPEI NAGATSUKI

Translation by Jeremiah Bourque
Cover art by Shinichirou Otsuka

Yen On
150 West 30th Street, 19th Floor
New York, NY 10001

Visit us at yenpress.com
facebook.com/yenpress
twitter.com/yenpress
yenpress.tumblr.com
instagram.com/yenpress

First Yen On Edition: June 2021

Yen On is an imprint of Yen Press, LLC.
The Yen On name and logo are trademarks of Yen Press, LLC.

The publisher is not responsible for websites (or their content) that are not owned by the publisher.

Library of Congress Cataloging-in-Publication Data
Names: Nagatsuki, Tappei, 1987– author. | Otsuka, Shinichirou, illustrator. | ZephyrRz, translator. | Bourque, Jeremiah, translator.
Title: Re:ZERO starting life in another world / Tappei Nagatsuki ; illustration by Shinichirou Otsuka ; translation by ZephyrRz ; translation by Bourque, Jeremiah
Other titles: Re:ZERO kara hajimeru isekai seikatsu. English
Description: First Yen On edition. | New York, NY : Yen On, 2016– | Audience: Ages 13 & up.
Identifiers: LCCN 2016031562 | ISBN 9780316315302 (v. 1 : pbk.) | ISBN 9780316398374 (v. 2 : pbk.) | ISBN 9780316398404 (v. 3 : pbk.) | ISBN 9780316398428 (v. 4 : pbk.) | ISBN 9780316398459 (v. 5 : pbk.) | ISBN 9780316398473 (v. 6 : pbk.) | ISBN 9780316398497 (v. 7 : pbk.) | ISBN 9781975301934 (v. 8 : pbk.) | ISBN 9781975356293 (v. 9 : pbk.) | ISBN 9781975383169 (v. 10 : pbk.) | ISBN 9781975383183 (v. 11 : pbk.) | ISBN 9781975383206 (v. 12 : pbk.) | ISBN 9781975383220 (v. 13 : pbk.) | ISBN 9781975383244 (v. 14 : pbk.) | ISBN 9781975383268 (v. 15 : pbk.) | ISBN 9781975383282 (v. 16 : pbk.)
Subjects: CYAC: Science fiction. | Time travel—Fiction.
Classification: LCC PZ7.1.N34 Re 2016 | DDC [Fic]—dc23
LC record available at https://lccn.loc.gov/2016031562

ISBNs: 978-1-9753-8328-2 (paperback)
978-1-9753-8329-9 (ebook)

10 9 8 7 6 5 4 3

LSC-MRQ

Printed in Canada

CHAPTER 1

IT ALWAYS BEGINS WITH A VISITOR

1

The instant Subaru Natsuki flew over the white boundary, his world turned upside down.

"—Wha—?! Whoa! Gah!"

This was the natural result when one sprinted at top speed. Whether traveling by car or on foot, no one could just instantly come to a stop.

Subaru pitched forward over his feet and plunged face-first into the grass. Instantly, he threw out his hands and rolled, breaking his fall to soften the unavoidable impact, then tumbled until he was sprawled on the ground.

His breath was ragged, and his vision flickered from the lack of oxygen. He could feel the grass pressing up against his back. Through gaps between the trees, he caught glimpses of the sky beyond. Subaru breathed in as much fresh air as his lungs would let him.

Then he thrust a hand toward the sky and clenched it into a fist.

"Oooaaahhh!! That was rough! Things got really bad for a minute there! But it's over! We made it! We hit the goooal!"

Though Subaru was covered in a sheen of sweat, his face lit up as he shouted with a sense of triumph.

His spirit had nearly been irrevocably broken on several occasions, but each time, Subaru refused to give up until he finally reached his goal. The number of repeated failures only made his ultimate success that much sweeter.

Finally, he could proudly face his mentor, who had taught him so much.

"Subaru, you've done quite well this time, I suppose."

As he basked in the moment, a girl entered Subaru's field of view. Strangely enough, she was upside down.

She looked lovely with her long, lustrous hair in extravagant curls and her elaborate dress. The sight of the young girl, who had distinct patterns in her light-blue eyes, brought a bright smile to Subaru's face.

"Oh, it's you, Beako."

"Obviously. Is it not my duty as a partner to praise you for your hard work day after day, I wonder? Also, Petra was rather insistent that I should bring you a towel."

"Ah, thanks. This is nice and cool. I feel alive again."

"Why not thank Petra directly, I wonder? That girl will probably leap with joy."

As Subaru set the damp towel on his head, Beatrice addressed him with an impassive face. However, he noticed a slight smile on her lips and couldn't help grinning a bit in return.

Even though he spent every waking moment with Beatrice, it surprised him how he still hadn't gotten tired of these kinds of little daily interactions yet. They only grew closer with each passing day.

"...Man, to think that it's been a whole year since Beako and I made a pact, huh."

"—? What brought this on all of a sudden, I wonder?"

"Nah, just thinking that time flies way too fast. And that I'm deeply moved by how cute you are today, too."

"You always say that, Subaru. But is Betty being cute not something to take for granted, I wonder?"

The fact that she took pride in the compliment was undeniable proof that Subaru had rubbed off on her quite a bit.

One year. That was how much time had passed since the string of incidents surrounding the Sanctuary.

It was a span of time that seemed so long and so short at once. In that stretch, some things had changed, while others had not. If the biggest constant was the bond between Subaru and his friends, then the greatest development had to be—

"—The sheer amount I've buffed up this past year. No one would recognize the old me anymore."

"Pffffft. Th-that was a good one… A priceless joke."

"I was being serious, damn it!"

Beatrice put a hand to her mouth as she broke into uncontrollable laughter. Subaru shrugged in a show of disappointment.

"Well, maybe I exaggerated a bit, but you don't need to laugh that hard. I mean, look at these biceps, Beako! They're rock-solid!"

"Fine, fine, I suppose. Betty will support you even if no one else will."

"That was not a vote of confidence! I've been trying so hard every day, too."

Sitting cross-legged on the ground, Subaru wrapped the cool towel around his neck as he gestured toward the area behind him with his chin. Gazing in that direction, Beatrice said, "True," closing one eye as she made the comment.

Behind the pair was a clearing where the forest had been cut open. This developed land was a trial Subaru had taken on with determination—in other words, he'd created his very own secret training facility.

Attracted by the idea of having a place to call his own, he'd secured a fair bit of space in the forest for his personal use. By utilizing wood from felled trees, he'd built a variety of attractions, including various hurdles to leap over and barriers to climb, turning the whole area into an obstacle course.

"The place might look like fun, but when people try to run around and bust through all the attractions within the time limit, its brutal design will make even adults cry… Damn, I made something pretty wild."

"Is that not an overstatement, I wonder? For that matter, only you and Garfiel refer to it as a secret base. Will the neighborhood children come by to play, I wonder?"

"You mean kids are going to treat it like an amusement park? Well, as long as no one gets hurt, they can play all they want. Plus, the master who drew up the blueprints should be satisfied with that."

Taking the challenge seriously served as a form of training, while tackling it with playful heart made it a fun excursion. The obstacle course contained great potential, and it being popular with children was a happy miscalculation.

"Actually, knowing my mentor, it's possible the whole point was to kill two birds with one stone from the very beginning..."

"He is certainly a difficult man to understand. He does know his manners, I suppose. The man should be praised for treating a Great Spirit with respect."

"I think that's not quite it, though."

Subaru poked at her apparent misunderstanding, then took a moment to think.

His mentor—Clind, the ultra-capable butler who had served the Mathers family for many years. He had helped Subaru so much in the past year and taught him a great many things, including how to hone his physique. Subaru's title for him was more serious than not.

In terms of ability and personality, Clind was more than worthy of praise, but—

"Why does Subaru refuse to allow Betty to go anywhere near Clind, I wonder?"

"It's not just you. Same goes for Petra and, depending on the situation, Emilia-tan, too."

Incidentally, there was no worrying where Ram and Frederica were concerned. For the record, Clind was harmless to Subaru, Roswaal, Otto, and Garfiel as well, for fairly obvious reasons.

"Anyway, it's fine even if this obstacle course is just a secret base in name only. Still sounds cool."

"I was shocked. The instant you called it that, Garfiel began helping you fell trees with that glint in his eyes... It's probably impossible to understand why the two of you find it so appealing, I suppose."

"It's something that calls to all men. Wait, but then what about Otto?"

Subaru and Beatrice both thought back to Otto's decidedly lukewarm reaction to the idea.

In any case, Subaru's prodigious growth was all thanks to the secret training base in the forest. It was only a ten-minute walk from the mansion, and no one except the people from the mansion ever came by. The only real downside was how often they would show up and get in the way of training.

"How ridiculous to consider this getting in the way. Is Betty not merely fulfilling her duty as Subaru's partner, I wonder? And what a chore it is, truly."

"Now you've done it. This is what happens to young ladies who get full of themselves!"

"What are you doing, I wonder?!"

Since she was being so cheeky and cute, Subaru used all his newfound strength to grab Beatrice and put her over his knees, patting her on the head as much as he pleased.

"You're terrible! Isn't this spirit abuse, I wonder?! What a heinous contractor!"

"Mwa-ha-ha. Well, you're the idiot who made a pact with a guy like me without putting anything in writing."

Subaru laughed as Beatrice pouted while she fixed her tousled hair.

When they first formed the pact, he thought he already adored her as much as humanly possible, but he had been revising that assumption on a daily basis. The so-called Beako Development Diary—a compilation of the days he shared with Beatrice—had already entered its fifth volume. Subaru was excited to see where their relationship would go next.

After all, an album of precious memories beat the hell out of a book filled with nothing but blank pages. And if it was going to be an album, then the more pictures and the more people he recorded, the better. That's why Subaru wanted to cram as much as he could into Beatrice's heart.

"In other words, Beako, my teasing is just another way I show my love."

"Did you say *teasing* just now, I wonder?! I will not let that slide!"

"I'd prefer it if you didn't casually brush aside the love part."

"There isn't much to worry about there, I suppose. I have great confidence that I am loved."

When Beatrice boasted with a smug look on her face, Subaru only replied with a smile.

He had no words to express the joy he felt when he saw how self-assured and full of life she was every day. There was only a deep, indescribable warmth that welled up in his chest.

"Master Subaru! Beatrice—!"

Both paused their play-fighting when they heard a high-pitched voice calling out to them. When they looked, a girl was waving as she ran over. The familiar voice and face belonged to an adorable young maid who epitomized the word *cute*.

"I'm glad to see that both of you are having fun. It's good to know you two are getting along."

It was Petra, putting a hand to her chest and smiling in relief.

Undaunted by the major incident that had occurred one year prior, Petra was currently working at the new Roswaal Manor. As expected of a growing girl, she had gotten a little bit taller and, in Subaru's opinion, a little more charming since then. That said, she was still very much a younger-sister type in Subaru's eyes.

"Hey now, I'm offended you call it playing around. I've been out here doing my best with training and everything."

"Well, at the moment, you seem to be patting Beatrice while she's sitting on your lap, so…"

"Whoa, it's not as simple as just wanting to give Beako head pats. First, you have to bring her out of a burning mansion and then gradually build up your relationship with her. Otherwise, it's impossible."

"Doesn't that mean no one but Master Subaru can ever…?"

Her exasperated tone and expression drew a wry smile from Subaru. That was when he remembered the towel around his neck.

“Oh, right. Petra, thanks for the towel. Pretty smart to cool it down like that.”

“Really? I’m glad it was helpful. Actually, I thought about chilling it with ice, but there was no time, so I asked Big Sis Emilia.”

“I like that practical part of you, Petra.”

He was fond of how Petra, despite her position as a servant, had no qualms requesting help from the lady of the household.

Such open praise elicited a “hee-hee-hee” from Petra, who blushed furiously before she remembered something.

“Ah, that’s right. Actually, I came here to bring you and Beatrice back.”

“What is it? Did you bake some super-tasty tarts or something?”

“What?! That is a matter of great importance, I suppose. I can understand why you needed to summon us so urgently.”

“Oh, come on, of course that’s not it. This is no time to play around.”

Puffing up her cheeks and pointedly raising a finger, Petra scolded the carefree pair. Then she grabbed Subaru’s hand and hauled him to his feet.

“There’ll be time for tarts later! More importantly, Big Sis Emilia is calling you, Master Subaru. Guests have arrived…and she wants you to be there when she greets them.”

“Visitors?”

Subaru cocked his head in confusion. He had no idea who it could be. Beside him, Beatrice made the same quizzical gesture as they wondered aloud.

“There are unscheduled guests, and the cute Emilia-tan is calling me over… Doesn’t it feel like something’s about to happen?”

“It’s the sort of pattern that leads to trouble, I suppose. Petra, tell us what kind of guests have come.”

“Errr,” went Petra as she tilted her head at the same angle as the other two. “One of them is a man who seems like he’s in a real hurry. I’d almost say he’s fidgeting like he’s scared.”

“Restless and fidgety, huh. In other words, he’s basically suspi… No, wait. Can’t go judging people based on appearances.”

"I've learned my lesson once already, so I don't do that, either."

"Ohhh, good girl, Petra. Not sure what happened before, but that's really nice of you."

"Last year, a stranger with a mean face came to the village. I thought he was a weirdo, but I was completely wrong, so…"

"An unexpected boomerang!! We'll have to talk about that first impression some other time…"

After surviving that verbal sneak attack, Subaru winked at Petra. After all, based on her report so far, Petra still had more to share.

"Anyway, there are other guests, too, yeah? Pals of restless-fidgety guy?"

Petra's cheeks grew redder as a trace of happiness came over her face.

"—He came with a cute kitty cat."

2

Viewed from the outside, the new Roswaal Manor looked just like a European-style mansion, closely resembling the old one that had burned down.

This mansion was actually considered the main residence, and it had been constructed more recently than the one that had been lost in the fire. Accordingly, it was more grandiose and occupied more space than the countryside mansion, which likely made maintaining the grounds all the more arduous for the servants like Petra.

"And here we are, back at this swanky manor."

After a quick ten-minute walk from the forest, Subaru and the others pushed open the double doors and stepped into the mansion's entry hall. Subaru assumed the guests they heard about must have been brought to a reception room or something.

"For starters, we should poke our faces over the…"

"Oh, hey! If it isn't Mister! How've you been?"

"Wha—? Whoa?!"

An energetic greeting and a sudden impact put an end to any other thoughts.

The voice was high-pitched, and something thumped into him at chest level. Subaru hastily reached out with his hands and caught something light. Quickly realizing who it was, the expression on Subaru's face changed from shock to recognition.

He remembered the super-soft fur and that ridiculously outgoing smile.

"I had a sneaking suspicion after hearing it from Petra...but it really is you, Mimi!"

"Eh-heh-heh-heh. It's been a while, Mister! How long has it been? Like, a year?"

The beast person wrapped up in Subaru's arms had bright-orange fur and wore a white robe. She was a demi-human, or more specifically, a cat-person. She was shorter than Petra and Beatrice, and she was undeniably cute as a kitten.

"Yeah, it's been a whole year. You seem to be having a good time. I'm glad."

"Yep! Mimi's having a super-good time! Also, Mimi's gotten taller! I'm basically an adult now!"

"What kind of grown woman jumps on someone's head the second they meet?!"

Mimi, who was now standing on the floor, puffed out her chest and swished her long tail.

She acted naive and had a super-friendly personality, but she was one of the leaders of the beast person mercenary unit known as the Iron Fangs and a powerful warrior many times stronger than Subaru. She'd also fought by Subaru's side during the hunt for the White Whale and once again later in the battle against the Witch Cult, during which she'd gone ahead and decided she and Subaru were war buddies.

"Well, you sure came a long way to get here. Oh right, let me introduce everyone. The cute maid here is Petra, and the embarrassed baby hiding behind my back is Beatrice."

"Ohhh, I get it! So it's Petra the maid, and your child!"

"Would you mind remembering me in a less unpleasant manner, I wonder?!"

In response to Mimi's questionable conclusion, Petra offered a graceful curtsy, while Beatrice shot a withering glare that broke past the bashfulness Subaru so enjoyed. Then Mimi went, "Oh!" Her eyes glittered as she stared at Beatrice. "Wow, that hair's incredible! How do you get it all curly-wurly? It's so cool!"

"It was all Mother's idea. This is the pinnacle of hairstyling—both practical and elegant."

"Uh, elegance aside, no way in hell it's practical. How many times has your hair gotten snagged in all sorts of places? I think you've had your share of problems with that over the past year."

Whether inside the mansion, outdoors, or nestled within Subaru's arms, Beatrice's hair constantly got in the way. By this point, Subaru's skill at disentangling hair was probably unmatched in the entire kingdom. He practically deserved a title like *Bea-trimmer*.

"Right, practical and elegant! I don't know what that stuff means, though!"

"Your gaze is like that of an uncomprehending chi… Hey, would you stop pulling, I wonder?!"

Bursting with curiosity, Mimi took great interest in Beatrice's curls. Mimi's movements were like a cat that had a mouse in its sights. Beatrice meekly looked to Subaru in search of rescue.

However, seeing a chance for Beatrice to make a new friend, Subaru left them to their own devices.

"Hey, Master Subaru. Beatrice looks like she's really concerned."

"Wrestling with your failings is what makes people grow. Beatrice has a tendency to give up without even trying, so this is her challenge. Let's stay quiet and watch over her like a good mom and dad."

"M-mom…? O-okay…"

Petra fell silent with a red face as Subaru stroked his nonexistent beard. The pair stood back and simply appreciated the warm exchange between Beatrice and Mimi.

"Incidentally, since Mimi turned out to be the kitty Petra talked about…that probably means the restless-fidgety man who came with her is Julius, doesn't it?"

Crossing his arms, Subaru felt in his gut that this premonition was most likely accurate.

It was plain to see that Subaru was very fond of Mimi personally. At the same time, she was part of the faction working under Anastasia Hoshin, one of Emilia's political rivals in the royal selection.

Another person working for the Anastasia camp was Julius Juukulius, a knight who had a complicated relationship with Subaru. At the very least, they didn't have the kind of relationship where Subaru was unconditionally glad to see him.

This being the case, he wanted to avoid seeing the man until he had some time to emotionally prepare himself, if he could help it.

"Mister, there's no need to worry! Julius isn't here today. Also, Hetaro and TB and the captain and the lady aren't here, either! Mimi's escorting all by herself!"

"Phew, that's a relief. But damn, Anastasia's crew has a deep bench."

Subaru still felt a certain wariness even after learning of the knight's absence. Surely, Anastasia wouldn't send just anyone to serve as an envoy to Emilia, a rival candidate in the royal selection. Anastasia was a big-time merchant, and the Hoshin Company she ran was a massive organization based out of the western city-state of Kararagi. Neither the quantity nor quality of her followers could be underestimated.

Subaru decided he had best sit down with this envoy and gauge him sooner rather than later.

"All right, this time, we really are going to the reception room… yes?"

"Yes. That's where I left the guest. Big Sis Emilia and the others are already there."

"Meaning it's Emilia-tan dealing with this guest, plus Otto and Garfiel, plus maybe Ram…? Better go rescue Otto before he dies of a stomachache."

"Is there anyone more pitiful, I wonder? His luck ran out the moment you caught him, Subaru."

"Hey, stop making it sound like I grabbed him and won't let go."

Beatrice wore an exasperated face as Mimi, in an unbelievably good mood, kept her left hand glued to Beatrice's right. With Petra leading the way, Subaru followed as they headed to the reception room on the second floor.

When the four of them arrived at their destination, they found a single girl standing in the hallway.

"Ram? Why are you out here?"

"So you've finally come, Barusu. You are quite late, aren't…?"

Ram was a beautiful maid whose charming appearance belied her razor-sharp tongue. Greeting their party with a demeanor reminiscent of someone speaking to her inferiors, she broke off midsentence to narrow her pink eyes. Then she sighed deeply.

"Indecent."

"You're the weirdo for thinking this lineup is indecent! How can you find this scene anything but heartwarming?!"

"Please stop basing everything on whatever passes for virtue in your brain. You would do well to remember this, Subaru. In Ram's world, only Ram's point of view matters."

"Wasn't there a lot of inconsistency just now between the first and the last part of what you said?!"

Decrying subjectivity with her own subjectivity was so self-centered that Subaru was at a loss for words. Ignoring Subaru's reaction, Ram crossed her arms as she shifted her gaze toward Mimi.

"Dear guest, if you stay away any longer, your companion will be quite worried."

"Ahhh, I guess I should head back, huh? Whoopsie—!"

"Yes, please do. Otherwise, it will be very bothersome, since your absence forced a certain Ram to leave the room to find you."

Judging by the conversation so far, it seemed that Mimi had raced around the mansion without getting permission from either the master of the house or her companion.

It was natural to assume that Mimi of all people wouldn't get up to any funny business even if left alone. Then Subaru turned to Ram as something occurred to him.

"You didn't look for her at all, did you? You've just been standing with your arms crossed in front of the room."

"Just a convenient excuse. The atmosphere inside is hard to endure. Otto will probably die if you don't hurry."

"I have to give it to you for not having even the tiniest sliver of guilt."

He had to admire her complete disregard for the fact that they had guests despite her supposedly being a maid.

For Ram to say that it was uncomfortable inside the room was sincerely frightening. Still, Subaru braced himself because he found the thought of not being involved even more terrifying.

"Thanks for bringing us over, Petra. Are you going to…?"

"Ah, I'll be busy baking some delicious tarts, so good luck in there, Dad."

"Agh… Since Mom's gone and said it, there's no backing down!"

Now it was Petra's turn to tease Subaru with more banter, like they were Beatrice's parents. Of course, Petra had a job of her own to do. Subaru couldn't expect her to keep him company on a whim. *It's not like she's abandoning me or anything.* At least, that's what he wanted to believe. Probably. Maybe.

"All right, let's go. Can't catch a tiger cub without going into the tiger's hole."

"You mean a butthole?"

"How vulgar."

"I didn't say that! Let's just go already!"

Ignoring Mimi's confusion and Ram's judgment, Subaru knocked on the door to the reception room. The door opened immediately, and a head topped with short blond hair stuck out into the hallway.

"Yo, awful late, ain't ya, General? Our bro's gonna wind up with a hole in his stomach any second now."

"Yeah, I know. Honestly, it's only a matter of time before it happens, but I'd like to keep him whole for as long as possible."

"No kiddin'! This is basically the *Arkel Lake Revolt*!"

Subaru and Garfiel exchanged smiles like little mischief-makers. Immediately swinging the door wide, Garfiel still wore that smile on his face as he gestured toward the interior of the room with his chin.

“Come on in. Nothin’s happenin’ without the general, so it’s a pain for the guest, too. Watching Otto and Lady Emilia welcome our visitor ain’t nothin’ but a comedy act.”

“Now, that’s a performance worth seeing… Gah!”

“Stop saying stupid things and go in. You’re in the way.”

After getting a literal kick in the butt from Ram, Subaru was forced into the room. Stumbling forward as he entered, several sets of eyes shifted toward him.

“———”

Relief, exasperation, and suspicion. This was pretty much what he had expected. He turned away from the two familiar figures to focus on the one regarding him suspiciously.

The visitor was a pretty boy with a handsome, delicate face. His lithe body was clad in exquisite ceremonial garments, and he had gathered some of his relatively long hair in a ponytail. He seemed about the same age as Subaru, though his face looked rather tense, and the monocle he wore over his right eye only added to the stern appearance.

“So this is…?”

When this guest made his inquiry with a hard voice, the beautiful girl sitting across from him nodded.

“Yes, that’s correct.”

The delicate, silver-haired beauty who wore a charming expression that perfectly reflected her wholesome spirit was none other than Emilia. It seemed like she only became more enchanting with each passing day.

She smiled slightly, gesturing at Subaru with a gentle point of her finger.

“I am sorry for the wait. This is my knight, Subaru Natsuki.”

Emilia introducing him as her knight left Subaru’s heart trembling. Whenever he heard those words, he often thought back to the time she had bestowed the title upon him.

The fond memory always bolstered Subaru’s frail, fragile heart.

“H-he seems to be rather ecstatic about something…”

“Subaru, stop making such a strange face. People will think there’s something wrong with you if you act like that…and why are you gripping my hand so hard, I wonder? Wait, it hurts! Ow, owww!!"

"—Whoa!! Ah, sorry, I zoned out a bit there without even realizing."

He had been so preoccupied with his thoughts that he'd almost crushed Beatrice's adorable hand by accident.

In any case, Beatrice was right. Their guest was already staring at Subaru dubiously. Deciding that this situation needed to be resolved sooner rather than later, Subaru cleared his throat and raised the customary salute of knights.

After standing up straight and composing his face, he put his right hand over his chest and willed his heart to calm down.

"Please excuse my poor manners. Allow me to introduce myself. I am Lady Emilia's knight, Subaru Natsuki."

"——"

The fact that he was clothed in a track jacket probably cost him points, but Subaru's salute had been drilled into him by a certain versatile butler until he got his seal of approval. It was as perfect as could be.

In the past, Subaru had scoffed at all the theatrics of knightly etiquette, but when he tried it for himself, he quickly became captivated by all the trappings. Though he had not been born into the position, the customs and attitude were slowly but surely guiding Subaru Natsuki closer to knighthood. It wasn't something stupid or just for show.

It seemed as though Subaru's greeting had impressed everyone present, save the guest. Emilia's smile was especially proud, which boosted Subaru's spirits so, so much.

Surrounded by these faces and apparently unwilling to endure any more silence, the visitor rose up and bowed his head.

"…Thank you for your courtesy. I'm here to… I have come to represent Anastasia Hoshin. My name is Joshua Juukulius."

"No, thank you. A fine name you have, Joshua…Juukulius?"

In the middle of exchanging perfunctory greetings, Subaru faltered when he heard the familiar family name. Seeing his reaction, Emilia pulled her hands to her chest.

"Ah, it seems you're surprised, too, Subaru. That's right, Joshua is apparently Julius's younger brother. It's *really* wonderful that both brothers are helping Ms. Anastasia, isn't it?"

Subaru's cheek twitched as he listened to Emilia's explanation, her violet eyes filled with admiration all the while. It was just as Mimi had said. Julius hadn't come himself, but—

"Sir Natsuki, is it? I have heard about you from my older brother, as well as from, shall we say…various rumors."

Almost seemingly taking advantage of Subaru's distress, Joshua spoke with some amusement. The sharp glint in his eyes and his refined yet biting attitude convinced Subaru that this was most certainly someone related to Julius by blood.

Subaru kneaded his brow in consternation before looking back up.

"I'm afraid to find out what he might've said about me to his family."

"There is no need for concern. My brother is an exceptionally impartial man."

These words drew a strained smile from Subaru. Joshua raised an eyebrow, unable to decipher his reaction.

That's exactly why was what Subaru wanted to retort, but he refrained.

"Anyway, Julius's younger brother, is it? Now that you mention it, that nast…er, that keen look in your eye, the sarcas…uh, the refined manner of speech, and the terribly…lovely hair color are all the same, huh?"

"Would you please stop with the unnecessary flattery? It's fairly obvious how bad you are at it."

Otto, chief domestic adviser of the Emilia faction, could not conceal his cold sweat as he asked Subaru to rein in his choppy attempts at praise.

"Dude, have you lost weight since I last saw you?"

"It has only been a few hours, but every day is a new struggle! Someday, I will undoubtedly succumb to the chills and stomach pain! Also, I completely heard your conversation with Garfiel earlier!"

"Well, I wasn't particularly hiding it. I don't intend to keep anything from you if I can help it."

"Could you try a little harder to hide *some* things?!"

Deflecting Otto's complaint with a superficial "yeah, yeah," Subaru smoothly took a seat at Emilia's side. Once there, he sat Beatrice down on his lap, moving his hands around her tummy to support her.

This put Emilia, Subaru (plus Beatrice), and Otto in a row on the reception-room sofa.

"Now, then. Sorry to make you wait. Could we continue the conversa—?"

"W-wait a moment, please! Who is this girl?!"

"—? Is something the matter with Betty, I wonder?"

Flustered, Joshua pointed at her, and Beatrice cocked her head quizzically.

"Wait, what…? Am I the only one who finds this strange?"

"No, I am quite sorry. Your reaction is only to be expected. If anything, this is a place where common sense goes to die."

When Joshua leaned forward with such force that his monocle came loose, Otto apologized with a sympathetic look in his eyes. It seemed that Joshua was not nearly as unflappable as his older brother.

Subaru also apologized even as he privately thought that this made Joshua the easier brother to get along with.

"Having Beako on my lap has become so second nature to me that I did it without thinking."

"It's so normal now that even Otto didn't bring it up. I'm flabbergasted, too."

"No one says *flabbergasted* anymore…"

Emilia had skillfully woven yet another outdated term into the conversation, but Subaru agreed with the message nonetheless. His and Beatrice's relationship had been normalized to the point that it no longer elicited witty quips from Otto.

"Sheesh, Joshua's so sloooow—"

Mimi cut in as she hopped over, settling into her seat beside

Joshua. She helped herself to the sweets on the table as she poked Joshua's cheek with her long tail.

"That's Beako! Mister and Miss's child—!"

"What?!"

"Right, right. This is my and Emilia-tan's adorable baby, Beatrice."

When Subaru took advantage of Joshua's shock, Emilia immediately slapped him on the shoulder.

"Goodness. Of course not. Now look. You've gone and startled Joshua. I may have kissed you, Subaru, but babies don't come from a kiss. I've learned that much, at least."

"Ah, sorry, Emilia-tan. It's really embarrassing, so could you stop revealing details like that so, um, bluntly? I'll stop messing around and introduce her properly."

Emilia's incredibly innocent openness quickly forced Subaru into submission.

Incidentally, Emilia's knowledge of baby-making had yet to progress past the *kissing doesn't make babies* level. Discussing anything beyond that was a high hurdle for Subaru, and the others generally agreed to a vague consensus of *we'll worry about it when she's older.* In the end, everyone was simply overprotective.

"See, this is what happens when you use Betty as the butt of a joke. Have you learned your lesson yet, I wonder?"

"Yes, I've thought long and hard about what I did wrong. From now on, I'll think up even better pranks."

"Errr, so this Lady Beatrice's actual position would be…"

"Ohhh, sorry, got off track again. Beatrice is my contracted spirit."

"Contracted…spirit…"

Putting his fallen monocle back in place, Joshua lowered his voice slightly in response to Subaru's explanation. The change in tone and the complicated emotions that reaction seemed to express made Subaru furrow his brow.

"Hey, dear guest. Ya got a problem with the general bringing his Great Spirit with him?"

Garfiel honed in on the young man's distress without the slightest hesitation.

"No," replied Joshua, briefly shaking his head. "I had heard the rumors, but I am merely surprised that Master Natsuki truly is a spirit knight. I believe you are well aware, but my older brother is also a spirit knight…previously the only one in the entire kingdom."

"Ahhh, of course we know that. He was a big…gnhhh, big…help to us…"

"Is that how badly you hate admitting he helped you?!"

Subaru wasn't quite that stubborn. This had more to do with the fact that whenever he thought back to how he had felt during the battle where he fought side by side with Julius, he found it difficult to reconcile those emotions with the pain of the wounds he suffered after his thrashing at the training square—plus a whole host of other annoyances.

"I see now. There certainly was talk about another knight who's also a spirit user, I suppose. If that person is your older brother, I offer my condolences."

"Condolences? What do you mean by that?"

"Is it not obvious, I wonder? His eventual downfall is inevitable. It is only a matter of when. At the very least, he can serve as a stepping-stone for Subaru and Betty's spectacular exploits… *Gahhh!*"

"Don't go picking fights out of the blue. Besides, my strength can't even compare to Julius's. I've got no chance against him on a level playing field. Who goes around challenging puzzle masters to a puzzle game? You obviously challenge them to a round of *Smash Brothers*. That's how we win."

After mussing Beatrice's hair for her provocative remarks, Subaru bowed in apology to Joshua. With her head still a complete mess, Beatrice followed suit.

"Sorry. We have no intention of insulting your older brother. For that matter, I am fully aware that my abilities are beneath his. Forgive my cute and vain girl, would you?"

"Yes, of course. It's only natural to be humble when compared with my older brother."

"Huh?

Even though it had seemed like they were getting the conversation back on track, Joshua's sudden haughty statement racked up the tension once more.

Not noticing the bewilderment around him, Joshua's monocle seemed to give off a concerning gleam.

"Yes, my older brother is an incredible man. At the young age of twenty-two, he is already recognized as one of the greatest knights in the kingdom and is effectively the second-in-command of the royal guard. Though he is currently not performing that duty to better serve Lady Anastasia, there is no doubt that my older brother shall become captain of the royal guard once she rises to the throne. Even Sir Reinhard, this generation's Sword Saint, cannot compare to my older brother when it comes to knightly virtues. Truly, my brother is a knight among knights! It would be ridiculous to even speak both your names in the same breath."

"...R-right."

The sheer force and speed of the tirade overwhelmed Subaru. Even Beatrice was taken aback.

"Apologies, I didn't get a chance to warn you. This is the second time he's gone on a rant."

Otto clutched at his head while whispering regretfully into Subaru's ear. When Subaru glanced around, he could see that Garfiel was obviously aggravated, while Ram had *now you see?* written all over her face.

He finally realized what had compelled Ram to flee the room. Joshua's obliviousness here was on par with Subaru's infamous episode during the meeting of royal-selection candidates.

Considering how Joshua's sole ally, Mimi, was too busy stuffing her face with sweets to pay attention, clearly someone else had to smack some sense into him...

"Hee-hee. Joshua *really* likes his big brother, Julius, doesn't he?"

But before anyone inevitably snapped, Emilia smiled at Joshua. She was completely unfazed by his intense demeanor.

After that comment brought him to his senses, Joshua went red in the face and put a hand to his ponytail in embarrassment.

"I—I am very sorry. I tend to lose my composure when it comes to my family..."

"Oh, that's no problem. Julius has been a great help to me, too. If you like, I'd love to hear more about you and Julius both..."

"Whoa there! Let's do that another time. Right now, we need to get down to business! Hey, isn't that right, Otto, Garfiel?!"

"—Eh?!"

When Subaru interrupted, forcibly changed the subject, and asked for aid, it was clear from the pair's reaction that they were clearly thinking, *Don't drag us into this!* Even so, the two immediately nodded, agreeing with Subaru. Though Joshua's eyes lit up for a moment, he seemed to have regained his self-control as he cleared his throat.

"W-well then, I shall recite the tales of my older brother's glory on another occasion. I better be, *ahem*... It is of the utmost importance to conclude this business and return to Lady Anastasia with all available haste."

"Yes, I am looking forward to that... Now, we've put it off for quite some time, but let's get to the issue at hand..."

As Joshua resumed acting as an envoy, Emilia seamlessly shifted back to Royal-Selection-Candidate Mode. Instantly, the atmosphere in the room became ever so slightly weightier. Emilia seemed like a completely different person.

Subaru and Beatrice weren't the only ones who had grown over the last year. Emilia had spent that time honing herself in all the fields a royal-selection candidate was expected to handle skillfully.

"—Representing Lady Anastasia Hoshin, I shall now convey the words of my master to you, Lady Emilia."

The noticeable change in the air brought a tenseness to Joshua's expression as he produced a letter from his pocket. He spread it out on the table, revealing its contents, which were written in black ink.

"Lady Anastasia wishes to invite Lady Emilia to the Water Gate City of Pristella."

"Pristella..."

Bewilderment lingered in Emilia's eyes as she rolled the name around in her mouth. Subaru was no different.

What was the true motive behind Anastasia's sudden request?

"The Water Gate City of Pristella, you say? Why ask us to go there?"

With their leader hesitant to reply, Otto took the initiative on probing for answers. Amusement crept into Joshua's golden eyes as he drew a thin smile.

In that moment, his face and expression made him the spitting image of Julius, which gave Subaru a bad feeling about what would come next.

"It would seem my master would like to invite you to a party. Lady Anastasia wishes to call upon Lady Emilia out of goodwill—and also to convey that she has found that which Lady Emilia seeks."

"What could that be?"

"—!"

As soon as Emilia took the bait, Otto's reaction was instant. It was obvious he was thinking *we've been had!* and Subaru understood exactly why; Emilia's reply had cost them the chance to discuss the matter among themselves first.

Still, Subaru couldn't see where this was going, either. Being late on the uptake had forced them to completely relinquish all initiative.

"—A specialist trader in Pristella seems to possess the type of high-quality magic crystal Lady Emilia desires. You are currently searching for a catalyst to call back a Great Spirit, are you not?"

And with that, the next steps were as good as decided.

3

"I feel bad for Otto that I just decided this all on my own."

When it was just her and Subaru in her bedroom, Emilia's eyes were downcast as she spoke.

Sitting across from her, Subaru wore a concerned smile.

"Well, Otto was pretty shaken up, but I mostly agree with your decision, Emilia-tan. What worries me is the idea of leaping into someone else's backyard without being properly prepared."

"But would Ms. Anastasia genuinely try something after sending Julius's younger brother as a messenger? I think that'd be crossing a *really* dangerous bridge for their side."

"You have a point. Sending a blood relative of their knight means they're acknowledging us as peers. I used to wonder why important people who were sent as messengers in *Taiga* dramas and stuff never got killed. Who would've thought I'd figure it out by living it?"

Subaru understood now that it was an issue of reputation. Anyone who became known for being untrustworthy would quickly find themselves surrounded by enemies. That was a poor way to conduct business, whether you were a Warring States–era samurai warlord or a royal-selection candidate. The powerful had to take care when it came to subterfuge.

In any case, the meeting with the envoy Joshua Juukulius had already come to an end, and evening had fallen on the new Roswaal Manor.

It'd be a shame for you to leave so soon, Emilia had said in an attempt to convince Joshua's party to stay for the night, but he had politely declined her offer and departed the mansion with Mimi in tow not long after.

He had received a favorable reply, so there was nothing left for him to do here.

Well then, when you arrive at Pristella, please visit the Water Raiment. That's where we'll... Ahem, *Lady Anastasia's party shall await you there.*

Later, Garf! I'll be waiting, so make sure you come, okay?

As they had said their farewells, Subaru couldn't help but notice the clear expression of relief on Joshua's face. Meanwhile, Mimi had been in an extremely good mood as she addressed Garfiel specifically.

Garfiel, who had been escorting their guests out while keeping a watchful eye on them, seemed to be wary. He probably suspected there might be ulterior motives to inviting him.

"There's no way Mimi is up to anything, so maybe she just likes Garfiel?"

"Mimi seems *really* fond of Garfiel. I might even be a little jealous."

"Yeah, she ranks high on the cuddly scale, that's for sure. I didn't talk to Joshua for all that long, either, but I get the feeling I can get along with him a lot more than with his older brother."

"Subaru, you are so stubborn. Are you still holding a grudge because of your fight with Julius at the castle?"

Emilia had a mischievous look on her face as she poked at his old wounds. Subaru winced as he recalled the unpleasant memory.

"I'll admit it's not something I can bring myself to laugh about just yet. I was young back then. I know better now...but I still think he went too far!"

"I think it's very uncool to cling to the past even though you've already made up and everything."

"Nghhhhh...I'm only human!"

Subaru stubbornly turned away when Emilia stared at him with her adorable face. She kept her gaze on him for a while, until finally, her endurance ran out, and she simply burst into laughter.

"Okay, okay. Goodness, Subaru, you really are a stubborn blockhead. But you can't get into fights with Julius in Pristella. You've become a fine knight, Subaru, and knights don't use their strength lightly."

"Yes, ma'am. The lady is always right, that she is."

Playing the fool to conceal his embarrassment, Subaru rubbed his nose with a finger.

"Anyway, I don't know much about this Pristella, but it's a famous city, isn't it?"

"You haven't been studying, have you? Pristella is one of Lugunica's five major cities and is located on our kingdom's border with the city-state of Kararagi. It's a *really* pretty city with canals all over."

"Interesting. Your explanation makes me wanna print it in a brochure. But man, a city floating on top of water, huh? I guess Venice is the closest thing I can think of. That'd definitely make it an impressive place."

When he thought of the waterfront cities from his own world,

Venice naturally came to mind. It also had canals crisscrossing the city's interior. Images of naturally flowing water winding its way through a stonework cityscape made him want to visit such an enchanting place at least once.

Subaru was projecting all that onto the city of Pristella, but the reality was a little different.

"Nah, that ain't right, Subaru. Pristella isn't a city on the water. It's usually known as the Water Gate City."

"Wait, what?"

"Yes, Pristella sits in the middle of a lake, so the city gets flooded when rain falls. That's why they have high walls to protect the city and several sluice gates to control the water levels. Those gates are famous, which is why it's called the Water Gate City."

"Somehow, my impression of this place suddenly went from a magical city of water to a watery prison…"

His mental image of a charming city was ruined when he learned about the high walls. He wondered why anyone would choose to build a city on a plot of land that demanded such radical safeguards.

"In the end, we still don't have a clue why Anastasia is asking us to visit a place like that… Hard to think it's just a social call."

"Hmm, is it not okay to believe they really might just want to get along?"

"Unfortunately, for better or worse, the royal-selection candidates all have their quirks. To be honest, there isn't a single one you can trust a hundred percent even under ideal circumstances, masters and servants alike."

Subaru carefully recalled and considered all the royal candidates and their respective knights before concluding every last one of them could be considered bona fide weirdos.

He trusted Crusch because of her character. However, because she had lost her memories due to an encounter with Gluttony, he actually couldn't rely on anything *except* her intrinsic character traits. Ferris was dangerous because he'd do anything for Crusch's sake, and Wilhelm's issues with his departed wife also made him an unknown element.

When it came to Anastasia, he still couldn't get a firm grasp on what she was thinking. That applied to the invitation they were currently considering, too. Though Subaru had very reluctantly come to trust Julius, that didn't change the fact that the leader of the faction was still none other than Anastasia. Also, she had a formidable private army in the Iron Fangs, and that could not be underestimated.

Felt's camp included Reinhard and Old Man Rom, both of whom Subaru considered decently trustworthy, but that didn't matter, since he still couldn't figure out Felt. If nothing else, now that she'd committed herself to fully participating in the royal selection, they couldn't let their guard down when dealing with that spirited, crafty girl.

If she and Reinhard had formed a close bond, the odds of claiming victory over them would become extremely slim.

And when it came to Priscilla's faction, their attitude was honestly the hardest to predict of all.

There was no mistaking that master and servant alike were far, far removed from words like *trust* and *faith*. Al and Subaru hailed from the same homeland, but Priscilla's knight was a man of strong loyalty. He probably wouldn't give Subaru any special treatment, and Priscilla's own whimsical, irrational character made her akin to a natural disaster.

In other words, even after a whole year had passed since the start of the royal selection, the other candidates remained inscrutable.

Learning more about them could be accomplished only by interacting more. That was another reason to accept Anastasia's invitation.

"I gotta say, I'm more scared than I want to be at the idea of owing a debt to Anastasia. For starters, how did they know what Emilia-tan wanted?"

Subaru murmured this with twisted lips, referring to the magic crystal Joshua had mentioned as a bargaining chip.

The high-purity magic crystal that had been the pretext for Anastasia's invitation was the kind of catalyst Emilia needed for a chance to form a pact with Puck once more.

To awaken Puck, who had fallen into a deep slumber after expending all his mana, she absolutely needed a magic crystal infused with great power. For a whole year, she had searched high and low for a suitable one to no avail.

"Everyone at the castle would've seen Puck, and they know I'm a spirit mage. We tried to keep the catalyst thing a secret, but it seems there was no hiding it after all."

"Just means people didn't keep it to themselves. Besides, even if we do end up bringing Puck back, from the others' point of view, that's basically us returning to square one. It's a good deal for them to get a chance to put us in their debt."

That said, if Puck really did return, the benefit to Emilia's mental state would be immeasurable.

In addition to that, Emilia's combat ability would go up as well, but that was just frosting on the cake. Her individual performance in battle would probably have very little effect upon the royal selection's ultimate outcome.

At most, it added more credibility to the camp's claims of victory over the Great Rabbit, which was considered more fictional horror story than anything else.

—The Great Rabbit, one of the three great demon beasts that had been soundly defeated at the Sanctuary.

Unlike the hunt of the White Whale and the battle with Sloth, the public had not acknowledged their struggle against the Great Rabbit. After all, there were no impartial witnesses, and the Great Rabbit itself had been exiled to another plane of existence, leaving no trace behind.

Subaru and the others had long since concluded that no one would believe their words no matter how hard they tried to convince the public. If there were no confirmed appearances of the Great Rabbit for several years thereafter, their claim could be strengthened with a formal report, but there was a distinct possibility the royal selection would be over by then.

"Well, it's not like people would believe we ran into two of the three great demon beasts in such a short time, let alone took both down. At the very least, we can pray that the third doesn't show up, too."

"—Yes, I agree."

The last of the three legendary monsters was said to be the Black Serpent. Putting his faith in the power of words, Subaru hoped with all his might that he would never come face-to-face with it. However, Emilia's reply had been strangely hesitant.

If he didn't know any better, Subaru would almost think she knew something about this Black Serpent…

"So about Pristella."

However, she moved on to the next subject before he could follow up.

Emilia's behavior made it clear that she didn't want to talk about it. Though that left him a bit uneasy, Subaru had learned enough about her heart to know better than to try and force the issue at a time like this.

"I wonder if it's all right to accept the invitation and go together just like we discussed earlier?"

"I think it'll be fine. Obviously, that means Emilia-tan will go, and of course, I'll follow you as your knight, with Beako as my partner. After that, Garfiel will come along as our muscle, and Otto will come as our adviser and out of pity. Really, I'd like to bring Petra and Frederica just in case, but…"

"You know we can't do that. Roswaal's busy gathering the western nobles for an assembly. It's already been decided Petra will go with him as part of her education…even though she *really* didn't like the idea."

"That's because Petra's hate for Roswaal is baked in. Ram doesn't say anything 'cause Roswaal finds it funny, but my heart's always beating hard whenever I'm watching them interact."

Ever since the series of events at the Sanctuary, Petra's feelings of distrust toward Roswaal ran deep. It was bad enough that it wouldn't be strange if she wrung out a sweaty towel over the tea she served him.

Of course, even if Subaru had seen her do something like that, he would pretend not to have seen a thing for Petra's sake.

"Then because we want Petra's mentor, Frederica, to also attend the assembly and keep an eye on her, that leaves Ram at the mansion… Aaand now I'm worried."

"There's no need to be concerned, Subaru. After all, the mansion still has—"

At that point, Emilia faltered as she lowered her violet eyes. Subaru knew very well what words would have followed, the words she'd tried to say.

It was guaranteed that Ram wouldn't shirk her duties. She had plenty of reason not to.

"Well, we should worry less about the mansion and more about what's in front of us… Right, Emilia-tan?"

"Mm, that's right. Also, I need to apologize to Otto for moving the conversation ahead without him."

"He's not the type to take that kind of stuff personally, but he is the type to drag things out. Let me talk to him. I'll say I scolded you until I broke into tears."

"Tee-hee, thank you."

Emilia smiled faintly as she watched Subaru wave his fist around. Then she touched the azure magic crystal pendant resting against the milky skin of her chest.

Its blue radiance declared that this was the cradle where Puck the Great Spirit lay as he slept.

It was her link with the family member whose existence she could confirm but, at present, with whom she could not speak—Emilia gently stroked the surface of the magic crystal with a slender finger, as if wishing she could talk to him somehow.

"I want to talk to Puck, and there's so much I want to ask him. That's why…"

Emilia sank into silence. Shutting her eyes, which had strikingly long eyelashes, she kept the rest of her thoughts unspoken.

Seeing her eyes tremble ever so slightly, Subaru quietly scratched his head. A vague understanding of what Emilia was experiencing was all that he could offer.

"Come back soon, kitty spirit. I've got a mountain of complaints with your name on them."

Though he griped, Subaru was also Emilia's knight, and he hoped her wish would come true.

4

"I will have you know, I'm always trying to do what's best for everyone!"

Slamming his wine cup against the table, Otto Suwen raged that evening.

After talking with Emilia and having dinner, Subaru paid Otto a visit in his room before his nighttime routine, only to find himself humoring the domestic adviser, who was drinking and had many complaints to get off his chest.

"He's been goin' at it this whole time. Even my ears are startin' to hurt."

Sitting at Otto's workbench with a feather pen in hand, Garfiel wore an exasperated expression. He was taking little sips of the cup of milk he had in his hand while lending his ears to his senior's complaints.

Garfiel had turned fifteen over the last year, meaning he could legally drink alcohol according to the kingdom's laws; however, he was surprisingly weak against it. Ever since Otto had tempted him to drink and subsequently gotten him dead-drunk, which had earned the merchant a baleful glare from Ram, the mere sight of a wine bottle was enough to make Garfiel frown.

Of course, Subaru also took to heart the laws of his original world and respected that alcohol was off-limits. He chalked up his having once engaged in a bout of drinking at the mansion as the result of his youthful exuberance.

Thus, Subaru could only sigh deeply as Otto got drunk and continued ranting.

"Don't be so sore about it. Emilia regrets how things went this time around. Sorry for leaping ahead without consulting you and stuff. To be fair, I think the result would've been the same even if she had talked to you."

"The result isn't everything, you know. The process itself is important. Deciding the outcome of a conversation before having the conversation is utter nonsense. This is why I insisted we must not surrender the initiative no matter what…and yet, we played right into our opponent's hand! That was the worst thing we could have done!!"

When Subaru tried to soothe him, Otto only got more worked up, slurring his words all the while. On top of that, even while drunk, he still presented a perfectly sound argument. Subaru had to admit he was impressed.

"Man, you've totally gotten used to being a domestic adviser. The way you deny it every time is kind of a running joke at this point."

"Yeah, you've changed so little that it's no fun. That ain't good, Bro."

"Well, the two of you have changed so little since I've met you that it's like a splash of water in the face!"

Subaru and Garfiel high-fived when Otto shot back at them for their perfect tag-team combo.

With the three being similar in age, a special kind of friendship linked them and naturally led to them spending a lot of time together at the mansion. Their banter had settled into a familiar routine that they had practically gotten down to an art form.

At present, Otto was spending his days employed as the chief domestic adviser of the Emilia camp. Armed with the formal education he'd received as a son in a mercantile family and his worldly experience as a traveling merchant, the calculating, quick-witted Otto was an excellent addition to the team. It was a miracle they'd encountered him before he ended up deceived, abandoned on the roadside, or sold into slavery.

Albeit, even as he continued work as a secretary, he often muttered to himself that "it wasn't supposed to be like this…" He really didn't know when to give up.

"And what exactly is that pitying look in your eyes for?"

"Well, you know, it's not like you can just back out now after getting to know so much sensitive information… So yeah, I was mostly thinking about what terrible luck you have."

"Could you really stop pitying me already?!"

"Hey, calm down, Bro. You're gonna spill your booze. And, General, don't tease him too much, all right? Last time, we decided we'd do ten Ottos a day."

"What are you two even counting?! Why are there ten in a day?!"

Otto was red-faced and shouting, so that was one Otto down.

Of course, Subaru and Garfiel weren't toying around with Otto for no reason whatsoever. This was a ritual with the objective of letting Otto yell like he was doing now and blow off all his steam from overworking day after day.

"If we don't do this, you probably wouldn't even be able to eat or sleep. Just leave the stress reduction to us!"

"I believe the possibility of this backfiring is rather high!!"

"Hey, hey, don't get so bent outta shape, Bro. If ya keep that up, I ain't gonna make any progress with this letter. Granny asked me to and all."

Garfiel pointed the tip of his feather pen at Otto, who had been cowed into silence. Otto was a man with the unfortunate physical condition of not losing his senses even when blackout drunk.

Subaru smiled wryly as he peeked at the letter Garfiel was penning.

"Whoa, that's some awful handwriting. Is Ryuzu really gonna be able to read this letter?"

"Ha! Don't make me laugh, General. How long do ya think me 'n' Granny have been together for? Granny can even read the stuff I write left-handed."

"That makes Ryuzu really impressive, but it's nothing for you to be proud of."

Poking fun at Garfiel's display of pride, Subaru faintly lowered the corners of his eyes.

Ryuzu was both Garfiel's grandmother and the representative of the Sanctuary—presently, she was not dwelling at this mansion but rather at Earlham Village, which was close to the old mansion. The reason was that she bore the duty of granting "an everyday life" to the twenty-four people who had been born just like her: replicas derived from Ryuzu Meyer, with bodies constructed of mana just like Ryuzu herself.

These replicas had been liberated from the Sanctuary and cast into the world like innocent babes. Stating that it was her responsibility to teach them about life, Ryuzu had parted with her two grandchildren.

Though it would be best if she could someday complete that duty so she, Garfiel, and Frederica could live together as a family once more, the circumstances demanded that this be put aside for the time being.

And it was this Ryuzu whom Garfiel was drafting a letter for. An unexpectedly prolific writer, he held unconcealable feelings for his grandmother, which resulted in him writing letters with frequency far beyond the norm.

"I have mentioned this before, but Ms. Frederica also sends letters, though I believe not even she writes as many as Garfiel."

"Well, all joking aside, Garfiel writes every day, so that has to be a mountain of letters."

Even so, Ryuzu was delighted to receive letters from both her grandchildren. Apparently, she stored every one she received like they were all precious treasures.

"Guess you could almost say I'm taking advantage of Ryuzu's way of thinking, couldn't you…?"

Subaru had been the first to approve of Ryuzu's desire to guide the other replicas. Perhaps it was a poor choice of words, but Subaru just didn't want them to stay "dolls."

Or perhaps that was Subaru's self-serving sense of guilt for having used the girls like sacrificial pawns once during a previous loop.

"General?"

"…Never mind. There's a lot to tell Ryuzu after what happened today, so I'm sure you won't have any problems with your letter. It's a lot worse to have nothing to write about. That's when you got no choice but to try and make up something funny."

"Ah, that would be pretty painful. If perchance you end up writing *Bro was boring* in a letter, I really will have to punch you to make up for it."

"Well, relax. I wrote that Bro's bein' plenty funny today. Ah, besides that, General, there's somethin' I wanted to ask ya."

After using his pen to point out the part about Otto, which earned him a grimace, Garfiel floated Subaru a question.

"I wonder what the enemy's target was this time around. Until now, the other candidates ain't been in any skirmishes, so why go openly pick a fight all of a sudden?"

"A fight… You sure have a simple way of looking at the world."

"As if ya need complicated logic for a fight. It all depends on what the other side wants. Settin' that pale dude aside for the moment… Despite her looks, the cat-person runt who came with him seemed pretty tough."

Garfiel might have called her a brat, but age-wise, Mimi was about as old as him. The reason Subaru didn't interrupt him with a wisecrack was because he saw the serious look in Garfiel's eyes.

"When I first met her, she gave me a real long stare. Kept that up the whole time we were talkin'. That, there's no mistakin' it's to figure out a good chance to pick a fight with me."

"…You sure? I'll admit Mimi's pretty strong, and it's a fact that she talks like a combat maniac, but, uh…"

She didn't strike him as the kind of cunning character to secretly scheme or rely on subterfuge. Her companion Joshua didn't seem well-suited for wickedness, either, in a good way.

"Anyway, if we're takin' 'em up on the invitation, we better stay on guard. General, that means you and Lady Emilia are banned from movin' around on your own. Bro may be one thing, but if our general or the lady get taken out, we're done."

"For the record, without me, everything would grind to a complete standstill, got it?! Good grief, I wish you would understand that and appreciate me more already!"

Otto sulked, but of course, Garfiel wasn't slighting Otto at all. Though he was not one to make a big show of saying so, Garfiel actually respected Otto a great deal. Given Garfiel's personality, under no circumstances would he refer to anyone so familiarly were that not the case.

It deeply moved Subaru when he thought back to when they'd first met and how far they had come.

"Wha—? What's the big deal with that strange look, General?"

"I was just thinking how glad I am to have you on our team. You've become really dependable, Garfiel."

"Heh, just leave it to me. I ain't much good at any hard thinkin', but I'll buy you time so you can. I'm countin' on ya for the rest, General."

Speaking those words, Garfiel grabbed his cup of milk and drank it dry, laughing with white all around his lips.

This went for Emilia, too, but the trusting gaze Garfiel turned toward Subaru was a strong restraint upon him. It made him think he had to work hard in order to do that trust justice.

"So with Garfiel, that puts us in a safe place fighting-strength-wise... but you're really coming, Otto?"

"Well, of course I am! If I am not there, I will not have any rest wondering what kind of harebrained conversations Lady Emilia and Mr. Natsuki might be having!"

The unreliability of the pair's negotiating ability to date was still in sharp relief. Emilia was as cooperative and sincere as she looked, and for all of Subaru's personality and stubbornness, he was unversed in the ways of the world. From Otto's point of view, they had to look like a wild duck paired with a green onion—easy pickings whether alone or together.

"Also, Pristella is a place deeply connected to Hoshin of the Wastes. As this is a legendary individual to all merchants, I had always wanted to visit it once someday."

"But you washed out from being a merchant a long time ago, so why bother now?"

"I did not wash out! Now, listen, if you think I'll remain your domestic adviser forever, you are sorely mistaken! My dream is to be a great merchant with my very own store! My presence here is nothing but a temporary stop!"

"Ain't no guarantee that there's a place you're gonna spend the rest of your life at ahead of that stop."

When Garfiel amusedly chimed in to tease him, Otto grimaced but made no retort.

Of course, to Subaru, having Otto tag along was a wish come true.

Whatever they might say out loud, neither the negotiations nor the camp itself would go anywhere without him. Everyone in the group understood that.

It was because Otto himself was aware of his own worth that he continued carrying such arduous burdens on his back.

"Well, it also feels like you're just a masochist, but I'll set that sentiment aside."

"I get the sense that is an even ruder form of acceptance, but perhaps that is just my imagination?"

"Yep, just your imagination. Either way, our rival is a great merchant and real sharp. I'm counting on you, Otto. Garfiel for the martial, Otto for the cultural, and me to keep things lively."

"Work harder, would you?!!"

Subaru's decision was made in accordance with the right man for the right job. Even if Subaru worked himself to death from that moment onward, he would never be as strong as Garfiel, and even if he cost himself sleep at night, he'd never be as useful an official as Otto.

But the position in which Subaru Natsuki stood was not so soft that he could simply rot on the vine.

"I'll do whatever I can do. That's the forward-looking way Beako and I are handling the situation after talking it over."

"Well, with Lady Emilia 'n' Beatrice there, ya should be all right, General. And I guess that means I gotta protect Bro. Just be careful, 'kay?"

"That somehow feels like I am the element of greatest concern… It really does not sit well with me."

Subaru turned serious, Garfiel acted like he was taking on babysitting duty, and Otto complained while bringing more wine to his lips bit by bit.

In so doing, their weighty conversation switched to the trivial, adding a pinch of spice as the night deepened.

"Well, I think I'll finally turn in for the night. How about you, Garfiel?"

"Me, I'm gonna stick with Bro a li'l longer. Letter writin' is done, but I see my chance to finally win at shatranj. Now that he's drunk, it should be a snap."

Replying as Subaru rose to his feet, Garfiel pointed to the game board on the table. Shatranj was a board game similar to chess or shogi. Otto was fairly skilled at this game, and Garfiel's eagerness to challenge him in a weakened state suggested he'd been on a big losing streak.

Incidentally, Subaru was pretty good at othello, but he was bottom-feeder tier at shatranj.

"Well, good luck. Don't stay up too late. You won't grow any taller like that."

"Hey, is that even true? I believed that and always went to bed early but don't think it works at my age."

"I'm not sure in your case. I think Frederica sucked some out of you."

"Damn you, Sis!"

Baring his fangs, Garfiel prepared for shatranj so he could direct the power of his anger toward the game. Subaru let a small smile slip, watching from behind as Garfiel set the pawns in neat rows.

"And don't drink too much, Otto. If you're hungover and useless, Petra's gonna get real scary."

"I feel as if that girl is being particularly strict with me of late. Say something to her, would you, Mr. Natsuki?"

"That she's too soft on the offense?"

"Could you not ask her to be gentler instead?!"

"No way, no how. Good night."

Waving his hand, Subaru left the room as the remaining pair huddled with the game board between them.

The color indicated by the magic crystal clock on the wall of the mansion corridor announced that it would soon be midnight. He'd lingered a little longer, making him later than usual.

"It was a talk among men. Gotta let something like that slide."

Letting slip those words of excuse, Subaru went not to his own room but in the direction of the west wing, where the women's bedrooms were.

And then—

"—Excuse me."

Subaru always knocked before entering the room.

He knew there would be no reply. Even so, was that any reason to abandon hope?

Or perhaps not forgetting to do so was simply to confirm that there was no reply—

—so that he might never, ever forget the heat of the unquenchable flame that continued to burn within his chest.

This room that gave no reply was a simple, unadorned bedroom.

It was arranged in a manner unchanged from the mansion's many other rooms, with only the most basic of furniture. The bed at the center of the room, the curtains over the windows, and the simple table with a flower vase on it were the only real furnishings.

The flowers in the vase were changed regularly, and the water was replaced on a daily basis. Even though he knew that the beauty and scent of the flowers brought no repose, this was an everyday routine for Subaru.

Subaru's sentimental actions were observed in silence by the other people at the mansion.

—I think that if he could easily set things aside and just move on, I wouldn't have come to an understanding with Subaru no matter how many times we argued. That's why I really *like Subaru as he is.*

It is a bad habit to be greedy when one is so lacking. Can Subaru be anything save rash and reckless, I wonder…? That is why, now that he is not alone, we shall indulge his avarice even so.

That's what the two girls closest to Subaru thought about his behavior.

"They're such softies. Also, Emilia-tan's suggestive comments push my buttons way too much."

He wished she wouldn't say *like* and *cool* so casually.

The words clearly conveyed her feelings, but there had been no romantic developments between Subaru and Emilia. Put simply, Emilia wasn't prepared to accept a confession, and Subaru's heart didn't seem prepared for it at all. Two years, maybe three— No, in the worst case, it might take even more time than that.

"It's kind of rude to come here and always talk about Emilia and the others. Petra or someone else would seriously scold me if they heard."

Perhaps when you got down to it, there really was no one in the Emilia camp who was more of a social person than Petra. The defining feature of Subaru and company was that every one of them sucked at interpersonal relations. The fact that a girl not yet thirteen years of age was ahead of them all made for a pretty pathetic tale.

"I've really got to wonder. If you…were awake, Rem, I don't feel like you'd be moving the needle all that much. Either because I'm useless at this whole relationship thing or because you always put me first."

As he spoke, Subaru pulled a chair over and sat down beside the bed.

The girl's sleeping face was exposed just enough that the moonlight filtering in through the gaps of the curtains made it stand out against the night.

He could make out her white cheeks, pink lips, and blue hair. Her beautiful figure was clad in a thin negligee. The chest of Subaru's Sleeping Princess rhythmically rose and fell.

—That was how this precious girl—Rem—had continued to slumber for more than a year.

"There's lots to talk about today. An uninvited guest dumped one hell of a problem in our laps. First, this morning, I did the usual—"

Subaru had a tender look on his face as he told the still-sleeping Rem his tale.

He spun his stories in a witty fashion, and the tone of his voice was very gentle. Speaking with great care, like he would with an infant taking a nap, he amusedly recited the day's events.

The girl offered no reply. Even so, these midnight trysts continued.

On nights when there was a great amount of news to share, Subaru often insisted on whispering dreamlike tales to the Sleeping Princess until the moon had largely run its course.

CHAPTER 2
THE WATER GATE CITY OF PRISTELLA

1

"As far as I am concerned, Lady Emilia's wishes should be respeeected. Fortunately, there are no urgent matters for her to attend to at the moment… Although, our competition's aim being inscrutable is some cause for conceeern."

Those were the thoughts that Roswaal shared with Emilia and Subaru after receiving the after-action report on the meeting with the envoy and the invitation to Pristella.

They were talking in Roswaal's study the day after the envoy's visit.

Roswaal had recently been devoting all his time and effort to maintaining dialogue with other regional power holders in preparation for the upcoming meeting with all the lords of the western marches.

Generally speaking, these people followed Roswaal's lead when it came to the royal selection, but they considered dealing with demihumans and half-elves as a separate matter and harbored deep-rooted insecurities about his open support for Emilia.

Over the past year, Roswaal had fought battles of his own with conversation and careful negotiation to consolidate the support of these lords. This assembly was the culmination of all those efforts, and hopefully, it would bring them closer to pledging their genuine allegiance to Emilia.

"I'm sorry that I'll be away from the mansion at such a crucial time."

"No, no, worry not. The coming assembly is merely extended preparation for the main event that is still to come. Bringing you to the fore now would be tantamount to foul play…or would you rather give us another masterful performance to silence the seething elites? Just like you did when you grabbed me by the collar and demanded I get my act together?"

"I think…that's still beyond me. All right, I understand. I'll behave."

When Emilia pursed her lips and lowered her gaze in apparent frustration, Roswaal nodded with visible satisfaction.

Though the sarcasm conveyed by his statement made Subaru want to say something, he held his tongue. Roswaal was dealing with Emilia far more openly than before. This was a million times better than her old treatment as a mere figurehead. At least, that was what Emilia had said.

For his part, Roswaal was putting vigorous work into the royal selection. He'd become far more dependable as a sponsor than before. But the remaining uncertainties about his true intentions balanced the scales.

"—Goodness. Master truly does not come off as a man who has learned his lesson."

Having watched that exchange in full, a tall maid lifted her face to the sky and let out a sigh.

The maid attending at Roswaal's side was Frederica. The beautiful girl with long blond hair and jade eyes somehow seemed to be in quite a good mood as she glared at the side of Roswaal's face.

"Perhaps you are enjoying everyone's company too much to notice, but I believe that it is rather unsightly to keep dredging up the past."

"My, what a severe review, Frederica."

"But of course. Incidentally, I must ask you to stop teasing Petra. She is accompanying you because she is a kind child, but please do not ask too much of her."

Frederica sharply objected to her master's behavior. When she pointed these things out, Roswaal shrugged. "You win thiiiis time," he went, his expression relaxing as he seemed even more amused.

—In the year since the incident in the Sanctuary, the attitude that the people at the mansion held toward Roswaal had changed.

Some were closer to him, some more distant, and some displayed a sharp drop in restraint toward him; Frederica's demeanor definitely leaned toward the kinder side.

"Either way, no medicine will cure Roswaal's personality at this point. So what kind of opposition are we expecting at the assembly?"

"Tolerable, one might say. If there is one concern, it is suuurely about young Petra, but Annerose shall be attending this assembly as well. In other words, Clind shall also be present."

As Roswaal shrugged again, his words made Subaru recall the sight of a particular girl.

Annerose Miload—a person distantly connected to Roswaal and an adorable girl still ten years old thereabouts. She possessed an aristocratic bearing unusual for her age, and though the lady of the household had Clind to support her, she was more than up to the task of leading the Miload family as its matriarch.

As Annerose was incredibly fond of Emilia, she would be a reassuring ally at the assembly. Though, on Subaru's side, Annerose being overly attached made his head hurt whenever he had to deal with her.

"My mentor is going as well, and he's extremely partial to Petra. I'm not sure whether to be reassured or worried."

"If you are concerned, why not escort the girl during her on-the-job training? She will surely listen to whatever Barusu has to say."

When Subaru's voice became uncertain, the last person in the room interjected.

Ram sat with her arms crossed in an insolent, un-maid-like fashion upon the sofa. She then brought a cup of black tea to her lips as she glanced toward him.

"Seriously, no one's had a sharper drop in restraint than you, Ram."

"I suppose that's true. Ram was too soft before. Are you saying that's simply a sign of how much I've let my guard down? How awful."

"Don't go putting words in my mouth!"

Ram turned a glare on Subaru, completely unfazed by his retort.

"But Ram does have a point. If you're worried, Subaru, how about we redo the assignments?"

"...Nah, it's fine. Petra herself said so. Plus, doing something like that really would be overprotective."

Letting her leave the nest was just as important as watching over her. He had to respect Petra's desire to go out into the world and seize this opportunity to grow. The least he could do was not get in her way.

"Yes, precisely, Master Subaru. Please rest at ease. I shall take full responsibility for looking after Petra. I shall absolutely not allow that man to get close to her."

"Of course Petra's important, but having you say that about my mentor gives me conflicted feelings."

Frederica, who doted on Petra, had little love for Clind, who would likely also be present at the assembly. Subaru expected that the pair would clash even while both treated Petra like a goddess.

Strange. Wasn't the conversation a moment ago about him being worried about Petra?

"By process of elimination, that means Ram will stay behind at the mansion. You do not miiind?"

"No, I shall do as Master Roswaal desires. You will be lonely without Ram, but please endure."

"Yes, I understand. I shall entruuust the mansion to you."

As Roswaal closed one eye and looked at her with his blue eye, Ram magnanimously pulled back her shoulders.

There had been a change in the relationship between Ram and Roswaal as well. Ram remained supremely loyal toward Roswaal, but one might say she'd become a fair bit pushier than before. Roswaal accepted this without a word of criticism. Though their interactions seemed familiar, it differed from the codependence they had previously shared.

To put it simply, they understood each other now—that's how it came off.

"What are you staring for? Do not lust for others indiscriminately. It is indecent."

"Just how much of an incorrigible bastard do you think I am, Big Sis?"

"———"

When Subaru posed that question, he saw a complicated emotion reflected in Ram's eyes.

It was not because she found the question difficult to answer. It was just that Ram always faltered whenever Subaru addressed her as Big Sis.

It was a clear sign she still didn't feel like an older sister. Her memories of her actual sister, Rem, remained lost. The days she spent with the little sister she loved most of all were nothing but a blank.

The fact that Subaru called Ram Big Sis even so was probably because he relied on her more than most realized.

"Now then, to be honest, I am somewhat anxiooous about sending Lady Emilia and young Subaru off on their own, but if they have Garfiel and young Otto accompanying them, it should be all right. With young Otto, there is no concern about awkwardly fumbling negotiations, and if all else fails, Garfiel can smash everything in sight and allow for an escape."

"That would be a *really* big problem, so I'll try my hardest to avoid that."

"No need to worry, Emilia-tan. Whether it's with Anastasia or Julius, I'm a top-class product when it comes to fogging up conversations. The gossip-lovin' Witch herself gave me her seal of approval."

"Sheesh, I don't think that's anything to be proud of."

When Emilia smiled wryly, Subaru gave her a thumbs-up and flashed his own mischievous grin. Of course, Emilia was well aware that Subaru was joking around in an attempt to put her at ease.

That exchange made Roswaal close his yellow eye. Then he looked at the entrance to the room.

"It would seem the conversation has concluded—well then, I leave protecting these four to you, Beatrice."

"Ngh!!"

Raising a yelp at those words was Beatrice, covertly hiding behind the door to the study. When Roswaal drew attention to her eavesdropping on the conversation through the gap, she gingerly poked her head into the doorway.

"H-how long did you realize Betty was there, I wonder...?"

"From the beginning. I considered letting it slide out of bemusement, but when I thought about it, I would hardly call this good behavior from a four-hundred-year-old child. Former or not, does this not bring shaaame to the title of librarian of the archive of forbidden books?"

"How infuriating! And will you stop calling me a four-hundred-year-old child, I wonder?! Unbelievable!"

Beatrice rushed into the room and stomped her foot at Roswaal's provocative remarks. All Subaru and the others could do was smile and watch.

Their current relationship could also be safely included in the *loss of restraint* category.

Finally, after she had a chance to vent her anger, Beatrice crossed her arms.

"At any rate, I would protect them whether you said to or not. Without Betty, who in this group of klutzes would you trust to get anything done, I wonder?"

"Ohhh, how reassuring. I am very much relying on you to lead these precious children by the hand."

"Hmph, you can count on me."

Puffing her chest out, Beatrice accepted the offered leadership role. With this, the conversation concluded at last.

Subaru, Emilia, Beatrice, Garfiel, and Otto.

They were the ones who would be heading to the Water Gate City of Pristella.

2

"Even with a fast dragon carriage, it will be a long journey that'll last more than ten days. There is no particular reason to rush, so let us put safety first and take our time."

When Otto spoke those words as he plotted the route for the journey, everyone agreed without a word of complaint.

Of the members heading to Pristella, Otto was the one most accustomed to travel. Indeed, compared with the other members, it could be said he was almost too used to it.

"I was a total truant, Garfiel lived all fourteen years of his life without leaving his birthplace, Emilia-tan spent a hundred years in cryo-sleep, and Beako's a four-century-old shut-in… I mean, what can you really say about a group like this?"

"Yes, yes, it is fine. Mr. Fulfew and Ms. Patlash will pull the dragon carriage together. No camping in the wild is scheduled, so that keeps the necessary travel equipment to a minimum."

"My body's gonna get dull if I'm ridin' a shaky dragon carriage the whole time, Bro."

"In that case, you can get off and run from time to time, Garfiel."

"I'll do that, then."

"You will?"

One of Otto and Garfiel's typical exchanges thoroughly confused Emilia. And that was how their journey to Pristella began.

That said, their itinerary proceeded in good order, and they spent their journey uneventfully.

They traveled on well-maintained highways, passing through multiple towns. Though they almost got into spots of trouble with other travelers at various rest stops, they managed to resolve things peacefully by strategically dropping the name of Marquis Mathers.

Of course, Emilia's presence was also a major factor. News about the royal selection had already spread throughout the kingdom, and many people knew she was one of the candidates.

Regardless of how people felt about it, it was a fact that Emilia had become too well-known for anyone to openly be hostile toward her.

Their journey continued in such orderly fashion for about ten days. It was a little too orderly, which was why—

"—Yes. This land dragon is very impressive. She deserves some praise, I suppose."

Sitting beside Subaru in the driver's seat as he held the reins, Beatrice swayed her legs as she casually commented on the ride.

Perhaps this wasn't obvious, but holding the reins wasn't only Otto's duty. To be fair, Subaru was dealing with a land dragon that he was incredibly familiar with, but he was certainly capable enough to be entrusted with driving their draft dragons without supervision.

However, this only really applied when it involved his beloved dragon, Patlash, and Otto's beloved dragon, Fulfew. He would also be fine with Rascal or Peter, the other land dragons being raised at the mansion.

The conditional driver, Subaru, smiled dryly as Beatrice put on airs beside him.

"If you're going to keep talking like a know-it-all, then you should switch with me for a bit. Patlash has enough motherly instincts that I'm sure she'll be kind to you, Beako."

"I shall decline. In fact, does the look in that land dragon's eyes not make it seem like she views Betty with some hostility, I wonder? Those are not the eyes of an ally. I suppose that talk of motherly instinct was a pack of lies."

"Hey, hey, I won't let anyone talk trash about Patlash, not even you. Emilia-tan, Rem, Beako, and Patlash are the only ones I won't let anyone bad-mouth."

"It seems rather strange that Betty is included on that list yet you refuse to let this slide."

"If anyone on the list says stuff like that, then she's the bad one."

As Beatrice made excuses, Subaru grabbed her by the collar and forced her over his own lap. He was about to proceed to tickle her when the wriggling Beatrice's hair grazed his nose.

What followed was a grand, spontaneous sneeze—and a heavy lurch of the dragon carriage.

"What the—?! Mr. Natsuki! Please take care on the road!"

"Sorry, sorry! Beako was horsing around too much. I'll be careful. Tickle-tickle!"

"Is it Betty's fault at all, I wonder?! Subaru decided all on his own to… Wait a moment, do not tickle me! Stop it… *Pfft*, hee-hee!"

Hearing the voices of the pair playing around on the driver's seat, Otto let out a heavy sigh inside the cabin. Seeing Otto so obviously worn out drew a little laugh from Emilia, seated directly opposite him.

"Those two really do get along well… Even though Subaru and Beatrice being on good terms like that was unimaginable not so long ago."

"In my case, I find it far harder to believe there was ever a time they were separable. Beatrice indulging Subaru and Subaru indulging Beatrice—it gives me a stomachache."

"You might have a point. But…I think it's a good thing. Everyone probably agrees that a smiling face suits Beatrice much better."

With a twinkle in her violet eyes, Emilia thought of the girl on the driver's seat. To Otto, her expression seemed like the one a loving older sister or mother might wear.

Though Otto was not uncivilized enough to say this out loud like a certain Subaru.

"Well, let us allow them to play while we engage in an important conversation. I have said this many times, but our preparations for the impending encounter with one of your fellow royal-selection candidates…is extremely lacking."

"So you're saying it won't just be a matter of repaying a debt."

"One year has passed in the royal selection, which is scheduled to be decided in three. Surely, each faction has largely finished shoring up its base by now. In our case, the assembly of the western lords shall secure us a good number of supporters. There's little doubt that the other camps are pursuing similar strategies."

"And that also goes for Lady Anastasia, I assume?"

The group had been intentionally keeping the fine details of what the other camps were up to away from Emilia. Developing Emilia into a proper statesman took priority over worrying about what their rivals might be up to—this was something agreed upon by the domestic policy team consisting of Roswaal and Otto.

Accordingly, after discussing the matter with Roswaal, Otto had been assigned the task of moving things to the next stage.

"First, let me speak of the present circumstances of the royal selection. In the beginning, it was viewed as a contest between Duchess Crusch Karsten, the favorite, and Anastasia Hoshin, the primary challenger. Including Lady Emilia, the three remaining candidates were viewed as…without mincing words, only there to fill in the other spaces."

"…Yeah, I don't think I can deny that. But based on how you phrased it, that means now…"

"Yes. At the very least, it is a fact that the public's opinion has gradually changed over this past year. The reason is that the three underdogs in this race have made notable achievements."

When it came to the Emilia camp, it was difficult to ignore the White Whale and Sloth.

The hunt of the White Whale was considered Crusch's achievement, but it was none other than Crusch herself who had stated that the contributions of Sir Subaru Natsuki had made it all possible. And though he had borrowed the strength of not one but two rival factions, the defeat of the Witch Cult that had followed had been achieved under Subaru's leadership.

These achievements had made Emilia's existence widely known among the people of the kingdom.

At the same time, this also spread the fact that Emilia had been born a half-elf, which for better or worse ensured that she was someone the people would keep an eye on for the royal selection.

And the other underdogs—Felt and Priscilla—had not been idle, either.

In particular, Priscilla's talent had flourished. She was the widow of Lyp Bariel, whose lands were on the border shared with the Empire of Volakia, with which the kingdom had engaged in skirmishes for many years. Priscilla had managed to make the most of this unfavorable situation, bringing the faltering and anxious regional power holders onto her side all at once.

With cunning that almost seemed to work like magic, she pacified the empire, made allies out of the local nobility, and proceeded to vigorously revitalize impoverished villages and otherwise strengthen her lands. Day by day, the people under her rule were regaining a sense of normalcy.

In addition to her ability to dance on any stage provided to her, she possessed beauty far beyond all norms. The south of the kingdom revered her as "The Sun Princess" with a fervor that seemed to increase with each day.

On the other hand, the Felt camp's one claim to fame was the knight under their banner, the Sword Saint Reinhard van Astrea; they had the most difficult starting position out of all the candidates.

Even with the overwhelming influence the Sword Saint held over the knights and the masses, his name alone wasn't enough to convince the kingdom's people that the master he served was worthy of the throne. Even in the Astrea domain, her base of operations, the regional lords regarded her with wariness when they weren't openly distrustful.

However, the girl named Felt had broken past those unfavorable headwinds in a manner none had expected.

From the very beginning, the strong-willed girl hadn't planned on lobbying the indecisive and cautious weather-vane nobles. Instead, she'd set her eyes on the people who had fallen out of favor—in other words, outcasts and pariahs.

By taking in the talented who were sidelined due to personality issues and those who regretted their dark pasts, Felt was able to assemble a formidable group. Her flexible thinking and unique perspective had revolutionized her territory.

She had little reason or inclination to rely on the rumors that she was a long-lost child of the royal family. She had a discerning eye for character, and assigning people jobs they were best suited to came naturally to her. In that sense, she possessed one of the most crucial qualities needed in any ruler.

And with that tiny spark, the lands surrounding the Astrea domain quickly became a beacon of prosperity. Felt's influence had grown so great that the local lords, who had been sitting on the fence, could no longer ignore her.

As her small footsteps had made a tangible mark upon history, no one in the kingdom could make light of her claim to the throne any longer.

"That is how things currently look. At the very least, no candidates have fallen out of the running over this past year. Ahhh, it is just..."

"What is it?"

"The only place where things have deteriorated is the Duchy of Karsten."

The pitch of Otto's voice dropped a notch as he elaborated. The reply made Emilia harden her cheeks. Closing one eye in response to her reaction, Otto continued.

"Duchess Crusch Karsten was considered the favorite, but rumors say she has lost her way over the last year, as if she has become a different person somehow. Previously, she was relentlessly active in public and private, and with the support of His Lordship the prior duke, it was considered a matter of course for everyone to acknowledge her. However..."

Whether in the royal selection or politics at large, Crusch's character seemed to have changed a great deal.

Her past determination had been so firm that it made her current shortcomings stand out all the more. Though she had formally taken on the important title of a duke, there were some who claimed she had finally revealed her true colors as an incapable woman.

"Apparently, His Lordship the former duke has been brought out of retirement and rushed back into service. After successfully hunting down the White Whale, it initially seemed like the royal selection had practically been decided...but no one can ever know when calamity may strike. Lady Emilia, please take proper heed of this."

"—I guess that's true."

Otto's admonition made Emilia lower her gaze, her violet eyes filled with melancholy.

Otto noticed that she couldn't seem to help but sympathize with her political rival, and he considered it a sign of fragility. It was inevitable that someone would be defeated. It would only invite hesitation if she let that weigh on her excessively.

Otto's experiences over the last year had taught him that this applied to politics as much as it did to commerce.

"Please do not dwell on it too much. This is only the beginning of such tales."

"Mm, thank you. I understand you're being considerate, Otto."

"That is good to know, at least—also it would be remiss of me to not note that the complete lack of any decline in influence whatsoever since the very start of the royal selection should establish just how terrifying the Anastasia camp is."

"Lady Anastasia has the backing of that big Hoshin Company. Apparently, the company began in Kararagi, but it's expanding into the kingdom."

"Yes. In other words, their financial clout is their primary weapon—their strongest card is simply to crush any competition through pure economic force."

Otto hung his head as he ran through the implication, fear settling in his heart.

Under no circumstances was his evaluation of her strength biased because he was also a merchant by trade. Making an ally out of a major businessperson was synonymous with allying a pillar of the economy. And so long as the economy continued to maintain the livelihoods society depended on, economic power was simultaneously the strongest offense and defense one could wield.

"Therefore, I believe that the Anastasia camp is the one we should be most wary of at the present. So for them to be putting us in their debt with that invitation... Do you understand just how much pain my stomach has endured?"

"...Finally, it's *really* sinking in. I am sorry for deciding all this on my own."

"If you understand, that is fine for the time being. If you can refrain from such rash moves in the future... I'll believe that you really do understand, so...!"

As Emilia bowed her head, Otto stroked his stomach and sighed. Thanks to the way that explanation broke everything down for her, Emilia, too, realized what kind of position she was in.

Of course, various things about the world of politics were difficult and complex.

She'd long understood that bracing her heart with phrases like *I'll try my best!* and *Let's do it together!* wasn't nearly enough to get by, but her eyes were spinning at the sheer amount she had to be concerned with.

She was happy to finally know what had been kept secret from her for so long, but in turn, her worries loomed larger.

"—It is not necessary to try to take it on all by yourself."

Reading what was in Emilia's heart from the look on her face, Otto flashed a pained smile.

"You might be the star of the show, but that does not mean you must do every little thing yourself, Lady Emilia. It is the same for this dragon carriage."

"Really?"

"Currently, it is Mr. Natsuki who holds the reins. Beatrice is watching Mr. Natsuki so that he does not slack off. Garfiel is above, on guard for anything in the area, and I am planning our itinerary. And with your voice thanking everyone for their hard work, we will move forward by hook or by crook as we head to Pristella."

Emilia's eyes opened wide as she took in Otto's roundabout analogy. Simultaneously, she found it funny how his meandering approach reminded her of a certain someone.

"Just now, Otto's way of putting that *really* sounded exactly like Subaru somehow."

"Ughhh?! Really? Oh no…could it be that it's spreading to me the longer I hang around him…? P-please don't scare me like that!"

"Hey, Otto! Having a fun little chat with Emilia-tan, are you? My main source of sustenance is Emilia-tan's adorable smile, so don't go nabbing my food!"

When the topic of their conversation suddenly interrupted them, it gave Otto a fright. Emilia reflexively laughed, and it wasn't long before Otto laughed, too, with a heartbreaking look on his face.

"Wait a…! Why are you two the only ones having fun?! That's super not fair! Beatrice, take the reins for a second. I'm going in!"

"What?! How is this okay, I wonder?! Stop it! Betty can't… It's tipping over! Aren't we about to tip over, I wonder?! That land dragon's eyes say it's about to happen!"

"Hey, General! What's up? The ride's shakin' real hard—is everythin' all right?!"

Hearing the commotion from the driver's position and overhead, Otto reluctantly rose from his seat.

It seemed that Sir Knight of Little Patience had reached his limits. Otto judged that it was best to politely yield his spot so he could soothe the land dragons.

"Otto."

As Otto thus began shifting from the cabin to the driver's seat, the call of Emilia's voice stopped him. What he saw when he turned around suddenly stole his breath away.

The trust Emilia placed in her smile struck him deeply within his chest.

"I've caused you a great deal of trouble, but I will do my best. I'm counting on you."

"—Yes, please do. I look forward to sharing whatever enjoyment you find along the way."

"That reply sounded a lot like Subaru, too."

Smiling wryly, Otto headed toward the driver's seat.

—This is why I work so hard.

Truly, master and servant alike were born swindlers. Otto had a need to rise to meet others' expectations of him, and it was like a disease that left him fatally vulnerable to people like Subaru and Emilia.

And as their banter continued like this, the twelfth day since departing from Roswaal Manor arrived.

—On that day, the Emilia party finally reached the Water Gate City of Pristella without incident.

3

Anyone who wanted to gain entry to the Water Gate City of Pristella had to pass through the main gate that oversaw virtually all traffic in and out of the city.

On the border between the Kingdom of Lugunica and the city-state of Kararagi flowed the vast Great Tigrasea River, which resembled an ever-shifting ocean. The city was constructed atop a lake fed by one of the tributaries of this massive body of water.

Entering the city required crossing a bridge that spanned this river and passing through a section of the circular curtain wall. There, all visitors had to present papers at the main gate that led to the city's interior.

When Subaru's party drove the dragon carriage directly to the gate, the official on duty explained the laws of the city and demanded they fill out entry forms. The details were similar to a vow that basically confirmed *I will act in accordance with local laws during my stay in the city.*

It almost went without saying that city laws were a binding authority separate from royal or noble law, but Subaru didn't take any issue with the city laws of Pristella at a glance. Most of them involved things like not inciting riots, not using magic within city limits without good reason, and so forth. After flipping through the pages, he quickly signed and handed the papers back.

Notably, the official became incredibly flustered when Emilia identified herself. That meant he must have known that Anastasia was already staying in the city and had panicked a little while wondering what in the world was going on.

"Suppose they can't help but be all nervous at having more than one royal-selection candidate pop up at the same time."

"But it does seem like Anastasia told the people at the gate to expect us ahead of time. They did let us pass right away, after all. Though maybe it was actually Joshua or Mimi."

"If you set aside his weird competitiveness, it's possible Joshua might've gone to the trouble, but I don't think Mimi would've."

He didn't think the cat-girl was capable of that kind of consideration. That wasn't an insult but merely his honest impression of her.

"She's cute, after all."

"Yes, Mimi is cute."

The mysterious persuasive power of Subaru's assertion made Emilia trade nods with him. To be blunt, he couldn't think of any other word to describe her. Also, for some reason, Beatrice stomped on his foot upon overhearing this. He didn't get it.

By the time he'd managed to restore Beatrice's sullen mood, he met back up with Otto and Garfiel, who'd stayed with the dragon carriage. It seemed that the check of the dragon carriage's cargo was going to take some time.

"They sure are strict for just heading into the place. Now it seems even more like a watery prison instead of a city of water."

"Truly spoken like someone who has little experience with life on the road. A traveling merchant would not even consider this a snag. At least they are honest enough not to demand something under the table."

"Under the table? Who the hell keeps anythin' special under that…?"

"He means a gift. Actually, it'd be bad if you take what I said literally, so just know that phrase means someone is asking for something bad. Don't let anyone catch you saying that, okay, Emilia-tan?"

Gift might have been technically correct in a broader sense, but given Emilia's position, even the hint of bribery was no laughing matter.

With that episode out of the way, Subaru and the others continued to an inner gate to finally enter the city proper. As the inner gate slowly opened, the scenery of Pristella gradually came into view—

"—Oooh."

After momentarily squinting from the dazzling light, Subaru spontaneously let out a breath of admiration.

And he wasn't the only one; Emilia did the same as she stood beside him. She opened her violet eyes wide as the beautiful spectacle before them left her at a loss for words.

"...So it turned out to be a city of water after all."

This view made him want to apologize for ever suspecting it was a watery prison.

When the prominent features of Pristella had first been described to him, Subaru had imagined Venice from his own world.

If one ignored issues of size, the circular city resembled a stadium for holding and watching sporting events. The elevation differed depending on the area's proximity to the city's center, and each stratum boasted its own orderly row of stonework buildings. A network of waterways crisscrossed the entire cityscape, and a particularly large one—better described as a canal—that ran through the heart of the city divided it into four parts. Subaru could see ferryboats in these waterways gliding in every which way, and the presence of what were essentially gondoliers stoked Subaru's curiosity and sense of adventure.

—This was the blue metropolis. The city of water. The Water Gate City of Pristella.

"Originally, Pristella was built on top of this lake using a combination of technologies from four hundred years ago."

Beatrice abruptly began a lecture about the Water Gate City as if to reinforce the feeling of wonder.

She glanced at Subaru and the others, who listened in rapt attention as she continued:

"It is constructed strangely, but if you think of the city itself as if it were built to be a trap, designing it to collect water at the center is only natural, I suppose."

"Calling the whole city a trap feels really spot-on. Was this place meant for demon beasts or something?"

"No records remain of exactly what this trap was intended for. But when gazing at the city like this, seeing how it looks today... does it even matter anymore, I wonder?"

Beatrice narrowed her blue-tinged eyes as she beheld the same stunning sight as Subaru and the others. It seemed like she had been deeply moved by the realization that learning about something academically and experiencing it firsthand were fundamentally different.

"...What? Why are you stroking Betty's head, I wonder?"

"Maybe because you just happened to be nearby. I wanna rub your head for you every chance I get."

"That doesn't make much sense, but that's quite enough patronizing!"

Though she fumed with anger, she made no move to bat his hand away. Still patting Beatrice's head, Subaru let out a breath of admiration for the city sights all over again.

"Damn, this is incredible..."

His honest appraisal elicited a wry smile of satisfaction from the soldiers who'd opened the inner gate for them. Seeing the reaction of people admiring the view was probably the biggest perk of the job.

Subaru could appreciate that feeling. It was a job suitable for the residents who took pride in their city's beauty.

"Huhhh, I see. Sure is a pretty place. Not the horrible thing Bro painted it out to be."

"That appraisal irks me slightly, but... Ahhh, everyone, we cannot remain halted forever when there are others behind us. Please get back in the dragon carriage for now."

Garfiel, fastest to recover, rubbed his nose as he shared his first impressions. Otto followed up by asking Subaru and the others to get a move on.

"Wow, not a very sentimental guy, are you? I thought you were a big fan of this place."

"Of course, for it is a land deeply connected to Hoshin, whom some even call the God of Commerce. Yes, indubitably it is a feast for the eyes. Have no doubt that I am deeply moved."

"But apart from that, you have more practical things to worry about? That's a sad way to live, you know."

Otto flashed a pained smile, but there were echoes of emotion visible in his eyes. Subaru didn't ask why Otto put both his hands together, but Subaru honored his stoicism by politely doing as he instructed.

"So now we go to the Water Raiment Inn Joshua mentioned… He said Anastasia and the others would be waiting for us there," Emilia said.

"Yes. The official told me of its location, so I shall guide the way. As travel within the city is chiefly by dragon boat rather than dragon carriage, we wouldn't be able to rely on the provisional dragon-carriage driver, Mr. Natsuki, to safely take us through the tangled paths here."

"I'll have you know that as long as I give Patlash a shake and a stare, she takes care of everything else."

Undaunted by Otto's assessment, Subaru winked at Patlash. The proud land dragon covered in inky-black scales quietly averted her face. For some reason, he got the sense that she would sigh if she could.

"Well, let's get movin'. Time to go!"

"Yes, into the Water Gate City!" "I suppose!"

Emilia and Beatrice added their voices as Garfiel pointed to the city and announced their departure from his vantage point atop the dragon carriage.

And so they took their first steps into the cityscape of Pristella. The streets were set at a fair incline. Seeing the scenery outside the windows scrolling by at a leisurely pace made for a pleasant ride.

"But even looking from up here, you hardly see any dragon carriages at all."

"Mm, I suppose so. In this city, the waterways are wider than normal streets. Even the shape of the city was decided with waterways in mind, so the roads seem to be *really* tangled."

"Ahhh, I see. So that's why there's all these labyrinth-like twists and turns."

Just as Emilia had said, the city had been designed to prioritize waterways, meaning that the streets for pedestrian and dragon-carriage traffic naturally had to either straddle them or take detours around them. It felt pretty inconvenient, but when Subaru saw the little boats heading down the waterways, it didn't seem surprising at all.

"Hum, hum, huhummm."

With the tranquil scenery filling her heart, Emilia began to happily hum. She had no ear for music.

The off-key humming served as background music as Subaru rested his cheek on a palm and watched the cityscape. Beside him, Beatrice sat on her knees as she gazed outside, a very childlike gesture indeed. And then…

"Ah, Subaru, look."

"Mm? Oh, ohhh…!"

When Beatrice called out to Subaru, a small boat was crossing a waterway—he raised his voice at the sight of the long-bodied, serpentlike creature drawing it.

Its torso came with short limbs and had a blue, slippery-looking surface. Its head looked more like that of a lizard than that of a snake, with sharp fangs and catfish-like whiskers. It was a water dragon—a dragon that dwelled near water.

"Unlike land dragons, which look like dinosaurs, these water dragons are like those from eastern mythology. Maybe I should call them shenlongs?"

"Would it be wiser not to, I wonder? Unlike land dragons, which easily get fond of humans, water dragons are famous for their difficult dispositions. It takes raising one from the time it hatches until it matures for it to recognize someone as a master, I wonder."

"That sure is a lot of time, considering Patlash and I got along from the first glance."

"It is a mystery even to Betty why she is so fond of Subaru."

Unfortunately, Subaru could only agree. Originally a land dragon owned by Crusch, Patlash was the reward Subaru took from Crusch following the hunt of the White Whale.

Without Patlash, Subaru wouldn't still be around. That was no exaggeration in the slightest.

"Hmph. These water dragons are nothing. My dear Patlash has a much more refined face."

"Subaru, why are you suddenly talking like Anne?"

The way Subaru burned with an oddly antagonistic spirit toward the elegantly swimming water dragon made Emilia give him a mystified look.

That moment, though the water dragon surely had not overheard their conversation, it abruptly turned its head in their direction. Then the water dragon jutted its head from the surface as it sent a high-pitched neigh slamming into the dragon carriage.

This was not an amiable neigh conveying, *Welcome to Pristella!* but the sort of sound that implied, *Stop staring at me, filthy outsiders!*

"That bastard, it's making fun of us, isn't it?! All high-and-mighty just because this is its home turf..."

"———!!"

It was Subaru whom Otto had asked to avoid unnecessary disputes, but Subaru's spiteful comments were interrupted by a sharp, vivid, awe-inspiring neigh—Patlash's howl.

In her master's stead, she had responded to the water dragon's provocative attitude, returning the favor in a gallant fashion.

He didn't know what meaning the neigh carried, but the water dragon seemed terrified by her reply, making a small sound as it sank into the water, immediately fleeing and taking the little boat along with it.

"Wait a second, Mr. Natsuki! Please do not make Ms. Patlash do strange things all of a sudden! I really do not want to get involved in trouble so soon after our arrival!"

When Otto called from the driver's seat, Subaru stuck his hand out the window and waved back. Then he blew a finger whistle of thanks toward Patlash. The pitch-black dragon responded with a ladylike sway of her tail.

"Awww. The water dragon looked cool, too, but I think Patlash is the best."

"...Well, does Betty not also think our girl is better than that vulgar water dragon, I wonder?"

Concurring with the pleased-looking Subaru, Beatrice seemed both proud and inconsiderate. After he put the girl on his lap, they continued raising voices of admiration over the cityscape for a little while thereafter.

"Come to think of it, it looked like the waterways split this city into four."

"Mm, yeah. The Great Waterway in the middle of Pristella divides it into four, and these sections are called the First, Second, Third, and Fourth Districts, respectively."

"Just doesn't feel right. How about naming them after the four gods Suzaku, Seiryu, Byakko, and Genbu?"

"Ahhh, that sounds kinda cool. Me, I'm all for that."

"I really do not understand Subaru's and Garfiel's taste. Ohhh..."

Garfiel peered in through the window and shared Subaru's enthusiasm. Beatrice shrugged at the pair when a sudden shudder surprised her.

The wind repel blessing ought to have meant they would not feel any effect from the dragon carriage shaking on bad roads. Such an impact even so meant either that the dragon carriage was being bowled onto its side or—

"—If we have arrived at our destination, yes? Meaning we have arrived."

Otto, poking his head into the cabin from the driver's seat, thus announced that the dragon carriage had stopped.

"Faster than I thought. We've barely gotten a chance to enjoy the city."

"Please do that on your own free time. I must speak to the innkeeper to have the dragon carriage, Fulfew, and Patlash stabled, so if the rest of you could… No, it is indeed best if you remain at the entrance."

"Why the correction? What, you're worried about letting us go ahead of you?!"

"I certainly am. I can barely contemplate what would happen if you meet Lady Anastasia at the inn before I am able to rejoin you. The marquis did say as much."

The only thing the culprits involved in the previous offense could do in response to Otto's words was to hang their heads in shame. From there, they unloaded only the hand luggage from the dragon carriage as Otto followed the guidance of the inn staff and brought the dragon carriage as well as the dragons behind the inn.

Seeing him and the dragons off, Subaru and the others finally headed to the front door of the inn—the Water Raiment.

"Now then, what sort of place should I expect this to be…?"

When Subaru looked up at the structure with high spirits, his mouth dropped open as he stiffened.

Beside Subaru, Emilia touched her own cheek with a finger as she gazed at the same inn.

"Somehow, the building seems *really* mysterious. This is the first time I've seen something like this."

Emilia's floaty impression was largely the same as those of Beatrice and Garfiel. However, Subaru was the only one who could not help harboring a different impression than them.

Of course he couldn't. After all, standing before him was—

"This isn't some ordinary fantasy-world bed-and-breakfast… It's literally a traditional Japanese inn…"

Before his eyes was a blocky building of wooden construction. The entrance had a wooden door with glass facing, the yard had a hedge, there was a path of cobblestones leading from the gate to the front door, and the roof was tiled.

This was a city that greatly resembled the famous Venice and came with matching architecture and furnishings. This was the last place Subaru Natsuki expected to encounter an unmistakably Japanese building in the form of the Water Raiment.

"—Seems like you're surprised. I was right to pick this place, hmm?"

An amused voice suddenly spoke up.

When Subaru turned toward the speaker in a daze, he caught sight of some teasing light-blue eyes peering at him from the other side of the hedge.

It was a beautiful girl wearing a white dress paired with an eye-catching fox-fur scarf. The cold season had surely already passed, but her attire had not changed whatsoever since the last time he'd seen her.

She had a rather small stature and long, wavy light-purple hair. An elegant smile came over her adorable face, and her big, round eyes somehow seemed bottomless.

There was no mistaking that this was the person who had invited Subaru and the others to this city—

"—Anastasia."

"Yep. Welcome to Pristella. And thank you for coming."

Anastasia Hoshin beamed as she greeted her guests in person.

4

"You've come such a long way. You must be tired from your journey… First, let's get you settled into your rooms. Then we can take our time to talk things over."

When Anastasia smiled and spoke those words, Subaru was too dazed to respond right away. He felt like they'd suddenly been ambushed just like Otto had feared.

If this continued, Anastasia would completely dictate the pace. That was how everyone must have fe—

"—Thank you for going out of your way to greet us in person. It's such a relief."

Everyone besides Emilia, apparently.

There was little doubt Emilia had been just as surprised, but her gentle reply snapped Subaru back to his senses. When he glanced around, he saw Garfiel regarding Anastasia with a wary eye while Beatrice was firmly holding on to Subaru's sleeve.

It seemed Subaru had been the slowest to recover. The impact of seeing a traditional Japanese inn here had a far lesser effect on them—you'd have had to know of it to be surprised by it.

"—Your face has gotten even nicer, huh…"

As Subaru took a deep breath to steady himself, Anastasia gazed at Emilia and murmured. Her light-blue eyes showed no hint of sarcasm, nor did her comment come off as belittling.

That tiny exchange showed that Anastasia noticed the ways Emilia had changed over the past year. Emilia must have been barely recognizable.

"Well, her cuteness is the same…actually, maybe that's gone up a level, too."

"It has been a long time, Natsuki. We last met when you were honored for hunting down the White Whale and the Witch Cult, I think? It's been a whole year since then, but I assume Marquis Mathers is the same as usual, yeah?"

"That certainly wasn't us at our best. Thankfully, we have managed to keep it together since then. At the very least, we haven't disintegrated midflight yet."

"That so, that so. Lovely news. I must say, I am glad that both of you came together this time. Julius seems eager to meet Natsuki as well."

When Anastasia made that comment with her hands placed together, Subaru openly grimaced. Emilia and Anastasia both broke into laughter, making him feel even more uncomfortable. He did think that Emilia's reaction differed from Anastasia's in terms of purity and mischievousness.

Of course, neither reaction was what he would have preferred. Apparently, it didn't matter how often he insisted that he and Julius didn't get along.

"Sorry to intrude on this peace 'n' harmony stuff, but should we just be standin' around all day?"

The one who cut into that warm and fuzzy atmosphere was Garfiel, who'd maintained his silence up to that point. Clacking his sharp fangs, he glared straight at Anastasia with his jade eyes.

The glint in his gaze was blatantly hostile, but Anastasia only deepened her smile.

"What a cute boy. It's plain as day he's concerned about Emilia and everyone."

"Heh, she's smilin'. But someday, you're someone we gotta sink our fangs into. Gettin' along now is only gonna make things harder later."

"I suppose that's true. Garfiel is kind, so I understand why he would worry…"

"Dah!! Who you talkin' about?! Really gotta watch what ya say, Lady Emilia!"

Taking unexpected friendly fire, Garfiel lost his composure after a failed attempt to restore some sense of tension to the conversation. Even so, he quickly rebounded and attempted to get back on topic, but—

"—Ah! Garf came! Why did the lady keep it a secret—?!"

A high-pitched voice overlapped with a flurry of sounds as the inn's wooden door flew open with great force.

The head poking in from the other side belonged to none other than Mimi, her adorable face full of joy. With a flutter of the hem of her robe, she bounded toward Subaru and the others as if leaping clear over a hedgerow.

"Good job finishing such a long journey! Mimi'll show you to your rooms—! And after, you need to explore the inn! There's really amazing stuff to see here!"

"H-hey, wait, you! Me, I still had more to talk abo… Wait, she's pullin' me along?!"

"Let's gooo! Let's go right now!"

With all the power in Mimi's tiny body, she dragged away Garfiel while he was still off balance. Of course, if he truly wanted to break free, he could have, but in the end, Garfiel was slowly but surely spirited away.

"Errr…Mimi is…*really* energetic, huh?"

"You have my thanks for putting it so politely. Mimi's impulsiveness has caused me quite a bit of trouble on more than one occasion… but even for her, that was rather insistent."

Emilia's words made Anastasia touch a hand to her cheek in exasperation as she wore a troubled smile. However, that lasted for only a moment. "I would like to ask one thing," Anastasia continued, her face turning serious. "That boy Mimi was teasing… Who is he? He's an upstanding person, I hope?"

The question carried an edge of wariness one might have about some pest buzzing around a cute daughter or little sister.

From that alone, Subaru deduced the true intent behind Mimi's behavior toward Garfiel. Simultaneously, he let out a long sigh as he grasped just how loved and cherished Mimi was in the Anastasia camp.

"…Mr. Natsuki, why do you have such an exhausted face all of a sudden?"

It was just then that Otto, returning after storing the dragon carriage, frankly spoke his mind when he caught sight of Subaru's haggard state as they reunited at the entrance to the inn.

5

Under the staff's guidance, Subaru and the others left their luggage in their rooms and rendezvoused once more at the inn's lobby.

The banquet hall of the Water Raiment boasted hardwood floors from wall to wall and a long table at the center. The floor wasn't completely covered with tatami mats, but the atmosphere closely resembled a Japanese inn all the same.

"But points get deducted for not reproducing screens and sliding paper doors. The staff aren't in Japanese outfits, either. I guess for the atmosphere and that hospitality mindset, we can give it a net seventy points."

"I do not have even the slightest idea what you just said… Are you all right, I wonder?"

"I'm just flapping my lips to try and stay calm. I think I'll be fine even without someone holding my hand, though."

"…Oh really? Just to be safe, I shall hold your hand for a while longer."

Beatrice was squirming on top of a square cushion that was placed on the floor as she held Subaru's hand. He didn't speak a word about how she was gripping somewhat harder than usual.

To Subaru's right side, Emilia was kneeling on another floor cushion with her knees facing forward and her feet out to the sides as she examined their surroundings, finding the sight rather novel.

"Somehow, this place has a *really* mysterious atmosphere to it… From the outside, I thought it was an unusual building, but that feeling only got stronger now that we're inside. I mean, sitting on the floor, taking your shoes off…"

"And the bedrooms have futons in them instead of beds. The closets have *yukata* in them, too."

"Huh, interesting. You seem very familiar with all this, Subaru."

"Truly. Just where did you study this much about the Kararagi style?"

As Subaru and Emilia conversed, Otto joined in from his seat beside Beatrice. Hearing him mention the term *Kararagi style*, Subaru furrowed his brows.

"You mean this inn is Kararagi-style?"

"Indeed it is. Jabaneez-style architecture is a Kararagi tradition… This inn's design appears to be heavily influenced by it."

"Jabaneez-style construction… There's no way that's a coincidence."

Though it sounded a bit strange, the obvious connection to Japan could no longer be chalked up as a misunderstanding. It was incredibly difficult to believe that such a thing had developed naturally without any influence from Japanese custom. There was no doubt in his mind that this "Kararagi style" had been influenced by Subaru's original world.

"In the first place, Hoshin, the hero who founded Kararagi, is the one who built Pristella, inextricably connecting the two. One might call this land the place that the tale of Hoshin of the Wastes' rise to fame and fortune began."

"...This Hoshin guy sure did a lot of stuff all over the place."

"If it were up to me, it would be Hoshin who would be called the Sage. In any case, his achievements are simply too awesome. Nowadays, Pristella is formally considered the kingdom's territory, but there was a time when it was cause of considerable territorial disputes between Lugunica and Kararagi."

According to Otto, the two nations had gone to war over it about a hundred years in the past. Geographically, Pristella was part of Lugunica's domain, but the fact that the famous national founder of Kararagi had built it loomed large. Once the drawn-out economic conflict simmered down, the current-day arrangement was born.

"So Hoshin's influence is big here... I guess it'd be safe to assume this Kararagi style is related to Hoshin, too?"

"It seems that way. In his era, Hoshin was someone who introduced revolutionary ways of thinking and ideas ahead of his time... He reshaped ideology, technology, culture—everything."

"Interesting."

Nodding at Otto's explanation, Subaru let out a very deep sigh.

He was sure of it now—Hoshin of the Wastes, the hero who had founded the city-state of Kararagi, was most likely someone who had been summoned from another world, just like Subaru and Al.

Much of the culture linked to Kararagi, and the so-called Kararagi style, fit the world Subaru knew far too well. All of it seemed to have roots there.

This made him the third person summoned to another world whom Subaru knew about—but the time periods differed drastically.

Hoshin came four centuries ago, Al twenty years earlier, and Subaru one year prior.

What meaning was there to the time differences? Why had Subaru and the others been selected?

Subaru still didn't know why he had been brought to this world. Even after coming to terms with the fact that he'd parted ways with his own world and his past during the Trials in the Sanctuary, nonetheless—

"—From the look of things, you seem to be appreciating the Jabaneez inn."

Abruptly, as if timed to coincide with a lull in the conversation, a voice called to them from outside the hall. A wooden door quietly swung open, bringing Anastasia into view.

She was not alone. She had brought a single man who promptly made an elegant bow.

"It has been a long time, Lady Emilia. Originally, I should have been the one to welcome you ahead of everyone else. I apologize for the tardiness of my greeting."

Swiftly after he appeared, the man's handsome face turned contrite and remorseful as he apologized.

Just the fleeting sound of his beautiful voice from across a wall would have melted many a woman. The twinkle in his amber eyes held a passion that clawed at the hearts of any who merely gazed upon them.

That was the kind of presence Julius Juukulius possessed. This was the famous Finest of Knights.

Emilia responded to Julius's bow with a gentle smile.

"Yes, it has been too long, Julius. I'm glad to see you are also doing well."

"I thank you for your generous heart. It is good to see that you have refined your own beauty even further, Lady Emilia. I must say that the loveliness of your eyes is a national treasure—nay, a treasure for the entire world."

That annoyingly roundabout way of speaking and his pompous attitude were what made him the most irritating man alive—or so Subaru privately complained as Julius turned away from Emilia, who wore a wry smile.

"It has been quite some time since we last met face-to-face. It seems you are in good health, Sir Subaru Natsuki."

"...Don't call me that. It's sending a chill up my spine. What's with the *Sir Subaru* stuff? Just talk normally."

"Even if you say that, it is a well-known fact that Sir Subaru has formally become Lady Emilia's knight. Setting the past aside, you currently occupy a proper position. I merely intended to treat you as a peer."

"*Merely intended*, my ass. It's ruining my mood, so cut the sarcasm, or I'll sic Beako on you."

"I see. It seems that though your position has changed, it has had little effect upon your demeanor."

When Julius insisted on propriety to the bitter end, Subaru scowled as he clicked his tongue. Seeing this, Julius's face broke into a slight smile, this time bowing to Subaru.

"Then let us try again... It has been a long time, Subaru Natsuki. May you strive every day not to bring shame upon the knighthood you have been granted."

"Ha, damn straight. I don't wanna get beaten senseless by someone 'cause I've gotten too big for my britches again."

"I am offended that you would speak as if it was an unprovoked assault. According to my memory, it was merely a sparring match between two people of equal standing with their honor on the line."

"You sure don't know when to shut up..."

However, as Subaru had been in the wrong on every level at the time, there wasn't much he could say that wouldn't make him come off as a sore loser. Instead, Subaru devoted himself to being rather petty and refused to let a single insult slide.

After studying Subaru's reaction, Julius went "hmm," closing one eye as if finding this development somewhat surprising. Then he shifted his gaze to Beatrice, who was sitting right beside Subaru.

Noticing Julius's amber gaze falling on her, Beatrice glared straight back at him.

"What do you want, I wonder? A lady is not to be stared at in excess."

"Forgive my great rudeness. I never suspected that a high-ranking spirit such as yourself would be attending."

"Betty is Subaru's partner, so is it not natural for me to be here, I wonder? Do not assume I am on the same level as lesser spirits who have no name worth mentioning. Just because you are appealing enough to make Betty's pure maiden heart flutter slightly, you would do well to not get carried away, I suppose."

"Wait, wait, wait, wait, *flutter*?!"

When Beatrice rose from her seat and puffed out her chest, Subaru hastily picked her up. The moment he seemed ready to whisk her far from Julius, Beatrice interjected, saying, "Calm down. It is not really a matter of appearance, I suppose. Besides, it is the disposition, not the face, that makes the man."

"That's no consolation! Wh-wh-why you… How dare you do this to my Beako…"

Subaru glared at Julius hatefully as he fretted over this apparent threat to his relationship with his partner. The sheer intensity made Julius widen his eyes, but his expression relaxed soon after.

"You should not misunderstand her. Your Great Spirit has no intention of betraying you. It is merely that the blessing within me… the blessing of spirit attraction naturally draws spirits to me."

"Could you get any worse?! Do you exist just to bring me suffering?!"

"You wound me. Of course, this blessing has been of great assistance to me. It is thanks to this blessing that one lacking in talent such as I was able to form bonds with the lovely buds, the lesser spirits of the six elements."

"Would Betty ever lose to such a blessing, I wonder? I will say this now. Subaru is much more…yes, much better than you!"

"Thank you! And please don't hurt me any further!"

Beatrice would never betray him; Subaru was confident of that much. At the same time, her inability to find a tangible reason for her loyalty gave him a palpable sense of defeat.

Whenever it came to Julius, Subaru always felt a sense of inferiority. That wasn't the only factor, but it certainly was the main reason he disliked Julius.

"As per usual, my noble knight is infatuated with Natsuki."

"That is a misunderstanding. I merely wish to advise him as his senior. Now that he is a knight of the kingdom, his conduct has an effect on the reputation of all knights."

"In other words, what you want to say is that since everyone is watching, get your act together so no one can look down on you? That's so roundabout. Your flaw is that you're never straightforward about things like this, Julius."

As Anastasia spoke in a teasing tone, Julius sighed briefly and hung his head. He'd no doubt judged that if his master carried on any further, he would become the butt of the conversation. It seemed like this was a common pattern.

For his part, Subaru had already gone through the wringer. Emilia gently patted him on the shoulder.

"I'm *really* happy to see that Subaru and Julius get along so well now."

"That's a hard comment to say thank you for, but thank you."

The world as seen through Emilia's eyes was a peaceful one. Taking that sentiment to heart, Subaru put Beatrice over his knees after sitting back down on the square floor cushion. Anastasia and Julius also took their seats at the long table across from them.

"Come to think of it, is it just the two of you? Everyone else…Well, we did catch a glimpse of Mimi earlier."

"As you guessed, Mimi is getting along very well with your blondie. Hetaro, who really loves his big sister, chased after them in a hurry, so I asked TB to take veeeery good care of things before they get more complicated. If this was a divide-and-conquer plan, you really got us good."

"Plan or not, reining in Mimi's your jurisdiction. What about Ricardo and Joshua?"

Subaru understood that Mimi and her siblings were strong, but it worried him that he hadn't seen the rest of the Iron Fangs, Anastasia's private army. Incidentally, that worry included Julius's younger brother, Joshua, too.

"Well, even during a leisurely stay, we're not just sitting around taking it easy. Ricardo and Joshua are both on errands away from the inn… Come to think of it, Joshua wasn't rude to you, was he?"

"Not as much as you. But you brothers definitely take after each other. If he was slightly better built, he could totally take your place. Hey, why don't you guys actually do that so you can just retire?"

"That's an amusing opinion, but it would be rather difficult. My younger brother has been physically frail from a young age. Nowadays, there is no concern over him taking extended journeys, but as his older brother, I have often worried about him since long ago."

Lowering both his gaze and his tone of voice, Julius seemed genuinely concerned for Joshua's sake. Subaru scratched his head and averted his gaze as he felt disgusted bringing up such a sensitive topic over something so petty.

Naturally, there was a pause in the conversation.

"Errr, I think it's good to be rekindling old friendships, but if we have everyone in order, we should probably proceed with the formal greetings."

Otto, who'd maintained his silence up to that point, decided to break the ice. Anastasia responded to his proposal with deep interest and turned her gaze toward him.

"Good idea. I've been wanting to give the shrewd domestic adviser I've heard so much about a greeting myself."

"Hey, hey, you got some bad info there. That mistake isn't like you, Lady Anastasia."

"I can imagine the source of that rumor, but having it treated as inaccurate hearsay so bluntly can really make someone overly self-conscious. Truly, it can!"

When the "shrewd" domestic adviser raised a cry of protest, Subaru only cutely stuck out his tongue. Watching this comedy act between Subaru and Otto, Anastasia made a small smile as she nodded toward Julius.

"Allow me to formally introduce myself. I am Julius Juukulius, assigned to Lugunica's Knights of the Royal Guard, but I am currently serving as Lady Anastasia's knight."

When Julius introduced himself and elegantly bowed, Otto nodded with an awed look on his face.

"And this is one of the Kingdom of Lugunica's royal candidates, the girl of genius who runs the Hoshin Company based in the city-state of Kararagi, Lady Anastasia Hoshin."

"My lady!"

"Why did you take a knee?!"

"Wha—?! Oh, no, it was so awe-inspiring, my body moved on its own!"

When Otto got too swept up in Julius's performance, Subaru slapped him on the back of the head.

"Look! Our Emilia-tan is a fine royal candidate! She's just as impressive as theirs!"

"Yeah, that's right. I'm a contender for the throne just like she is. I'm *really* trying my best."

"Just look at that cuteness. That was E M T through and through!"

"I must say it feels extremely awkward that I am calmed by such a sight…"

The usual frivolities restored Otto's calm, which caused him to question his state of mind. Then he turned to face the other party, his mood apparently restored.

"Overdue as it may be, I shall introduce myself as well. My name is Otto Suwen, and I am serving as domestic adviser to Lady Emilia… Yes, through some twist of fate, that is my role."

"It seems like you have trouble accepting that for various reasons, huh."

"Honestly, I should be a traveling merchant. Really, why did it end up like this…?"

"That sounds rough. Well, if anything happens, you can depend on me. I won't do wrong by you."

Anastasia spoke with a sorrowful tone, but this was plainly an effort to pluck Emilia's domestic adviser from them. As if hoping to avert this, Subaru stood up and presented Beatrice in front of Otto.

"Incidentally, let me properly introduce her, too. She's my contracted baby girl… Uhhh, I mean, this is Beatrice the spirit."

"The incidental treatment offends me, but you may know my name, I suppose. Betty is Beatrice the Great Spirit, and as you can see, I am of a completely different rank, level, and cuteness than your run-of-the-mill spirits. Now that you have a firm understanding of this, might I request black tea and sweet pastries, I wonder?"

"Uphold your dignity till the end, sheesh."

With Beatrice unable to separate herself from that mascot-character feeling at the very, very end, Subaru tugged on her curls and pulled her back onto his lap. Then he motioned to Otto to move the discussion along. "Yes, yes," said Otto in response as he took the lead. "Though it is uncouth of us to force the conversation forward, there are a number of things we would like to confirm."

"Tee-hee, that's fine. It's my duty to indulge my guests. Do as you please."

"In that case…might I ask you the reason for this invitation to Pristella?"

"No need to be so wary. I'm not planning anything. It's been a year since the royal selection began, right? We're both in similar circumstances, so I thought I'd give us a chance to talk things over."

Otto's question got right to the point. Anastasia stroked the scarf on her neck.

Anastasia's demeanor and way of speaking were gentle, but the tone of her voice was a pretty ornament with which she concealed her true intent. Finding her hard to deal with, Otto licked his lips; the smile of the great merchant across from him, veteran of countless battles, deepened further.

"Based on recent reports, I feel as if you have lured us with blatant bait, however."

"*Bait* is such a negative way to put it. If I'm going to invite someone, then I should at least have a proper gift prepared. That's all it is. And if I am giving a gift, then it might as well be the best gift possible."

"...And how is it you know what the other party desires?"

"Tee-hee, that's a trade secret. That's no good, Natsuki. Trying to find out anything and everything about a girl... Isn't that rude to the two people beside you?"

Covering her mouth with her sleeve, Anastasia leaned forward and teased Subaru about his question. Subaru spontaneously groaned with a "gnnnh" as he was cowed into silence. Beatrice simply sighed, which didn't exactly make him feel better.

"It's not like we tried to keep our search absolutely secret. There isn't much we could've done if she simply heard about it from someone."

Emilia was indifferent as she spoke in the stead of her pathetic knight. Her words made Anastasia widen her eyes. Emilia tilted her head a little as she gazed into those light-blue eyes.

"More importantly, I think if Lady Anastasia tells me where I can find what I'm looking for, it's perfectly fine to be happy about it. That seems to be the best way to go about this."

"What a friendly reply. I don't have any intention of telling you anything just yet, though."

"But that means you'll tell us in the future, right? Thank you. I don't know what I can do, but I'm sure I will return the favor."

"———"

Emilia's smiling reply made Anastasia close her mouth. Glancing at this, Julius's expression relaxed ever so faintly. "Grrr," went Anastasia, glaring at her own knight over his reaction. "What's so funny, Julius?"

"Nothing. It is merely that I rarely get to see someone exceed Lady Anastasia's expectations like this. I believe that your genuine reactions are quite beautiful."

"Well, you certainly have a way with words... I see I still have a long way to go, too."

Regaining her composure thanks to Julius's comment, Anastasia turned toward Emilia once more.

"Let me correct myself. Even though a year has passed, you have stayed the same down to your core. Doesn't being like that cause a lot of trouble for Natsuki and the others around you?"

"Mm-hmm, it's true. I'm still lacking in so many areas, which makes it harder for everyone. I really have to catch up. I'm trying very hard, though."

"Let me correct myself further. You are even softer than before. You make me seem like a villain."

Anastasia let out a sigh, followed by a grinning smile. The sudden change in her demeanor made Emilia widen her eyes this time. After watching this, Anastasia looked at Subaru and Otto.

"Make sure you lend her your strength, all right? If she doesn't put up much of a fight, it'd mean trouble for me as well, so…"

"I intend to eagerly give it my all, but my basic policy and personal style is to spoil her with praise."

"Which is why the rest of the burden falls to me. Ha-ha…how did it end up like this?"

Subaru gave a thumbs-up as Otto's expression grew increasingly morose.

Anastasia shrugged at the sharp contrast in the pair's appearances.

"Well, it's fine. Seems like there's no need to worry whether you boys know how much a favor is worth."

"A favor, is it? Favors are excellent. You do not have to keep it in stock, nor does it expire by a certain date."

"That's right. And more than that—"

Anastasia agreed wholeheartedly with Otto as the two merchants locked eyes.

"—You don't have to put a price tag on it."

Their voices were as one. Anastasia smiled, and a listless smile came over Otto as well. Subaru felt like he'd heard such an exchange once before, but apparently, it was a maxim among merchants.

Whatever its practical application, the words made merchants sound strong.

"Now then, I suppose I'll get to what you've been waiting for. The thing Lady Emilia is searching for…is a magic crystal that can serve as a catalyst for a spirit mage, with the added conditions that it must be colorless and have a high level of purity, correct?"

"Yes, that's right. Could you tell me more about it, even if it's just something you've heard of in passing?"

A sense of expectation rested in Emilia's violet eyes as Anastasia indicated she was moving on to the main topic.

When they had first arrived in Pristella, Emilia's demeanor had been somewhat reserved. After all, frankly speaking, the sought-after magic crystal in question was Emilia's personal problem.

What overcame that faint hesitation was her hope of being reunited with her family at last.

To her, a chance to see Puck again was also a ceremony heralding a new beginning.

Anastasia smiled broadly at the expectations clearly welling up in Emilia's chest.

"The magic crystal you seek is owned by the son of a great merchant following his father's footsteps here in the city. He has quite some talent in business himself, but in this city, he is more famously known by something other than his name."

Anastasia paused, as if building anticipation for what might follow before finally proceeding.

"—I believe they call him The Man Whose Heart Was Stolen by the Songstress?"

6

"The Man Whose Heart Was Stolen by the Songstress…or the Songstress Maniac for short? Weird nickname."

Subaru gazed at the waterway with a quiet look on his face as he muttered.

The overly tranquil time of the Water Raiment conference—though it seemed grandiose to call it that—had come to an end, and Subaru's party was in front of the inn, preparing to head out.

Their next goal was to visit the Songstress Maniac and negotiate for the magic crystal.

Anastasia had actually ended the meeting immediately after presenting her information about the magic crystal's owner.

Not only that, but she'd also contacted the other party in advance, apparently having already made all the arrangements for a visit. Her sheer thoroughness left Subaru unable to do anything save bite his tongue.

"Of course, whether the negotiations go well is up to us, but…the problem is whether the other party is sane, right? This Songstress Maniac just has to be a weirdo."

"I wouldn't be so sure. Your heart was stolen by a single woman, and you publicly pronounced this fact without hesitation—do you not find your behavior at the meeting of royal-selection candidates quite similar?"

"Not that it's some kind of dark secret, but could you not bring that up just to get under my skin?"

Subaru's scowling demeanor left Julius shrugging in exasperation.

At the moment, only Subaru and Julius were in front of the inn. Subaru had finished his preparations swiftly, while Julius had arrived in order to see him off.

Subaru wanted to meet back up with Emilia and company as soon as possible. He already missed Beatrice's warmth.

"We last met at the honors ceremony, but…how have you been over the past year?"

"Stop acting like we're buddies sharing recent news. Now, what do you know about this Songstress and the guy who's obsessed with her?"

"I have not actually met them in person, but both are famous individuals here in Pristella. Not a day passes when this city does not hear the Songstress's voice."

"The heck is that about? Is this some recital they hold all the time?"

"Hmph. You will soon understand."

Subaru grimaced when Julius snorted and flashed that smug

smile. Julius's habit of unnecessarily building suspense only fueled Subaru's irritation.

"I'll pay you back for being a pointless pain in my butt some other time… Anyway, what is this Songstress Maniac's deal? I gotta say I'm not expecting much from meeting him in person."

"There's no need to be concerned; he is a man worth speaking with. However, if I had to warn you about one thing…I believe Lady Emilia would not be a problem, but perhaps it would be wiser not to bring Lady Beatrice with you."

"What is that supposed to mean?!"

When Subaru immediately asked for a response, Julius was at a loss for words for once as he quickly averted his gaze. Subaru could sense his distress. Maybe this Songstress Maniac guy had a grudge against spirits?

"If he hurts Beako somehow, I'm not confident I'll be able to hold myself back."

"No, surely, he would not treat her poorly… She might be the recipient of an excessive welcome, however."

"What do you mean by…? Wait. Don't tell me he's a lolicon…?"

"I do not know what you mean by that term, but…"

Julius trailed off at the end as he searched for an appropriate word within his own vocabulary. However, even a knight as elegant as he could not magically produce something so elusive.

Either way, the true reason for Julius's concern was clear, causing Subaru to clutch his head.

"My mentor was already a handful as far as troublesome lolicons go…"

Really, Clind had an aesthetic all his own. Subaru was mostly troubled by the fact that Clind and the Songstress Maniac might well have something in common.

Clind prized youthfulness and treasured the childish spirit. In other words, someone with a youthful appearance but a mature mind would be of no interest whatsoever. Accordingly, Clind did not find Ryuzu appealing at all; in contrast, he held Emilia in high regard. Furthermore, he practically treated Beatrice like a princess.

"My Beako is an all-rounder who's attractive to your run-of-the-mill pervert as well as the exacting tastes of people like Clind…"

"Why is it I feel as if I am being treated rather rudely again, I wonder?"

Beatrice, who had arrived just in time to hear his comment, puffed her cheeks up in a fit of pique. Seeing Beatrice there like that with no sense of danger, Subaru raised his voice, saying, "Get some sense, dummy! I'm just worried about you! Wake up and realize that you give off a dangerous level of charm just by existing! Be careful so I don't have to worry this much! Damn it, you're so cute…!"

"Eh, ah, mm… W-well, it's only natural that you would worry about that, I suppose. Tee-hee-hee."

Even though he'd just warned her about her carelessness, Beatrice simply grasped Subaru's hand with delight. For the moment, he decided to firmly hold on to her hand and never let go. He needed to be especially careful in this city.

"Incidentally, Beako, you came by yourself? Wasn't Emilia-tan in the same room as you?"

"Emilia and Otto are searching for Garfiel. He must be taking a stroll inside the inn, I suppose. In the meanwhile, Betty has come here so that Subaru wouldn't get lonely."

"I see. You're cute even when you're condescending."

Stroking Beatrice's dazzling hair, Subaru turned his gaze toward the inn. Garfiel was no doubt engaged in arduous combat with the three siblings at that very moment.

If worse came to worst, abandoning Garfiel and departing immediately was an option.

"Then again, leaving without him would make it pretty meaningless to have brought him as an escort. No, wait a sec. When you think of it as him drawing away three of the enemy at the same time…"

"It is not good to think so belligerently. Even if that were the case, who would be my opponent? Hmph, you, perhaps?"

"You laughed a bit just now, didn't you? You don't think I can cut it? I'll have you know—Beako 'n' I are dangerous when we put our power together. You'd be struck with awe, okay?"

"Precisely. You would be astonished, I suppose."

When Julius made a provocative remark, Subaru grabbed Beatrice and pushed her to the fore. When he saw Beatrice puffing her chest out, Julius raised both hands in apparent surrender.

Then during that exchange among the trio, a voice called out to them—

"—Brother, I have just returned."

A young man waved his hand as he climbed up from a waterway onto a footpath. The new arrival had a delicate face with a monocle—Joshua. Seeing him made Julius stand straighter with a smile.

"So you made it in time. Thank you for your hard work, Joshua."

"Not at all. Please feel free to leave this much in my hands any time you wish. Also…"

Hearing his older brother's thanks, Joshua's expression relaxed. After that, he looked at Subaru and Beatrice. Instantly, keenly, and very blatantly, the temperature in his yellow eyes turned cold.

"…Both of you, thank you for coming all this way. I believe you have already spoken to Lady Anastasia. I am sorry that I was unable to join you."

"Mm, don't sweat it… I heard you were out to take care of some kind of business."

"Yes. By the command of Lady Anastasia, I went to the trading company to…prepare a dragon boat for you. Please make use of it during your time in the city."

"Dragon boat!"

The statement was delivered in an oddly chilly tone, but the content made Subaru's eyes sparkle. Behind Joshua, in the waterway from which he had just emerged, Subaru saw a water dragon with its outstretched head turned their way.

"A pilot has also been provided. I employed Hoshin Company connections to secure a trustworthy person."

"That's being very thorough. What's really important is that this is the stuff of dreams and fantasy, so thanks for setting all this up."

"Pay it no heed. I mentioned it already, but this was on Lady

Anastasia's orders. If anything, I sought to finish preparations as early as possible to keep my older brother from dealing with Sir Natsuki any longer than necessary, but…"

"You're one hell of a blunt guy, aren't you?"

Joshua's overly forthright nature brought a strained smile to Subaru's face. But Julius was the one surprised in his stead. He raised his shapely eyebrows, apparently unaware of the enmity his younger brother had held toward Subaru until this moment.

"Joshua, all of them are Lady Anastasia's guests of honor, him included. Rudeness toward him is a slight upon the honor of Lady Anastasia, our liege. Refrain from this in the future."

"…I—I am very sorry, Brother."

After getting a scolding from Julius, Joshua clenched his jaw as he bowed his head. Julius sighed at the sight, glancing at Subaru and Beatrice with an apologetic look in his eyes.

"I am sorry. I apologize for our impropriety. Normally, my younger brother would absolutely never behave in such a manner… Perhaps the change in environment has him more worked up than usual."

"Not that I mind, but if it's really because this is some new, unfamiliar place, then you need to keep a firm grip on the reins as the older brother. I don't wanna have both siblings nipping at my heels, Big Bro."

"Hmph, I shall keep that in mind."

When Julius returned to normal and wore his usual smug smile, Subaru shrugged in exasperation. As he did, Beatrice went, "Ah," her voice trickling out as she held Subaru's hand and trained her gaze toward the inn.

Just as Subaru turned to see what had caught her attention, the door to the inn was flung open as several people emerged.

"Hey, General! It's terrible ya just abandoned me like that! This ain't no joke!"

Garfiel came first, his sparkling golden hair all a mess as he clenched his fangs. He'd apparently been at Mimi's mercy for quite a while.

"Sorry to make you wait. We just couldn't find Garfiel and the others any sooner."

"They left signs of mayhem throughout the entire inn, so we had to look everywhere."

Behind Garfiel, Emilia and Otto spoke of the difficulties their search party had to overcome.

Just as Anastasia had said, Mimi had whisked Garfiel away, which drove her two younger brothers to take up pursuit and interfere with their date, resulting in scuffles that had apparently broken out all around the inn.

"That was hell. If Bro hadn't come, I'd still be runnin'."

"So you've been savoring a meowtiful festival. Satisfied?"

"*Satisfied*, my ass. Those little bros tried to kill me as soon as that runt dragged me off. I was racin' around like *Gehanon's Fleeing Feet*, damn it."

"Well, those two little brothers seem to be obsessed with their sister to the extreme. You didn't counterattack?"

"They were on a rampage 'cause they were worried for their big sis, right? No way I was gonna make 'em cry over that."

Garfiel had steadfastly chosen to not raise a hand upon his sister-loving comrades.

Either way, thanks to timely aid, he had finally been freed from the sibling trio, meaning the Emilia camp was assembled at last. Preparations were in order to pay the Songstress Maniac a visit and engage in direct negotiations.

"Joshua arranged a dragon boat for us, so it's a boat trip from here on out."

"Wow, seriously? I *really* wanted to ride one. Thank you, Joshua."

Bringing her hands together before her, Emilia smiled and voiced her appreciation. Joshua's cheeks reddened slightly as he tried to respond.

"N-not at all. Your words are wasted upon me. I merely did as Lady Anastasia bade."

"We are grateful for your thanks. Please enjoy your boat trip, Lady Emilia."

The two brothers reacted to her gratitude in very different ways, which Subaru interpreted as a sign of how accustomed each sibling was to this sort of thing.

Having bid the Juukulius brothers a farewell, Subaru and the others began climbing aboard the dragon boat.

The dragon boat was the size of a small rivercraft and could accommodate seven people including the pilot. The good-natured, weathered-looking pilot lent them a hand, and when he saw that everyone was aboard, he gently launched the boat.

"The size of the boats is apparently set by city law, y'see. It's a compromise 'cause they gotta consider not just pilots like us but the comings and goings of other vessels, too."

The swarthy-skinned pilot gave that explanation as Subaru and the others looked at the boat like it was a novelty.

Subaru hadn't given it much thought, but unlike the dragon carriages speeding down broad highways, something like traffic rules needed to be set for the waterway boats that were the chief means of getting around the city.

"It's my first time crossing the water by boat. Somehow, it has my heart racing."

"Seriously? Ahhh, but it's not like this is a sea or anything."

"What's a sea?"

"It's like a…never-ending puddle of water. My homeland had that all around it, see."

"Huh, that's incredible. It's nice that you'd never run out of water in a place like that."

Emilia's eyes glimmered. Subaru smiled at her childlike impression of his birthplace.

Unfortunately, using seawater to supplement insufficient drinking water was spectacularly suicidal conduct. As it would be fruitless and complicated to explain that, he decided to simply appreciate Emilia's cuteness.

In the meantime, the dragon boat followed the waterway's current, picking up speed as it proceeded into the center of the city.

A dragon boat heading down the left lane of the broad waterway gave Subaru pause.

Mysteriously, the flow in the waterway's right lane was heading upward. Just what strange physics were at work here?

"Tee-hee-hee. Surprised? Actually, I know why. Look at the edge of the city."

When Subaru had that question in his mind, Emilia proudly pointed far into the distance. Looking in that direction, he saw that the circular outer wall surrounding the city was connected to some stonework towers. There was one giant stonework tower for each of the cardinal directions—west, east, south, north—it was impossible to miss them.

"Ahhh, I was wondering about that. What are those towers?"

"Those are the control towers that regulate the flow of water inside the city. Apparently, the towers themselves are complex metia that use the power of water magic crystals to control the current. It seems like the city's huge water gates are operated there, too."

"Heh, so those are giant metia! That's really something."

Nodding at Emilia's explanation, Subaru now knew the mysterious mechanism behind the waterways flowing in the city. The Water Gate City of Pristella really was different from other cities in quite a few respects. Beginning with its laws and its standing as a completely independent city, there seemed to be many things he ought to study about it.

"Incidentally, please be careful. Sullying the water is a grave criminal offense in this city. This goes especially for Garfiel, who has been gazing at the water with a frightened face for some time now."

"It ain't that I'm scared of the water. I just don't wanna end up like some waterlogged cat."

"Then could you stop holding on to my cloak with all your strength? Judging by the sound, it might well tear soon."

Sitting in the center of the dragon boat, Otto sighed at how Garfiel couldn't seem to calm down at all. The exchange brought a smile to Emilia while Beatrice simply shrugged.

"Goodness, everyone is too worked up. Would you behave yourselves and learn from Betty's ladylike example, I wonder? Subaru thinks so as well."

Beatrice winked toward Subaru as she sought his agreement. Then Subaru gave Beatrice a little nod.

"—ad."

"...What did you say just now, I wonder?"

It was Beatrice alone who overheard the murmur so small, it was almost inaudible.

When her expression stiffened and she took a step back, everyone else turned their attention to Subaru. Looking over each of their faces in turn, Subaru smiled.

"This is bad. I think I'm gonna throw up."

—In an instant, complete pandemonium broke out on the boat.

7

"Are you finally better, I wonder?"

"Nah, just a little longer... Whoa, this is bad. The world's spinning. It's still going... Crap, I thought I had this under control, but it's no use... I guess some things never change."

Subaru gazed at the current of the waterway as Beatrice stroked his back.

They were on a footpath by the Great Waterway, which ran through the center of the city. He understood why passersby were smiling as they watched the two of them sitting together in a corner.

They likely mistook them for close siblings—that, or recent arrivals who thought the Great Waterway was quite a novelty.

"Not that either of those assumptions is wrong, though... *Bleh.*"

"If you are going to retch in the middle of saying something foolish, you can at least behave yourself and catch your breath. There's no need to be concerned. I shall stay with you, I suppose... Get well soon."

Beatrice was gentle and reassuring to the frail, blue-faced Subaru. Indulging in her kindness, Subaru focused on steadying himself, wanting to recover as soon as possible.

Some fifteen minutes had passed since Subaru's sudden bout of seasickness on the dragon boat had caused an uproar.

Having gotten off the dragon boat midway, Subaru was left with no option but to rendezvous with the others at their destination by foot, with Beatrice staying close to him to keep him from setting out before taking time to recover.

Of course, Emilia had offered to wait until he felt better, but—

"Lady Anastasia has already made arrangements for the other party to grant us his time. The tardier we are, the worse the impression we make, and I would like to avoid giving Lady Anastasia a reason to ridicule us."

This was the merciless opinion of the domestic adviser who had neither blood nor tears to spare. Thus, Subaru had been abandoned by the party.

That said, on top of having no idea how long his recovery would take, Subaru's pride wouldn't allow the issue of his seasickness to slow Emilia down. Then again, he had the sense that his pride had already been shattered to pieces. At any rate, he agreed that Otto's judgment was the right one.

"It's the nightmare from when I rode the ferry on that field trip to the ocean in elementary school all over again...or did they know about my seasickness and took advantage of it to separate me from Emilia-tan...?"

"Is Emilia someone who would be rendered helpless from the lack of one bumbling Subaru, I wonder? Then what is Garfiel here for?"

"Suppose you're right. Besides, Julius wouldn't tolerate some underhanded move like that... That guy is always the most chivalrous person in the room."

Julius's nobility was inflexible. Subaru had no reason to doubt him on that point. Due to that, Subaru didn't feel a strong need to be overly concerned about any conspiracy by the Anastasia camp.

"*Pfft*, Subaru, do you not trust that man a great deal, I wonder?"

"Huuuh?! No, no, there's no way! I mean, what I wanted to say is that his twisted personality won't let him, no more and no less! That's it—let's go already!"

After shouting his protests and pouting, Subaru jumped to his feet.

He rotated his arms and legs a little, confirming there were no lingering effects from his seasickness. His limbs felt a little heavy, but if that was the extent of it…

"I'll just hold Beako's hand and cancel it out with heartwarming energy."

"You seem to be in quite high spirits. Well, Betty will take care of you whatever happens, I suppose."

"Yeah, I'm counting on ya. Anyway, let's hurry and meet back up with everyone before Emilia-tan becomes sad and lonely."

They were already affectionately holding hands as Subaru winked at Beatrice. In turn, Beatrice's very presence seemed to say *leave it to me!* as they set out toward the trading company.

"Come to think of it, we've been focusing on this Songstress Maniac guy, but I wonder what kind of chick this Songstress is? A city of water with a songstress, plus Emilia-tan and Lady Anastasia, two royal candidates—it all sounds like some major drama's about to break out."

"I do not know what you mean by drama, but Betty has an interest in the Songstress as well."

"Ohhh, come to think of it, Beako really liked it when Liliana came to the mansion, too, huh?"

Subaru nodded and broached previous events when Beako displayed her interest in the Songstress.

It was about one year prior, before the royal selection had begun in earnest. Just a little after the demon-beast uproar had been mopped up, a minstrel came to stay at Roswaal Manor.

This minstrel was the same Liliana he had just mentioned.

She had a few…troubling personality quirks, but setting that aside, her singing voice charmed all the girls at the mansion to no end. That included Beatrice, long back before she'd opened her heart, as well as Emilia, who was second to none when it came to giving her honest impressions.

—And Rem had been a part of the unexpected new fad, too.

"———"

"...Subaru, shall we go this way, I wonder?"

Subaru briefly fell silent, and Beatrice saw a flash of emotion in his black eyes. When she pulled him by the hand, Subaru lightly sighed and slowly followed her tiny back, grateful for her silent thoughtfulness.

Their destination was a trading company that stood on the edge of the Great Waterway at the border between the First and Second Districts.

The city's layout prioritized waterways, meaning the paths were unusually inconvenient for pedestrians. But Beatrice leisurely led him through the city streets, walking as if they were as familiar as her own home.

After several detours around some waterways and countless bending paths, he crossed the waterway hand in hand with Beatrice.

"Look, Subaru. Is that not a magnificent water fountain, I wonder?"

"Ahhh, yeah... Is this some kind of park?"

When Beatrice expressed her admiration, Subaru spoke those words while gazing at a city park that enshrined a beautiful water fountain.

It had a green lawn, a meticulously maintained flower garden, and a large, beautiful fountain sending up dazzling sprays. This was a place that epitomized tranquility, a place of calm and quiet repose.

Had he the time, he would have considered taking a nap right then and there. Yes, if only he had the time.

"But right now, we don't have a minute to lose. Hey, Beako. You've been projecting this whole *leave it to Betty, and you can't go wrong, oh-ho-ho* energy—but you have no idea where we are, do you?"

"*Sigh*... Honestly, bringing that up when there's something so beautiful to see is rather heartbreaking. Are you incapable of relaxing, I wonder? As your partner, Betty feels quite embarrassed."

"The old you would've tried to desperately hide your mistake while your face went beet-red. You've become a little cheekier lately. It's enough to make Daddy cry."

Who was the bad influence who had transformed her into such an expert at making excuses?

He ignored the fact that had Otto been present, the adviser would have almost certainly made a witty remark, for Subaru and Beatrice had become thoroughly lost. Though there was some truth to the claim that Subaru didn't know how to take it easy, they really couldn't afford to take their time wandering around.

If possible, Subaru wanted to rejoin Emilia and the others before the negotiations for the magic crystal were wrapped up.

"In that case, would it not be best to politely ask someone to show us the way, I wonder?"

"Ohhh…I never thought I'd live to see the day that Beako would say the words *politely ask someone*. How you've grown…"

"Oh-ho-ho, Betty is not one to remain at a standstill forever."

Seemingly forgetting that it was her poor sense of direction that had gotten them lost in the first place, Beatrice proudly puffed out her chest. Since she was basically a walking mass of weaponized cuteness, Subaru refrained from pointing out anything rude and simply stroked her head.

Then Subaru started looking for someone to ask for directions. However—

"…What's going on? How is there not a single person in this park when it's the middle of the day?"

"I suppose this is rather strange. One would think a large throng of humans would be napping in a place like…"

Unable to spot any sign of life nearby, Subaru and Beatrice cocked their heads in confusion. Then Beatrice trailed off midway as she stared toward the back of the park.

Curious about her reaction, Subaru turned in the same direction when he suddenly realized something.

"—Do you hear that? A song?"

The flowers of the park rustled in the wind. There was the soft sound of water flowing along the waterways.

With this natural harmony as a backdrop, the distinct sound of a musical instrument and a person's singing voice tickled their ears.

Because of the distance, they could hear only snatches of it. Though they were but fragments of a dancing tune and music, the sounds clawed at Subaru's heart.

Naturally, Subaru's—no, Subaru's and Beatrice's feet were both drawn toward the singing.

"———"

Then when they arrived at the source of that enticing melody, the pair was overwhelmed, forgetting even to breathe.

—At the deepest part of the park, a lone girl was singing in front of some kind of monument.

The girl had brown skin. Her stature was short.

She had a cheerful face and big, round eyes with bright-yellow irises, and her hair was tied in twin braids with the ends hanging from each side of her head. Her hair and body were adorned with ornaments made from tree fruits and animal bones.

In the singing girl's arms was a lyulyre—a stringed instrument somewhere between the size of a guitar and a ukulele. With that and her voice, the girl put on a performance of stunning skill, her throat trembling as she wove the song.

It was the energy the music carried that was overwhelming.

A wind and tremor that should not have existed, a blazing heat that should have been impossible to feel, and uncontrollable surges of happiness, anger, sadness, joy—this was what consumed Subaru as the song enraptured him.

And it was not only Subaru who felt this way. Nor was it merely him and Beatrice.

As the girl continued to sing, an audience of some fifty people had gathered around her. Their breaths were hushed as they listened to the song, just as entranced as Subaru and Beatrice.

Finally, the girl's song reached its climax. The audience's emotions reached their zenith—

"—No money, no future, no dream, only vanity. Ahhh, what do I see? I see the darkness behind my eyelids. There is nothing beyond the darkness. It is over, over, and it all comes to an end."

"Hey, when you listen to the words, this is a pretty horrible song, y'know?!"

"Hyaaa?!"

The lyrics, which contained neither dreams nor hopes, made Subaru raise his voice as he snapped back to his senses.

That instant, the girl cried out in surprise as she nearly dropped the instrument she was holding, which obviously interrupted the performance. The heat that had permeated the place dissipated all at once.

The change in atmosphere made Subaru go pale as he realized he'd done something bad.

"Oh crap, I failed to read the mood just like old times! Beako, let's hightail… Owww?!"

"Stupid Subaru! It is ruined! What terrible manners… Could you be any worse, I wonder?!"

Before he could beat a strategic retreat, he felt sharp pain as nails dug into him. When he looked, his assailant turned out to be a red-faced Beatrice. The genuine anger in her expression made Subaru keenly understand that if Beatrice was grading him, he'd just spectacularly failed. And—

"Er, ah…a song?" "The park… I was in darkness until just now." "No, back then, I couldn't help it…" "When I grow up, I'll smack Temion and save Draphin!" "I wanted to cheer on her dream…" "Oh, Tina…" "Lusbel…"

—the audience members who had been captivated by the song gradually began returning to reality. Some had broken into tears because of the music, and there were boys and girls who had found that the song lifted their spirits.

And as they came to their senses, the crowd slowly turned toward Subaru, who was standing a short distance away.

Subaru's body went rigid when he caught sight of the glints in their eyes.

"—Don't ruin the moment!!"

The next instant, Subaru paid for his thoughtlessness as they hurled whatever they could get their hands on at the poor boy.

8

"Ow, ow, ow…that was horrible. Beako, how do I look? Am I bleeding anywhere?"

"Why should I care, I wonder? This time, not even Betty will take Subaru's side."

Beatrice harrumphed and turned her head away from Subaru, who was sitting cross-legged on the grass. Apparently, she was really holding a grudge over Subaru's rude interruption. She wasn't going to let him off the hook this time.

After ruining the recital earlier, Subaru had endured a hail of insults and projectiles from the enraged audience. If he was being perfectly honest, it had been a year since he'd been that sure death was coming for him.

Fortunately, thanks to the singer pacifying the crowd despite being the greatest victim, Subaru had escaped with his life. He'd managed to get away with nothing worse than being trodden on by the majority of the listeners as they departed.

"My left foot feels like it's swollen to twice its size. I'm scared to take the shoe off."

"I will not use any healing magic. Perhaps a little pain will help you reflect on your actions?"

"That's ice-cold, Beako… Well, it'd be a waste of the mana you painstakingly gather up every day, and I get it. It's not good to assume you can just rely on healing magic whenever you get hurt."

Nodding in agreement, Subaru stomped his aching left foot against the ground.

Since coming to this world, he'd gotten used to a life without scrapes and bruises, but it was true that he might have started taking healing magic for granted. Forgetting about wounds and pain led to arrogance. It was something to be wary of.

"Now then, since I've apologized to Beako, I should properly apologize to the offended party."

After that light exchange, Subaru finally turned back toward the monument.

The audience there had already departed. There was only one person left save for Subaru and Beatrice. It was none other than the singer who had finished baring her heart through song.

"Sorry that our conversation kept you waiting after I interrupted your singing like that. I never thought… Huh?"

Subaru closed his mouth in the middle of his apology. The reason was the palm that filled his vision. The girl had thrust her hand right into Subaru's face. And then—

"I have it. Listen to this— Doowop doowop, the difference of years in love."

Leaving the surprised Subaru and Beatrice behind, the girl rhythmically slapped her musical instrument with her fingers. Then she clicked her tongue as a cue to break into song, accompanied by a ferocious melody.

"Hey, do you see it, do you feel it? The difference between the years of love in you and me. People call it strange, but I don't mind at all. My worry is always the difference in years of love between you and me. Hey, wait. Please, wait. A little longer, until I grow a little taller. I don't care about a difference in years. The distance of love between you and me, the distance of soft, enchanting love—"

"The space between lovers shrinks and quietly becomes burning love. Then at last the stork comes past, with a child and a tale of love and bright futures!"

"Ehhhhh?!"

The song the girl suddenly belted out made Beatrice's eyes spin, but when the battered Subaru joined in as the song was wrapping up, the spirit found that it was beyond her ability to cope.

Of course, none of this had been rehearsed in advance. It was an act of reflex, but of course Subaru was a master of such things.

As the girl finished her song and offered zero explanation for it, he gave her a high five as they pointed to each other.

"W-will you hold on a moment, I wonder?! Why…? Why did Subaru just break into song and dance? And is it not very strange that you seem to find this all very normal, I wonder?!"

"Hey, hey, what are you talking about, Beako…? Music transcends borders, y'know?"

"What fine words! I, Liliana, am so deeply moved that my chest trembles. Not literally, but still!"

"I-it's unacceptable that you two are making it seem like Betty is the one who's gotten something wrong…"

These two weren't just going at their own pace; they had a *my way or the highway* attitude, and Beatrice had lost nearly all will to fight it. Subaru gave the spirit's shoulder a couple of pats as he turned to face the brown-skinned girl.

"Right. Just to be clear, don't get the wrong idea about my relationship with Beako. She and I have gotten real, real close, but even if Beako got taller, that isn't going to put her in my strike zone."

"Ehhh, but girls change over time! And I'm a great judge of character. I suppose you could chalk that up to life experience?"

"Beako might look like this, but she's already four hundred years old. I wonder if she'll ever change?"

"Oh, cooome on. There's no need to make things up just because you're embarrassed"

It was the truth, but it was so unbelievable that she immediately assumed it was a lie. Subaru figured correcting her would be too much trouble. More important, there were higher priorities than clearing up the misunderstanding around Beatrice's age.

Namely—

"It's been a while, Liliana! This was a total coincidence, but the most important thing is that you're doing well."

"Not at aaaall! Meeting you two in a place like this leaves me so embarrassingly, frustratingly happy that I can barely contain my exciiitewend!"

"She bit her tongue rather hard, I suppose."

Elegantly bowing with her musical instrument in one hand, Liliana smiled as an alarming amount of blood spilled from her mouth

ぺこり…
PEKORI (BOW)
ぶしゅー
BUSHUUU (SPURT)
DARADARADARA (DRIP)

even as she smiled. The bite must have had shocking force. Liliana pressed a handkerchief to her mouth, quickly dyeing the cloth red.

"Pardon me, I really did a number on myself there."

"I can tell. You seriously haven't changed at all. Kinda makes me more worried than relieved, honestly."

Subaru let out a deep sigh as he experienced a complex mix of emotions that came with this reunion.

Liliana was an old friend of Subaru and Beatrice's. She was both the performer in the park and the minstrel who had spent several days with them at Roswaal Manor.

During her stay, Liliana had brought singing, music, and her various personal issues to the mansion. In the end, these issues were resolved, and she departed from the mansion safe and sound.

"Who knew that we'd run into you here in Pristella. From what we saw earlier, it seems like you're in peak form, too."

"Yes, rest at ease. Since that time, my ample sensitivity has exploded even more, and I have devoted everything to polishing my skills further, so I have nooo trouble earning a living wage even in a city like this."

"The way you said that sounded kinda shady and even a bit dirty. I mean, isn't it bad for you to be in this city?"

"Hmm? Why?"

Liliana gave Subaru's words a mystified look. Subaru sighed at her oblivious reaction.

"You're technically a minstrel, right? But now, this city is home to some huge competition they call the Songstress. Ain't that bad for business?"

"I am not *technically* a minstrel; I am a minstrel down to every strand of hair and drop of blood! Also, also, it's so flattering how worried you sound. It's making my body throb aaaaall over."

"Whoa, what's with that way you're moving your body? It's creepy!"

"Did you just call an adorabibble girl creepy?!"

Thanks to her squirming while wiping a fair bit of blood away,

Liliana's face was left covered in strange splotches. Unsure whether he should call attention to her ghastly makeup, Subaru ultimately decided to prioritize advancing the conversation.

Of course, the conversation itself was rather strange. Based on what he had just heard, it was almost as if—

"Give up, Subaru. Is it not time to face reality, I wonder?"

"Hold on, Beako. I still want to cling to even the slightest possibility until the very, very end. Any way you slice it, this girl can't be the Songstress. That'd be total blasphemy."

"Ah, the Songstress you heard about? That's me. Ahhh, it makes me so blushy blushy."

"That's exactly what I was afraid of!!"

As Liliana's face became doubly red, Subaru clutched his head and shouted at the top of his lungs.

Being forced to confront a truth he didn't want to acknowledge—that Liliana was the Songstress—shattered Subaru's expectations for the rumored singer. Beatrice reacted in much the same way; she had a face like a child who had been full of hopes and dreams, only to have a promise to go to an amusement park dashed due to rain.

"Well, we saw for ourselves that the girl's singing voice is quite formidable. So Betty's eyes…or ears did not lead you astray after all, I suppose."

"I guess you have a point there… No, wait. If you're the Songstress, then the madman they call the Songstress Maniac is…?"

"Ahhh, you're referring to Mr. Kiritaka, yes? There's no mistake, none at all!!"

"Uuuuugh, so he's here, too?"

The name Liliana spoke so cheerfully made Subaru clutch his head once more.

Kiritaka was another individual who had visited the mansion during Liliana's stay. He also happened to be one of the problems Liliana had brought to the mansion; in short, he was Liliana's stalker.

From a certain viewpoint, he could be mistaken for a patron of Liliana's, enamored by her artistic talent, but as it was not Liliana's skills he was obsessed with but Liliana herself, he was definitely a stalker.

That said, Liliana ended up leaving the mansion with him, and everything had been settled peaceably.

"Come to think of it, there was talk of him inheriting some trading company. Don't tell me…"

"He is indeed the young owner of the Muse Company, which runs this city."

"So he even runs the whole city! That's incredible!"

Kiritaka's unexpected jump in status just didn't click with the impression Subaru had gained after seeing him in the flesh. Kiritaka was living proof that someone could change a lot in the span of a single year.

"It's almost enough to make you believe that Liliana could become a songstress in just a year."

"Heh-heh-heh. I am honored by your praise. But, but, but bunnies shouldn't just say anything they liiike."

"—?"

As if saying *Why, you sly dog*, Liliana ribbed Subaru with her elbow, which made him flick her forehead on reflex. "Adahhh!" she cried out like some kind of peculiar creature as she reeled.

"What are you doing all of a sudden? Don't surprise me like that."

"H-how brazen of you to flick someone right in the forehead! But I shall forgive you! After all, I have heard the rumors… Right? Sir Subaru Natsuki, the Moppet Mage."

"Geh!" "Geh, I say!"

The words Liliana spoke with a sparkle in her eyes made Subaru and Beatrice yell simultaneously.

Since having knighthood conferred upon him, Subaru Natsuki was permitted to call himself Emilia's knight in name and fact, but during that past year, he was better known by his "infamous" nickname.

The reasoning was that the knight of the half-elf reportedly spent all his time with a little girl, an individual shrouded in mystery.

"Word has it that you were of extraordinary help in the hunt for the White Whale under the banner of Duchess Crusch Karsten, becoming the benefactor of Wilhelm the Sword Devil in the process! And directly after, with the cooperation of two royal-selection candidates, you destroyed one of the Archbishops of the Witch Cult, which has continued to terrorize the world! A new hero's overwhelming march forward made four centuries of stagnant time move again!"

"Aaaargh!"

With the expression of a charmed maiden, Liliana put her hands together and rattled off Subaru's achievements. Though some were gross exaggerations, they were all based in truth, so there wasn't much room to protest. Ambushed by this physically embarrassing tirade, Subaru groaned in what seemed like physical pain. Meanwhile, Beatrice made a tiny snort and puffed up with a satisfied look.

"Afterward, it is said he ran all about from east to west in service of The Freezing Witch, together with a young child who is a powerful magic user. You did all that, yes, Sir Subaru Natsuki?!"

"Oh-ho. This girl understands things rather well, I suppose. Yes, Betty's partner, Subaru, shall sweep aside the famous names of yore and rise to even greater heights hereafter, shining like a brilliantly gleaming star. If you understand this, then you would do well to praise and revere us even more, I suppose!"

"Tee-hee—!!"

"Don't get cocky."

When Beatrice turned arrogant and made Liliana bow down before her, Subaru grabbed the spirit by the collar and lifted her up. Suspended like a kitten, Beatrice said, "Nya!" as her overbearing lecture was interrupted.

"Sheesh. Liliana, don't let Beatrice take you for a ride like… Wow, what a beautiful groveling technique!"

"Heh-heh-heh. In my life as a wandering traveler, I have polished the Liliana style of prostration. Not only do bandits spontaneously let me go, but they also want to donate to me, making my travels highly successful."

"Invest your points in minstrel-related stats, would you?"

That said, even as a singer, her talents were sufficient to earn her the name of Songstress.

Subaru had heard that many geniuses excelling at a single talent were eccentrics, and Liliana most certainly fit that description. Her lack of inhibition just barely fit under what was tolerated even for those of great talent, though.

"Subaru, just how long do you intend to treat Betty like a cat…?"

"Oh, sorry, sorry. Beako's as light as a wispy dandelion seed, so I totally forgot."

Gently setting the dismayed Beatrice upon the ground, he stroked and messed up her hair. Liliana widened her big eyes at the sight of Subaru and Beatrice behaving so intimately.

"It really seems like you two have become very close somehow. When I spent time with you at the mansion previously, your friendship was more difficult to pick up on."

"Well, there have been a lot of twists and turns since then. Even now, those are some precious memories for Beako and me."

"Indeed, I suppose."

It was because of the times when neither was honest with each other that the present had come to pass.

Liliana exhaled slightly at Subaru's and Beatrice's words.

"—You really have become a hero, haven't you, Sir Subaru Natsuki?"

"———"

"Do you recall the promise you made when we last met?"

Quietly, the atmosphere surrounding Liliana changed. Somehow, her voice sounded dignified, even holy, making Subaru feel like she'd suddenly wrapped a hand around his heart.

She displayed a passion that rivaled that of her singing voice.

"I am a minstrel. I am a wanderer who travels to every land to spread my songs. For one such as I, destined never to remain rooted in one place, there is something I must not fail to achieve, namely…"

"…The world's newest legend, was it?"

"Yes."

Liliana nodded at Subaru's words. This had been the objective of her journey since their first encounter. To a minstrel, who left behind nothing tangible when she departed, there was no way to leave her mark upon the world, to prove that she had lived, save through song. Creating a song that would be passed down through the ages was her life's ambition.

And that had led her to a single answer—

"—Sir Subaru Natsuki, you have become a hero, just like you promised. I could not be happier."

Though Liliana was never serious about anything but music, there was not the slightest hint of mischief in her words now.

In response, Subaru closed his eyes. He had no intention of responding to Liliana's earlier recitation of his exploits with a show of humility, passing them off as something anyone could have done.

He understood that no one would praise him for behaving like that. All the same—

"Sorry. I'm not a person who deserves to be called that just yet."

"Eh?"

When Subaru stared straight at her and told her that, Liliana's eyes shot open.

Subaru clenched his fist as he continued.

"I know that I'm only a little more reliable compared with before. I still have a long way to go. My journey's only just begun. There's still things I need to accomplish and things I need to make up for."

Subaru Natsuki had become a knight with the sole intent of supporting a lovely girl.

For Subaru Natsuki to become a hero, he needed to bring the Sleeping Princess back to his side, she who had refused to abandon Subaru when he was still weak and foolish.

And—

"———"

Beatrice squeezed Subaru's empty hand, respecting his way of life.

That was why Subaru Natsuki would do it. He'd borrow everyone's strength and see it through.

"So hold off on that promise to make a song about me until I've wrapped up everything. After that, I'll tell you about it as much as you like. It ain't cool to rush ahead to the end."

Whether a hero's epic or a fairy tale, a story ought to have as good an ending as possible. If they could reach a happy ending after everything was over, then who wouldn't want to talk about it? Even Subaru wouldn't say no to bragging about something like that.

"——"

As she listened to Subaru's reply, Liliana had hung her head at some point. With her face turned downward, Subaru could not read her expression; Subaru lowered his own eyes, figuring he must have hurt her.

Just as Subaru reflected, wondering if he could have said it in a different way—

"...ord."

"Excuse me?"

"—I have your word—!!!"

"Whoaaa?!"

Suddenly, Liliana lifted her head and thrust her fist toward the heavens, leaving Subaru taken aback. Liliana proceeded to close the distance with a red face and ragged breath.

"Y-you—you said it just now, didn't you?! Someday, you will speak to me of your legend as much as I like! In other words, the Legend of the Moppet Mage is mine and mine alone!"

"W-well, I'd like you to do something about that title, but yeah."

"Then my ultimate victory is assured! Hip, hip, hooray! Mwa-ha-ha-haaa!"

Wearing an expression of excitement and delight that was rather unseemly, Liliana threw her lyulyre high into the sky. She caught it, then promptly dropped it. She didn't care. She was overjoyed.

"Hey, is that any way to treat your instrument?! And you call yourself a songstress?!"

"O-o-of course! Isn't that ooobvious? I can't do anything with this. It's my precious; I love it so much! See, I'm kissing it! Smoochie, smoooochie—!!"

"You're really something… In terms of shock factor, you might be the second coming of Petelgeuse."

"Oh-ho, I do not know who that is, but it seems you hold this Petelgeuse in high regard. If we should ever have a chance to meet, perhaps I shall gain a worthy rival for life!"

"He's an Archbishop of the Seven Deadly Sins in the Witch Cult."

"Now that's a legend to take your breath away! Oh, you're the best!!"

Despite exposing so much skin that you'd think she was a dancer, Liliana pulled out something resembling confetti from who knew where and tossed it in the air as she showered Subaru with more praise.

Subaru sighed deeply when he saw that Liliana had truly reached a feverish pitch. Where had the solemn, dignified atmosphere she'd shown for one brief moment disappeared to?

"What Betty and Subaru saw was probably some kind of daydream."

Subaru smiled wryly at Beatrice's comment and waited for Liliana to calm down.

It would be another five minutes before Liliana morphed from a peculiar creature back to a human being.

9

"I see, I see, you have business with Mr. Kiritaka's trading company! Actually, I'm here in this city right now thanks to him. I can guide you there."

"Awesome, that'd be a big help."

Having somehow regained enough humanity to engage in conversation, Liliana patted her chest as she declared she would help Subaru and Beatrice. After they explained that they were lost and had business at Kiritaka's trading company, they'd ended up procuring her services as a guide.

"It's just that he told me he had an important business meeting today, so I should stay outside, you see!"

"Guess you would be a distraction for a serious business meeting. I get that."

"That makes sense, I suppose."

"Huh?! Against my expectations, are you actually agreeing with him? I'm woundeeed!"

Liliana gaped in vivid dismay, but hers was likely a needless worry. After all, the other party in the important business meeting Kiritaka had spoken of was no doubt Emilia.

Kiritaka was greeting a royal-selection candidate and had his own position as a merchant to consider. It would be difficult to have Liliana, who was liable to act up the moment she saw some familiar faces, attend such an important meeting.

"In other words, it's because of how you usually behave. You reap what you sow."

"What kind of remark is that?! Wait, I have it. Please listen—rough waves, tall waves, the waves of society."

"Though deeply intriguing, we do not have time to listen. Could you guide us there right away, I wonder?"

"Boo-hoo, the waves of society are rough, tall, and so cooold. Also, we're already here!"

Pretending to sob and weep for a moment, Liliana's face immediately brightened up as she rushed forward. Then she spread her arms wide in front of the large building before her.

"This is the Muse Company you've been waiting foooor!"

As Liliana spun around as if she was dancing, Subaru raised his eyebrows as he stared up at the establishment behind her.

A stonework structure, the office of the Muse Company, stood between Pristella's First and Second Districts. From what he'd heard, most of the traffic in the city was concentrated in these two districts. The fact that the building was situated on strategic ground between these districts proved the strength of the Muse Company's influence within the city.

"Even Anastasia said he was pretty good. It's enough to make you almost forget his image of being a pampered rich kid..."

As a matter of fact, the man was leading one of the largest trading companies in a major city. There was no mistaking that in the last year, he must've straddled the line between life and death, though in a very different way from Subaru. Just because Emilia was an acquaintance didn't mean Kiritaka was likely to cut her any slack at the negotiation table.

"Hooowever, there's no need to worry! The bonds we share will overcome that somehow! Leave it to Liliana Masquerade to use obligation and sentiment to smash the scaaales!"

"Smash them? Just what do you intend to do?"

"It's rare for me to speak so plainly, but it means I'll put in a good word for you!"

Adopting a peculiar pose, Liliana winked clumsily as she replied to Beatrice's question. Her answer left Subaru going "ow?" as he tilted his head.

"It's nothing hard! Mr. Kiritaka has a real soft spot for me, so I'm sure if he hears from me, this business meeting will be all smooth sailing. How does that sound?"

"That doesn't exactly inspire confidence… Are you sure about this?"

"This much is nothing at all. Sir Natsuki and I are old friends, right, right?"

When Liliana shot him an even clumsier wink, Subaru sank into thought.

It felt more than a little unfair, but the chance that Liliana putting a good word in with Kiritaka would be effective was certainly high. Seasickness had caused Subaru to be late, but it might have opened an unexpected door as well.

"Okay, let's go with that plan. I'm counting on you, Liliana."

"Yes, milord—! As you command!"

When Subaru indicated he'd go with the idea offered, Liliana looked extremely enthusiastic as she raised a tight fist.

However, seeing Liliana like that seemed to make Beatrice more than a bit concerned.

"Subaru, is this really all right, I wonder? Betty is uneasy."

"I'm painfully aware of how you feel. But I wanna bet that this is our silver lining. I don't want to end up doing nothing more than being the vomiting, seasick jerk."

"Does anyone actually think of you as a vomiting, seasick jerk, I wonder…?"

At any rate, seeing that Subaru had made up his mind, Beatrice said no more. She seemed unable to hide her worry, but they would try trusting in Liliana's stage presence just this once.

"And so Liliana makes her dramatic return. Where is Mr. Kiritaka?"

After Liliana psyched herself up, she shoved open the door to the Muse Company at the head of the group. There was a receptionist right inside the entrance on the first floor, who widened her eyes at Liliana's words.

"Ah, the president is in a business meeting with some guests… Um, Ms. Liliana, why are you here? This is a problem."

"Getting that treatment from the very start is already making me worried. What sort of impression did you make here…?"

The receptionist's nervous words were plainly tinged with concern and bewilderment. She was treating Liliana less like a pest and more like she wasn't sure how to deal with a dog that hadn't been housebroken.

"Sure about that? Didn't you hear that some of the guests the president is meeting with were running late?"

"Yes, I am aware of this. A man and a mop…a young woman."

Subaru was pretty sure the receptionist was about to say *moppet* while looking at Beatrice, but she was apparently a polished professional. She made a quick recovery and bowed deeply.

"The president is with the rest of your party on the second floor. Allow me to show you…"

"Hold on, just leave that part to me! I have something to say directly to Mr. Kiritaka!"

Liliana's statement, burning with a sense of duty, made the receptionist look at Subaru. He nodded back.

"Liliana and the president here are both acquaintances of ours. Thanks for the concern."

"...Understood. Do be careful."

After Subaru spelled it out for her, the receptionist had no option but to back down. Her parting words provided a glimpse of her conscience. Subaru acknowledged her concern and then headed toward the second floor.

"So what sort of business do you have with Mr. Kiritaka today?"

"I can't believe you've been so confident even though you didn't even know that much, but it's about an arrangement for a magic crystal. The Muse Company deals in magic crystals, so you must've heard some details, right?"

"Oh, yes. I did hear they found a gemstone of rare beauty recently... Is that what you mean?"

Apparently, word of it had reached Liliana's ears as well. This rare gemstone was likely the magic crystal they were after.

Subaru admired Anastasia's thoroughness in getting hold of such information as the trio arrived at the reception room. Then when Subaru stood in front of the room that had a RECEIVING GUESTS sign hanging from the door...

"—So I'm asking if you would please hand over that magic crystal."

Hearing a voice clear as a bell through the door, Subaru learned that the business meeting was at an impasse.

Both sides already knew each other, so the pleasantries of their reunion must have ended quickly, and they'd gotten right to the heart of the matter. Since Emilia was making her plea, the real negotiations over the terms were no doubt beginning.

"Bingo, Liliana. Now we just have to pick the right moment to..."

"Excuuuse meee!"

"What are you—?!"

When Subaru tried to wait for the right moment, Liliana immediately flung the door open. Boldly asserting her presence, she marched directly into the room.

Inside, Subaru could see five men and women in total. Sitting in tall chairs side by side were Emilia, Otto, and Garfiel, making three.

Facing them were a young man who had meticulously combed blond hair and was good-looking overall, plus a man in a white suit standing behind him.

The good-looking man was Kiritaka Muse—the young head of the Muse Company who ran the city even while being known by his other identity, the Songstress Maniac.

There was a table among the five, upon which magic crystals small and large of various types were lined up. It very much looked like everyone was in the middle of a business deal. Kiritaka was understandably shocked at the intrusion.

"L-Liliana? Why in the world are you here?"

"Isn't that obvious?! Because justice always wins!"

Replying with an answer that wasn't an answer, Liliana pointed straight at Kiritaka. She proceeded to aim her finger at Emilia and the others, who were just as surprised by her sudden appearance.

"I can't, can't, *can't* believe you would drive me away when you knew Lady Emilia and her friends were coming—such villainy, such cruelty! This is much too much—I might even burst into tears!"

"Er, ah, I'm sorry about that. But, my dear Liliana, I want you to listen to me."

"Noooo! I have no ears for you! I have no affection left for Mr. Kiritaka! But along the way, I was able to recover thanks to Master Subaru Natsuki, the Moppet Mage!"

"You're bringing me into this?!"

Spinning around like a dancer, she indicated Subaru with a flourish. All attention within the room instantly gathered upon Subaru. Beside him, Beatrice touched a hand to her forehead.

By this point, Subaru was beginning to regret all his choices that had led up to this moment, but—

"Nah, not yet. I should still be able to turn this around."

"I owe a debt of gratitude to the magnanimous Master Natsuki as well as *his* master, Lady Emilia! Mr. Kiritaka, this is a chance to show what kind of man you really are by making it easy for them! Won't you play a role in my dream?!"

Completely unaware of Subaru's struggle, Liliana made her proposition to Kiritaka in a spectacularly brazen fashion. Now completely swept up in her momentum, Kiritaka furrowed his brow.

After a little thought, he asked Liliana, "A role in a dream?"

"Noooo! *My* dream! To leave behind a song about the newest legend in the land! That is what Master Natsuki is here for, and he has promised that when he succeeds in this business deal, he will cooperate with my dream by answering my questions about anything and everything no matter how embarrassing! Liliana was nearly brought to her knees!"

"Eh, eh, eh? W-wait a— That's not what I—!"

Liliana had subtly altered his promise inside her head for her own convenience, which threw Subaru for a loop. According to Liliana, he'd already agreed to be the subject of her highly anticipated tale of valor.

It was more or less true that he'd intended to share his story, but the level of heroics she expected had apparently changed drastically.

"So please, I ask kindly for your consideration! Make Liliana a womaaaan!!"

"Think about what you're saying!!"

When Liliana began to storm closer to Kiritaka, Subaru grabbed her and hoisted her into the air from behind. If he let her rampage continue, Liliana the Songstress would turn this into her own impromptu stage. Beatrice and the receptionist had been right to worry. Liliana really was a drama queen.

"Ah, what are you doing?! Hey, hey, let me go! Oh, for crying out loud!"

"Pipe down! Ahhh, sorry to intrude… Er, more like sorry for bringing someone who intruded, I guess? Anyway, I'll get her out of here so you guys can pick up where you left off…"

"———"

Still holding the thrashing Liliana aloft, Subaru tried to leave the room. But before he did, a slender figure swayed as it stood up. This was Kiritaka.

Moving as if he were a vengeful spirit, he grabbed one of the magic stones in the lineup displayed on the table. Then he shifted his eyes toward Subaru—they looked fiendish.

"…na."

"Wha?"

"D-d-d-don't touch my Lilianaaa!!"

The next instant, Kiritaka's voice went shrill as he hurled the blue magic stone in his hand.

Just before pure energy exploded, Subaru immediately went from carrying Liliana to casting her aside. That was all he had time to do. An instant later, he was enveloped in blue light.

The explosive sound and the shock wave that blew the reception room apart announced that negotiations had fallen through on the first day.

WAH!

CHAPTER 3

AN UNEXPECTED, UNPLANNED REUNION LONG IN COMING

1

"I am sorry it turned out like this after so long apart. Even normally, our young master is rather edgy, but when Ms. Liliana gets involved, he is liable to lose control, as you saw for yourselves."

At the entrance to the Muse Company, Kiritaka's bodyguard spoke those words and bowed his head to Subaru.

The bearded man calling himself Dynas seemed fair-minded and acted accordingly, in contrast to his stern visage. The sight of him apologizing drove home his message that he felt genuinely regretful about his employer's act of violence.

"This is the second time you've bowed your head to us like this, huh? At the time, you guys were almost as edgy as Kiritaka was."

"…Ms. Liliana caused you a fair bit of trouble back then as well, did she not?"

With those words, Dynas made what came off like a self-effacing smile, which deepened Subaru's own troubled smile.

Just like Liliana and Kiritaka, this wasn't his first time meeting Dynas, either. He, too, had been staying at Roswaal Manor during Liliana's visit. His—no, their objective had been Liliana herself, so at one time, he and Subaru were something close to enemies.

"And Kiritaka's the one who mediated at the time… Is that really the same guy?"

"Small wonder you would ask that. Normally, the young master is excellent, setting his illness aside."

Dynas put his hand to his forehead as he sighed. *Illness* was quite an odd way of putting it.

Really, Subaru had underestimated Kiritaka's obsession with Liliana, which had even earned him a title as ominous as the Songstress Maniac. He never would've thought Kiritaka might lose himself during a business meeting and become so riled that he'd blow up an entire room of his office building.

Of course, the failure of the business deal was due to Subaru's thoughtlessness and Liliana being even worse at reading a room than he expected. On further examination, Subaru realized he was just as bad as she was. Why had he ever thought two people like that could be of help in a delicate negotiation where reading people's reactions was the most important thing?

"I don't even understand it myself… Anyway, from your position as a bodyguard, how does Kiritaka look?"

"His mood will likely recover tomorrow… I want to think so, at least. I am sorry, but he is not presentable at the moment."

"Well, I suppose that figures. Now, as for the Songstress in question…"

Trading sighs with Dynas, Subaru turned around. Liliana, who'd come to see them off just as Dynas had, was exchanging words with Emilia and the others.

"Really, Mr. Kiritaka can be such a pain. To think that even though Lady Emilia and Master Subaru came to visit after so long, we won't get a chance to speak—it's so irritating!"

Consumed by her own anger and fury, Liliana's face made it clear she was totally unaware that she was a major part of why the meeting had come to an early close. Emilia and Beatrice were gently soothing Liliana all the same.

"Normally, it's the other way around, right?"

"One should not expect normalcy of any sort from Ms. Liliana. Ahhh, may I have a moment, young miss?"

Interrupting the exchanges, which Subaru didn't know whether to call charming or shameless, Dynas patted Liliana on the shoulder and addressed her.

"I am sorry, but I simply must ask Ms. Liliana to restore the young master's mood. His schedule is packed today, so please save the rest for tomorrow."

"—. ——. ————. ——————. I understand."

It took her a fair bit of time to clue in, but even Liliana yielded to Dynas's earnest plea.

As a result of the combined efforts of the Emilia camp's Moppet Mage and the Songstress, negotiations had been spectacularly fruitless, dashing any hope Subaru had for a triumphant return.

"Shit, what silver lining was I even thinking about? All I found was more cloud…!"

"Is that all you have to say for yourself?!"

Waving enough that their hands nearly fell off, Liliana and Dynas bid them farewell and parted ways. When Subaru muttered to himself as the party was walking home, Otto sent spittle flying as he interjected.

Adjusting his hat after that outburst, Otto proceeded to vent all his pent-up anger.

"Why, in front of a man they call the Songstress Maniac, did you act so familiar with the very same Songstress? Thanks to that, talks broke down right when we were on the very verge of striking a deal!"

"Er, I thought I'd try and improve things because everyone seemed to be at an impasse…"

"There was no impasse whatsoever! We were working out the terms in a gentlemanly fashion!"

"Ehhh, you seriously mean I made a big fuss over nothing?!"

Naturally, even Subaru had to repent over turning his own worries into misfortune. Otto must have found the other party pretty responsive during negotiations. His dismay at seeing all his work ruined was considerable.

Depending on Liliana's efforts, perhaps Kiritaka would be willing to talk again the next day.

"Even if he does, it would be wise to assume he will make his terms more onerous."

"Uggghhh."

That sound was Subaru's only possible response; Otto had read what was in Subaru's mind and hit him right where it hurt most.

Then Emilia clapped her hands, saying, "Yes, that's far enough. Otto, there's no need to be so angry. It's not as if Subaru had any bad intentions, or he'd never be this down about what happened."

"Emilia-tan… Yeah, that's right. You really understand, don't you? Go ahead and say more."

"Subaru, you should properly reflect on what you've done. It's not fair. I wanted to speak more to Liliana, too."

"Huh?! So you're on Liliana's side and not mine?!"

As Emilia sulked, Subaru reeled in shock, feeling as if he'd been cut down from behind.

Watching the almost playful exchange between master and servant, Otto let out a sigh at the familiar sight.

"Setting aside that Mr. Natsuki should absolutely reflect on his actions… Negotiations have come to a standstill. For the moment, we should return to the Water Raiment and review our plans, but…"

"What is it?"

"Actually, I have some business to attend to, so I must depart for a while."

When Otto raised a finger and spoke those words, Subaru and Emilia both went, "Business?" as they tilted their heads.

"Yes. After coming all this way, it is advantageous to create connections that normally I could not. So for today, I will be going around and greeting people."

"An unflappably devoted professional, huh…"

Perhaps Otto was simply good at switching gears. Or maybe he kept a couple spare brains tucked away somewhere. Either way, Subaru had to admire his dizzying methods.

"Yes, about that, Otto. You don't need me with you when you go around and greet people like that?"

"A fine question, Lady Emilia. However, if you were to arrive without sending word ahead, everyone would be conflicted, since they'd be unable to give you a proper welcome. Refraining from rash actions is also a form of consideration. Much like how Lady Anastasia spoke with the Muse Company for us."

"I see… Mm, understood. I'll remember that, Teacher."

Emilia's reply brought a tired smile to Otto's face. Then he said, "Go home straightaway," as if he was speaking to a child, before leaving the party, vanishing in the direction of the Second District.

"Emilia-tan, what's with that *Teacher* thing just now?"

"Hmm? Oh, Otto has been teaching me quite a lot lately, including when we were on the carriage ride here. That's why I call him Teacher. Is that weird?"

"Nah, it's not weird; I'm just jealous. You can call me Teacher, too, okay?"

"But Subaru is my knight, not my teacher…"

"Gaaah, so cute…!"

Emilia's adorably conflicted look and hushed words left Subaru weak in the knees.

"The general and Lady Emilia both took a pretty big likin' to that Songstress chick, huh."

Garfiel joined the conversation with both hands entwined behind his head. He, the only one among them unfamiliar with Liliana's songs, crinkled his nose.

"Me, I wanna hear her stuff, too, if it's really that good. I've gone through a ton of books, but ya can't know what a song is like from just readin' about it, so I dunno what I'm missin'."

"Right, Garfiel wasn't at the mansion when they paid us a visit."

"So this'll be the first time you hear Liliana's song, huh…? It'll probably rock your world."

"Serious? That's some heavy billin'."

The way Subaru and Emilia talked about her music drew an expression of surprise and expectation from Garfiel.

Liliana's songs really did have that kind of power. Subaru previously had a few chances to listen to minstrels other than Liliana, but none of them held a candle to her.

It was beyond all doubt that Liliana was gifted enough to be called a songstress.

"I guess for that talent, the gods took a few too many things from Liliana in exchange?"

"A rather cruel thing of them to do."

"I don't really get what ya mean by that."

Beatrice's face showed how deeply she agreed with Subaru's murmur. Garfiel, the only one left in the lurch with just tangential information to make guesses from, clicked his tongue, seemingly pouting as he glared at the water's surface.

Incidentally, the four were taking the long way back to the Water Raiment on foot. Unfortunately, if they went by dragon boat, there was a rather high chance that they'd have to leave Subaru behind due to his seasickness again.

"It's such a pretty city that I think it's nice to have a chance to walk around. Like Otto said, we don't really have anything left to do today."

"I sure caused you a lot of trouble…"

"Ah, I didn't mean to blame Subaru. I'm only a little angry."

"So you *are* angry! I mean, of course you are!"

All that said, it was a fact that he wanted to take his time before returning to the inn where Anastasia would no doubt pry into everything that had happened. Subaru had no reason to object to a detour.

"The only worry besides that is whether I can escort Emilia-tan back to the inn safe and sound."

"Do not be concerned. Betty will watch over you, I suppose."

"Just to say this out loud, it wasn't only me who dropped the ball today; this involves you, too."

Beatrice was nonchalantly shirking responsibility for the failure of negotiations, but her passive participation made her an accomplice all the same. That her face showed no recognition of this was cute, though.

"No need to worry, General. My nose remembers the scent of the road all the way back to the inn. Even if I can't smell the building, I know the scent of that rowdy kid, so we ain't gettin' lost."

"Heeeh. Hooo. Hmmmm."

"Hey, what's with that reaction?"

Garfiel suspiciously crinkled his nose at Subaru's suggestive reaction.

He was mostly curious about the way Garfiel brought up Mimi. Mimi's actions were so impulsive that they were hard to understand, but he figured she had nothing but goodwill toward Garfiel. Their ages matched, too, so Subaru expected some interesting developments would come as time went on.

Incidentally, Garfiel continued to get the cold shoulder from his own target, Ram. It looked to Subaru like the only love Ram held for Garfiel was the sort one had for family.

"Either way, Garfiel, I wish from the bottom of my heart for you, my little brother, to be happy."

"Huh? What's this all of a sudden, General? Well, not that I hate that or anythin'..."

When Subaru patted his shoulder with a warm look in his eyes, Garfiel tilted his head in confusion and gave a blunt reply. Subaru genuinely hoped that his innocent little brother found happiness in this city of water.

"I have to say, this really is a splendid city. Everywhere I look feels like it's calming and peaceful."

On the way back, Emilia seemed to be in a very good mood as she savored the scenic beauty of the watery metropolis. The waterways cutting through the center of the city might have been slightly inconvenient, but they certainly did not fail to impress.

"According to Beako's explanation, the founding of this city wasn't exactly for peaceful reasons..."

"But whatever the reasons at the time, how we feel right now is still real, right?"

When Emilia stopped atop a bridge and gazed at the Great Waterway, Subaru was enchanted by her smile.

From her charming expression to the words she spoke, she was happy. Whatever the reason, that moment was genuine.

—Because what's important isn't where you started; it's where you end.

"I hear ya, Mom."

"Did you say something?"

"Just remembering some magic words from the woman I respect the most in the world."

Even as time passed since Subaru had heard those words, they still gave him courage even now.

Forgetting something didn't mean losing it forever, and he was determined to hold on to whatever he could remember. For one more day, Subaru Natsuki lived on, pulled forward by the feelings he had inherited.

"I suppose we should really head back. The mysterious way the inn's built is *really* on my mind."

"Jabaneez construction, huh? To be honest, I'm interested in that, too. For a different reason than Emilia-tan, though."

"Is that so? Tee-hee. We'd better hurry, then."

Letting go of the handrail on the bridge, Emilia smiled and took a step back. Perhaps it was because she was too giddy from sightseeing that she lightly bumped into someone passing by as she did.

"Ah! I'm so sorry."

Emilia hastily turned around and bowed her head to the passerby she had bumped into, a man whose entire body seemed white.

He had bleached white hair and a white suit. His height was around the same as Subaru's, and their physiques were a close match as well. In short, he was a man without any visible distinguishing features.

The man in white shook his head to Emilia's apology.

"You need not be concerned. I was careless this time as well—I was momentarily enchanted by you."

"...Errr."

"Your beautiful silver hair, yes. I once tried to make a woman with hair as beautiful as yours my bride. Remembering this fondly, I found myself unable to avoid you."

In contrast to Emilia's apology, the man's reply somehow sounded unnatural. His speech seemed intended to sound persuasive, but the sense of hubris was stronger.

"Okay, stop. That's far enough."

That was the moment Subaru put himself in front of Emilia, motivated by the forthright heart of a knight and the pure heart of a man in love.

"Well, it seems like both people were careless this time around. I'll lecture our girl for being thoughtless later, so please kindly allow us to leave it at that for today."

"Wait a second, Subaru. That's no way to speak to someone who…"

"Go with it, 'kay?"

When Emilia shot him a look of protest, Subaru winked back at her.

Getting into some weird quarrel here ran the troublesome risk of others realizing Emilia's identity. He felt more like a celebrity's manager than a knight at the moment, but that was beside the point.

"A mutual encounter and a mutual apology. That's common courtesy in a city of water, right?"

"Thank you for your politeness. For the time being, I have little reason to pursue the matter. Should we meet again, it will simply be the whims of destiny bringing us together once more."

"Yeah, I agree. Well, here's hoping destiny makes our paths cross again in the future."

As the stranger was speaking poetically, Subaru replied like a delusional middle schooler as he took his leave.

Pulling Emilia along by the hand, Subaru let out an audible breath of relief and looked in her direction. When he did, he saw Emilia glancing back a bit, the stranger clearly still on her mind.

"I was definitely a little rude back there, but given your position, I hope you understand."

"Eh? Ah, no, no. It's true that Subaru's behavior was a little poor, but it was because I was careless in the first place. But that's not it. I…"

Her words trailed off. There was a faint hesitance in Emilia's eyes.

"—I feel like I've met that person somewhere before."

"An acquaintance of yours? I think I should know most of them already."

"Yeah… I'm not too sure myself. I wonder who he is?"

It had to be really bugging her, because Emilia glanced behind her one more time. However, the man had already crossed the bridge, and all she could see was his fast-receding back.

Though it was tugging on something inside her mind, her search for answers seemed to have been in vain.

"Hey, General. Ya look pretty shaken up. Wha, worried some pretty boy was gonna steal her away?"

Garfiel, who had already crossed the bridge and was waiting for them, greeted Subaru with a wave and a question. Subaru understood why Garfiel and Beatrice wanted to give him and Emilia some space, but even so, he sighed over Garfiel's carefree attitude.

"Idiot, this ain't the time to goof off. What are we gonna do if some weirdo hangs around and you're not there? Emilia-tan's gonna be in a pinch if it's not someone I can handle."

"Puttin' your body on the line to protect her—that's how the general shows he's a man, am I right?"

"Using my body as a shield? I don't think I'm really built for that. As a human being or as a shield."

Garfiel flashed a grin in response to Subaru's almost humble self-assessment.

Garfiel seemed to be taking that as modesty on Subaru's part, but from Subaru's perspective, it was plain fact. If anything, Garfiel held Subaru in too high esteem.

"Hey, relax. Me, if I think a guy's trouble, I'll send him flyin'. On that score, the guy just now is an amateur. The way he walks and moves… Ain't even worth talkin' about."

"…Well, I guess that's fine."

One of Garfiel's odd specialties was his ability to discern an opponent's combat potential from their physique and movement. Subaru could personally attest to that; Garfiel had sniffed out his middle school kendo experience.

If Garfiel guaranteed that it was fine, Subaru was probably worried over nothing.

"In that case, let's go, Emilia-tan…or is he still on your mind?"

"—. No, I'm all right. Sorry for being weird about it. Let's go back."

"Sounds good. Don't worry—when we get back, you can hug Mimi or something and take your mind off it. Hey, I'll be satisfied hugging Beako, so you don't need to pout like that."

"Did Betty not refrain from saying anything about it, I wonder?!"

Subaru's words made Beatrice's face redden. Upon seeing this, Emilia broke into a beaming smile.

Then she gently touched her hand to her lips.

"I suppose so. If I hug Mimi, I'll feel *really* relieved. I'll do just that."

Thus, having seemingly swept her concerns away, she set out walking once more. Beatrice and Garfiel followed behind her. Then Subaru began to join them.

"———"

Abruptly, Subaru stopped and turned around, gazing in the direction of the bridge.

The man in white was standing on a city street on the opposite side of the crossing. He turned around and looked directly at Subaru.

Finding his gaze supremely creepy, Subaru walked off after Emilia and the others at a rapid clip.

It felt like the man's gaze coiled around him, remaining glued to his shadow until Subaru rounded the corner.

2

After that, the stroll back through the city of water proceeded without incident.

From time to time, Emilia gazed at the surface of the water and seemed to sink into deep thought, but whenever someone pointed this out to her, she immediately glossed over the conversation with a smile.

Emilia was terrible at hiding things, so it was easy to understand that the man from earlier was still bugging her. However, Subaru was certainly mindful of the man himself. That was because—

"Beako."

"I know. Did Emilia and Garfiel not notice because both their heads are in the clouds, I wonder? They both require a great deal of supervision."

When Subaru called her name, Beatrice shrugged in visible exasperation.

The concern on Subaru's mind, the one Beatrice had just affirmed, was how the man from before had reacted to Emilia. A year after the announcement that she was running for the royal selection, Emilia was no longer using the "ID blocker" robe when going outside, as she had done without fail previously.

I think that it's really *strange for someone who's trying to get everyone to accept her and who has to work so hard to become the king to walk around hiding her own identity.*

That was what Emilia had asserted, and certainly, it was a sound argument. Accordingly, Emilia had decided to stop relying on the power of the coat, exposing her adorable face, meaning there was no concealing that she was a half-elf anymore. Even so, the prejudice against a silver-haired elf ran strong and deep, so for better or worse, many of the people who saw her had strong reactions, be they good ones or bad.

"The guy earlier didn't have either. He talked like he knew Emilia, but he didn't give his name… Am I overthinking this?"

"If Subaru pays no heed, Emilia will be far too vulnerable, so it is perfectly appropriate, I suppose. Betty shall also keep watch around Emilia as much as possible."

When Beatrice announced that he could depend on her, Subaru gave her a short "gotcha" in thanks.

This watery metropolis was massive, and he didn't think their chances of bumping into that man again were very high. But it was still more than possible that the stranger would initiate contact on his own. There was nothing to lose by being cautious.

"After all, it's because I didn't think things through enough that today's negotiations failed, so…!"

"Was that not also caused by the natural disaster called Liliana, I wonder? Repent, but only in moderation."

"Hey, General, let's hurry back to the inn already. If we go at Beatrice's walkin' pace, the sun'll go down before we get there."

"Would you refrain from saying such impudent things, I wonder? You are younger than I am."

Subaru and Beatrice had fallen behind the front of the group while whispering to each other, prompting Garfiel to call out to them. When his rude remark left Beatrice peeved, Garfiel went, "Sorry, my bad," with a smile before suddenly stopping. "—The hell? Someone in the direction of the inn smells really angry."

Turning his head toward a corner in the road ahead, Garfiel audibly sniffed the air as he murmured. A moment later, sure enough, they heard voices arguing farther down the street.

It sounded like two men were engaged in a heated argument.

"They seem like they're going at it pretty hard. The excitement never stops in this town."

"That sounds more convincin' from the general who made a big shot blow up his own room with a magic crystal. It's like the saying *You can boil a pot with the cries of an Azula bird*, ain't it?"

"Pheasants don't have cries, so I wonder if they'd fit the saying… Emilia-tan?"

Subaru was feeling guilty at the mention of what happened at the Muse Company, but beside him, Emilia broke out into a little run. She didn't look back as she spoke:

"Those voices just now—I think one of them sounds like Joshua's!"

"For real? If we're connected to one of the parties, we'd better hurry."

Even if that wasn't the case, Emilia's personality meant she still wouldn't stand by and do nothing. Chasing her around the curving corner of the road ahead, Subaru and the others also hurried back to the front of the Water Raiment.

As they did so and the Jabaneez-style structure came into distant view, in front of the establishment were—

"Don't make me repeat myself! Stop givin' me lip and get your master out here right now!"

"Faced with someone as crude as you, I refuse to call Brother, let alone my master. Please obediently take your leave of this place while I am the only one dealing with you!"

"Ya just don't get it, do ya, brat? I'm gonna give ya a good thrashin'!"

A concerning argument raged between Joshua, who barred entry to the inn with both arms spread wide, and a seedy-looking man angrily shouting at the youth. The man had a wiry physique, and both his words and bearing had a violent edge to them; it seemed only a matter of time until his short fuse ran out.

"That's far enough!"

Then before Subaru could ascertain the opponent's might, Emilia inserted herself between the two. The interruption made the man flinch and left Joshua gazing in shock as well.

"L-Lady Emilia?!"

"If your business is done here, then you should leave. More importantly, what happened? Don't bother people by kicking up a fuss in front of an inn like this. Calm down and talk this out properly."

With words that sounded like she was scolding a pair of bickering children, she cleared away the tense atmosphere, which had been primed to explode from the slightest spark. Sensing that a fight had narrowly been averted, Subaru let out a tentative sigh of relief.

"So tell me what happened. Ready, set, go."

"Er, ah. It would seem I have given Lady Emilia and everyone else cause for worry..."

Under Emilia's earnest gaze, Joshua glanced over at Subaru and the others as he hesitated for a moment.

Perhaps he was concerned that entrusting mediation to a rival camp meant putting his own in its debt. Of course, such haggling would never dissuade Emilia even if he spent the next hundred years trying.

"It ain't complicated. We got invited here, but this brat is runnin' his mouth, sayin' we can't go in. Why wouldn't I complain about it?"

Perhaps not caring for the impasse, the man gruffly explained his side of the dispute. The man focused his narrow eyes on Joshua as he shot him an intense glare.

The look on Joshua's face said that the gaze had rekindled his willingness to fight.

"I have told you over and over. If you intend to pass yourself off as a noble, you should at least make the deceit more convincing. A tiny bit of grooming cannot hide the unsophisticated ignorance oozing out from you!"

"Ya really don't hold back, do ya?! I ain't involved in this kind of trouble 'cause I wanna be! I'm tired of bein' sent on errands like this! Awww, hell, there ain't no point even talkin' to you!"

Faced with Joshua's obstinacy, the man clutched his own head and grumbled out loud. It sounded like the situation was truly beyond salvaging, frustrating Emilia after she had gone out of her way to intervene.

"Hey, Subaru, what should I do…? Subaru, what is it?"

"Er, this might just be my imagination…but I feel like I've seen this guy's face somewhere."

The man Joshua was arguing with made a sour expression when Subaru, responding to Emilia's question, pointed a finger at him. Then the man realized something, going "aaahhh?" as he glared back at Subaru with a foul look. "The hell are you goin' on about? What, you lookin' for a fight, t…oooo?!"

"Ohhh, his voice sure went really shrill at the… Aah!"

While glaring at Subaru, the man's face suddenly filled with shock; seeing that expression, something finally dawned on Subaru.

He really did know this man. He was a lot cleaner and better dressed than when Subaru had last seen him, but…

"Larry! It's Larry, isn't it?! Whoa, what are you doing in a place like this…? How've you been?"

"Don't talk to me like we're best pals! And who the hell's Larry?! I'm Lachins—that's my name, damn it!"

"So it is La-something."

"Shaddap!"

When Subaru wrapped an arm around his shoulder in a spontaneous act of camaraderie, Larry—or rather, Lachins—violently shook him off. With that incongruous exchange going on, Emilia asked, "Is he an acquaintance of yours?"

"Yeah. An old acquaintance from the royal capital back when Emilia-tan and I met for the very first time. When I got lost in an alley, he and his friends surrounded me, and I almost got stripped bare."

"Huh, really…? Er, stripped bare?"

"And the next time I was in the capital—right, I was with Priscilla when I got in a tangle with them, and after, they came back with more friends to try and return the favor. I really have a lot of memories with this guy…"

"From what Betty is hearing, he is nothing but trash."

Emilia and Beatrice had different reactions to Subaru's nostalgic comments. Listening to all this, Joshua's gaze turned grave, and Lachins, feeling the tide turn against him, lifted up both hands in apparent surrender as the blood drained from his face.

"W-wait, wait, wait. Yeah, maybe all that happened, but nothin' real bad happened either time, so it's ancient history, right? Let's just call it water under the bridge and talk this out, yeah?"

"Er, I wouldn't exactly mind, but you can't act so guilty at a time like this or you'll make it into a national-defense issue…"

Lachins was trying to salvage the situation, but by any stretch of the imagination, he was at a disadvantage here. It seemed like the smart thing to do was tie him up and make him spit out whatever he was planning to do.

"On that note—Garfiel. Restrain him and… Uh?"

"———"

Subaru wanted to rely on Garfiel's brute strength, but there was no response. Wondering what the big deal was, he looked over to find Garfiel's gaze not on Lachins but trained toward the street in front of the inn.

Subaru saw Garfiel open his jade eyes as his pupils shrank to points out of wariness. Every hair on his body was standing up as he stood ready, claws, fangs, and muscles all clearly tense.

Realizing from one glance that something had set off Garfiel's fighting instincts, tension raced through Subaru and the others as well, since something was clearly afoot.

And so Subaru and the others turned toward the source of Garfiel's alarm—

"—Lachins. I wondered what had happened when you didn't return. Is there some kind of trouble?"

For an instant, Subaru was sure that what stood there had to be a blazing flame.

It was a red, flickering fire— No, that was a hand waving. This was a human flame. No, just a human being.

With hair so red that it could be mistaken for a roaring fire and eyes so blue they seemed to contain the skies themselves, the tall man wearing all-white garb had such a handsome face, it seared itself into your soul for all eternity from a single glance.

There was no mistaking the sensation that shot through Subaru's entire body. This was what happened when an ordinary person set eyes upon a hero.

That's exactly what this chance encounter was.

The only thing you could mistake him for was an open flame. The man's name was—

"—!!"

Just before Subaru said the name aloud, all sight of Garfiel vanished from his side.

With a roar that started at the back of his throat, Garfiel's arm grew bulkier as sharp claws sprang from it. He proceeded to swing it in a frontal attack with incredible force at the man who had just appeared.

There was no time to stop Garfiel. It was a preemptive strike that closed to point-blank range in an instant. A direct hit with such a vicious blow would easily slice through an iron plate. As his claw drew near to the side of the man's handsome face—

"—My apologies. It would appear that I have startled you."

With a voice that had the echo of a troubled smile, he blocked the strongest attack Garfiel could muster.

"———"

The superhuman spectacle left Subaru speechless, and Garfiel went rigid with shock.

The man's upraised hand had stopped Garfiel's mighty arm. The bestial claw, swung without a shred of restraint, had been blocked by the man's hand as if they were arm wrestling. The only reaction the man showed was the wry smile spreading across his serene face.

This man was playing by different rules and operated beyond any notion of common sense. There was no doubt this was—

"—Reinhard."

Subaru seemed out of breath. His whisper brought another soft smile from the young man. Instantly, the sense of surprise and tension that Subaru had felt up to that point was forcibly melted away, changing into sweet relief.

With just a smile, Reinhard could instill absolute peace of mind into people. That was proof of just how incomparably strong he was.

Then the young man nodded once to Subaru—

"Hi, it's been a while, Subaru. I have heard the rumors. It's good to see you in fine health."

Yes, the Sword Saint Reinhard van Astrea was apparently delighted at being reunited with Subaru, friendly as always.

3

"By the way, Subaru, I know it has been a whole year, and there are many things I would like to speak about, but..."

"A-ahhh, yeah, what is it?"

"First, could I have you stop him? He is your friend, yes?"

As he spoke, Reinhard was looking at Garfiel, whose arm Reinhard was still keeping locked in place. Of course, Reinhard had no hostile intent, nor any reason to continue. In other words, the reason Reinhard hadn't let his arm go yet was because Garfiel was still ready to fight.

"Calm down, Garfiel. This is Reinhard, my…friend. You don't need to worry."

Grasping Garfiel by the shoulder, Subaru hesitated momentarily before deciding how to categorize Reinhard.

Instantly, Subaru's final memory of Reinhard from a year prior came rushing to mind. It was a bitter memory; Subaru had driven him away when he'd come to apologize for not stopping Julius from giving Subaru a thrashing at the training square.

The Subaru of the present keenly understood that his past self had only been lashing out at anyone within reach.

"It is as Subaru explained just now. I am his friend, Reinhard van Astrea. I would be grateful if you told me your name."

Paying Subaru's internal conflict no heed, Reinhard readily called Subaru a friend. On top of that, he let Garfiel's arm go and looked him straight in the eyes.

Under that gaze, Garfiel pulled his arm back and let out a deep, long sigh.

"—Garfiel. Garfiel Tinzel."

"I see, so you are Lady Emilia's shield. I am pleased to meet you. I'd wanted to meet you at least once."

As he spoke, Reinhard reached out in search of a handshake. There was no hint of sarcasm in his words whatsoever. There was nothing there save simple praise and delight.

After everything that had just transpired, Garfiel's shock must have been tremendous.

"—Ah?"

A dazed voice trickled out from Garfiel.

While Reinhard waited for a handshake, Garfiel moved a single step—backward.

That fact, that he had subconsciously retreated, made Garfiel open his eyes wide when he realized what had happened. This was the first time he had ever experienced anything like it.

"______"

Seeing this, Reinhard's eyes flickered slightly with a touch of sadness. But he still pulled back the hand he had offered without delay.

"I am sorry to have offended you. I shall be more careful in the future."

When he said that, Garfiel shook his head as if something bitter had reached his lips.

"Reinhard, I'm so sorry. Are you hurt?"

It was then that Emilia hurried over with a little run to apologize for Garfiel's sudden act of violence. The overly calm way Reinhard had dealt with it made Subaru momentarily forget that it was problematic conduct indeed.

This was the sort of thing that normally threatened to trigger open warfare between two rival factions.

"Lady Emilia, I am sorry to not have been in touch. Fortunately, thanks to Garfiel's aim being very precise, I was able to stop him without any problems. I am relieved we are both fine."

"Yes, I'm glad. It's quite a relief."

But Reinhard acted as if it was nothing—it probably really was nothing from his perspective. He was already assuring Emilia that Garfiel's impropriety was not an issue, either.

Emilia patted her chest, relieved by his reply. Then she went, "Right, right," clapping her hands together as her violet eyes glimmered. "I heard all about Felt. She's *really* been getting a lot done, hasn't she?"

"Compared with Lady Emilia's spectacular exploits, they are still rather minor, enough that she often berates me for being unable to properly support my liege. In particular, she heard about Subaru's deeds."

"Tee-hee-hee. That's right, Subaru's amazing. I'm very proud of my knight."

When Reinhard gave her a compliment that was perfectly sincere, Emilia proudly puffed out her chest. Subaru was half-proud and half-embarrassed that she talked about him like that.

Either way, the cordial exchange showed that things had largely calmed down, so Subaru chose that moment to clear his throat.

"We've strayed a lot, so to get the conversation back on track… You know this Lachins guy?"

Reinhard's arrival had been so momentous that Subaru had to specifically point out Lachins, who had been completely forgotten. "Yes," answered Reinhard, nodding in response to his question. "Currently, he is working as a retainer for Lady Felt. There are numerous areas where he is still lacking, but he has his good points, and Lady Felt has taken a liking to him."

"Felt hired that guy?!"

"Perhaps this leaves you feeling conflicted. I was also at the scene when they tangled with you in that alleyway, Subaru. But a great deal has happened since then… The three of them are currently in the middle of reforming their ways. I would like you to give them a chance."

"Errr, well, I'd be lying if I said it didn't bother me at all… Wait, she hired the whole trio?!"

Subaru looked toward the heavens as he realized just how many tricks fate was playing on him when it came to the three he had once pegged Larry, Curly, and Moe.

On the first day he was summoned to this other world, he'd had repeated fateful encounters with a certain gang of three thugs. He hadn't paid them any special mind since those days from long ago, but who would have thought they would be reunited like this?

"Hey, hey, hey, ya see! I was right all along, damn it!!"

It was just then that Lachins, who had kept his mouth shut ever since the tide had turned against him, regained his vigor. He jabbed his finger at Subaru, Emilia, and then Joshua.

"All of you, doubting someone who comes to visit like that! Apologize! Now, on your hands and knees!!"

"Lachins, I have said this so many times, but you lack awareness as a retainer. Now I understand what brought this situation to a head. Unfortunately, it is difficult for me to support you."

"Whose side are ya on here?!"

"I am the ally of justice. And in this case, I believe that leaves you no choice but to apologize to the younger brother of my friend."

Reinhard responded to Lachins's shouting dispassionately. Then he shot Joshua a quick smile. Joshua returned the gesture, nodding with a tense expression.

"It has been some time, Sir Reinhard. I apologize for the great rudeness caused by my ineptitude..."

"That fault lies with us, Joshua. I am sorry our envoy created such a major misunderstanding. Lady Felt is extremely grateful for Lady Anastasia's invitation."

"Hearing you say that is salve upon my wounds..."

The stubborn look on Joshua's face made plain that his response was superficial. Reinhard offered a wry smile at his demeanor when Subaru went "just a sec" and raised a hand. "Based on what you just said, is it safe to assume Felt's here with you, too?"

"Yes, that's right. Lady Anastasia invited her. *Let us engage in profitable exchange of information*, she said. This being Lady Anastasia, I assumed she was trying to secure some kind of angle, but..."

Trailing off, Reinhard gazed at Subaru and Emilia in turn.

"To think that Lady Emilia and company are here as well. Contrary to my expectations, this may not even be the end of it."

"Are you saying there's even more surprises coming?"

"I am saying that is quite possible. How about it, Joshua?"

When the flow of conversation turned to Joshua, the one in league with the mastermind of this whole gathering, the young man put his fallen monocle back in its proper position. "Hmm, I wonder," he said, playing dumb. This was a clear sign he had regained some of his usual composure. Reinhard nodded and looked at Lachins next.

"Lady Felt is in the middle of looking around the city with Gaston and the others. Please tell them I will be speaking to the people here in advance as instructed."

"Yeah, yeah. What, you don't need to head back, too?"

"If I am with her, Lady Felt will complain that she cannot do as she pleases. It is just...Mr. Rom is not with her at the moment. If

Lady Felt attempts to do something dangerous, stop her with all your strength. If anything happens, raise the signal. I shall rush over in five seconds."

"The fact that you're serious is scary as all hell."

Sullenly sticking out his long tongue, Lachins raced off like he was fleeing the scene. Along the way, he didn't forget to shoot an angry glare toward Joshua, the one he'd been arguing with. The guy really was pettiness personified.

"Now then, let's head inside. We've gotta go tell Anastasia that *Reinhard and friends came over!* and stuff, right?"

"Well, I think that is Joshua's job, but we're all here, so let's go together."

When Subaru consented to Emilia's proposal, Joshua followed suit, and everyone entered the inn. The one thing tugging at Subaru's mind was Garfiel, tailing the group with the same gloomy expression. It was obviously because of what had happened earlier. Subaru mulled over what to say to him when—

"Is it not a good opportunity for Garfiel to learn that there exists someone above him, I wonder?"

"Beatrice..."

Noticing Subaru's gaze, Beatrice gently grasped his sleeve and whispered to him.

"Since leaving the forest, Garfiel hasn't faced any serious resistance save the moving of heavy objects. It is good medicine once in a while, I suppose. Think of it as a learning opportunity and let him be."

"It's true that the only time his life was really on the line was with the ground spider. I guess it's a disease that most boys get at a certain age... All right. I'll quietly watch for now."

"Shall you, I wonder?"

For the moment, Subaru and Beatrice reached a consensus concerning Garfiel's anguish. "Also," said Beatrice before she continued. "About that Sword Saint...Betty prefers not to get too close to him."

"—? What's this all about? Don't tell me it's because he's too attractive like Julius was?"

"Too *dangerous* is more accurate, I suppose. In any case, please do what you can."

Beatrice avoided getting into the details as she quietly and quickly got as far from Reinhard as she could. However, she immediately came to a halt. The reason was that Emilia had gone "um?" and tapped Joshua's shoulder as he led them down the corridor. "Joshua, I think the reception hall is in a different direction…"

"I am sorry. However, Lady Anastasia is currently receiving guests, so I cannot bring you directly to the reception hall."

"I see. Guests…"

Listening to Joshua's reply, Emilia put a finger to her lips and sank into thought. In her place, Subaru murmured, "Guests, huh… Meaning guests besides Emilia-tan and Felt's envoy, Reinhard?"

"…You will understand soon enough. There is no need to stare at me with the eyes of a wild beast."

"Hey, *wild beast*'s going too far. I don't look hungry and feral enough for that."

"You will understand soon enough without you raising your voice like a demon beast."

"That's even worse than before. Which demon beast you talkin' about anyway? Dog, whale, rabbit. Pick one."

Subaru went through the bestiary of detested demon beasts that lingered strongest in his memories. Lately, he'd been wondering where to rank spiders, too. Also, he felt like there was something like a charbroiled lion in there somewhere, but the impression it had left was somehow thinner than the rest.

"Whale, you say?"

As Subaru dug deeper into his memories, Reinhard murmured quietly beside him. When Subaru responded, Reinhard slowly shook his head side to side. "By *whale*, may I take it that you mean the White Whale, Subaru?"

"…Yeah, that's right. The worst whale there ever was. It's a straight-up miracle I got through that fight without dying."

Really, Subaru thought it was a true miracle that he hadn't racked up more deaths fighting against the White Whale.

He'd resolved to die many times over. He'd tasted death many times over. That was how menacing the demon beast was, and the damage it had inflicted was hard to forget. Even in the present, the sacrifices continued to torment Subaru's chest.

"Would you mind telling me the details about the White Whale later? That beast is not an unrelated matter to me. Though I'm sure it will be a long talk once we begin."

"Sure. You don't need to tell me about any circumstances that are hard to talk about, either."

Somehow, he could guess the reason behind Reinhard's clouded expression.

To Subaru, the battle with the White Whale was also the resolution and recompense for one man's obsession with the beast that had lasted for over a decade. And he could guess at the relationship between that man and Reinhard. Subaru didn't have any way to know exactly what had happened in their pasts, however.

Naturally, it wasn't something he should ask out of idle curiosity. He knew that much.

"Thank you."

Therefore, that was the only reply Reinhard could offer in return.

No more was needed. That was enough.

"We have arrived. Please wait here in the tearoom until Lady Anastasia's meeting is finished."

Joshua announced that they had reached their destination right as their conversation was over. Seeing the sliding screen partition for what had been dubbed the tearoom, Subaru felt his Japanese spirit throb.

What a calculating use of the Japanese spirit, he mused, but such casual thoughts lasted for only a few seconds.

"I am sorry, honored guest. May I leave some other guests here until the rest of your party returns?"

Apparently, someone else was already in the tearoom, and Joshua was addressing him through the screen. When he did so, there were obvious signs of someone stirring within.

"—Feel free. I am doing nothing here except gathering dust."

When the sound of the replying voice reached his ears, Subaru furrowed his brow; then surprise set in.

It was a familiar voice, one difficult to ever forget. More importantly, he'd been thinking of the man only a moment prior.

Subaru seemed to be the only person in that place who was surprised— No, Reinhard was the sole exception among the others. His soft visage hardened ever so slightly, and bewilderment entered his blue eyes.

Not noticing that hesitance, Joshua slid the screen to the side. The paper screen door opened, revealing the small interior of the so-called tearoom.

Then the individual kneeling in a traditional fashion upon a square cushion turned his tranquil eyes toward them—

"—Grandfather."

"Reinhard?"

The initial voices of grandfather and grandson overlapped.

This was an unexpected reunion between the Sword Saint and the Sword Devil of the famed Astrea family.

4

The people gathered in the reception hall of the Water Raiment were distinguished in multiple ways.

"I have to say, I'm surprised that Reinhard and Mr. Wilhelm are family. Now that you mention it, both seem to be very good with swords."

"That completely absentminded way of looking at things is so E M T that it hurts."

Assembled around the long table in the center of the room, the respective camps were sitting on square floor cushions in traditional Japanese style. Emilia and Subaru were quietly whispering to each other in a corner where they sat side by side. She might have been nervous, but the contents of her words did not display any particular sense of tension at all.

"Betty is paying close attention, but it will be of no use if anyone makes a sudden move. Subaru, you should focus on not receiving cold stares from everyone present, I suppose."

"It hurts to hear you say that because I used to get plenty of experience with exactly that."

Sitting on Subaru's other side, Beatrice offered those words of caution.

Incidentally, Emilia was sitting with her legs to the side, Subaru was sitting cross-legged, and Beatrice was sitting on her knees. This was the result of Subaru daring her to try it, but Beatrice's knees were already beginning to shake.

"Either way, Garfiel is here should anything happen, and with the people present, this is a needless concern regardless."

With her legs at their limit, Beatrice shifted them to the side. Subaru glanced at Garfiel, who was sitting defensively in a corner of the room.

The encounter with Reinhard had to still be on his mind in various respects, but he seemed to have his hands full with Mimi clinging to him. Subaru hoped that Mimi would help distract him a little bit.

At present, the main figures from multiple camps were seated in the large reception hall, and other associates were on standby at the edges of the room. That was why Mimi's brothers were also present. Seeing his older sister glued to Garfiel's side, Hetaro was staring daggers at the offending boy, while TB's face made it clear he wanted nothing to do with this fracas.

Incidentally, Joshua was at the edge of the spectator seats, his already white face looking even paler than usual.

Out of everyone who had gathered in the hall, the one to kick things off was Reinhard, who started with a bow.

"We are truly grateful for the invitation you have offered us. Lady Felt's arrival to the inn is slightly delayed, but as she shall arrive forthwith, allow me to give you our formal greetings in her stead."

"No need to be so stuffy. Considering this invitation was on short notice from me, that's plenty… Though there was much more overlap in arrivals than I expected."

The hostess, Anastasia, softly smiled as Reinhard engaged in the courtesies expected of an envoy. Reinhard nodded in response to Anastasia's words; then he turned toward Julius, who was sitting with a smiling face at Anastasia's side.

"It has been a while, Julius. Since our earlier visit to the Hoshin Company, I believe?"

"Yes, I suppose it has been. I am sorry for imposing upon you like this. However, it is a good chance to see how everyone is doing. Such opportunities are difficult to come by."

The mutual friends exchanged greetings that were few in words. Reinhard was also seated at the table.

Somehow or other, the seating order had been neatly arranged by camp, with Anastasia, Emilia, a representative of the still-absent Felt camp, and finally—

"—It has been quite some time since I have met all of you like this, has it not?"

Speaking with a willowy smile was a woman with a beautiful face and long, lovely green hair.

A kindness rested in her almond-shaped, amber-colored eyes, and her alluring figure was dressed in navy-blue attire. It hardly required mentioning, but this person in the long-skirted clothing was the very image of ladylike grace.

People who knew the old her would scarcely believe she was the same person.

"It's been a long time, Lady Crusch. I believe the last time we met was at the honors ceremony?"

"Yes. That it has. I am sorry for having caused you such trouble on that occasion. It was only afterward that I heard of everyone's efforts. I wasn't the least bit surprised."

Replying to Emilia's greeting was Crusch, giving a rather soft-seeming response.

Her previously gallant and decisive demeanor had been lost along with her memories. With her old fearlessness still yet to return, she was the portrait of an aristocrat's beautiful daughter.

"Really, it's been nothing but surprises. I heard it at the honors ceremony, but after the White Whale and the Witch Cult, it was the Great Rabbit next? Subawu, are you out of your mind?"

Sitting at Crusch's side and jabbing at Subaru was the beautiful, kitty-eared girl——or rather, young man called Ferris.

The greatest healer in the kingdom, he'd also worked part-time as Subaru's physician. There was an edge to his otherwise teasing words that made Subaru sit up slightly straighter.

The cause of Ferris's anger toward Subaru was obvious.

"I'm sorry for ignoring your warnings, using magic, and smashing my gate…"

"I drilled it into you that meowch, and in the end, you still rode your broken gate into the ground. It wasn't worth treating you at all. Even now, it wouldn't be strange for it to rupture and go poof if Beatrice wasn't here. You really, really have to treat it with more care."

"I get it already. But there ain't a guy in the world who can make Beatrice happier than I do."

Ferris's tone was flippant, but his warning was dead serious. That's why Subaru replied with equal seriousness. The fact that Beatrice was pounding his shoulder while red in the face was a small price to pay.

"I have to say, I'm amazed that even the Crusch camp got called over. If I hadn't used up all my surprise after running into Reinhard outside earlier, I would've had one hell of a face for you to look at."

"Awww. That is quite a wasted opportunity. But it's really something to have so many invited guests gather here today. Even I'm astonished it's this many."

"That is only natural, as there was no specific date set. It is rare to have a chance to meet everyone at once like this, so we should consider this accident of timing as the blessing it is."

It was the final member of the Crusch camp, Wilhelm, who spoke of this coincidence as a good opportunity.

Crusch was sitting formally on her knees, while Ferris was sitting with his knees apart in a rather feminine fashion. Wilhelm was also sitting formally on Ferris's other side, but in spite of his butler's attire, his gentlemanly demeanor seemed a perfect fit for the distinctly Japanese ambience.

By some quirk, the seating arrangement of the camps had put Wilhelm and Reinhard right next to each other, which was a sight that was bad for the hearts of Subaru and everyone else aware of their relationship.

"Those two aren't meeting each other's eyes, are they…?"

Subaru mentally nodded to Emilia's very quiet whisper.

Pairing Wilhelm and Reinhard meant grandfather and grandchild were seated side by side, but the two hadn't spoken a word to each other from the moment of their unexpected reunion in the tearoom to the instant they were all called over.

A stifling silence had descended on the tearoom, enough that even the Emilia camp, brimming with oblivious people, hadn't tried to render any support. When Joshua came back, he looked like an angel to them.

Either way, Subaru deduced that there were complicated circumstances where the pair from the Astrea family was concerned. Otherwise, the feelings haunting Wilhelm during the hunt of the White Whale couldn't be explained away.

—Why had Wilhelm borrowed the power of Crusch's family and not his own?

For that matter, why hadn't Reinhard joined the battle to avenge his own grandmother?

"______"

Deep down, Subaru badly wanted to ask.

But probing would only rub salt into the pair's wounds and hurt them further. Both might have been in rival camps, but to Subaru, one was a precious friend and the other a person he deeply respected and to whom he owed a great deal.

Trust was a castle built atop a pile of sand. Subaru wasn't like Roswaal. He'd stand firm.

That was why he simply held out hope that someone would make the conversation naturally flow in that direction.

"Incidentally, why did Lady Anastasia call everyone here?"

"Oh, you're so suspicious. My objective really is that I just wanted to speak with you all a little. That's why I didn't invite unreasonable people over."

"Unreasonable…?"

Emilia frowned as she prompted back. But it wasn't because she was unaware who Anastasia meant just now. In the first place, there was only one camp absent.

"So I take it that you did not invite Lady Priscilla and Sir Al?"

"They do things completely their own way, so I couldn't come up with any excuse to ask them here. At least with Felt, we got a chance to know each other a little better during that incident with Black Silver Coin, right?"

"We caused you a great deal of trouble on that occasion. However, you are absolutely right."

When Anastasia rather easily confessed that she'd left one camp out, Reinhard seemed to agree and backed off with no sign of resistance.

It was then that Emilia raised her hand, seeking another opportunity to speak.

"Just now, you used the word *excuse*… Does that mean you convinced everyone else to come using various reasons like you did with us?"

"If you're going to come anyway, I should at least prepare a proper gift. All I did was just as I told you before, Emilia, nothing more."

"What we want most… But for Crusch and them, that would be…"

When Anastasia replied with a cutesy smile, Subaru glanced over at Crusch and company.

What Emilia wanted was a magic crystal to use as a catalyst to call back Puck. And considering the problems facing Crusch and the others, the thing they wanted most was information about—

"We came to Pristella because Lady Anastasia claimed to have some information concerning the incident with the Archbishop of Gluttony."

"—!"

Crusch had a look of determination on her face. Her words made Subaru unwittingly rise to his feet.

He couldn't ignore this kind of news. Subaru glared at Anastasia as if by reflex, whereupon Anastasia flashed a strained smile and stroked the scarf around her neck.

"It's not as if I'm trying to be mean to you, Natsuki. It's just that there's an order of priority. I can sell this to Lady Crusch and company higher than I can to Natsuki… Am I wrong?"

"…That's the thinking of a merchant all right. It doesn't sit well with me, but I can…understand."

"Coming from you, that's quite impressive."

"Oh, shaddap. Don't poke me when I'm only just holding it together."

Expensive merchandise was sold to the highest bidder. That was just a merchant's natural way of thinking.

Subaru barely avoided exploding in the face of Anastasia's lecture. However, if Julius landed even one more hit, Subaru was in real danger of blowing up for real.

"But you know… That's just…"

Subaru looked at Anastasia, trying to find some handhold to cling to. Perhaps he should have directed his plea to Crusch for even the slimmest possibility of awakening Rem, the Sleeping Princess, from her slumber.

However, faced with the fragile look on Subaru's face, Anastasia let out a deep breath.

"There's no need to put on such a sad face. Don't worry—I won't hide this secret from only you."

"…R-really?"

"It's no lie. But you should know that this is a request from Lady Crusch and her people. They're all goody-goody sorts who don't believe it's right to keep the information to themselves."

As Anastasia shrugged, her words left Subaru flabbergasted as he turned toward Crusch. As he did, Crusch looked back at him, trying with all her might to keep her expression firm.

"Naturally. Of course, I wish to settle the affair of my own memory with Gluttony personally. However, I understand that Master Subaru's fondest wish is to help that girl."

"Crusch…"

"Besides, I believe that the more we are united on this matter, the better. Our opponent is a cunning Archbishop of the Seven Deadly Sins who has continued to evade all attempts to hunt him down. I shall not hold a grudge regardless of whose blade reaches him first."

The joking way Crusch put the last part left Subaru bowing his head as relief flooded him.

No doubt it was very much her full intention to settle things with the one responsible for stealing her past. Her consideration for Subaru, who had a similar objective, made her bend even on this.

Even with her memories lost, the soul of the fair and just woman named Crusch Karsten was in no way diminished. She remained true to her own way of life.

"Really, thank you. I'll do my best to live up to those expectations. Somewhere, somehow."

"Even so, we will likely be first. I do not intend to yield to anyone, either."

As Subaru voiced his determination, Crusch puffed out her chest, undaunted.

Her demeanor made Subaru and Crusch exchange an out-of-place smile. Her knight, Ferris, looked upon this without being amused whatsoever.

"Grrr, you seem to be having a lot of fun, Lady Crusch. You need to stop being so fond of Subawu. He should be satisfied with one flower in each hand right *meow*. He doesn't need any more."

"Ferris, is that not a rude thing to say? Master Subaru is not so unfaithful as to make eyes at just anyone."

"Yeah, cut it out, Ferris. It's true that Crusch is cute and beautiful, but the line going forward from my heart is… Well, it splits into two midway, but it's still straight and na— Ow, ow, ow?!"

"No one else would call that a straight line, and that lack of self-awareness makes it even worse."

When Subaru tried to chime in on the Crusch camp's master-servant dispute, Beatrice gave his ear a mighty pull. But when Subaru objected with a tearful face, Beatrice feigned innocence.

Off to the side of that exchange, Crusch lowered her face, cheeks faintly flushed for some reason.

"Oh, dang. Emilia-tan, did I say something weird even for me?"

"Mm, did you? I think you're always saying similar things to me, though..."

"Well, yeah. So what's with this reaction...? Maybe if I hold Emilia-tan's hand, the answer will come to me. Can I hold your hand?"

"Work hard and think for yourself this time."

When the hand he was unable to grasp slapped him on the forehead, Subaru frowned in silence. After watching the pair's exchange, Ferris discreetly brought his lips close to Crusch's ear.

"See, just look at them. Subawu is indiscriminate. He'll try that with anyone at all if you give him the chance. It's an illness, *meow*. You shouldn't pay it any attention."

"Understood. I'll be more careful. *Phew*, that really surprised me."

After taking Ferris's advice to heart, Crusch took an unexpectedly deep breath and put a hand to her remarkably ample chest.

The gesture was adorable in every way and convinced Subaru that Crusch doing unexpectedly feminine things was incredibly appealing. Setting that impression aside, Crusch and Ferris smiled at each other like a pair of best friends.

"So to put things back on track...my people are in the middle of sorting out the information Crusch and Natsuki desire. It should be tidy enough to hand over by tomorrow or the day after, so can you hold on a little till then?"

"Seriously? I just can't stop the urge to speed this up. Can't you give us anything in advance, even a small bit?"

"*Rushing keeps you in Rizzi's debt forever.* Not good to flirt with total loss, is it? So calm down."

"Ggggh..."

Chided with a saying that probably meant *haste makes waste*, Subaru groaned and sat back down. Emilia and Beatrice both put a hand on one of his shoulders.

At any rate, it seemed that everyone had a reason of their own to come to Pristella.

"—Heh, well, isn't this quite a group? According to Lachins, it was only Ms. Half-Elf and Anastasia, but I guess not."

The door to the reception room forcefully slid open, and everyone's gazes assembled on the girl boldly crossing the threshold.

The girl had bright, glimmering, dazzling blond hair and big, round red eyes. What looked like little fangs peeked out from under the lips of her confident, smiling face, which gave off a mischievous charisma. She was still a small girl with a delicate physique, but her femininity seemed to have faintly increased.

However, as typical, her clothing style was straight out of the slums, and the always-energetic Felt burst onto the scene with her core remaining wholly unchanged.

When she surveyed the faces of those assembled, she seemed very relaxed as she closed one eye.

"Even though it's been a year, it's surprising how little you've all changed. Well, I suppose the same goes for me."

"—Lady Felt, if I may?"

Felt sighed, as if her expectations had been dashed, then immediately broke into a smile. The change in her expression was bewildering, but then Reinhard gently stood at her side.

Reinhard knit his refined eyebrows as he gazed at Felt, his own liege.

"A proper set of attire for going out in public was provided to you. What happened to it?"

"Ha! Who'd go along with your taste in outfits? Sightseeing was just the most convenient way to find a change of clothes. Understand my personality already, Reinhard dear."

"Truly, you are so…"

Unbelievable, Reinhard broadcast from the way he covered his face. Felt straddled the threshold of the room, looking positively delighted at having pulled a fast one on the man who was the nation's hero and its strongest warrior.

Then when she turned her head toward those assembled in the reception room again, her confident expression softly vanished.

"I am truly grateful that you have invited me here today. Let us have some productive discourse as fellow royal-selection candidates—okay, formalities over! Deal me in, 'kay?"

After offering a glimpse of conduct so refined as to be enchanting, Felt swiftly reverted to being a mischievous rascal. The way her uninhibited personality stomped all over decorum left Subaru, at least, feeling good on the inside. The girl's energy had only grown over the past year.

"I have to say, what a weird city, and this is a weird building. All the novelties everywhere wore me right out."

As she spoke, Felt happened to sit cross-legged on the square cushion Reinhard had been using. Reinhard drew a separate cushion over for himself, putting her between the awkward grandfather-grandson pair.

Of course, this hadn't been deliberate on her part, but it was just like her to do something like that purely by instinct.

"A novelty… If that is what you think of it, then I'm happy. Actually, I have other reasons for picking this inn, too… Wanna hear them?"

"Don't just build suspense. It's a bad habit of yours."

Felt raised the corners of her lips as she jabbed a finger at Anastasia's transparent scheme.

The very casual exchange between the two was a sign of how they had closed the distance between them. It seemed that some encounter Subaru was unaware of had greatly improved the relationship.

Acknowledging Felt's request, Anastasia touched a hand to her mouth as she smiled.

"I just can't beat you, Felt. Actually, this inn has a large, wide…hot spring."

"By *hot spring*, you mean a huge bath?!"

Felt's eyes glistened as she practically leaped to her feet.

"A bath sounds great! Back in the slums, a chance to soak in hot water was hard to come by, and I loved it. Hey, you've finished all the important talk, right?"

"The greetings have already ended…but, Lady Felt? Do not tell me you deliberately came late to the inn hoping to avoid serious conversation…"

"Ha, not listening. Hey, sisters, let's go to the bath already, bath!"

Ignoring Reinhard's reproachful comment, Felt addressed Emilia and the others. Emilia was surprised she had called out to her, but it didn't take long for her to smile in return.

"Mm, a bath is fine with me. I *really* want to see what this big bath is like."

"I suppose you are right. We are tired from a long journey, so that might well be best."

Emilia seemed excited, and even Crusch agreed with an elegant smile. Of course, neither Felt, originator of the proposal, nor Anastasia, boaster of the hot spring, was going to object.

"Wait, seriously, a hot spring? With these girls and this setup?"

"Hey, Mister, don't get in the way of our fun. All right, it's settled, so let's go!"

Felt folded her arms toward Subaru, who had been left scrambling after she started dictating the pace. Then an especially mischievous smile came over her face.

"Today, we bathe! Then we eat! I'm not talking a word about anything else!"

A manly declaration indeed.

5

In the end, Felt had the last word, and it was decided that everyone would split up, reassembling in the large reception room once more at dinnertime.

That said, it wasn't as if Subaru objected to Felt's proposal, either. If anything, the offbeat plan to switch things up was so good that he admired her for coming up with it.

Subaru had just found the possibility of gleaning information on an Archbishop of the Seven Deadly Sins in a place he never expected it. He wanted to earnestly address this and other worrying elements that concerned the camp as a whole.

The most obvious issue was Garfiel having hit a wall.

Beatrice had told Subaru to wait and watch as Garfiel overcame it with his own strength, but—

"—General, sorry, but do ya mind if I head outside for a bit? I don't think there's anythin', but I better stick an ear out anyway."

After the initial end of the meeting in the reception room, the men gave a send-off to the girls, who were on their way to the big bath, then were left to their own devices. That was when Garfiel came to Subaru with the request.

"Garfiel, worries or not, you're damn strong."

"But I ain't the strongest. That ain't good enough."

That was the last thing Garfiel said as he turned away and walked out of the inn.

Considering his role as their escort, Subaru should have stopped him. But he did not. He trusted that Garfiel of all people could make a recovery of some sort in one night.

—Therefore, Subaru could sub in for him for that one night, couldn't he?

"He calls me General and treats me like his older brother. This is the least I can do for him, right?"

In fact, Garfiel's other honorary older brother would've been here if he wasn't walking around the city that very moment—or walking and drinking, rather. That meant it fell to Subaru alone to do what he could for their little brother.

"Damn you, Otto, not being here when I really need you… Seriously, what an Otto."

Praying his younger brother wouldn't grow up to be like that, Subaru headed to the large reception hall when it was time for dinner.

When he did so, he saw the girls, who were back from bathing, as well as the men rendezvousing with them at the appointed time—

"B-Beako, your outfit…!"

"Oh-ho, how is it, I wonder? Today's Betty is a different flavor than the norm."

Beatrice wore a smug face as she greeted Subaru. Her cheeks were faintly reddened from her recent bath, driving her cuteness to even greater heights, but that wasn't what surprised him.

Beatrice was always seen in her extravagant dress, but he was floored by the sight of her in a *yukata*.

"Ohhh, incredible, just incredible, so they even have *yukata* here! And it looks really good on you! Beako, you're so pretty! Beako, you're so lovely! Did you manage to put it on all by yourself?"

"It's only natural, I suppose. To Betty, such a feat is more trifling than a cupcake."

"Heh, that figures! Well, that's what Beako would say, but is it true?"

"Tee-hee, don't doubt her. It's true. Beatrice only tripped on the hem twice."

"S-slander, I wonder?! Subaru, between Betty and Emilia, which one do you believe?!"

"The moment you asked that question, you already lost."

That was the normal judgment to make, for Beatrice was predictably dishonest while Emilia was entirely too honest.

Emilia softly smiled as Beatrice's face became redder still. She was in a *yukata* as well, with her still-damp silver hair tied up neatly behind her head.

This gave him a perfect view of the nape of her neck, which was truly marvelous. She smelled nice, too.

"Subaru, you seem to be breathing heavily through your nose. Do you have a fever?"

"A slight fever of love, maybe. Emilia-tan, can I braid your hair?"

"That's fine, but I think we're about to sit down for a meal. Do you mind doing it after?"

As Subaru touched the tip of her bundled hair, Emilia pointed to the table as she pushed her counteroffer. He grudgingly backed down, which was when he abruptly noticed that all the eyes in the room were gathered on them.

"What, did something weird happen?"

"I'm thinking, it's really hard to pick up how much distance there is between Mister and Miss. That didn't feel all that sexy, and the last time I saw you, your relationship was pretty horrible."

"Please do not dredge up what happened at the castle. It doth make my chest hurt."

Subaru deeply bowed to Felt, who was sitting cross-legged in a *yukata* as he made his plea.

"Ha! What's this all about? I guess Mister really got his act together, huh?"

His reaction made Felt laugh and look up from the book she was reading, which was something he normally wouldn't picture her doing at all. She closed the book, which had a pressed flower as a bookmark, and said, "Come to think of it…" She tilted her head before he continued. "I heard in the bath that my piece-of-junk knight bullied your blond boy? Sorry about that. I'll set him straight."

As she spoke, Felt used the book in her hand to thwap Reinhard on the shoulder. She showed little sign of restraint, giving the red-haired knight's brows a constrained look.

"Lady Felt, that manner of speaking will invite speculation. He and I simply had a misunderstanding, and I was a little rough in the way I handled it. That is all… As a matter of fact, he is tremendously powerful despite his young age."

"That patronizing lack of self-awareness really isn't convincing. I mean, you're basically merciless toward anyone who shows any promise. You always leave Gaston and the others half in tears after you're done working 'em over."

Reinhard's assessment of Garfiel's worth made Felt stick her tongue out with an exasperated look on her face.

But at the very least, Subaru understood that Reinhard's words were his true beliefs. He'd said that because he genuinely respected Garfiel and acknowledged his might.

Perhaps that was the most dangerous part of his character.

"Incidentally, Lady Felt, about that outfit…"

"What, it's not somethin' a royal-selection candidate would wear?

Look around—all the other girls are wearin' the same stuff, damn it. I can't be the only one to complain about it."

"No, not at all. I only meant to say that it suits you very well."

"Shaddap."

However, it was incredible to see just what vivid invective Felt directed at Reinhard.

He was the man most trusted and respected by the kingdom's people. Virtually everyone sincerely praised him as a knight among knights. A sweet word from him would be enough to make many a woman swoon, but Felt batted it aside like it was so much garbage.

Subaru was becoming genuinely concerned that things weren't going quite as swimmingly with them as the rumors would suggest.

"On that score, our side's pretty close to ideal…though Crusch's people take number one on that list."

"We what now?"

When Subaru put a hand to his chin in thought, Crusch directed a questioning look at him.

Of course, Crusch was no exception and wore a *yukata* as well—in a different manner than the dresses she commonly wore now, the thin *yukata* fabric, which was draped elegantly over her figure, heightened her feminine grace.

He knew that the outfits were originally worn as nightwear for evening revelry, but they were top-notch for charm as far as Japanese clothing went.

"Yeah. You and Ferris are really close, but you guys don't have that kind of relationship, right? I'm in a slightly different situation because of the ulterior motives I started with, but you guys have, like, a picture-perfect relationship."

"When you put it like that, I feel like blushing, tee-hee. Yes, Ferris?"

"Ferri very much has ulterior motives where Lady Crusch is concerned, though."

Instantly, Ferris's statement made the air in the reception hall freeze over.

Crusch's expression remained locked in a charming smile, while

Ferris gazed at her with a grin. Incidentally, Ferris was also wearing a *yukata*. He'd changed into one at some point, and it suited him just as well as it did any of the girls. At any rate—

"Sorry for exposing a secret no one needed to hear. Let's eat?"

"Please do not unearth bombs and attempt to flee like that!"

Crusch lamented with tearful eyes as Subaru tried to retreat to dinner.

Perhaps it came as a bolt from the blue as far as she was concerned, but Subaru hadn't been deliberately searching for explosive secrets like that, either. *What to do?* thought Subaru as he let his gaze wander.

"Ferris, I cannot approve of you startling Lady Crusch like this."

The one comment that changed the mood all at once had come from Wilhelm, who had been holding his silence.

Sitting formally in a *yukata*, the Sword Devil's words made Ferris touch a finger to his own lips.

"Oh no, even Old Man Wil doubts Ferri's feelings?"

"Respect, affection, romance. Cease courting chaos by teasing the lords and retainers in attendance. I am compelled to note that preying on someone's naivete is not adorable in the slightest."

"Boo. You're so strict, sheesh."

Wilhelm's gravitas-filled lecture made Ferris pout and surrender. After that, Ferris contented himself by snuggling his face against Crusch's shoulder.

"You don't have to get all worried like that. Of course it's a joke. Ferri having all kinds of ulterior meowtives with Lady Crusch would be bad on so many levels."

"Y-yes, I suppose it would. Phew, you surprised me. Because I cannot use my blessing properly at the moment, I feel like I might be misunderstanding your feelings about many things, Ferris."

"—That's not the case at all."

Crusch was breathing a sigh of relief, but the look in Ferris's eyes that moment tugged at Subaru.

For an instant, an intense emotion filled his eyes. It might well have been his personal brand of agony.

Though he acted in a frivolous manner, the suffering borne by

Ferris over the last year was probably comparable to Subaru's. He painfully understood the regret and anguish at Ferris's very core.

"Errr, preparations for dinner seem to be in order, so would you mind bringing it in?"

Having waited for a natural lull in the conversation, Joshua instructed the inn employees to set the table. As they got to work placing one dish after another atop the long table, surprised reactions sprang up all around.

The varied cooking was something Emilia and the others had never before seen, but Subaru's reaction was for a different reason—he was shocked by the unexpected familiar sights.

Since this world had no seas, cooking with fish meant fishing from rivers. Naturally, this meant there were few truly large fish, making sashimi dishes and the like quite hard to come by. Therefore, seeing such a wealth of fish dishes in a place like this was all the more surprising.

"We can eat it just like this?"

"How do you like it? Never seen it before, have you? Everything here comes from the Great Tigrasea River nearby and is prepared by experienced cooks. It's good enough to qualify as a specialty here at the Water Raiment."

It seemed that culinary traditions not bound by the Kingdom of Lugunica's common sense were still being passed down. Either way, one dish emerged after another based on Japanese cuisine, further deepening Emilia's and company's bewilderment.

The first one to break through their hesitance was not Anastasia, hostess of the banquet, but rather—

"Here! Like this! This is how you do it right!"

Unfortunately, the utensils were forks, but Subaru thrust his into some sashimi of a fish he didn't recognize, applied the soy-sauce-like seasoning, and tossed it into his mouth in one go.

Then as Emilia and Beatrice went "ah!" in surprise beside him, he licked his chops.

"Deeeelicious! Ahhh, it's been so long since I had sashimi! This is the best! You're the greatest, Anastasia!"

"I-it's tasty?"

"It's a masterpiece! The fish is fresh, so it tastes incredible! It's a shame. If you had sushi vinegar here, I could try copying my dad's sushi-chef pal and make some *nigirizushi*!"

"Sorry, I don't understand what you're saying… But I see. So it is tasty, then."

The gist of Subaru's stream of consciousness had apparently gotten through. Emilia chose to believe only the most critical part and did as he had, putting soy sauce on the sashimi before trying it herself.

When she did so, Emilia opened her round eyes wide. "Mm—!" she went, happily clenching and waving a fist.

Seeing the same honest reactions from master and retainer alike, the others in attendance put their hands on the food one after the next.

"Grrr, Natsuki, there you go spoiling my fun again…"

Anastasia had had her thunder stolen, leaving her ever so slightly dissatisfied. But Subaru's and Emilia's idyllic reactions finally made her expression relax.

"Goodness, there's no helping you children… Hey! Leave some for me!"

The dinner party was host to various worries, and certain faces were not in attendance, but even so, all who did participate were able to enjoy a brief respite.

—For that one night, the moon and the world seemed willing to allow a tranquil moment when all regular concerns could safely be postponed.

6

As they mutually agreed to forget they were political rivals for the time being, the night wore on.

The dinner in the reception hall came to an end, and Subaru finished bathing before returning to his room. The staff seemed to have laid out futons during the guests' absence, so everything was ready for a good night's sleep.

"Subaru! It seems that an intruder snuck in during the time Betty and others were gone!"

"Yeah, looks like the futon you made a big mess of got all tidied up. What a vandal."

Chiding Beatrice for her unnecessary wariness over the two futons lined side by side, Subaru gently tucked the sleepy-looking girl into bed.

Incidentally, ever since forming a formal pact, it had become the norm for Subaru and Beatrice to share a room. Anastasia had arranged separate rooms for them, but Beatrice would crawl into Subaru's futon in the middle of the night regardless, so he politely declined the offer.

Of course, this was not because Beatrice was too much of a child to be able to sleep alone, but because much of the mana drawn from one's Odo was generated during sleep, it was nothing more than consideration for Subaru's physical condition.

Therefore, it is not because Betty wants to be with Subaru. Would you not take this the wrong way, I wonder?

That was what Beatrice had told him shortly after forming the pact.

In this case, it really didn't matter what her true intent might be. Subaru had become very accustomed to hearing the sounds of someone else sleeping nearby over the past year. And it helped him stay warm on cold days, too.

"Is that a mass of green poison, I wonder…? You won't get away lightly if you eat it…"

She must have tired herself quite a bit, because Beatrice was swiftly dragged into dreamland as soon as she got into the futon, moaning in fear from the trauma of the wasabi from supper that evening.

Savoring his partner's adorable sleeping face, Subaru gave his back a good stretch in the middle of the room.

"Now then, how about I take a little stroll until I get sleepy?"

Tightening the belt of his *yukata*, Subaru headed out of the room in high spirits. He hadn't settled on a destination, but he had no intention of walking as far as beyond the inn, figuring that he would get some air out in the garden.

He imagined the scenery, which greatly resembled a Japanese garden, would look great under the moonlight. Looking up at the round moon through the corridor's window, Subaru squinted at its silver light.

It was a quiet night. In terms of defenses, the hot-spring inn had sections that were overly exposed, but given the lineup staying there at the moment, he could only pity anyone foolhardy enough to try to break in.

I do not think anything will happen, but if something does occur in this district, I will hurry over. Please rest at ease.

Such were Reinhard's reassuring words when they parted ways in the hall.

The fact that he'd used the word *district* rather than *inn* was so reassuring, it was downright scary. Given his personality, it was possible he was being modest just choosing to not use the word *city.*

"Reinhard, huh..."

Thinking of his friend, who quite possibly might still be on guard even at this time of night, Subaru lowered his eyes—it was hard to forget how unpretentiously Reinhard had agreed he was Subaru's friend.

During the unexpected reunion earlier in the day, Subaru had reforged his broken friendship with Reinhard. But that didn't mean that the terrible things Subaru had said or the loathsome attitude he'd shown on that fateful day in the past were permissible.

Friends should be equals. That was what Subaru believed. Whatever Reinhard thought of the matter, Subaru owed him a debt. How could he call himself Reinhard's friend without repaying it?

Wasn't there something, anything at all, that Subaru could do for the sake of his friend Reinhard?

"______"

As he pondered such thoughts, his feet brought him to the garden, whereupon Subaru's breath caught at the sight that greeted him.

Under a black sky and a silver moon, with clouds draped over the moon to lend the place an even more bewitching allure, he saw a single person standing there, enjoying the refreshing breeze.

The man had a sturdy back and a head and beard dyed white. Subaru knew only one person with those distinguishing features.

"—Mr. Wilhelm?"

"Sir Subaru? Did I alarm you?"

Wilhelm had probably sensed a human presence long before Subaru noticed him. Addressing Subaru, Wilhelm put his arms through the sleeves of his indigo-colored *yukata* as he turned around. The gentleness of his gaze matched his outfit remarkably well.

The sight of the Sword Devil putting his hands through the sleeves of a *yukata* as he stood in a Japanese-style garden somehow came off as picturesque.

"It is a quiet night, yet you were unable to sleep?"

"—. Nahhh, it's not actually like that. I just thought I'd give this garden a look at night. I figured it'd be a good view, so that's what I was aiming for."

"I see. Then it was rather boorish of me to intrude on such a solemn nightly occasion."

The way Wilhelm spoke those words with a sentimental smile and a soft voice left Subaru scratching his cheek. For Subaru, hearing Wilhelm's voice was immensely reassuring. For some reason, it also made him blush a little.

Wilhelm was the person Subaru respected most in this world.

There were many people Subaru wanted to stand alongside, compete with, and be considered equal to, but it was quite possibly Wilhelm alone who made Subaru think *I wanna look up to him* while harboring something akin to envy.

Wilhelm was pretty much Subaru's ideal, both as a person and a man.

Therefore, as Subaru scratched his cheek, he shook his head at Wilhelm's modesty.

"No, no. You're not intruding at all. If anything, the Sword Devil suits a Japanese garden so much that it's carving a photograph into my heart for eternity. I like seeing people under a moonlit sky."

So far as Subaru knew, the person best suited for a moonlit sky was without a doubt Emilia.

Her silver hair twinkled and glimmered in a way the sun's rays never did. Emilia's beauty was like fleeting moonlight. That's why Subaru hoped to one day become a star that nestled up to the moon.

Accordingly, Subaru found the sight of the Sword Devil standing under a moonlit sky symbolic of his aspirations.

"You should whisper such words not to me but to a woman. What a waste."

"With my face, even if I say flowery lines like that, it won't get me very far, and those phrases don't work one bit on the girl whose heart I want to tickle most right now."

"One must choose words for the sake of the woman one cares for most… That frustration is part of the joys of love."

Wilhelm's teasing tone made Subaru's shoulders sag in a comedic fashion.

"Ohhh, it's been a long time since I've seen you with that love-story vibe. So Mr. Wilhelm had times like that, too, huh?"

"But of course."

When Subaru bowed reverentially according to established custom, Wilhelm said, "Well then, I suppose it cannot be avoided," looking particularly pleased as he began to tell his tale.

He gazed with his blue eyes at something far in the distance as he recalled a beloved memory.

"I am clumsy with my words even today, but my past self was far worse. A man lacking in words. When I first met my wife, the issue of a man with thoughts of nothing but swinging a sword in his mind must have bored her to tears."

"But the missus enjoyed talking to you anyway, right, Mr. Wilhelm?"

"My wife was a profound woman. Even as she suffered under the weight of the destiny she carried upon her slender back, she never spoke one word of that to others. That was probably why I was attracted to her from the first time I ever laid eyes on her…but I was so foolish at the time not to realize any of that."

Wilhelm's voice held a whiff of regret and shame, no doubt from embarrassment at what an unsociable person he once was. Getting this rare reaction out of him helped Subaru feel at ease.

"Who'd have thought Mr. Wilhelm was, you know, unsophisticated like that once?"

"I truly had offered up every part of my being to the sword. When I gripped a sword, I forgot all other thoughts, immersing myself as if that was what gave meaning to my life—it was my wife who reminded me of the reason why I chose to walk the path of the sword."

"Is that when you first realized you liked the missus, by any chance?"

"…It seems you have seen right through me, Sir Subaru."

Subaru responded to Wilhelm's listless murmur with silence.

Wilhelm probably didn't realize what kind of face he was making just then. That he was comfortable showing him such a face made Subaru deeply proud.

Wilhelm's eyes, the creases on his cheeks, the tone of his voice, his gestures… Every part of him was saying one thing. Even at this very moment, from the instant he had first met her, he loved his wife—Theresia van Astrea.

Seeing that face, anyone would realize he was still in love.

"—!"

Without his knowledge, Subaru had come to the verge of tears while looking at Wilhelm's expression. Heat was rising into the back of his eyes. For some reason, his chest got hot like this when he looked at the face of someone in love. It would really put Wilhelm in a bind if he started crying at a place like this, wouldn't it?

"It is as you say, Sir Subaru. It was then that I realized my feelings for my wife."

As Subaru lowered his head to conceal his tears, Wilhelm continued to recount long-gone days. Accepting his generosity, Subaru listened to the man's tale as the ache inside him only grew stronger.

"Swinging the sword was everything to me. But it was the thoughts I had before swinging the sword, and the thoughts I had from swinging the sword, that made me all that I was. My wife realized that about me as if it was a matter of course. From then on, when I swung my sword, I thought of my wife."

"You still do even now?"

"—Then and now, what links me to my wife is the sword."

Wilhelm paused slightly before weaving the words in response to Subaru's question.

As Wilhelm faced Subaru with the moonlight at his back, his eyes had grown damp from complex emotions. He felt pride. He felt regret. He felt hesitance, passion, and shame. Bravery and tragedy were present, too.

—But behind all these emotions was love.

"So long as I grip a sword, my feelings for my wife shall no doubt persist. Accordingly, when I die, I want to die with a sword in my hand. To me, that is nothing less than continuing to be with my wife."

Wilhelm was too clumsy, too blunt, to love her in any other way.

Subaru drew in his breath, taking many shallow breaths as if he was gasping for air. His tongue was numb, and he felt like his lungs were convulsing. But he pressed on his chest to suppress his beating heart and forced his tongue to move.

That moment, with Wilhelm gazing into the distance before his eyes, he had to say it.

"Please don't say ominous things like *when I die*. Mr. Wilhelm, you're young, almost too young, and it'll be a real problem if you're always thinking about retirement."

"Sir Subaru?"

"Crusch and Ferris are both super dependent on you. Crush must struggle with not being able to remember her memories, and Ferris doesn't let it show, but he must be stretched pretty thin from supporting her any way he can, so they need you, Mr. Wilhelm. Besides, even I—!"

"———"

"Even I have lots of things left I want Mr. Wilhelm's help for. Maybe this is a naive way to think when it comes to political rivals. But I…"

—Subaru liked Wilhelm.

Wilhelm kept his feelings for his departed wife close even as he struck down his foes. That was why Subaru respected him as a man.

Even if Wilhelm had no awareness of it, even if amid repeated loops Subaru had spent no more than ten days as his apprentice, Subaru admired Wilhelm's strength.

Subaru was frightened to hear words that acknowledged death emerge from Wilhelm's mouth.

—Even more than before, Subaru was sensitive to death among the people he personally knew.

His promise with Roswaal was one reason, and it was also the effect of Return by Death altering Subaru's own thoughts. When he thought of someone he knew dying, he lost all control over his emotions.

It was enough that he had secret fears where Emilia and Beatrice were concerned.

"It seems that as is typical, I chose my words quite poorly."

As Subaru stood stiff, Wilhelm closed the distance between them with a pained smile. Drawing closer one step after another, the Sword Devil ended up right before the edge of the porch on which Subaru stood.

Then his blue, steely gaze pierced Subaru's flickering black eyes.

"Sir Subaru—that may be a virtue of yours, but it is also a weakness."

The words held no echo of a smile. But nor were they scornful scolding.

Somehow, it sounded as if he was debating a point like an elder speaking to his junior.

Or if Subaru was to put it more precisely, the tone was like that of a grandfather speaking to a grandchild.

"My wife was very much the same. It was a bad habit of hers to suppress her own feelings, prioritizing the hearts of the people all around her and always placing herself last."

"Bad habit, you say… Nah, to begin with, I'm not that saintly a guy. I'm not wishing for everyone everywhere to be happy or anything like that. I'm a guy who thinks that if I can just make sure the people around me are happy, that's enough."

"The issue is that the range in question is *the people around you.* My wife did not wish for it, but she possessed a power unsuited for any single person to wield. Her hopes and her wishes extended far beyond the reach and breadth of that power."

Wilhelm's wife, Theresia van Astrea, was the previous generation's Sword Saint.

Over the last year, even Subaru had become versed in the history of her brief career. She who had led the charge that ended the Kingdom of Lugunica's civil war that threatened to destroy the country, a hero and national savior—that was Theresia.

Subaru Natsuki could not possibly compare his heroic deeds with hers.

"I understand what you're saying about your wife. But there's no way in the world that applies to me."

"In times of peace, my wife was an ordinary woman who enjoyed looking at flowers. The heroes whose names are passed down through history did not continue being heroes in their daily lives. And, Sir Subaru, the extent of your name, and the reach of your hand, is far greater than you currently imagine. Hereafter, it shall only be more so."

"That's not…"

"I am certain of it. For all you are unable to do alone, Sir Subaru, I believe you are a man who can gather others who cannot do these things alone, either—and in doing so, you will make success possible where it was not before."

"———"

Subaru was in shock. That was all he could feel in response to the exaggerated worth Wilhelm had assigned to him.

Subaru wasn't strong, he lacked intelligence or wisdom, and he was half-hearted and weak-willed to boot. Precisely because he couldn't do anything alone, he had to talk other people into doing all kinds of things and always survived by the skin of his teeth over and over again, nothing more.

Why was it Wilhelm considered Subaru so valuable in spite of all that?

"Perhaps you are not yet aware of it for the time being. I suppose those who do not realize your worth yet are many. However, someday, you, too, will understand, and so will everyone else."

"I'm a puny, helpless guy who's no good at anything, though."

"Yes. And it is that puny, helpless you, who is no good at anything, whom I like."

Punctuating his words with a brief pause, Wilhelm nodded with satisfaction.

"And the number of those who think the same shall surely grow."

"———"

Subaru let out a deep breath.

Wilhelm really was exaggerating. The words were so unrealistic that they couldn't possibly be true. No one could have faulted Subaru for laughing out loud.

That he did not do so was because it was none other than Wilhelm saying it.

"—It seems I have rambled too much. I apologize for having kept you here for so long."

Seeing the melancholy Subaru harbored, Wilhelm bowed his head as if suddenly seized by embarrassment. But Subaru, seemingly regretting that he had made Wilhelm feel that way, shook his head from side to side.

"I'll give what you said just now some proper thought…and I'm kinda sorry. The original point of all this was to listen to stories about your wife."

"Not at all. It has been a long time since I have been satisfied… Well, perhaps not quite that, but I am glad to be able to speak of my wife. Neither Lady Crusch nor Ferris have had much time for such things of late."

"I just accidentally learned something because Mr. Wilhelm hasn't had his fill of telling romance stories!"

"I've clearly gotten a little too sentimental. It is finally time to put an old man's long stories to rest."

Wilhelm flashed a wry smile as he moved a foot from the garden onto the porch. The atmosphere said that the tale was over, so Subaru nonchalantly offered his hand to help Wilhelm up to the corridor.

"______"

Wilhelm accepted Subaru's hand and climbed up onto the corridor. Feeling the weight of the elderly swordsman's body through his arm, Subaru suddenly recalled the situation in the reception hall for an instant.

Simultaneously, the thoughts he'd had on his way to the garden came back to him.

Perhaps this would be very insensitive and brash of him. Yet, even so—

"Mr. Wilhelm. It's not my intention to go from someone sticking his nose into another camp's domestic affairs to thoughtlessly trampling on the hearts of others, but…"

"—. Yes, I am listening."

"…Can't you get along with Reinhard? You're family, aren't you?"

He could imagine the complexities that probably surrounded the relationship involving the grandfather and grandson of the Astrea family.

Perhaps crudely intruding upon that would cost him the trust he had built up with Wilhelm. But this was what he thought: What value was there in a relationship you merely clung to, not saying anything for fear of hurting the other?

And if Wilhelm intruding as he had done was meant to make Subaru think precisely that…

"A thought occurred to me while speaking with you, Sir Subaru."

"______"

"Why is it that I am unable to talk like this with my own grandson?"

This was the source of Wilhelm's agonizing remorse.

All expression vanished from Wilhelm's face. He was expressionless but hardly emotionless. These were powerful, powerful emotions locked away deep inside a hardened shell—these were undoubtedly regrets.

"I am a man of many regrets. However, there are three regrets I have amassed over the course of my own life for which I have absolutely no excuse. One of them is the cause of the current rift between my grandson and me."

"But that frustrates you, doesn't it, Mr. Wilhelm?"

"I am not allowed to feel frustration over this. That is the weight of the words I pounded into my grandson…into Reinhard at the time. They were egregiously, unforgivably…foolish."

While emotionless on the surface, there was a fire that raged inside Wilhelm that seemed like it would scorch his very soul.

These were the hellish flames of anger that had continued to blaze over those long years in Wilhelm's unforgiving heart. The fires of regret had combined into one great conflagration, the flame charring Wilhelm, not permitted to cease until he was turned to ash.

"For the sake of avenging my wife, I averted my eyes from this regret. And now that I have avenged her, I know this is truly the time to approach him."

"But the courage just won't come?"

"To my great shame. Thinking my grandson hates me even now, I cannot bring my feet to move."

Wilhelm lamented from the bottom of his heart how disappointed he was in himself.

Seeing the old man seemingly shrink dramatically, Subaru was seized by shock. Then after the shock wore off, he couldn't help bursting into laughter.

"Sir Subaru?"

"S-sorry. I didn't mean to laugh, but I couldn't hold it in."

Wilhelm was making an incredulous face, but it was Subaru who found what he said hard to believe.

There he'd been, resigned to the possibility that the relationship between the two was so hopeless that it might only grow worse, and yet.

"Mr. Wilhelm, it sounds like you don't think you deserve to call yourself Reinhard's grandfather or something."

"Yes, it is as you say. Even though I know I am in the wrong, I find myself unable to take a decisive step forward. Such cowardice leaves me greatly frustrated with myself, but…"

"Yeah, you don't look like anything more than a grandpa afraid of being hated by his grandkid."

"…What?"

Wilhelm's expression, clouded up to that point, registered surprise as he blinked hard. That reaction kept Subaru's grin lingering on his cheeks.

"I don't know much about the reason things went sour between the two of you. I might be off the mark for all I know. But from my outsider's point of view, you and Reinhard genuinely want to patch things up. In that case, it's a lot better for the one doing the apologizing to go first."

"Surely, Reinhard will refuse to forgive me."

"If he won't forgive you right away, keep apologizing until he does. In the first place, apologizing isn't about someone forgiving you, is it? You apologize because you want to. The desire to apologize is selfish and arbitrary. I mean, the person apologizing is the one who did something bad in the first place."

"______"

This time, it was Wilhelm's turn to be bewildered by Subaru's shocking leaps in logic.

Of course, Subaru was well aware of how selfish and arbitrary the irrational argument really was. Even so, it was something that Wilhelm, scared of speaking to his grandson and frightened of taking the first step, really needed. What he needed in that moment was the ability to be willfully ignorant, to brazenly act as if past regrets never happened, and a brash willingness to be caught up in the moment.

And Subaru Natsuki was a master of all these dubious skills.

"So yeah, apologizing all of a sudden after so many years have passed will make someone think, *What's with this guy?* But over the course of apologizing a bunch of times, that'll start changing. Hard to tell whether it'll become *This guy's beyond help* or *This guy's so annoying*, though."

"I believe that would count as a change for the worse."

"But it's still a change. Wouldn't any progress at all be better than keeping things horribly frozen in place like they are now?"

The popular image of Subaru was that he was someone who started out giving a whole slew of people the worst possible impression of himself. To Subaru, being surrounded by people who thought the worst of him was no big deal.

Besides, Subaru saw a chance for victory. After all, Reinhard—

"—Reinhard told me he wants to hear about what happened during the fight with the White Whale."

At the end of all those flippant words, Subaru revealed the fact that would probably become the key.

Reinhard had certainly asked Subaru about it on the way to the tearoom.

"I don't know what the White Whale has to do with you two not getting along. But if it is connected, Reinhard knows it's Mr. Wilhelm who struck the White Whale down. He knows that you spent over a decade to avenge his grandma, too."

"———"

"He probably hopes it's high time for things stuck in the past to start moving, too."

There was no way for Subaru to know how Reinhard truly felt.

In fact, it still wasn't clear to him how they'd ended up friends in the first place. There were even times that he worried they'd become friends too easily. Part of that was probably due to his belief that Reinhard had never felt powerless or uninformed.

—But there was no way that was true. There was no doubt Reinhard also had things he worried about.

Even Wilhelm, who looked superhuman from Subaru's point of view, was just another man, another grandfather, another flawed human being with problems and baggage.

Was it so wrong to think Reinhard was the same?

If Reinhard was such a man, then there was something Subaru could do for him as his friend.

He hoped that all it would take was a single act of meddling.

"I wonder if my grandson…if Reinhard will listen?"

After a brief pause, Wilhelm wrung that question out of himself. Subaru smiled, because this was the exact trigger for taking the first step forward that Wilhelm had been looking for.

"First, you talk to him until he's sick of you. If he brushes you off, that's fine, too. I mean, I always approach Emilia-tan with the mindset that I might only succeed once out of a hundred tries."

"Unbelievable—"

Listening to Subaru's advice, the unexpected revelations made Wilhelm shake his head in disbelief.

Then the old man lifted his gaze, peering up at the silvery moon floating overhead.

"There is no besting you, Sir Subaru."

It was clear from his voice that he was smiling.

CHAPTER 4

NOISY TRANQUILITY

1

The next morning, Subaru, who had woken up in high spirits, was standing in the garden as the morning sun shone upon it.

Savoring the sensation of the cobblestones beneath his soles, Subaru filled his lungs with the refreshing morning air, going "Nnn—!" as he stretched his back. The sight drew a small smile from Emilia, who was standing next to him.

"What is it, Subaru? You're in a *really* good mood this morning. Did something nice happen?"

"Emilia-tan's wavy braids are super cute this morning, so it was totally worth spending a little time on them before bed last night."

"Is that so? I'm so glad. You kind of seemed to have something on your mind last night."

Smiling as she made that remark, Emilia gently stroked her wavy silver hair.

Just as they'd planned it the night before when Emilia's braids were undone, Subaru had given her silver hair a soft wave. Her normal hairstyle was cute, of course, but a beautiful girl had the special privilege of changing the accent of her charm from time to time.

Still, it was fact that he had caused so much trouble the day before. And of course he was still reflecting on his failure at the Muse Company, but this was this, and that was that.

"I'll just have to accept it with the gravity it deserves… Beako, what's with you this morning, pouting like that?"

"I am not pouting or anything of the sort. Would you refrain from making such arbitrary claims, I wonder?"

Averting her face, Beatrice sat on the porch as she gazed at Subaru and Emilia.

It's nothing, she stubbornly projected, but the girl had said barely a word since waking up this morning, and on top of that, she'd been constantly glancing around in unease. Even if she said *don't worry*, Subaru couldn't help but do so.

"It's not cute when you're stubborn like that. If something happened, then just spell it out. It could be important, right?"

"That's right, Beatrice. If there's something worrying you, let's all worry about it together. I'm becoming dependable, you know."

"I am of a mind to object to some of Emilia's words. But…"

Casting a suspicious look at Emilia as the girl pressed a hand to her chest, Beatrice broke down under the two's gazes. She touched one of her hair rolls, then twirled it around her finger as she spoke.

"Actually, one of the inn staff members said something yesterday, I suppose. This employee told Betty alone that *at this inn, something inhuman appears at night* in a hushed whisper."

"Ohhh, something inhuman?"

"At first, Betty laughed it off, I suppose. But just to be sure, she put her mind on guard. And then sure enough, did something not happen last night, I wonder?"

"Thump, thump…"

Captivated by Beatrice's tale, Emilia pressed a hand to her chest as her eyes darted this way and that. From that reaction, she was really getting into it as Beatrice's voice grew more heated still.

"In the middle of the night, Betty awoke to a strange presence. And did she gently slip out of the room, so as not to awaken Subaru as he slept with a stupid look on his face, I wonder?"

"Don't stare at people's faces when they're sleeping. It's indecent."

"I—I was not staring! Was my glance not as light and graceful as the snow, I wonder?!"

Beatrice had just incriminated herself in a panic, but she was cute, so Subaru decided to let it pass without comment.

"At any rate, Betty pursued that presence. Then just beyond the entryway, I found the source of that aura…"

"You found it? And then what?"

"Did I confront that pale face floating in the darkness from the front, I wonder?! This face noticed Betty as well, and we entered a contest of stares… The battle continued on, one step forward and one step back!"

"A staring contest! And then, and then?"

"Oh-ho, but Betty is a Great Spirit, so the foe ultimately fled in terror, I suppose."

"I'm so glad—what a relief. I was worried Beatrice might have died right there…"

Having gotten far too invested in Beatrice's ghost story, Emilia's concerns were rather exaggerated. In the first place, if Beatrice were dead, just who was the adorable creature right before them?

That said, Subaru admired the fact that the story was fairly well thought out.

"So what actually happened, Otto?"

"Er, when I was on the verge of being sick just outside the entryway, I noticed Beatrice staring daggers at me… She vanished while I was crouched and feeling miserable, however."

It was just then that Otto entered the garden with a wobbly gait. Upon hearing the truth about last night from his lips, Beatrice muttered, "That cannot be…" in absolute shock.

It was said that fear made the wolf—or in this case, a drunken Otto—seem larger.

While Beatrice struggled to reconcile her memories with reality, Emilia tried to comfort her by stroking her head. Probably, the inn staffer who had told her about the apparition had quickly discerned that Beatrice possessed a rare and precious disposition; specifically, she was a *really cute when teased* character. Given the adorable red face he was looking at now, Subaru could only call this a job well done.

"Incidentally, you weren't back for dinner last night, either, so what were you up to?"

Keeping the charming Beatrice in the corner of his eye, Subaru cocked his head questioningly as he looked at Otto's pale face. Otto's pallor seemed drained of blood so early in the morning as he wobbled to the edge of the porch and sat down.

"I told you before we parted ways, did I not? Since we happened to have come all this way to Pristella, I wanted to meet people with whom it would normally be very difficult to sp-eak wi—ughhh."

"Sounds like you're living dangerously. You seem about as drunk as the first time we met, man."

"...In the case of Mr. Natsuki, I was not drunk when we first met, I believe?"

"If that's what you remember, then it's probably true. For you, at least."

Otto seemed to have no recollection of such an event, and at present, his memory was correct. Their first meeting from Subaru's point of view and from Otto's point of view differed greatly in place and subsequent developments. But Subaru had no intention of trying to explain over and over the happenings during various circuits of a loop that had been lost for eternity.

Deciding to move on, Subaru shot Otto's suspicious face a wink.

"Anyway, make sure you aren't a bad influence on Beako, or it'll affect her development. Well, I do understand that you were trying your best for the group, though."

"This, I did all on my own agh— I had other reasons for doing thish."

"—?"

"More importantly..." Bitterly twisting up his pale face, Otto scanned the garden. "I do not see Garfiel anywhere. It is unusual for him not to at least poke his face out, is it not? He is always the first to rise, howling from the peak of a mountain or something."

"That's because he couldn't find any other high ground to howl from. Errr, jokes aside, he's in a bit of a sensitive state at the moment. For the time being, be gentle if you run into him, 'kay?"

"To be perfectly honest, I wish I was the one being treated gently at the moment… Ugh, my head hurts…"

Subaru flashed a troubled smile at Otto's Groggy status as he wobbled and crumbled down onto the porch.

"So now that Otto is here, too, what are our plans for today?"

Hugging a sullen Beatrice from behind, Emilia inclined her head and posed the all-important question. Her words made Subaru go "right…" as he touched a hand to his chin. "There's the issue of renegotiating with Kiritaka for sure. What was the plan again, kidnap Liliana and trade her for the magic crystal?"

"Where did that drastic plan come from?! Did you really reflect on anything you did yesterday?!"

"Sorry, my smidgen of resentment toward Liliana affected my proposal."

Subaru apologized as Liliana's blissful face came rushing back to him, but Otto was too busy suffering from the effects of his own shouts on his hungover head to pay much attention. After moaning for a while, Otto continued with tears in his eyes.

"First of all, we are scheduled to visit the Muse Company at fire time today. I would be grateful if we could have White Dragon's Scale mediate, however…"

The name Otto mentioned was referring to Kiritaka's bodyguard, Dynas. White Dragon's Scale was the name of the mercenary company he was part of, which was currently hired to serve as Kiritaka's personal guard.

Although, in Subaru's mind, Dynas seemed less like a bodyguard and more like a private secretary whose main purpose was to deal with the Liliana issue.

"For the time being, I must ask that Mr. Natsuki remain here. I shall accept no rebuttals."

"*Why*…is what I'd like to say, but I'll keep it under wraps. Even I know the talks will go smoother without me there…but then what's the point of me coming to Pristella?"

"To play with Beatrice? It's good to make as many memories with her as you can."

"Is Betty somehow being treated lightly for some, I wonder?! I raise an objection!"

Beatrice's indignant protests were for the most part ignored, and with that, the afternoon plans were tentatively set. They weren't very involved plans, though; the gist was that everyone except Otto had free time.

"Well, how about I take Emilia-tan and Beako to a public park?"

"Eh? Shouldn't I be going together with Otto?"

"Today, I am only going to obtain a promise to reopen negotiations, you see. Bringing Lady Emilia along for this type of visit would be lacking in etiquette. Having you return ahead of me yesterday was for the same reason."

After explaining his reasoning to Emilia, Otto added, "However..." and shot Subaru a suspicious glance before continuing. "I do not know what Mr. Natsuki is scheming in citing such a reason."

"Calling it scheming makes it sound like I'm up to no good."

That was all he could muster. Otto was impressive as always—even his misses were still somehow on target.

Not that Subaru was actually scheming, but he did have a plan. It was a plan that relied heavily on luck, however.

"After I got off the boat yesterday, I found this really pretty park along the way. I was like, I wanna take a walk through there with Emilia-tan, with Beako in the middle and us holding her hands."

"Wow, that sounds fun. But should we really take it easy like that? What do you think, Teacher?"

"I can hardly say no when my pupil is looking forward to it quite this much. Well, assuming he comes back before you go, at least take Garfiel with you... Just do not cause any commotions."

"Why are you looking at me when you say that? Say that to Beako. She's the one you want."

"How accurate is that, I wonder? Betty is the oldest one here, so it's fairly obvious who should lead the way."

Mistaking what Otto was concerned about, Beatrice put her hands on her hips with a confident flourish. The way she completely missed the point was adorable, so Subaru affectionately stroked Beatrice's head all over.

And as Subaru and company enjoyed the peaceful, friendly atmosphere—

"Yo, everyone's together, huh? Pretty nice morning, ain't it?"

Felt raised her hand in greeting as she stepped into the corridor.

"Morning. I was wondering this yesterday, too, but what are you reading?"

"Ahhh, I have a bet with Reinhard going. He's gonna give me questions on what's in the book, and I'll answer 'em. If I don't win this, I probably won't be able to see Ilya next time I'm on break…"

In other words, Reinhard was using Felt's competitive spirit to educate her, all in the name of a bet.

What a pain, said her grimace. Felt lightly hopped down into the garden. Then the royal-selection candidate pointed at Otto, who was just managing to bring himself to a sitting position.

"That green Mister wasn't here yesterday, was he? He's with you guys?"

"Yeah, he is. This is our domestic adviser. Well, he's a lot like what Larry is to you."

"I am not quite sure what you mean, but I am fairly certain you didn't mean anything good!"

Though there was some rudeness implicit in his statement, it had introduced Otto more than sufficiently. At the end of that exchange, Felt tilted her head and asked Subaru, "Who's Larry?"

"I mean that Lachins guy with you. They're minor acquaintances of mine. That's why I lovingly call the trio Larry, Curly, and Moe."

"Heh, sounds fine to me. So Lachins, Gaston, and Camberley are Larry, Curly, and Moe to you? Has a nice ring to it—fits 'em surprisingly well!"

"I'm surprised at the miracle of what happened to me a year ago, too. Wish it was a different miracle, though."

He raised a toast to himself for dubbing them well at the time. Incidentally, since Felt apparently liked the terminology, he raised a toast to the Three Stooges, who would continue to be known as Larry, Curly, and Moe forevermore.

"By the way...," said Felt afterward as she glanced between Subaru and Emilia. "What's that weird dance you've been doing for a while now? Playing some kind of game?"

"Hey, hey, don't call it a weird dance. These are radio calisthenics, a completely respectable workout."

Felt had a mystified look as Subaru explained the activity that he and Emilia were doing together. The Emilia camp had assembled at the garden that morning precisely so they could do radio calisthenics.

Regardless of whether they were on a trip or whatever their itinerary, they never missed morning calisthenics.

"Good health is the secret to a long life, so this exercise routine is beloved by everyone from little kids to the elderly. When Emilia becomes king, she's going to make it national law to do these every morning."

"That's right. It feels *really* good to do this every morning with everyone."

"Yeah...? If it was up to me, anyone who planned to make that public policy definitely wouldn't get to be king..."

As she watched them go through the exercises, Felt murmured with a frown on her face.

It was sad that she didn't see the appeal of radio calisthenics, but even if people hated the activity at first, most got used to it as time wore on. As a matter of fact, an unprecedented radio-calisthenics boom was already spreading the exercise routine from the Mathers domain to various other regions.

"Now that I think about it, I heard lots of weird festivals are spreading from that Miss's lands. There's some weird dance involved, playing around with hollowed-out pumpkins, and something about women baking sweets and giving them to men?"

"Right now, it's treated as some weird custom from the boonies, but I wanna make it my project to spread these customs nationwide. On that note, it'd be nice to have someone like Anastasia cooperating when planning events and stuff."

It was considered an open secret that the modern iteration of Valentine's Day was a conspiracy hatched in the chocolate corporate world. In other words, a lot of money could be up for grabs, so he felt like Anastasia would pounce at the chance.

When Felt saw Subaru sink into thought with a serious look on his face, she glanced at Emilia and spoke in a quiet voice.

"Hey, is Mister always like this?"

"Yeah, Subaru's like this most of the time. When he looks like he's just kidding around, he's actually thinking really hard about all kinds of things. Then again, sometimes he looks like this when he really is kidding around, too."

"I have no idea why you sound like you're proud of him for that."

Felt cocked her head in puzzlement when Emilia seemed to take a strange sense of pride in Subaru's behavior.

Every so often, when Emilia interacted with people who were ostensibly younger than her, it was sometimes difficult to tell who was actually older, which was an issue of Emilia's mental age. This was one of those situations.

"Come to think of it, you're all alone, Felt. Where's Reinhard?"

"I ain't a kid, and havin' him around me just means I gotta listen to him fuss. Besides, not that I like admitting it, but if I call him, he'll get here in one second."

Judging by how Felt's face stiffened as she said that, she probably meant it literally and not a joke. That sort of thing really drove home how extraordinary Reinhard truly was.

"But from what I saw yesterday, it seems like you learned how to get along with Reinhard… Maybe *get along* isn't the right way to put it… It seems like you guys worked things out even though you had a rocky start."

"Oh, really? I thought Felt and Reinhard got along very nicely from the start…"

"Hey, are those actual gemstones in this Miss's eyes? You'd better polish 'em right so they see straight, 'cause I'm one scary girl when push comes to shove."

Felt's strangely poetic metaphor made Subaru appreciate how much education and growing she'd benefited from since they last met.

"Well, I can't deny what Mister said about it, though. Not like I can just be irresponsible forever or anything. Now that I've decided I'm doin' this with him, he's my responsibility, so…"

"—Lady Felt, you called?"

"I did not!!"

Instantly, Reinhard emerged out of thin air.

When Reinhard suddenly appeared behind her back, Felt roared with anger at him. Her high-pitched voice made Reinhard raise an eyebrow. Then he addressed her.

"Lady Felt, it is still early in the morning. This is not my mansion, so please do not cause trouble to those around us by raising a ruckus…"

"Oh, shut up—don't lecture me! And what's the big deal with you anyway?! You say you'll come in a second when I call you, and then you come when I'm not even calling at all!"

"Good morning to you, Lady Emilia. And morning to you, Subaru. A fine day."

"Don't ignore me when it's convenient for you, damn it!!"

When Reinhard crisply smiled and offered a morning greeting, Subaru raised his hand in return. Furious at Reinhard's reaction, Felt grabbed him by the collar and shook his head around.

Of course, given Reinhard's strength, he could have easily brushed her off, but she still kept a hold of him.

"You see? Felt and Reinhard get along *really* well."

"I guess you're right. That's a classic getting-along-nicely scene."

"Somehow, those words are creepy enough that I could just die! I don't like it!"

Grinning and agreeing with the smiling Emilia, Subaru smoothly ignored Felt's shouts. Instead, Subaru looked at Reinhard as Felt was manhandling him.

He'd lowered the corners of his eyes in a consternated look, and he wore a troubled smile on his face, but the sight was so natural somehow that Subaru oddly felt a sense of relief.

Simultaneously, he had a sudden thought—these two had also spent the last year challenging the royal selection as master and retainer.

"Well, hate to spoil the lovely moment, but how about we go get some breakfast?!"

"I'm not accepting this!"

Listening to Felt's high-pitched voice, Subaru looked up at the clear blue sky and gave a mighty stretch.

First the night before, then a morning like this—it was going to be a great day.

He had no rational basis for thinking that, but he felt confident nonetheless.

2

"—Good morning. Oh, you all seem to be getting along rather nicely."

Anastasia greeted Subaru and the others as they entered the reception hall, smiling mischievously as she spoke.

From her point of view, seeing the Emilia camp and the Felt camp together must have been a surprise. But Subaru was just as surprised by her greeting. The reason was the glossy outfit she was wearing.

The sight of Anastasia, wearing a different outfit with her usual scarf around her neck, made Emilia and the others go "wow" in astonishment.

"Good, good. It seems I've succeeded in surprising you this morning. I'm so happy."

"That outfit is splendid. Is this what you were talking about in the bath yesterday?"

"Yes, this is a kimono. It's like a *yukata*, but it takes a little longer to put on."

Anastasia proudly twirled on the spot, splendidly putting the blue-dyed clothing on display. The dancing, falling petal pattern on it was also very charming. Subaru could only be amazed at Kararagi's ability to reproduce it.

"So those clothes are some kind of Kararagi tradition?"

"Yes. The design of these clothes has been passed down by tailors since the era of Hoshin and is one of the few pieces of culture from that time."

"The era of Hoshin, is it?"

Once again, this mysterious person, Hoshin of the Wastes, stood before Subaru.

Just like Subaru and Al, he was probably an other-worlder from the same homeland, summoned four centuries prior—

"Once this is all wrapped up, I really need to look into this Hoshin guy a bit..."

At this point, Subaru had no intention of complaining about the phenomenon of being summoned to another world.

He'd long since passed the stages of understanding and acceptance.

He knew neither the process of the summoning nor the goals of the summoner, but he'd accepted that the summoning was a one-way trip and that there was no convenient way to travel back.

His questions about those things were as innumerable as stars in the sky, but what Subaru wanted to know most at the moment was what kind of marks the one summoned long before him had left upon the world and what became of him. That was all.

"Lady Anastasia, you are even more beautiful this morning. I was worried that you would not allow even me to see you like this, but it seems that was a needless concern."

"Eh-heh-heh, this was the jewel up my sleeve! The finished product only arrived in Pristella just a little while ago, you see. It was a real pain hiding it from Julius, heh-heh."

Afterward, meeting up with Julius in the hall, Anastasia showed her clothes off to her own knight, and Julius lavished her with fawning praise, filling Anastasia with satisfaction. Then she cocked her head to the side.

"Oh? Mimi and the others aren't with you?"

"Ricardo has not yet returned this morning while out on the business he mentioned. As for Mimi…it would seem she has been leading Lady Emilia's retainer Garfiel all around."

"Eh, Mimi's with Garfiel?"

When Emilia's eyes went wide at hearing the name of one of her own, Julius said, "Yes," with a nod. "Garfiel and Mimi have not returned to the inn since last night. When they learned of this, Hetaro and TB ran into the city with all haste."

"You heard about this from Joshua, and I'm only hearing about it now—that's how I should take this?"

Anastasia put her hands on her hips, checking with Joshua, who had followed Julius in and was hiding behind his back. The words left the young man with the delicate face downcast, bowing his head with a pathetic expression.

"I—I am very sorry. I was… I desperately tried to stop them, but Hetaro refused to listen to reason. And TB was also concerned, so…"

"That's because when Mimi's there, Hetaro doesn't see anything else around him. If TB's with him, it should be fine… In his place, there is something I would like to ask of you, Joshua."

Smiling at the cowed Joshua, Anastasia patted the young man's shoulder as he lifted his head.

"I really had meant to entrust this to Hetaro and the others, but I want you to pick up a letter at the main gate—it's a very, very important letter."

As she spoke those words, Anastasia glanced in Subaru's direction. In his mind, the suggestive gaze overlapped with the conversation in the hall the night before, spurring him to say something.

"I'm begging you, Joshua. You're my only hope."

"What need is there for you to ask that of me?! Lady Anastasia has already given me her instructions!"

Brushing off Subaru's hands, which had been grasping both his shoulders, Joshua headed for the sliding screen door with rapid steps. And then—

"I shall do as instructed. Leave it to me. I shall complete it without fail in TB and the others' stead!"

—with conviction, Joshua made this declaration to Anastasia and raced out of the hall. Anastasia gently touched her scarf when his ponytail vanished from sight.

"He really could have done it after eating breakfast, though..."

She wore a strained smile as she remarked on this youngster's apparent loyalty and hunger for glory.

"—I am sorry that we were a tad late. It would appear we are the last ones."

Crusch, with her long green hair all tied up this day, was the last to arrive at the reception hall. She remained dressed in a ladylike fashion, with a floral hair ornament and a white ribbon vividly adorning her green hair.

No doubt it was Ferris, appearing in the hall after her, who did the coordinating. With light steps, Wilhelm followed immediately behind Ferris, wearing his usual butler's outfit.

The sight of the tall elderly man made Subaru's shoulders grow tense. He recalled the many words he had exchanged with the Sword Devil under the moonlight the night before.

"——"

As Subaru reminisced, it was precisely then that Wilhelm spotted him, and they exchanged gazes. Subaru's breath caught in his throat as Wilhelm quietly greeted him with his eyes.

Subaru interpreted the message as *you need not be concerned*.

"So it seems we are all assembled. There are several faces missing, but still..."

"That goes for our Garfiel, too. If he's with Mimi, that's fine, but that harebrained son of ours..."

To be accurate, it should really be *tigerbrained*—but naturally, even Subaru was worried about Garfiel not returning by morning or failing to stay in touch. Perhaps he'd gone off somewhere to heal that difficult-to-shake sense of defeat.

And if Mimi really was with him, Subaru could only hope that things didn't get out of hand in some odd fashion.

"Well, be it worries or work, it can wait until after we've had some food. *Rohallo lost because of an empty stomach*, they say."

Clapping her hands, Anastasia invoked what seemed to be a common saying as she took her seat. Emulating her, Subaru and the others similarly sat down, divided by camp as they rested upon square floor cushions.

"Could you please bring it in?"

Seeing that everyone was seated, Anastasia called out to the people waiting behind the screens. As she did, several inn staffers brought plates in, placing them atop the long table.

The long table was quickly filled with huge black objects—only for even more iron plates to be set down.

"Today we shall enjoy some traditional Kararagi folk cooking—it's time for a *daisukiyaki* feast!"

Anastasia made her pronouncement with great vigor as she swiftly rolled up her sleeves.

Everyone in attendance was surprised by how she quickly set to work as the staff swiftly placed oil upon the iron plates and then brought a cart, which had all manner of condiments in round containers sitting atop it, into the hall.

Daisukiyaki—the echo of that word, the large iron plates, the dishes… Glancing among all these, Subaru realized the true nature of the culinary tradition before him—

"—Y-you mean this is *okonomiyaki*?!"

Passed down in Kararagi as *daisukiyaki*, the Japanese dish of *okonomiyaki* boldly made its appearance.

3

"Subaru, look! Look how prettily it turned over! I'm so proud of it! Eat up!"

"I suppose it came out well enough. Subaru, I went through all the trouble of frying this *daisukiyaki*, so you might as well eat it."

Emilia's face was one big smile, whereas Beatrice's was a little shy as both served up some curious-looking *daisukiyaki*, which they themselves had cooked and which now sat on the iron plates before them.

"Both of you should learn to taste your own cooking before serving it to people."

Following Subaru's rather sound advice, the pair did as he suggested and promptly writhed in agony. Incidentally, Subaru could boast about his *okonomiyaki* to an extent, but he was not the most skilled in the Emilia camp.

"Lady Emilia, Beatrice, both of you can have some of what I fried. Ahhh! Lady Emilia, frying it too lightly will ruin your stomach. Beatrice, you used too much sauce!"

Thanks to Otto's feverish efforts, the Emilia camp was at least able to secure a decent breakfast.

Glancing at the spectacle, Subaru shifted his gaze to the homemade cooking of the other camps.

"Lady Felt, I have prepared the next dish."

"Ohhh, nicely done, nicely done. Looks like at this rate, you're gonna be fryin' lots. I'm pretty grateful for your skill in cooking and making sweets, gotta say."

With the Felt camp seated directly across from Subaru, he had a front-row seat to Reinhard producing one dish of high-end *daisukiyaki* after another with incredible skill, before watching all the food disappear into Felt's stomach. As over five *daisukiyaki* dishes had already vanished into thin air, where Felt stuffed them into her tiny body struck Subaru as one of the deeper mysteries of life.

"Now, now, now, now, now, now—! This is some real, genuine *daisukiyaki* I whipped up!"

But of course, Anastasia had put on quite a performance given her deep knowledge of *daisukiyaki*. She'd raced between two separate frying pans, successfully creating two hunks of what appeared to be charcoal.

It was a valuable life lesson. Enthusiasm alone wasn't enough.

"As expected of you, Lady Anastasia. However, I prefer it when the frying time is a little briefer. Though it pains me to add to your time and trouble..."

"It's fine, it's fine, leave it to me. For a boy, you sure have a delicate tongue, Julius."

Unlike Subaru, who urged the cooks to eat their own food and repent for their culinary sins, Julius ate the hunks of charcoal without complaint and only after finishing every last bite did he suggest improvements. Truly, his demeanor toward his liege was chivalry itself. Subaru had absolutely no desire to follow suit.

"Ahhh, Lady Crusch—! Ferri fried a pretty one. Here, here."

"Why, yes you have. But I shall not be defeated. Ha-ha, behold."

Yes, it was Crusch and Ferris who were involved in relaxed, flirtatious same-sex bonding. That didn't properly describe their relationship, but this was typical for them, so Subaru decided it would be prudent to not intrude.

Either way, as befit their impressive dexterity, the *daisukiyaki* on their iron plates were remarkable—Ferris had even taken the time to give them kitty ears.

"*Fwoo.* Okay, it's time to make you eat Ferri's *daisukiyaki* made with love. Lady Crusch, please open your mouth and say *ahhh.*"

"Eh, eh? Um, errr…a-ahhh…"

Thanks to the tender rich-girl aura Crusch gave off, Subaru got the distinct feeling that he should stop watching. Off to the side of that pinkish scene, Wilhelm was working on his own *daisukiyaki*, but—

"Mmm…"

Turning over the pieces, the Sword Devil groaned as they broke apart and clung to the iron plate. They had probably been left to cook for a bit too long; Wilhelm seemed to be exhibiting unexpected clumsiness.

"I feel like I'm seeing something I was never meant to see. But that being the case… Er."

"Hey, Mister, what you fried looks pretty tasty."

Right as Subaru thought he'd offer Wilhelm a helping hand, Felt cut him off. Her eyes glimmered as she gazed at the Puck-shaped *daisukiyaki* that Subaru had fried with his own two hands.

"Nah, I'm sure your guy can cook palace-chef-level *daisukiyaki* on an industrial scale already. Not that I know if palace chefs actually make *daisukiyaki*…"

"Well, you have a point, but sometimes, you just wanna eat something different, right? Even though he's cooking on an iron plate like this, everything that bastard makes comes out elegant…"

"Then, Felt, why don't you try the *daisukiyaki* I ma…?"

"I'm talking about eating *food* here. Why don't you go and play with the little shrimp over there, charcoal-burner?"

Emilia, finally getting the charcoal-maker treatment, slinked over to Beatrice so she could commiserate with the glum spirit. Subaru wore a concerned smile when he saw how dejected they were.

"Hey now, don't tease my Emilia-tan and my Beako like that."

"So not just the Miss but the little shrimp, too… Oh right, that's right!"

Quickly sidestepping Subaru's reply, Felt proceeded to lean toward him.

"Hey, I thought I'd come out and ask. I heard some amazin' rumors about you, Mister. So be real with me: How many of those things are lies?"

"Come on—don't assume most of it is lies from the very start. It almost sounds like that's what you're hoping for."

"But there's no way I can believe all that stuff. I mean, I heard Mister sliced the White Whale in two all on his own, smashed the Witch Cult with his bare fists, turned the Great Rabbit into fried rabbit…and ate it!"

"The info sorta, kinda matches, but there's a lot of chaff mixed in, damn!!"

If Subaru could manage that all by himself, he'd have been made a national hero or even become king by now. He would have just taken the throne by force and made Emilia his queen so they could flirt forever.

"—Hmph."

But Subaru's strong wisecrack was greeted by a slight chuckle from off to the side—from a pair of voices at that. The voices belonged to none other than Julius and Wilhelm.

"—? Why are Mr. Finest and Grandpa laughing? Did I say something funny?"

"It's not just that you said something funny; it's that the whole situation's hilarious. Everything you mentioned rates my contributions way too high. Like, at that point just gimme a Nobel Peace Prize."

He didn't actually know what winning a Nobel Peace Prize entailed, but at any rate, it was what came to mind when he thought of respectable commendations.

Subaru had been recognized at the honors ceremony, but because he didn't really have a firm grasp of how much that was worth, he had little grasp of exactly how his achievements had been graded.

It was then that Wilhelm picked up where Subaru and Felt's conversation had left off.

"Not at all. Where the hunt of the White Whale was concerned, Sir Subaru's contributions were incalculable. Without Sir Subaru, my long-cherished desire would never have been fulfilled. I swear this to be true upon my very sword."

"It is the same with the Witch Cult incident. That victory was over and done and thanks to none other than his leadership. The assistance that others as well as I had provided were not contributions worthy of boasting about."

Wilhelm and especially Julius's blunt assessments left Subaru at a loss for words. After, what belatedly arrived was ferocious heat. Subaru's head and ears were burning from embarrassment.

"C-cut it out, guys! Don't put me on a weird pedestal like that! You all know what shameful shit I get up to when I get full of myself!"

"The results of your efforts after that more than made up for your own shame. There is no need for you to dwell upon that moment forever. Your future exploits are completely separate and should be greeted with pride."

"What you have accomplished are things no one else has ever done before. Until my final days, I shall take pride in having galloped across the battlefield alongside you."

"—Ah."

Killed by praise.

Up to that point, Subaru Natsuki had died over and over. But this was the first time he had glimpsed death in such a frightening manner. Subaru was learning what it meant to be slain by praise.

He felt so embarrassed that he honestly thought he might die at any moment. Subaru looked in search of aid toward Emilia, then Beatrice. However, the pair merely offered him adorable smiles with Subaru sandwiched between them.

"That's right. Subaru worked *really* hard. I'm truly proud, and happy, to have made that Subaru my knight."

"W-well, is that not all a matter of course for Betty's partner, I wonder? If anything, the surrounding rabble have been slow to realize just how incredible Subaru is."

He never dreamed their support would be so unanimous. The frightening degree of indulgence was making Subaru's head spin.

And there was not a single person in the hall who refuted these assessments. Indeed, the gazes turned toward Subaru were gentle and kind, one and all—

"Looks like a lot of stuff happened, but Mister's nature ain't changed a bit. What a relief."

"Oh, shaddap! Hey, everyone, don't praise me too much! You're gonna make me like every one of you!!"

When Felt neatly tied things up like that, Subaru's voice exploded as he neared his limit.

Instantly, the gentle atmosphere in the great hall was shattered as the voices of all present burst into laughter.

"______"

Amid that uproarious laughter, Subaru snuck a glance Wilhelm's way.

Subaru hadn't aimed for it, but the atmosphere in the hall was remarkably good. Even with careful planning, it would have been difficult to create a moment better than this for bridging gaps and creating mutual understanding.

"Mm."

Abruptly noticing Subaru's gaze, Wilhelm lifted an eyebrow. Subaru used his eyes to indicate the broken-up *daisukiyaki* by Wilhelm's hands, then motioned with his chin—toward Reinhard.

Realizing the import of the gesture, Wilhelm quietly drew in his breath.

Beside him, Reinhard was mass-producing *daisukiyaki* for Felt's sake once more. The gap in skill between grandfather and grandson was like the distance between the clouds and mud, which was exactly why Subaru thought that this could be a turning point.

Wilhelm's blue eyes grew unsteady as he wrestled with the complex emotions warring within him over and over—gloom, reluctance, hesitation, indecision.

But Wilhelm would surely overcome them all, taking a step forward and—

"*—Citizens of Pristella, good morning to you. The morn feels wonderful, does it not?*"

That was the moment they heard a voice coming from outside the inn—no, it was coming from the very sky itself. Emilia and the others' surprised reactions made it plain that the sudden voice was no private hallucination.

"Ohhh? The heck is this? Some bastard out there has a super loooud voice."

"Oh, Felt, of course not. This happens each morning in this city... This is a metropolitan-government broadcast using a metia."

"A metia broadcast..."

After Anastasia replied to Felt's carefree murmur, Subaru mulled the explanation over under his breath.

Metia was a general term for a magic item put together with some kind of magical technology. Some of the objects, such as the one being employed for the broadcast, functioned much like technology back in Subaru's original world.

He guessed that this metia worked like a bullhorn or a speaker system.

"There is a broadcast every morning? For what purpose?"

"I have heard it is preparation for emergencies. Given the construction of the city, there are very few evacuation routes available, so people familiarized them with broadcasts in hopes of avoiding a general panic in case of a real emergency."

"Hmm, I see *meow*. Very logical."

Julius's comprehensive explanation left Crusch and Ferris impressed. Subaru was equally impressed. This was the first time he'd heard of anyone treating a metia as genuinely useful and a critical part of a city's infrastructure. As far as he knew, there was virtually no precedent of using metia for practical purposes. Conversation mirrors just barely made the cut, and even these seemed to be almost exclusively possessed by the Witch Cult, leaving him with a poor impression.

But that impression vanished in an instant. He simply chalked it up to strange timing that he hadn't heard of this before.

"Incidentally, Mr. Kiritaka is both the broadcaster and the provider of the metia."

"Eh?"

With not a shred of ill will on his face, Otto added to the static in Subaru's mind.

Subaru sank into thought for several seconds. The back of his mind flipped through his memories of Kiritaka like a revolving lantern.

"No way." "Could anything be more impossible, I wonder?" "Oh, Otto, you can be so funny sometimes."

"I can understand Mr. Natsuki and Beatrice, but even Lady Emilia?!"

Subaru and Beatrice's conclusion and Emilia's laughter left Otto dumbstruck. During that time, the broadcast continued, and certainly, words from a somehow familiar voice were reaching every part of the city.

Of course, Subaru had heard from people over and over just how capable and respected Kiritaka was, but the impression he had from directly meeting the man loomed far larger in his mind. The appraisals and the real thing simply didn't match up. Even this broadcast seemed—

"And this morning, too, I offer this trifling... Nay! I shall grant you all a wonderful blessing! It is time for Ms. Liliana the Songstreeeessss!"

"Ah, it's totally him."

The tension snapped midway as Subaru's memories and the broadcast suddenly aligned.

In fact, he—no, they had interfered in what would have been a historic moment. That was hardly their fault, but Subaru was already pinching Kiritaka's cheeks in his own mind.

There was a noise of the broadcast metia being passed around, and then they heard a tiny throat-clearing sound.

"Hi, everyone, it's Lilianaaa. Being treated like a songstress is a burden as heavy as a mountain, but as I truly want to delight you with my singing and music, please support me with your joyous cheers during our brief time together—!"

Liliana's voice reverberated so vividly across the city, Subaru could picture exactly what kind of pose she was making.

Instantly, expectant looks sprang up all around; in particular, Emilia, Beatrice, Anastasia and company's faces were bright, knowing full well just how wonderful Liliana's singing voice was. It was probably only Subaru who had a somber, clouded expression among all of them.

Mysteriously, Kiritaka's voice had sounded a bit odd over the metia, but Liliana's seemed to have no problem coming through. This was probably due to differences in speaking and compatibility with the metia.

Or perhaps Liliana's voice truly had been blessed by some goddess of song.

Then when they heard Liliana ready her musical instrument, expectations in the hall swelled even more—

"Now, I shall sing. Please listen—this is the 'Love Song of the Sword Devil,' the second act."

"Wha—?"

The song was beginning as Subaru almost commented aloud on her selection.

The broadcast carried the beautiful melody throughout the entire city, seemingly straight to their hearts. Engulfed by the music and the singing voice, Subaru only had ears for the "Love Song of the Sword Devil."

Liliana really was a star-crossed songstress—but for all her character flaws, she had a truly magnificent singing voice.

4

A conflicted atmosphere coursed through the reception hall as the reverberations of the "Love Song of the Sword Devil" lingered within the city.

The word *incredible* was nowhere near sufficient to describe Liliana's song. As a matter of fact, had there been no other issues, Subaru would surely have gone straight to showering Liliana's song in praise and immediately diving into conversation about it.

There was only one issue—she had selected the "Love Song of the Sword Devil."

It was the tale of the Sword Devil, a man enamored with the sword and the one who pursued the Sword Saint. This was nothing short of the heroic tale of Wilhelm in his youth, the tale of how he and his deeply beloved wife came to meet.

In other words, thinking back to Subaru's conversation with Wilhelm the night before, this song could not have had worse timing… at least for Wilhelm, who continued to harbor feelings for his wife that had not diminished even one iota.

Of course, there were none in the hall unfamiliar with Wilhelm's relationship to the "Love Song of the Sword Devil." Even Emilia's cheeks hardened; even Felt's face was grave.

Accordingly, Subaru turned a gaze of concern toward Wilhelm, who was surely feeling considerable heartache—

"______"

The forthright look that had returned to his blue eyes, like a lake without a single ripple disturbing its surface, made Subaru unconsciously draw in his breath.

For a single instant, Wilhelm nodded toward Subaru's black eyes. Then he slowly turned to his left, where his young red-haired grandson was seated.

"—Reinhard."

As if to slice the concerns as well as Subaru and the others around them away, Wilhelm carefully spoke that name aloud.

Reinhard opened his eyes wide as he looked at Wilhelm. In turn, Wilhelm received Reinhard's gaze head-on.

A silence fell between the pair— No, it enveloped the entirety of the reception hall.

Expressions of urgency came over everyone as they sensed that a fateful conversation between grandfather and grandson was imminent. Within the room, the only sound was that of the *daisukiyaki* already frying atop the hot iron plates.

And while it was still unclear whether the silence had lasted for an instant or the span of several breaths—

"You see…"

"Yes, what is it?"

"…I am not frying this very well. If there is a knack to this, could you teach it to me?"

That was what Wilhelm said with curt, halting words.

Just how much courage did Wilhelm summon to spit those words out? Subaru had some idea. Apparently, Crusch and Ferris recognized this as well, being as wide-eyed as he.

From the side, Subaru watched complex emotions ripple across Reinhard's face as he listened to his haggard grandfather's words.

Reinhard closed his eyes in sorrow, or perhaps some undefinable emotion, then swept it away with a deep breath. From there, he slowly relaxed and said—

"—Yes. I understand, Grandfather."

As the tension palpably drained from his eyes and mouth, there was no longer any doubt that he was smiling.

This was not the hero's smile that Reinhard used to set people at ease on a daily basis. This was an expression that only belonged to the young man named Reinhard, not the Sword Saint.

Wilhelm was taken aback. Then he slowly lowered his head.

He couldn't immediately accept it. However, even if it didn't seem real at first, a connection had surely been made.

The long, deep chasm that had opened up between the pair, between grandfather and grandson, might still require as much time to fill as it had taken to dig it. But now that they had bridged that gap once, all there was to do now was fill it with acceptance.

Tracing that future in his mind, Subaru, feeling a flood of emotions, tightly clenched a fist.

After all—

"—Oh, no you don't, Father. Isn't it too convenient to pull that after all this time?"

Suddenly, a red-haired man opened the screen door and peered into the hall.

The sheer malice in his words stunned Subaru, who forgot the very passage of time in his shock.

5

The greatest of moments had been ruined in the vilest way possible.

The red-haired man's action could be considered a type of evil—no, it was cruelty.

A faint whiff of alcohol wafted from this flushed man as he stroked the stubble on his cheek. A repulsive smile came over him. His age seemed to be around forty, give or take.

The reason these little gestures and askew grooming instilled even greater disgust than necessary was because his outward appearance was fundamentally handsome. It was a striking rejection and sullying of beauty.

The deep-rooted sense of malice from the tall man's appearance was making Subaru sick.

"...Who the heck are you?"

"Aaahhh?"

As all the others in the hall held their tongues, Subaru was the first among them to raise his voice. He moved a hand behind his hip, grasping hold of something as he made a threatening sound, blood rising to his head in indignation.

That moment, everyone should have been wishing for reconciliation between the awkward pair. Subaru felt nothing but anger for the man who'd interfered.

His friend and the man he admired were making progress on repairing their relationship, until—

"Answer me. Who the hell are you?"

"...Those're some nasty eyes ya got there, brat. You got any idea who you're picking a fight with, huh, greenhorn knight?"

"Don't make me laugh. You're the one picking a fight. I'm just taking you up on the offer."

Subaru stood up then and there, finally approaching his limit.

Beside him, Beatrice quietly sat, putting her hand within easy reach of Subaru. His reliable partner approved of the flames of anger welling up in Subaru's heart.

Looking down at Subaru, the man had an annoyed look on his face as he raggedly scratched his head.

"What a noisy brat. Hey, Sword Saint, Julius, or hell, even Argyle—cut this rude brat down."

Pointing at Subaru with his scratching hand, the man ordered Reinhard and the others in a casual voice. Subaru could only interpret his arrogant statement as contempt for all three.

This time, Subaru seriously made ready to swing his arm and smack the man across the face—

"I must object."

—but just before he could act, Julius held Subaru's shoulder in check, forcing him to stop.

Julius, who had risen at some point, stood directly to Subaru's right while grasping his shoulder. Turning to glance at Subaru, he set his jaw firmly. Then he glared at the red-haired intruder.

"Currently, I, Ferris, and Reinhard are on special duty and relieved from our normal responsibilities. Accordingly, even the vice captain does not possess command authority over us at the moment."

"Right, right. Ferri is Lady Crusch's servant both in name and fact right *meow*. So I cannot obey your command."

Seizing the opportunity provided by Julius's assertion, Ferris hugged Crusch's arm as he gave his irreverent reply. Crusch was momentarily surprised to find her knight wrapped around her, but she immediately looked at the man with a sober expression.

When Subaru looked around, the other people in the room had similar expressions as they drew close, making no attempt to hide their hostility toward the interloper.

Of course not. This was the man who had wrecked the reconciliation between grandfather and grandchild that everyone had been watching with bated breath.

"Hey, hey. What a scary lot. Obviously, that was a joke, so don't get all worked up over nothing. Even if I am a vice captain in name only, I'll uphold the rules of the knighthood at least."

"In name only…?"

Subaru knit his brows at the word choice of the drunkard with a thin smile on his lips. Hearing Subaru's murmur, the man shot him another gaze of ridicule.

"That's right, in name only. I am none other than Heinkel the Idle, the despised, ornamental vice captain of the royal guard of the Kingdom of Lugunica."

"Don't get passive-aggressive with that idle and despised stuff."

"Gah-ha-ha! It hurts my ears to hear that. It hurts, it hurts, it hurts so much, I can't stand it…so shut your mouth, damn brat."

"—!"

The gloom and darkness brimming in those eyes sent a chill running down Subaru's spine.

This wasn't the same fear he felt when confronting a powerful being, such as the White Whale or a Witch. No, this was a separate, more personal feeling of revulsion.

"Calm down, Subaru. You mustn't get caught up in the vice captain's rhythm."

As Subaru drew in his breath, Julius addressed him. The words made the man—Heinkel—shoot Julius a somber smile.

"Ha! That's the Finest of Knights for you. Such refined conduct and careful choice of words. If those actually amounted to real power among knights, you'd have a proper following of your own."

"I am honored that you would praise me so, Vice Captain Heinkel… Incidentally, what business brings you here on this occasion? According to memory, the vice captain should have been assigned the duty of garrisoning the Royal Palace in the capital."

"Such graceful sarcasm. The castle's security won't be affected due to my absence, especially with the great Captain Marcus taking care of it…and it ain't like there's a royal family to protect now, is there?"

"Heinkel!"

It was Wilhelm who rose and shouted in anger at Heinkel's statement, which, considering the place, was insolent to the extreme. The Sword Devil had an incredible look on his face as his lips openly trembled.

"Heinkel…"

"I heard you the first time. I'm not old enough to be hard of hearing yet. Well, just let that slide as the ramblings of a drunk. More importantly…"

When Wilhelm raised his voice, Heinkel shrugged with an innocent look on his face. Then he surveyed the interior of the room with eyes just as blue as Wilhelm's.

"Not inviting me to the celebration for the hunt of the White Whale… What's the big idea? How cold and callous can you be? It's a big job that took over ten years to complete. I had just as much right as anybody to join the celebration and share in the happiness. Ain't that right, Father of mine?"

"Heinkel, I…"

"Reinhard! You feel the same way, don't ya?"

"———"

Adopting a face oozing with malice, Heinkel dug right into Wilhelm's heart.

The old man's expression registered pain as if he was being sliced with a blade, but Heinkel cared not. His voice interrupted Wilhelm's protest, directing his malice toward its next destination: Reinhard.

Those words made Reinhard, who had maintained his silence to that point, finally meet Heinkel's gaze.

"Thanks to Father, the burden on your shoulders got lighter, didn't it? This is your magnificent grandfather, the man who avenged his wife, my mother, and your grandmother. You didn't even say one word about him doing a good job, did you? After all..."

Breaking off his speech, Heinkel smeared a healthy dose of poison onto his blade of words. Then he spoke again.

"...he's the one who avenged the predecessor you let die, isn't that right?"

—This man's face, more than any other Subaru had ever seen, deserved to be called...*repulsive.*

Heinkel's words, his face, his demeanor, his voice, his gaze—every single thing emanating from his entire existence was drenched with nothing but malice.

This was a man of pure contempt, a man whose repulsiveness was his reason for being.

"Stop this, Heinkel! You... Even for you, this is...!"

"Stop trying to pretty it up after all this time, Father. You don't have any right to criticize me. After all, the first one to scold Reinhard for killing his predecessor...was none other than *you.*"

"—!"

Heinkel's words were like a curse craftily brewed by distilling all the hatred in the world. And the content of those words was a denunciation Subaru could not bear to hear.

The guy was spouting nothing but lies. It was wrong. It was false. It was obviously made-up.

It simply couldn't be. And yet, neither Reinhard nor Wilhelm...

"———"

Neither of them opened their mouths to deny it.

Why? All they had to say was one word: *no.* If they swept it all away as made-up garbage, Subaru would believe them without any doubt whatsoever.

His friend in arms and his respected mentor versus a drunken excuse of a man—there was no need to anguish over whom to believe.

That was why Subaru desperately wanted the two to speak the one word that would make this all go away.

"Gone quiet 'cause the truth's inconvenient for ya? That's how it's been for fifteen years. Father hasn't changed one bit, either. If he hasn't changed, no way we're patching things up. You think Theresia van Astrea would allow something as simpleminded as that?"

Silence descended upon the hall as Heinkel's curse persisted.

The name he invoked was that of Wilhelm's wife and Reinhard's grandmother—

"—My dead mother has cursed us, all three generations of Astreas. We're not allowed forgiveness."

The man called the prior Sword Saint, Theresia…his mother.

That made him Reinhard's father and Wilhelm's son.

"Heinkel van Astrea…"

Saying the name aloud, Subaru could feel its weight.

He'd grasped who Heinkel really was. There was no mistake; the man before him carried the name of the Astrea family line—even though his character was nothing like the Astreas whom Subaru knew.

"Don't add *van* to it, brat. I never got the sword name. It's Heinkel Astrea."

Overhearing Subaru's troubled murmur, Heinkel clicked his tongue.

In an instant, pain appeared on Heinkel's face. Perhaps this was simply the first time he had allowed it to be seen since he'd arrived. Now pain ran through his eyes, which had held nothing but dark delight when he disparaged his family earlier.

Thinking that this did not amount to consolation of any kind, Subaru instantly cut it aside, but—

"So what is it you came for?"

"Emilia?"

Everyone in the hall who had witnessed Heinkel's various words and actions received a jolt.

The first among them to come forward and pose that question was none other than Emilia.

The girl stood in front of Subaru, her silver hair billowing down her back as she voiced a soft-spoken anger. Subaru could keenly feel on his skin that her ire was genuine.

She always became upset when others were hurt for no good reason.

When she watched Reinhard and Wilhelm get hurt, it had roused her anger.

"...Well, well, so this is Lady Emilia. I've heard the rumors. You're apparently some kind of poor little half-demon princess burdened with a battle she can't possibly win."

"I'd like to discuss with you what you think of me at a later point, but I am not speaking of it now. I have only one question. Why have you come here?"

His provocative statement was meant to ridicule Emilia, but Heinkel looked taken aback when his effort backfired.

Subaru understood why the other camps within the room were shocked by Emilia's bold demeanor. Considering how Emilia had acted the previous day up to this morning, of course they were surprised by the dramatic change.

This was why she pretended to be scatterbrained to conceal her true nature...is what some might believe, but that would be a lie. This was simply the kind of person she was.

"Everyone is gathered here because they were invited by Anastasia. But for everyone to be here at once is already coincidence, and I do not think you would simply happen to plan a visit at a time like this. That's doubly true for someone who's a high-ranking member of the Knights of the Royal Guard. What is the meaning of this? Tell me."

"Tch, she ain't like the rumors at all..."

"Answer properly."

Heinkel clicked his tongue and furiously scratched his head—clear signs that Emilia was overwhelming him.

Emilia was angry, but in no way did she resort to a show of force. Her formidable presence was thanks to the indomitable spirit she possessed, not the overwhelming store of magical energy she was emanating.

"Wow, you stormed in all full of yourself only to get shut up by one chick glaring at ya, huh? Hey, Pops, that's really uncool of you."

"You have a point. If he wanted to entertain himself with amusing conversation, he should have gone to watch the Songstress. The stories there would have been much funnier and more bizarre."

"My, is that so? Then this uncouth individual should leave and by all means spend some time together with the oft-rumored Songstress."

"—!"

Backing Emilia up, Felt, Anastasia, and Crusch all chimed in.

Just as Emilia had done, the three other royal-selection candidates lashed at the boorish interloper with the sheer intensity of their commanding presence. Feeling the pressure coming from all four, Heinkel's cheek twitched.

It was almost as if...he was unworthy of standing on this stage. Compared with the people who had earned their right to be there, the gap between him and them was yawning indeed.

"Are you satisfied, vice captain? If you have no other business, I believe it would be mutually beneficial for you to depart from this place as soon as possible."

Julius made that suggestion as he beheld the contrast between the color of Heinkel's face and the rising temperature from the women.

In one sense, he was offering Heinkel a lifeboat. The thought crossed Subaru's mind that if possible, Heinkel's spirit should be broken then and there, but he wanted to avoid dragging out this conversation.

He didn't want to have Heinkel in the same room as Reinhard and Wilhelm any longer.

"Ughhh..."

"Vice captain, your decision. If possible, it would be best for all sides to refrain from speaking of this any fur..."

"—That will not be necessary, commoner."

The voice that called out was uncommonly charming, filled with the arrogance of one who looked down upon all others as a matter of fact.

The stunning voice compelled the hearts of anyone within earshot to submit and imposed the speaker's absolute sense of superiority on them, completely overwriting their perceptions of worth and value.

Everyone in the hall shifted their eyes toward the closed screen door behind Heinkel.

Already, not a single person paid Heinkel any more attention. Perhaps that was because their attention was gathered solely upon the sunlike heat approaching from beyond the threshold. And then—

"It would seem that the riffraff have been assembled. Marvelous. You have prepared a place suitable for my personal attendance. For this, and this alone, I commend you."

Her cleavage was provocatively exposed. She was clad in a dress as red as blood. Her arms were wrapped around her chest, propping up her substantial breasts and freely baring her lustrous skin while she flashed a sultry smile.

Her crimson eyes seemed to set all aflame. Her gaze seemed to make sport of everything. Her enchanting charisma was bewitchment made manifest, ready to enthrall every male in the world and make them her slaves.

Beyond a certain point, beauty could become violence. Her very existence was the embodiment of those words.

And her name was Priscilla Bariel.

With this, the fifth and final candidate for the royal selection had arrived, apparently uninvited, to the feast.

6

"I must say, however, you certainly are holding this event in a remote place. It was highly inconvenient locating suitable transport to cover such a distance. Well, the sights of the city and the odd structure of this inn do suit my tastes."

Concealing her lips behind a crimson fan, Priscilla snickered as she surveyed the hall.

The people shocked by her sudden appearance could not muster a response to her statement. Seeing this, Priscilla knit her shapely brows in displeasure.

"What is with this poor reaction, when I have bothered to walk here with my own two legs? Is it not proper custom to touch your heads to the floor and greet my arrival with deeply moved tears?"

"...Where do you get off acting like a big-shot princess? A scene like that would only happen in a dictatorship."

"Mmm?"

Subaru had unwittingly interrupted Priscilla's self-centered dictum. Overhearing his murmur, Priscilla inclined her head and gazed squarely at Subaru with her red eyes.

"...Who might you be? This is a room for fools ignorant of their station attempting to compete with me for the throne. Why is a vulgar peasant such as you mixed in among them?"

"Is she serious?"

Subaru dejectedly slumped at the genuine, threatening disdain trained toward him.

She gave no sign that this was a joke, nor any hint of sarcasm or ridicule. In other words, it was just what it seemed. Priscilla was completely unaware of Subaru's very existence.

The way they had met ought to have left something of an impression, but she'd already forgotten him entirely.

"Hey, Princess. Even for you, isn't that horrible? Maybe he doesn't stand out to a princess like you, but to me, this bro of mine is plenty interesting, okay?"

Then as if to split asunder the terrible, stagnant pall hanging over the hall, a voice casually called out to Priscilla.

The voice was fairly muffled and was accompanied by a faint metallic clinking. A lumbering noise came in from the corridor as a one-armed man appeared to stand at Priscilla's side.

The man's head was covered in a pitch-black steel helm, with the rest of him clad in crude clothing that had a rustic, bandit chic to it. This was Al, both Priscilla's retainer and a man in the same position as Subaru—he had also been summoned from another world.

Al, who was naturally traveling with his liege, wearily shrugged in Priscilla's direction.

"Come on, you remember, right? This is the guy who seriously shamed himself in front of a massive crowd when Princess and the others declared their beliefs back at the castle. That's this bro right here. You grabbed your belly and laughed a ton, didn't you?"

"I have no memory of such a thing. In the first place, would I ever do something as tactless as grasp my belly and laugh? Do not confuse nobility such as mine with that of these country bumpkins. Next time, I shall remove your head from your shoulders, Al."

"Well, there you have it, Bro. Sorry, I just can't cut it. You're gonna have to work hard and raise your affinity points up from scratch again."

"You had a whole year, so you could've raised your speech ability a little bit more, damn it!"

Al apologized to Subaru as he swiftly gave up on trying to remind his liege of their first meeting. The frivolous way he went "sowwy, sowwy" felt like he hadn't changed one bit in the last year, leaving Subaru with little to do but sigh at the steadfast master and servant.

"Being able to change like you is the privilege of the young, Bro. An old guy like me can't do that, no, sir."

"Man, I was just about to revise the rankings on my *do not turn into adults like these* list—though some exceptions apply."

In contrast to Al's flippant tongue, Subaru ended his reply by glancing Heinkel's way. The man, completely abandoned as everyone's attention went elsewhere, shot Priscilla a servile smile.

"You're late, Lady Priscilla. My liver was freezing, wondering if you'd ever show up..."

"Do not chirp at me, commoner. If I command you to dance, it is your duty as a commoner to dance until I command you to cease or until your demise. Should you misunderstand this and seek to 'correct' me, your death for your conceit shall be neither brief nor painless."

"Ghhh..."

Heinkel's face had momentarily brightened at the prospect of turning things around, but Priscilla's sharp tongue-lashing shut him up. But Subaru raised his eyebrows as the pair's conversation made him harbor suspicions.

"Priscilla, is he with you?"

"...Who granted you permission to address me without title, vulgar peasant? Even though I am as generous as a compassionate mother, it is quite limited in regards to such behavior coming from anyone but a child."

"Princess."

Al called out to Priscilla as she shot a cruel look toward Subaru. The whiff of supplication contained in his voice caused Priscilla to close one eye and let out a sigh.

"I know not why, but my servant has taken a rather odd liking to you. I will refrain from removing even a single layer of skin off your head, so you should thank Al— No, you should revere me. I shall overlook your impertinence this once."

"...I'm grateful for your enormous generosity. Now answer my question."

"Whether this commoner is with me or not, was it? In that case, you assume correctly. It is precisely that. I summoned him and dispatched him to this place."

"—!! What for?!"

"If I must name a reason, then it is because I thought it would be amusing."

Subaru was aghast. Bringing an uninvited guest who proceeded to ruin a grandfather's opportunity to reconcile with his grandson—Priscilla had created this situation for a terrifyingly cruel reason.

As Subaru gazed at Priscilla in dazed silence, she explained further.

"Yes. Such awkward and pitiful attempts to smooth over warped family bonds… There is no way I could calmly allow such an unsightly performance to continue. Accordingly, I have altered the script more to my liking. Quite a spectacle, was it not?"

"Priscillaaa!"

Her actions had been beyond vicious, and the way she casually talked about it sent Subaru flying into a rage.

Spectacle. That was what this woman had called it. Inflicting deep wounds upon the hearts of Reinhard and Wilhelm, a few short steps away from going back to being family… She'd called that a spectacle.

"Quit it, Bro. There's nothing gained from us going toe to toe here. Princess's personality being twisted isn't new. Just think of it as bad luck…the stars being out of alignment."

"If you get that, rein her in, damn it. *Stars*, my ass. You've gotta be kidding me."

As Subaru's blood ran hot, Al halted him with a push of his right hand. Having only one arm, he couldn't draw his sword like that—he was making it clear that he had no intention of fighting.

Subaru clenched his teeth tight. He realized he was the only one in the room who'd forgotten himself in a fit of anger. Obviously, this went for the royal candidates, but there was no sign of Julius or Ferris being agitated by events, either.

Of course not. This was a graceful assembly of the rising stars aiming to be the next generation to carry the burden of the throne—not a single person among them wanted allies who might give in to their emotions and hurt others in a fit of rage.

"But isn't that saying you can hurt people emotionally all you want and it's okay…?!"

"Subaru…"

When Subaru put his nigh-unendurable anger into words, Emilia called out to him with shaking, forlorn eyes. When he noticed the sensation of his sleeve being pulled, Beatrice was there, too, holding Subaru's hand.

Accepting the pair's sympathy, Subaru sighed deeply with a bitter face.

"It would seem that the mongrel has ceased its baying. Today, I have come merely to make an appearance. Now that I have seen your tearful faces, I do not have any particular reason to remain."

"Well, isn't that fine and dandy…? You're the only one I didn't tell about what I was doing here. Where did you hear of it?"

Anastasia cut into Priscilla's crowing over having raised such a great ruckus. Wariness resided in Anastasia's pale blue-green eyes as a wry smile spread across her lips.

"And here I was sure that I hadn't slipped up and told any child with loose lips…"

"Drop the pretenses, you sly fox. When something enters the ears of men, it is inevitable that it shall trickle forth like drops of tears. As the numbers increase, so do the openings. You are not the only one who keeps a close eye on the movements of others."

"Heh, now that surprises me. I didn't expect that out of Priscilla of all people."

The sarcasm mixed with admiration made Priscilla spread out her fan as she broke into derisive laughter.

"Were I a fool who sees only what is on the surface, I would be no different from you commoners. As people competing with me for succession rights, surely you are not attempting to disappoint me with a poor performance, yes?"

"…You truly are a hard one to put a finger on."

Exasperation was apparent in Anastasia's voice as she sighed at Priscilla's remark.

Subaru completely agreed with Anastasia on that point. He'd misjudged Priscilla as someone who didn't see the other candidates as actual rivals and assumed she strictly followed her own path.

But judging from her actions on this day, Priscilla had acquired accurate intelligence, prepared countermeasures, and set her plan in motion without any disdain for detail—and so she had brought this most horrible of developments about.

"This old man, he's Reinhard's dad, right?"

Then after having ignored the course of the conversation to that point, one voice wedged itself in with complete disregard for the current situation.

It was Felt who had raised her voice while stabbing a fork into the *daisukiyaki* on her plate. While she merrily stuffed her cheeks, her mouth was marred with sauce as she glared at Priscilla.

"You were acting all chummy back at the castle before, so between that and the talk just now, I get it. It's not like I know all about this guy's family situation…but the old man's relationship with you, now that's different."

"…Oh? And what opinion would a mere girl from the slums deign to hold about me?"

"Ain't like this has nothin' to do with me. The Astrea family is Reinhard's to inherit, right? That's my so-called lifeline, and this old man has it in the palm of his hand."

As Felt elaborated, Reinhard stiffened his cheeks as he sat beside her. One glance at his reaction was enough to convey to Subaru and the others the enormity of this matter.

Felt was an orphan with no other backing. She had no other substantial support save that of Reinhard's family. Over the last year, her activities had been centered upon the Astrea domain, allowing her to raise her name as a royal candidate bit by bit. But what would happen if that sure footing collapsed?

What if the control of the Astrea family and the real clout within it was actually held by Heinkel?

"Heh, so your puny head finally caught up? That's slow even for you bunch of half-wits."

Heinkel sneered as Felt finally grasped what he was thinking.

"That's just how it is. The Astrea family inheritance is in my care. I don't have any intention of handing it to Reinhard, and I never did! Not to Mr. High-and-Mighty Sword Saint who's oh so busy for the nation! I wouldn't dream of entrusting it to someone with such a troublesome and annoying job!"

"Big talk for a lord in name only. You bastard, do you even know what kind of state you left your lands in? You and the folks around you were all doing whatever you damn well pleased."

When Felt growled as low as she could, Heinkel mocked her, saying, "Ooh, scary." His provocative words and gestures only added to the disgust and disdain already suffusing the room.

Having endured far too many malignant slights, Reinhard finally lifted up his head. He was still striving to maintain a neutral expression as he looked not at his father but toward Felt.

"Lady Felt, I…"

"Reinhard."

Reinhard was about to say something, but then he stopped. The cause was Felt thrusting her fork toward the tip of his nose. Reinhard's eyes wavered as his liege's action sealed his lips. Then without even a glance Reinhard's way, Felt—

"—Shut up and put on your war face."

Reinhard opened his eyes wide as Felt casually issued a command. But it was the change in him immediately after that shocked everyone else.

"—Yes."

Reinhard nodded solemnly as light returned to his blue eyes. Though his own father had derided him and wrecked his moment of reconciliation with his grandfather, the pain that had clung to him was gone, at least for that single brief moment.

"…If it's not one thing, it's another. Stop messin' around."

Heinkel clicked his tongue as things once again started going awry. However, after shaking his head, a wicked smile immediately returned to his face.

"Say what you want; your sense of danger is spot-on, oh great master of Reinhard. The Astrea family is mine. And I don't support you."

To ensnare others and hurt them with cruel speech—with no objectives save these, Heinkel swung his words like a blade.

"No one needs me to spell out just who I support, I'm sure. You've worked so hard over the last year. The results are marvelous. And now I'm going to take everything you've built up and hand it to Lady Priscilla as a present..."

"Commoner."

"Aah? Yes, Lady Priscilla? I'm in the middle of an important conversation here."

"Silence."

The tyrannical act that immediately followed made everyone gasp.

With no more warning than that one word, Priscilla flashed her fan out toward the wide-eyed Heinkel's skull. The folded fan sliced through the air, inverting his body with incredible force and slamming him onto the floor. The impact made Heinkel's eyes roll, rendering him unconscious in a single blow.

But Priscilla's chastisement did not end there. She kicked up the fallen Heinkel with the tip of her shoe, then drew back her hand while he was airborne. And then she began to swing—

"Princess, your tantrum's gone far enough. He'll die."

Priscilla glared at Al with her red eyes as he grasped her wrist and called for her to stop. But Al's action was the right one. Heinkel would have died if he hadn't stepped in.

After all, at some point, a beautiful crimson sword had found its way into Priscilla's hand.

The gleaming blade featured an undulating pattern to it. One could tell from a single glance that it was no normal weapon. It had appeared in Priscilla's hand in the blink of an eye and vanished just as quickly.

Seeing this, Al slowly released Priscilla's hand.

"Sheesh, gimme a break here. You even drew the Sun Blade. It's bad for my heart... *Bnnnfh!!*"

"You are most rude, Al. Whose permission did you obtain to touch my jewellike flesh? It is your business how you deal with your dearth of womanly attention and seething desire, but do not even dream of sullying me in the process."

Slamming her freed hand into Al's gut, Priscilla made her retainer groan in anguish. She let out a snort, gazing down upon Heinkel with cold eyes as he lay there pathetically on the floor.

The uncaring cruelty in those crimson eyes was frightening indeed.

"Though it is not my wont to grant mercy to those committing gross acts of impropriety…Al's words do have some merit."

"If you think that, I'd kinda prefer if you treated me a little more gently."

"Do not say that. I am not a demon. Later, I shall grant you the reward of being permitted to lick my foot."

"Can you stop talking like that'd actually make me happy?! You'll cause all kinds of misunderstandings!"

Priscilla paid no attention to Al as he pleaded on bended knee. Instead, she clapped her hands together.

"Schult, carry that commoner out of here. It would be a waste to discard him just yet. Attend to his wounds."

"Right away, Lady Priscilla!"

Appearing the moment she issued the summons was a pink-haired boy who'd apparently been waiting in the corridor. Subaru had seen this person at Priscilla's mansion once previously; he was a boy with adorably curly, fluffy-looking hair.

The young, still growing butler raced over to Heinkel with tiny steps.

"Pardon my rudeness, Lord Heinkel."

With those polite words, he grabbed hold of both of Heinkel's legs and dragged him into the corridor. The method of transportation caused Heinkel some bumps here and there, but Schult faithfully performed his job without a single word of complaint.

Seeing the youth's professionalism on display, Al prodded the eye slits of his helm as he made a passing comment.

"Our lovely boy Schult is always so lively, isn't he? You really need to praise him more, Princess."

"It is only natural that I should be served with all of one's spirit. That is what I love about Schult. I shall properly reward him. Schult, too, shall be allowed to lick my foot."

"That image is waaaay too indecent. Give him a different reward, I'm begging you."

"Hmm. Then the honor of sleeping while snuggled up and embracing me, perhaps?"

"...Well, that much is fine, I suppose. I almost wanna trade places with him now."

At the conclusion of that carefree exchange between master and servant, Priscilla returned her gaze to the hall once more. Among the people in the room, she turned her eyes toward Felt and the grave face she wore.

Come to think of it, those two had glared at each other like this back at the castle, too. Perhaps their compatibility was horrible by nature.

"So was the old man serious just now? He's gonna drive me out and take back his place as lord?"

"If it was so, what would you do about it? Cry into your pillow and politely back down?"

"Ha! Don't make me laugh. No matter what anyone says, that's the last thing anyone'll catch me doing. If there's no inheritance and I get driven out of the Astrea domain, it makes things reaaal simple, doesn't it?"

As she spoke, Felt's face contorted into a ferocious smile as she gestured at Reinhard.

"He'll just make that old fart hand over the inheritance. He's pretty laid-back, but he's a hell of a lot more reliable than that jerk. That bastard'll be retiring in no time."

"——"

Regardless of whether it was realistic or not, it was a remarkably satisfying declaration.

Felt's proclamation made Priscilla narrow her eyes. Then Priscilla covered her lips with her fan once more.

"There is no need to take that commoner's words at face value.

Even if rights to the domain were changed on paper, the trust of the populace would remain yours. The masses may be made up of ignorant fools, but their very foolishness means they are slow to forget a grudge. As the only value of the talentless rabble is to callously employ them as pawns, this renders them unusable."

"...Then why'd you bring that old man with you?"

"I have already told you. I brought him for nothing more than my own amusement. In that sense, he has already proved his worth."

With absolute faith in her own standards, Priscilla spoke without hesitation as she surveyed the room.

She was set in her ways. Surrender and serve or confront her with an iron will; there were no other options.

"——"

And the four candidates who stood in opposition to her did not hesitate to assert their own will.

Receiving their gazes, Priscilla nodded with profound satisfaction.

"Very good. My victory is inevitable. Therefore, I desire that the path be as turbulent and entertaining as possible. Fan my flames, you who oppose me—those are the supporting roles you are all meant to play."

That was Priscilla's bold pronouncement to her four rivals one year after the royal selection had begun.

This was her judgment of the changes that had taken place over that year. This was the conclusion drawn by the crimson eyes of Priscilla Bariel, who had unshakable faith in the belief that the entire world moved for her own convenience.

"I'll make you regret that pride."

Felt's abrupt declaration of war reflected the views of everyone present.

7

—Even when things settled down, it was impossible to restore the hall's atmosphere to what it had been before.

After Felt addressed her, Priscilla exited the reception hall with Al in tow and a satisfied look on her face. Coming from Priscilla, that amounted to delight at having achieved her goal.

Considering the damage she had inflicted upon Subaru and the others, her actions were selfish to the extreme.

In the end, the respective camps that had gathered for a meal rose up, dispersing without a single attempt to resume their pleasant chat—and without Reinhard and Wilhelm reaching a peaceful reconciliation.

"We are truly fortunate that Garfiel was not there."

Those were Otto's parting words as he left for the Muse Company on his own.

He certainly had a point. If Garfiel and other hotheads had been present, carnage might well have been unavoidable. Thanks to that, Heinkel had escaped with his life.

Of course, had he lost his life in the ensuing clash, the reputation of his killer and their master would have fallen to the level of dirt.

"Don't tell me she made a mess of the place aiming for that… I'm overthinking this, right?"

The frightening mental image of Priscilla's blazing eyes seeing through every possibility arose in his mind. He felt that if he denied it, passing everything off as nothing but coincidence, it was tantamount to accepting that her success was thanks to her good fortune.

"Cool it, you clown… In the end, I'm the only one who blew his lid."

Looking back at the events that had unfolded in the hall, Subaru truly thought his lack of self-control was pathetic.

Even Felt had acted in a logical manner; Subaru had been the most emotional person in the room. He must have been a source of great anxiety for Emilia and Beatrice, too.

In an attempt to dispel his agitation, Subaru was walking around the inn, striving for mental calm before going on the scheduled stroll with Emilia and company.

The creaks of the wooden floor seemed to reflect the creaks he felt in his own heart. Finding them exceptionally irritating, Subaru marched with heavy steps as if it would help him understand.

"Do not take your frustrations out on the floor. It will cause problems for the inn workers."

Subaru had been staring intently at the floor when a voice called out to him. Looking around, he spotted Julius watching him from the garden. Subaru had arrived at the edge of the garden at some point without even realizing it.

The man looked oddly picturesque as he touched a hand to his slightly unruly purple hair, which was being caressed by a refreshing breeze.

"You are not together with Lady Emilia and Lady Beatrice?"

"Well, you can see that. Neither of them is a child, and they're both at an age where they want some private time. Even I have enough delicacy to respect that. Besides, we're going on a date later."

"There are several terms I have not heard before, but I believe I understand. It would seem even you can learn how to be considerate."

"Ghhh, why you…!"

Though Subaru had been quick to pick a fight, it was Julius who had landed the first substantial blow, causing Subaru to lose his cool. But his irritation instantly dissipated when he saw Julius's expression.

Julius's eyelashes were quivering, somehow seeming like he was biting back remorse.

"I am sorry. If you really did lack empathy and thoughtfulness, you wouldn't have been so distressed talking to the vice captain earlier—if anything, I should be thanking you."

"All I did was lose my temper like an idiot while everyone else thought things through and kept their cool."

"That is not so. It was only because of your display of anger that those around you were able to maintain their calm, nothing more. I am no exception. Your rashness served a valuable purpose."

"You're not really trying to praise me, though, are you?"

Subaru grimaced at the words lavished upon him.

"I get it. I need to be calmer and remember to keep my cool. That's how a knight should act, isn't it? I'm aware that I don't think far ahead enough. After all, I had it marked on every report card I got in elementary school."

"...Certainly, if it is chivalrous conduct one seeks, your actions cannot be praised. However."

Julius abruptly broke off his words. When Subaru realized what he was doing, his eyes shot open in surprise.

"Uh, what are you doing?"

"Precisely what it looks like."

"Well, from my end, it looks like you're bowing to me."

Julius had gone down on one knee, solemnly lowering his head.

This was not a knightly salute, nor a custom among nobles. He was simply acting as an individual person.

"You have my gratitude. I wanted to thank you for your righteous indignation in that setting."

"...I don't know what you mean."

"If one is devoted to chivalry, one must strive to behave in a knightly fashion regardless of the circumstance... One can never act out of emotion, even if his friend is being disparaged or humiliated. But you were not bound by such things."

His head still bowed, Julius added more words of thanks for Subaru's recklessness.

The unexpected response made Subaru blink several times over. However, finally—

"So you're basically thanking me for getting angry in your place—man, are you stupid or what?"

When the still-irritated Subaru vented, his words caused Julius to lift his head. Receiving the brunt of Subaru's anger, he let his lips curl into a self-deprecating smile.

"Stupid, you say."

"Stupid and a bad joke. Why do I have to be angry instead of you? I'm pissed at myself for the fact that I got angry. It's not like I tried to smack that bearded face for anyone else but myself."

Subaru was genuinely exasperated with Julius, thinking he had gotten it all wrong.

His temper tantrum was nothing as noble as the righteous indignation Julius made it out to be. Subaru knew practically nothing of the issues surrounding the Astrea family. That's why he'd selfishly gotten upset over his own selfish assumptions, nothing more.

"If you didn't like it, you should've gotten angry, too. Because it was just me, he blew me off, but if you had joined in, that dad of Reinhard's would've run with his tail between his legs."

"Figurehead or not, he is the vice captain of the Knights of the Royal Guard. It would be reprehensible to act with such rudeness toward a direct superior."

"You're not directly under him at the moment, and just now, you called him a figurehead, didn't you? How inflexible can you be, man? The whole time you were dedicating yourself to chivalry, were you also putting armor around your heart, too?"

Pressing Julius into silence, Subaru folded his arms and lifted his face toward the heavens with a snort.

It was an infantile argument. Even though he was being thanked, Subaru was lashing out at Julius simply because he didn't care for it.

"Armor over the heart, you say…? Hmph, that remark cuts quite deep."

"For me, it sounds like a pretty cool thing to say, but don't think too hard on it. Just the words of a fool."

"No, I shall take them to heart. It was pleasant to think I had been saved by you, a thought I would never have even imagined a year prior."

"Just so you know, I still have nightmares about that once in a while."

"Hmm… Were it possible, I would like to avoid a situation where we reunite in your dreams on a nightly basis."

"I'd also far prefer to do this and that with Emilia-tan instead! There's no room for you in my dreams!"

With the appreciative atmosphere from before gone, Julius returned to his normal tone of voice as he ran a hand through his hair. Disgusted with himself for being relieved by the change in attitude, Subaru forcibly switched topics.

"About Beard-face back there… Seriously, the vice captain is Reinhard's dad?"

"I suppose it isn't surprising that you would have doubts, but it is true. That individual is indeed Heinkel Astrea, vice captain of the Knights of the Royal Guard of Lugunica."

"What's the reason for that? Is human resources blind, or did no one even question whether he'd be a problem?"

"The answers are all in what you overheard. Of course, there is no lack of dissenters who doubt the vice captain's worth, both from the leadership and from within the royal guard itself. As a matter of fact, the position of vice captain was assigned for decorative purposes. Surely, there are none who have witnessed him actually engaged in his duties."

When Julius shook his head and replied, Subaru conjured the mental image of some high-ranking bureaucrat stepping down to take a cushy job in private industry. That seemed a fitting description for Heinkel's situation—an important, high-paying job that required little actual work.

"Don't tell me he used his influence as the dad of the Sword Saint to land that position?"

"…That is also part of it. But the greatest reason lies not with the vice captain but with Reinhard…or perhaps it is more accurate to say the Astrea family."

"The Astrea family… Does that include Wilhelm too?"

"Well, that man is Master Wilhelm's son and the current head of the Astrea family. He is also Reinhard's own father. What would happen to the kingdom if such an individual rebelled due to discourteous treatment?"

As he rattled off another explanation, Julius strove to keep his replies as emotionless as possible.

Listening to his words, Subaru sank into thought for several seconds. Then he immediately arrived at the answer.

The reason that man, Heinkel Astrea, was treated so favorably by the kingdom was—

"—If Heinkel revolts, that'd mean the family of the Sword Saint becoming an enemy of the kingdom. So he's being treated like a big shot to maintain good relations…? In other words, the kingdom doesn't trust Reinhard, or Wilhelm for that matter?!"

If that was the case, Subaru could only think of such treatment as a grave insult toward Reinhard and Wilhelm both. Considering the pair's personalities, how could anyone think they might betray the kingdom?

"Your anger is justified. However, those in charge of the kingdom must consider all possibilities."

"As if that's even possible!! There's no way something like that could even…!"

"…Master Wilhelm is the former captain of the Knights of the Royal Guard."

When Julius took a step forward and spoke those words, Subaru's breath caught, his body coming to a halt.

"Fifteen years ago, someone abducted a member of the royal family from the Royal Palace. At the time, Master Wilhelm was in charge of the search for the abducted royal as captain of the Knights of the Royal Guard."

"So? Even I've heard about that kidnapping."

A kidnapped royal—would that mean Felt? That incident was supposedly the whole justification behind her taking part in the royal selection. Why was Julius digging up that surreal story?

"I also know that the abducted kid was never found. But what of it? Does that mean Wilhelm has some sort of grudge against the kingdom because he had to take responsibility and quit the knighthood?"

"That is not so—however, the 'Grand Expedition,' the effort to bring down the White Whale that included the prior Sword Saint, took place during the time Master Wilhelm was absent from the capital to conduct the search."

The words Julius spoke made Subaru's mind go blank once more. Sliding into that blank space were words he recalled hearing from Wilhelm at some time or other.

Wilhelm had said he had been unable to be with his wife at the time of her death.

"Because of the incident, he couldn't be there when his wife died, so he holds a grudge against the person responsible?"

"I do not know Master Wilhelm's true intentions. However, the facts remain that the search was aborted, the Grand Expedition itself ended in failure, and Master Wilhelm resigned from the Knights of the Royal Guard. The guard surely would not have recovered if it were not for Captain Marcus exhausting every effort to do so."

"Like I care about what happened after! I'm talking about Wilhelm here. What do you think? Does he still hold a grudge about his wife, and…?"

Did Julius suspect that Wilhelm might rebel against the kingdom?

Did he think that this person, Wilhelm van Astrea, was that kind of human being?

How could someone look at him and think that about a man so forthright about his love that he'd offered up everything for it? Couldn't you tell from looking at his eyes, his back?

And why were the people Subaru liked exposed to such undeserved prejudice?

"Why can't everyone understand he's not that kind of person…?"

Demanding to know why in a choked voice, Subaru glared at Julius. Accepting his withering gaze head-on, Julius's eyes somehow seemed envious as he looked back at Subaru.

Subaru knew. He was well aware his anger was misplaced and aimed at the wrong target.

In the end, Julius had just objectively recited the tale. In no way did Julius himself doubt Wilhelm, nor was he one of the people who doubted Wilhelm.

After all, Julius had thanked Wilhelm after the battle with the White Whale one year prior.

He'd praised Wilhelm for pursuing his greatest wish for fourteen long years.

"…Sorry. I'm an idiot."

"No, you are not in the wrong. What you say is correct. It is I who is in the wrong—and so I shall remain, without a chance to rectify my mistake."

Lowering their gazes, both of them closed their eyes as they wrestled with such unbearable thoughts.

The seeds of distrust about Wilhelm's true intentions still remained. They weren't the sort of thing that could be immediately solved with words and actions.

"...Does this go for Reinhard, too?"

"The situation is different in his case—at one time, Reinhard did whatever Master Heinkel told him to. It was not a period that could be dismissed simply by saying, *well, they were father and son.*"

Averting his gaze from Subaru, Julius seemed regretful as he spoke.

But without touching upon any of the details, Julius took a deep breath and continued his explanation.

"When Reinhard became independent, such behavior came to an end. However, enough happened that a concern remains within the kingdom. Namely, could such a thing not come to pass once more?"

"...So to make sure Heinkel doesn't give Reinhard insane orders, the kingdom's trying its damnedest to keep Heinkel in a good mood?"

"Perhaps it is something far worse. In the end, this is nothing more than rumor, but I shall convey it to you nonetheless—to you, who expressed indignation in that situation as Reinhard's friend."

With that worrying preamble, Julius quickly scanned their surroundings. Having confirmed no one might overhear, he turned back toward Subaru. And then—

"The vice captain is suspected of involvement with the royal-abduction incident fifteen years ago."

"—?!"

"There is no conclusive proof. But the fact remains that I have heard suspicions surrounding a number of circumstances."

"Is that even possible? I mean, for him to be involved in the kidnapping."

"Whether it is true or false matters little. An individual who is suspected of such things could potentially command the kingdom's greatest warrior any way he wishes. This is seen as problematic."

Possessing the title of Sword Saint was a spectacular honor—however, the revelation of this situation made Subaru feel as if it was not so much an honor as a curse.

"I mean, if that's true, then it'd be Heinkel's fault Wilhelm wasn't able to be there when his wife died."

"...That is not the half of it. I have heard that at the time, it was Lord Heinkel who recommended that Lady Theresia, who had already laid down her sword and retired from active duty, participate in the Grand Expedition."

"He threw his own mom onto the front lines against that demon beast?!"

"We have records remaining from that time. The vice captain refused to join the Grand Expedition, nominating Lady Theresia to join the battle in his stead."

As Subaru learned more about this incident, he couldn't help but be stunned.

Heinkel had sent his own mother to take his place on the field of battle. There, his mother had been killed in action. To protect himself against his father, who was unable to be with her upon her death, from wielding his blades in vengeance, Heinkel used his son's talent as a shield, spending his own peaceful days in depraved indolence.

It couldn't be. A human being actually capable of such a thing couldn't really exist.

It wasn't because Subaru wanted to affirm Heinkel's humanity. He couldn't accept the theoretical possibility that a human who was able to live so shamelessly could even exist.

"...I am sorry. I should not have spoken of such things when you were not emotionally prepared for them."

Julius apologized in a morose voice when he noticed how Subaru was shocked and speechless.

Subaru had only been listening, and he could barely control himself. There was no way that Julius could possibly keep his composure when he had to be the one conveying it all. For someone like Julius, who constantly strove to be rational and logical, this behavior was particularly strange.

"...It's not like this is your fault. I'm the one who made you say it."

"It is not an attitude worthy of praise. To look at someone else's family and speak with a mixture of rumor and prejudice is extremely insensitive; they are actions that a knight should be ashamed of."

"But you made sure to see it through, right? Because you're Reinhard's friend."

When Julius berated himself, Subaru shook his head side to side.

"I don't know how long you've been his friend, but I get that you're worried about him. That's why it's natural to be ticked off. I don't think there's one thing strange about that. I don't think it's right to politely back off just 'cause it's another family's private business, either."

For anyone who knew Julius, suspecting him of being an inconsiderate busybody was the height of foolishness.

Subaru Natsuki knew what exactly kind of person Julius Juukulius was. What was there to gain from suspecting friendship?

"I've told you before, right? There's no need to obsess with being a well-mannered knight all the time. Right, maybe you should strip off that armor and try being Juli for a while. Maybe being more flexible like that would help you do a whole bunch of things better."

Juli was the false name Julius had employed when cooperating with hunting down the Witch Cult. Given his position, Julius couldn't be seen joining a band of mercenaries, so he had offered the false name in a desperate attempt to hide his elegance behind his back. In the end, it was a name so useless that even Julius himself forgot to use it, but at the time, Julius had allowed himself to diverge the strict rules of knighthood.

"Juli, you say? That is quite a nostalgic name you have pulled out."

"It's the sort of one-and-done plot twist you forget in an instant. I'm proud of myself just for remembering it."

"...But when you say not to be bound by chivalry, you suggest a very difficult thing. It is not as if you are unaware of what they call me."

"That whole 'finest knight' thing is why you're always so stiff, right? When you get in the bath and take all that armor off, make sure you do some extra stretching before you put it back on again."

On the spot, Subaru proudly bent his hips and touched his palms to the ground. He meant to show off how limber he had become over the past year.

"If you intended to best me with that little display, I can only sigh at your incredibly lacking powers of observation."

"Whoaaa?!"

After a quick remark, Julius opened his legs wide, one in front and one in back as he assumed an extreme pose in front of the triumphant Subaru. Subaru gaped at how far Julius's long legs could stretch. Without moving anything else, he brought his hips to the ground with ease.

The detestable man easily surpassed Subaru in every possible area.

"W-well, I'm still really good at singing and playing the lyulyre!"

"I truly cannot see the significance of winning such a contest, but I am somewhat familiar with musical performance."

"Gah! There it is! Even I know that when a guy like you acts humble, it means he's super good at it! Ain't no way I'm joining a band with you! You'll steal the vocalist spot from me in no time!"

"—I see."

As Subaru continued airing out his grievances, Julius returned his stretching legs to their proper positions and stood up. When Julius let out a short sigh, Subaru knit his brow; faced with that stare, Julius swept his own hair back, a triumphant smile coming over him as he gazed up at the sky.

"So when Juli looks up at the sky, standing in the bracing wind, this is what it feels like."

"Wha—?"

"Now that I think about it, the sky always looked different back then. I feel like I am only just recalling that."

"I don't get you. You really are one smug bastard."

Intentionally ignoring the atmosphere that had been building, Subaru sat down on the raised floor running along the garden's edge. Only flashing a troubled smile in reply to Subaru's insult, Julius half closed his eyes, seemingly dazzled by the rays of the sun.

A new mood had swept away the dregs of their awkward conversation.

Of course, that didn't wipe away Subaru's memory of what they'd discussed, and the stiffness remaining in his heart would not relent. Even so, he could be cooperative enough to not let it drag them both down.

—If anyone had been watching from a distance, they would have seen nothing but a normal pair of friends.

CHAPTER 5
THEATRICAL MALICE

1

When Subaru's conversation with Julius, part momentous and part silly, had run its course, Subaru departed from the Water Raiment with Emilia and Beatrice in tow.

"Hey, Subaru. You seemed to be getting along *really* nicely with Julius in the garden. What did you talk about?"

"I wouldn't say we *really* got along or anything, but what do you think we talked about?"

"Where to go to play next time or something?"

"What are we, school buddies?!"

Unfortunately, their relationship was not nearly as friendly as Emilia imagined, and even if Subaru and Julius did attend the same school, the natural energies inside a school would keep them from ever being friends.

In one sense, a school was as much an exclusivist, discriminatory society as any system of nobility.

"Thinking of it that way, bridging social classes is a really tough thing to do in either case."

"There's no need to keep it that secret. You can just come out and tell me."

"Hey, we really were just scouting out the enemy a bit. The rest was just some chitchat about the world around us."

"Isn't that something friends do?"

When Emilia curiously tilted her head, Subaru tilted his, too. "Who knows?" he said.

Viewed objectively, it did seem to resemble friendship, but there was no way Subaru and Julius shared that. They were something worse than friends, but Subaru couldn't put his finger on what exactly.

"Well, we're not friends. That much I'm sure of."

"So stubborn..."

"He really is, I suppose."

Emilia looked exasperated while Beatrice simply sighed and agreed with her. For some reason, the two were so in sync that it made Subaru feel like he was being left out somehow.

In any case, setting aside whether he was friends with Julius or not, he had no intention of telling Emilia about the details of what they'd discussed—namely, the problems of the Astrea family. He didn't want to thoughtlessly divulge someone else's private family circumstances, but the biggest reason was the burden that knowing such information would inevitably create.

The deep-rooted problems of the Astrea family were not the sort that outsiders could approach half-heartedly.

Julius had been keenly aware of this when he revealed the details to Subaru alone. Julius had judged him as someone with enough consideration not to burden his own liege with such knowledge.

The fact that Julius had thought that much of him had left a strange feeling in the pit of his stomach, though.

"So, Subaru. I'm happy you invited me on a stroll, but what are you up to?"

Then as Subaru wrestled with an unsettling feeling that he struggled to identify, Emilia smiled and asked him.

For a moment, Subaru raised an eyebrow in surprise, but he immediately shrugged to try and gloss that over.

"Hey, that makes it sound like I'm plotting something. I'm not up to anything. I just wanted to have a lovey-dovey time in this crazy-beautiful city of water."

"Hmm, so that's what you're going with? Subaru, honestly, you're so stubborn and hardheaded. Even I won't fall for your sweet talk in a situation like this."

When Emilia pouted, Subaru put a hand to his forehead with a resigned look on his face. When he glanced at Beatrice for aid, who was in between Subaru and Emilia and holding one hand of each, she pretended not to notice—it seemed she had no intention of taking his side.

Meanwhile, Emilia's gaze was relentless. Subaru promptly crumbled.

"I get it; I'm raising the white flag. I wanted it to be a surprise for you, Emilia-tan."

"A surprise… You mean, you were planning to startle me with something kooky?"

"No one says *kooky* anymo… Hey, I'm sorry, sorry!"

When Emilia puffed her cheeks up in anger at Subaru reacting like he always did, this time, he surrendered for good. Afraid of what might follow otherwise, Subaru suppressed his feelings of disappointment and put everything on the table.

"It's really not anything I'd call a scheme, though. Right now, we're heading for a park in the middle of the city, the one where Liliana performed yesterday."

"Wow, really? Then maybe Liliana will sing there today, too?"

"Your eyes are so cute when they sparkle like that. Well, I'm interested in Liliana's songs, too, but I also want to do some scouting and give Otto some fire support."

Subaru had no idea just how much trouble he'd caused for Otto, off on his own for solo negotiations with Kiritaka, who Subaru had angered with his botched plan from the day before.

It was absolutely not that he lacked faith in Otto's negotiating skills.

"Of course, I have just as much faith that he never gets lucky except at the very last moment."

"That does not mean you need to do something as ominous as rely on Liliana again… Well, things with Puckie are riding on this, so I understand why you want to take your chances, I suppose."

Even Beatrice, torn between the previous day's failure and her partiality for Liliana, did not object to something that would ostensibly help Puck. However, that opinion brought a stern look over Emilia's face.

"But it sounds like you're using Liliana, and that's just…"

"I know. I thought Emilia-tan would feel that way, too. I really don't like saying this, but…"

"Yes?"

"I guess I should say it anyway… Emilia, now and in the future during this royal selection, we can't afford to not be calculating or to ignore the pros and cons of choices and people. Of course, I want you to be able to stay true to yourself."

"——"

As Emilia worried about various implications, Subaru tried to dispel her concerns.

There was no mistaking that Emilia's honesty, sincerity, and the way she always believed in the good of others were some of her strongest virtues. However, Subaru felt that a virtue founded on ignorance was a weakness all the same.

If that virtue was truly a part of who she was as a person, then eliminating ignorance would pose no danger to her way of being—Subaru wanted Emilia to learn and become stronger without losing sight of herself.

That had been Subaru's wish when he vowed to remain at her side ever after.

"Well, even ignoring all the benefits and stuff, you did make a promise to chat with Liliana. You get along really well with her, Emilia-tan, so it's not like you're doing anything bad."

As Emilia continued to mull over it, Subaru relaxed his tone a little and tried to introduce some levity. Emilia lowered her eyes, which were rimmed with long lashes, and sighed slightly.

"Mm, I understand. I'll try to keep what you said in mind, too. Thank you for always being here, Subaru."

Emilia nodded with an earnest look on her face. "You got it," replied Subaru.

He'd conveyed everything he wanted. The determination he saw in her and her response was enough. At the same time, he felt a small pang of regret over sticking his nose into something that clearly wasn't his business.

"Ahhh, maybe I said something pretty weird. Know what? Let's forget meeting up with Liliana and go on a date instead. I think doing some water-dragon cruising would be pretty romantic."

"I'm not sure what you mean by *cruising*, but you'll get seasick if you get on a dragon boat, won't you, Subaru? I don't really want to walk around the city carrying you on my back."

"Besides, the park is already right in front of our noses. Would it not be a waste to turn back now, I wonder?"

Though Subaru was on the verge of giving up, Emilia and Beatrice opted to stick it out to the end. The public park had indeed come into view; this time, Subaru had fortunately arrived at his destination without getting lost.

Water gushed up from the fountain, turning into a spray of water that glimmered in the sunlight as an ephemeral scene unfolded before them.

This day, a great throng had assembled near that water fountain rather than the commemorative statue.

"Feels like these recitals hold their popularity day after day, but..."

The fervent audience's energy suffused the air in the park, but it was strikingly different compared to what it had felt like the day before. The main cause was probably the hands clapping in time with the music and singing.

"Wow, it looks *really* lively."

"So it would seem. Unlike yesterday, this all sounds rather rowdy, I suppose."

While Emilia was delighted, Beatrice cocked her head dubiously, sharing some of Subaru's doubts.

Liliana's song choices for her performances often contrasted greatly with how she normally behaved. The metia broadcast from that morning was no exception. With song and sound, she lured the audience into another world, giving a bewitching performance that charmed all five senses.

However, the song they were currently listening to seemed ever so slightly different from usual.

It had the unsettling feeling of some foreign entity adding an impurity to the mix.

"______"

As if trying to determine what that dissonant element was, Subaru had unconsciously joined one edge of the audience.

Male or female, young or old, there was a vortex of passion surrounding everyone enchanted by the Songstress's song. Wedging themselves into their ranks, Subaru led Emilia and Beatrice by their hands as he plunged deeper and deeper.

Then the instant he emerged onto the front row, his face contorted amid thunderous applause.

The beautiful timbre of the lyulyre's final twang signaled that the song had reached its end and that it was time to bid the intoxicating music farewell.

Then the Songstress who had just put on a stunning performance turned around to reveal a smiling, satisfied face.

"Such wonderful dancing! Seeing footwork like that almost made my eyeballs fly out!"

"And your performance was quite entertaining. You have done well. It has been some time since a performer of the arts has amused me so."

A woman in red smiled charmingly as she exchanged a firm handshake with Liliana the Songstress.

Watching this unfold, Subaru let out a long breath as one phrase rose in the back of his mind.

—Danger: do not mix.

2

"I was so moved." "What an amazing dance." "I wanna see that again!"

Commenting as if they were being filmed for a TV commercial, the audience members waved to the Songstress-dancer duo and dispersed. They were every bit as touched as the crowd from the day before.

Hearing their praise made Liliana flare her nostrils in a satisfied and very un-Songstress-like manner. Unexpectedly, Priscilla's lips were curled up, showing she was in an exceptionally good mood as she fanned herself beside Liliana.

"And here I was thinking Priscilla wasn't the type to care what others thought…"

"My, oh my, oh my?! Is that Master Subaru and Lady Emilia over there, and Lady Moppet as well?!"

Right as she said her good-byes to the last of the audience, Liliana noticed the remaining three people left in the park and made her pigtails bounce. How she managed that was totally beyond him.

As Liliana raced over, practically flying through the air, her words made Beatrice narrow her brows.

"I believe I heard *Lady Moppet*. Exactly what might she mean by this, I wonder? Subaru, explain."

"Go ask her; she's the one who said it. Here, have a sugar plum and behave."

"Do you think you can…*lick, lick*…distract me with this, I wonder? *Lick, lick*…"

As Beatrice rolled the candy around in her mouth, Subaru left her behind. He turned toward the pigtailed Liliana darting about in front of him and grabbed her hair with both hands. "Gah!" shouted Liliana. But it did stop her from moving.

"Yesterday got all crazy, meaning we couldn't keep our promise, so it's good you were here today, too. Actually, don't tell me… Does Kiritaka show you out the door during work every day?"

"Why would you put it like that?!! It is nothing of the sort.

Certainly, Mr. Kiritaka devotes his heart and mind to his job whenever there's work to be done, but he always tells me that he wants me to be happy doing whatever I like outside!!"

"So you *do* get thrown out a lot."

Kiritaka had his own unique issues, but this was his way of keeping things in order. It made sense—if Liliana was at his workplace, there was no way anyone could hold a proper conversation.

And if she had to spend her day somewhere, then holding recitals was a fine use of her time, but—

"—Since earlier, you have been staring intently at me, have you not? 'Tis most rude."

Liliana puffed out her nonexistent breasts, which was a lot like stroking a nonexistent beard. Beside her, Priscilla crossed her arms to proudly display her ample bosom, snorting toward Subaru with visible scorn.

"Though it is only natural to be enthralled at the sight of my dance, it is unbearable to have such an obscene gaze turned toward me. Even if my charm does make others lose their way, the likes of you are only permitted to appreciate it from a distance."

"Just so you know, I didn't watch you dance, and I don't have any fetishes like that. I prefer pure and lovely girls like Emilia-tan. Girls as over-the-top as you actually make me less excited."

"What a pitiful man to pick that thin half-demon over me. However, I am not so narrow-minded as to disallow bad taste. If you know not what true beauty is, it cannot be forced upon you. But someday, I shall pry open that narrow-minded world with my own two hands."

Their values clashed, but Priscilla's philosophy robbed Subaru of all willpower to shoot a response back. Priscilla considered it a matter of fact that she was the center of the universe; Subaru's idea of common sense held no meaning whatsoever.

"But that means Priscilla was dancing, right? I *really* didn't expect that."

"You should curse your fate for allowing you to miss it. I do not dance, save when the mood strikes me. And that is rarely the case. This artist's song was simply that alluring."

"For real? So you're a Liliana fan, too…?"

Subaru acknowledged that Liliana's singing was incredible, but not nearly to the extent that everyone else seemed to. As far as Subaru could tell, every girl who heard Liliana sing became her ally. She had a perfect record.

Honestly, if she could woo even Priscilla, her status was pretty much unassailable.

"But to have Lady Priscilla and Lady Emilia both come here, candidates for the royal selection that's the glimmering issue of the day, Liliana is grateful and even moved to tears!!"

Even with the uneasy atmosphere that came with two rival candidates meeting, Liliana's powerful ability to set her own pace was undaunted.

Of course, even she understood that relations between Emilia and Priscilla were delicate at best. The profound silliness of her statement was no doubt intentional.

"Mwa-ha-ha-ha, so my songs are that incredible? Oh wooow, I'm gonna blush!"

"On second thought, maybe she's just being herself."

Liliana's bashful reaction gave Subaru renewed doubts. He concluded with a shrug that he had simply been overthinking things. After that, Subaru abruptly noticed that Priscilla was alone, lacking even a single escort.

"You're by yourself? Not with Al or the shitty bastard or your cute butler?"

"Schult gets lost whenever he walks out the door. He is earnest and adorable to console, but that is all, really. Having Al at my side means putting up with his annoying little comments, so I left him behind. As for the shitty bastard, I would not know."

"So you also call him that, huh…?"

Subaru was surprised by her unexpectedly blunt replies. He was similarly surprised at just how poorly she treated Heinkel even after taking him as a follower.

Granted, he obviously deserved such treatment, but why bring him into the fold, then?

"No doubt that's also 'cause it amuses you."

"Reasons are such trifling things. To begin with, he came to me with an offer, and I accepted, nothing more. I shall use him for my entertainment while I can, but if he ceases to have value, I shall discard him instantly. That is the extent of how much I care."

"Nah, I wonder about that... If you didn't care about him, you wouldn't have beaten him down like that, would you?"

For that matter, had Al not intervened, she might well have sliced him apart then and there and walked away. Subaru figured Reinhard would've probably intervened and stopped her short of that, though.

"Come to think of it, you've broken my jaw with a kick once before, huh..."

At one point during the loop at the capital a year before, Subaru had once been kicked by Priscilla when he'd procured her ire. His memory of being in a near-death state from a single one of her kicks came flooding back.

Thinking of that, he could accept the overwhelming combat strength she'd displayed back at the hall.

"Isn't it dangerous for you to ditch Al and the rest of your crew like that?"

"And what, pray tell, would suddenly become a threat simply because my three retainers are absent? About the only advantage of their presence is to have eyes to see directly behind me."

"So your dancing with Liliana here was just coincidence?"

Emilia's question made Priscilla fold her arms with an audible snort.

"Unlike the dull streets of the capital, this city's sights are salve for my tedium. I was enjoying the flow of the water when this artist's song reached my ears."

"I mean, wow, yeah, I didn't know what to expect when she suddenly came in and started dancing. Usually, I give people who get too worked up a good smacking with my song, and most of the time, they settle back down right away...!"

"You really don't act like a songstress at all..."

Driving interlopers back with your song was way too rock and roll.

Besides, the only word he had for Priscilla suddenly breaking into dance was *shocking*. Considering how rapt the audience was, it must have been quite the performance.

"To gather the hearts of so many people and leave me behind is self-centered to the extreme. However, such is the appeal of your music. How about it? Would you care to serve as a singing girl at my side?"

"Oh, thank you, thank you so very much!! I am honored and very, very proud that you praise me so! But! But! I must respectfully decline!"

Priscilla's invitation showed she had taken a liking to Liliana's singing even more than Subaru had first assumed. Liliana responded with a smiling face and a refusal with virtually no hesitation.

Instantly, the park was enveloped by an aura that pricked Subaru's skin. His body tensed up on its own.

Liliana had made a frighteningly, spectacularly momentous decision in a flash. She understood nothing about Priscilla's character or the instant and even cruel threat Priscilla could pose. She was totally oblivious.

"Oh, you refuse me? Why do you refuse my invitation?"

Like clockwork, the tone of Priscilla's voice dropped an octave as she responded, her crimson eyes running cold.

Even Subaru, who wasn't the target of her ire, felt like a blade had been pressed to his throat.

In that situation, where a single word could cost her life, Liliana stroked her musical instrument with her hand.

"I am Liliana the minstrel. Though I have stopped in this city for a time, I am destined to wander again before long, traveling wherever the wind carries me. It is an occupation and way of life of not being bound to any one land or one person."

"And so you decline my invitation."

"It was the same for my mother, my mother's mother, and their mothers before that. It is our family's way. We leave nothing behind, save for our songs in people's hearts. Just as one cannot fence in the wind, no one can keep us in one place. Your invitation makes me happy, but I must decline. Even I do not know where my songs shall echo. I leave that up to the wind."

Raising her musical instrument high, Liliana spoke the words proudly, not a single reservation upon her face.

Her usual demeanor—the way she made fun of everything and consistently got on people's nerves—was nowhere to be seen.

There was only the simple pride of the creature known as a minstrel—those who passed down tales through song.

"———"

After listening to Liliana's answer, Priscilla kept her arms folded and one eye closed. Then her remaining eye shot straight through Liliana, her gaze redder than an incandescent flame.

When even this failed to make Liliana falter, Priscilla abruptly let out her breath.

"—Very well. Your resolve is commendable. Forgive me; 'tis I who was rude."

"Not at aaaall. I'm really sorry I couldn't accept."

Priscilla's remark made Liliana proudly thrust her chest out as if it was the obvious thing to do.

Subaru could only be amazed. He never thought Priscilla would actually accept someone else defying her will.

"What is it, filthy peasant? What is the reason for this distasteful face you are showing me?"

"Hey, there's nothing on my face except surprise. I was scared because I thought for sure you'd slice Liliana in half for refusing your invitation..."

"A ridiculous concern."

Priscilla spat out her reply with a snort, but was it true?

Until she heard Liliana's reply, Subaru had no doubt whatsoever that Priscilla's bloodlust was balanced on a knife's edge. Wasn't Liliana spared only because it didn't happen to tilt in the wrong direction?

"But I'm a little surprised by Priscilla, too. I thought she was the sort of person who would do anything to get something she wanted."

It was then that Emilia spectacularly stepped upon the land mine Subaru had painstakingly tiptoed around.

Emilia's blunt impression made Priscilla sigh with displeasure.

"Lowly half-demon, would you cease your prattling? Just what do you know about me when you see with such clouded eyes? Rudeness and insult can be forgiven only so much."

"This girl is an expert at being all talk. If she has enough spare time to criticize and lecture others for their outward appearance, would she not be better served spending it reflecting on her own words and deeds, I wonder?"

"Beatrice..."

When Priscilla's merciless words brought a conflicted look over Emilia's face, Beatrice squeezed her hand. When she shot back at Priscilla in Emilia's stead, Priscilla looked like she'd noticed the girl for the first time.

"Such brave words for a little girl. I shall have you know my tolerance is not dependent on age. Do not beguile yourself with the notion that I will turn a blind eye to your rudeness because of your youth."

"Your advice is unnecessary. Do you even realize, I wonder? Little girl, Betty may be cute, but do not think that is all there is to see."

Instantly, sparks of hostility flew between Beatrice and Priscilla.

Both were wearing dresses, but their compatibility couldn't be worse. Of course, Subaru was on Beatrice's side, but just the fact that she was picking a fight with a royal-selection candidate made this problematic.

"Beatrice, it's okay. I'm all right."

"Why try to stop me, I wonder? Surely, we cannot simply let her slights pass in silence."

Fearful of the problem growing larger, Emilia tried to rein in Beatrice, but the spirit refused to budge. After hearing her comment, a realization dawned on Emilia. The same went for Subaru.

Beatrice wasn't angry because Priscilla's attitude or insults had bothered her personally. She was angry because Priscilla had belittled Emilia.

Emilia was deeply moved by this. Of course, Subaru was, too.

"Beatrice, it's fine. I mean it. I'm *really* grateful, though."

Emilia used the hand Beatrice wasn't holding to stroke her on the head. The action made Beatrice momentarily gaze at Subaru and Emilia alone, a tearful look in her eyes.

But this was for only a single moment. Immediately after, Beatrice glared at Priscilla with renewed heat.

"I will do as Emilia wishes, I suppose. You should be grateful."

"Surely, you speak for yourself. Count your adorable appearance among your blessings."

With ragged breaths, Beatrice got a hold of her temper; Priscilla responded in kind by suppressing her ghastly aura.

Subaru almost felt like the last line was just pure praise for Beatrice's looks. The gist was, *You're cute, so I'll let it go this time*, which was fine and well with him. Priscilla's thinking remained a mystery.

"You really are a woman I can't understand one bit..."

"But of course. I do as I please more than any other. It is a gross conceit to even attempt to understand me."

"So now it's my fault...? In the first place, this all started because you wanted Liliana for yourself."

In the end, it was unclear just what had made Priscilla allow Liliana to slip from her grasp.

Seemingly gleaning the question from the doubts on Subaru's face, Priscilla hid her own lips behind her fan.

"Everything in this world is mine. Therefore, I need not personally own everything that is beautiful, proud, and valuable in order to appreciate it. It is sometimes best to leave them as they are. That is all."

"______"

"If this entire world becomes my garden, where little chirping birds sing matters not. It would not only be crude but quite unpleasant to place every one of them in birdcages to protect them from all outside dangers."

This was the first time Subaru had ever heard Priscilla break her aesthetics down into a digestible form.

The sheer scale of her inaccessible, overwhelmingly aloof rationale left Subaru at a loss for words.

It wasn't that he failed to understand the meaning or the logic. She simply perceived things on a fundamentally different level.

Subaru thought that this difference, or perhaps the very scale of it all, was terrifying. But at the same time, those feelings of terror were accompanied by the awe that came from gazing up at an overpowering being.

He wasn't sure, but maybe that was why Al stood by Priscilla.

"Now, now, now! With everyone having calmed down a notch, how about I present to you a song in honor of our friendship?! But noooo! Not one song, but maybe two or even three!"

With swift pulls of the strings of her lyulyre, Liliana made an abrupt proposal.

"This time, Lady Priscilla should simply enjoy herself without being concerned about dancing!! And, Lady Emilia, it looked like earlier you arrived just as the song was ending!! This time, we shall joyously celebrate our reunion, and you shall see for yourself how Liliana's unique singing voice lets her make off like a bandit in this city!"

"My word."

"Wow, really?"

"The result isn't elegant at all, but you are satisfied with this?"

Setting Liliana's assertion aside, the fact remained that her song was currently the key to a peaceful resolution.

At present, Emilia and Priscilla stood side by side with an odd sense of distance between them as they prepared to listen to Liliana's performance. It was in that situation that Liliana beckoned Subaru over with her hand. Then when Subaru approached, she whispered in a low voice.

"Could it be that Lady Emilia and Lady Priscilla don't get along too well?"

"Are you kidding? It should be kinda obvious based on their positions. Incidentally, there's pretty much no such thing as a person who gets along well with Priscilla, and she treats Emilia-tan like *that*."

"My oh my, this is quite a serious matter!!"

Liliana gazed up at the heavens, the tails of her hair furiously bouncing, much like a dog warily wagging its tail. Maybe they were connected to her nerves or something. He had a sudden urge to grab them, pull them, and twirl them all around.

"But, but! Here, I shall do everything in my power to seduce them both with the power of music! Ah, just now, you thought of something dirty because I said *seduce*, didn't you? You can't do that—it's indeeecent!"

"I'm beat, so could you not make me feel admiration and disdain from the same damn line?"

Even as he sighed, Subaru admired how Liliana could show such consideration amid her fits of madness.

Her goal of sweeping away the bad atmosphere with a song was something he could appreciate. As a matter of fact, it irked him a little that Liliana's voice made such a thing actually possible.

"After the song, we'll have a pleasant chat, so could you prepare some snacks, Master Natsuki? Do you not think that sweets will make everyone happy and bring us all closer together?"

"Not particularly."

"After the song, we'll have a pleasant chat, so could you prepare some snacks, Master Natsuki? Do you not think that sweets will help make everyone happy and bring us all closer together?"

"What is this? Are you an NPC who just repeats your lines until someone picks *yes*?"

When Liliana stubbornly asked the exact same question without a single change in tension, tone, or even word choice, Subaru gave in and selected *yes*. Liliana's face brightened, but surprisingly, her proposal was not a terrible one.

If the atmosphere improved, maybe they could have a proper conversation with Liliana and Priscilla.

"So while Liliana's singing, I'll head off to buy some drinks. Emilia-tan, stay here, behave, and don't get into any fights while I'm gone."

"Well, I don't want to have an argument with Priscilla, either. Don't worry—it'll be fine."

Subaru reminded her to be careful just to be on the safe side, and Emilia responded with a buoyant smile. Of course, even if Emilia wasn't looking for a fight, there was no denying the possibility that Priscilla might offer one regardless.

"Beako, take care of Emilia-tan if anything happens."

"I understand, I suppose. Next time that whelp says something out of line, I shall reduce her to ash."

"Don't pick a fight with her, either, okay?"

After entrusting Emilia to Beatrice, who was possibly a much greater cause for concern, Subaru got ready to leave the park for the time being. But before he did—

"Priscilla, any foods you can't eat?"

"How unexpected that even an unremarkable man such as you understands how to be considerate. Very well. If you must present me with something, you should prepare something appropriate. Present me something boring, and I shall slice off the hand with which you offered it and place it upon your head."

"It's not like I lost at rock-paper-scissors to be the errand boy, so you've got no right to take it that far!"

Subaru decided then and there that if anyone was selling a delicacy advertised as only for the bold, that's what he'd give her.

For her part, Priscilla knit her refined eyebrows at Subaru's response.

"Rock-paper…scissors?"

She tilted her head while murmuring in confusion.

If she'd forgotten about Subaru, maybe she'd forgotten about rock-paper-scissors, too. In many ways, she was a very hard woman to get along with.

"Subaru, be careful."

"If something happens, would you immediately call Betty, I wonder?"

After Emilia and Beatrice saw him off, Subaru waved and rushed out of the park.

When he tried to wink at Liliana, he was thwarted because she had closed both eyes.

"Oh..."

A little after that, right when he was reaching the entrance to the park, he heard the melody of the lyulyre echoing behind him.

With that sound at his back, Subaru quickened his steps as he headed toward the shopping district.

3

—And some ten minutes later after Subaru left the park...

"Man, I'm just a chicken. Really, I am."

As he exited the store, Subaru glanced at the products inside the bag, and his shoulders sagged.

After setting off in the name of procuring sweets, Subaru had found some appropriate stores and finished his shopping in short order. Along the way, his interest had been temporarily drawn by "gina jelly," a strange Pristella specialty, but he hadn't summoned the courage to buy it for Priscilla.

It sounded better to say he was fearful of worsening relations between the camps, but he'd simply chickened out.

"But it looked kind of like eel jelly... I'm not brave enough to taste test this one, but I liked that stuff."

Berating himself for his complex personal biases, Subaru jogged until he reached the street that led back to the park.

Fortunately, in the ten or so minutes he'd been away, Beatrice hadn't warned him about something going awry in the park. They were probably in the middle of the recital without any problems.

Even though he understood that, he instinctively wanted to return as soon as possible. But—

"Oops, my bad."

—after rounding a sharp corner a little too fast, he nearly bumped into someone as soon as he entered a public square. After narrowly evading the passerby, Subaru immediately apologized as the other party raised a cry of "aah?" with a foul-sounding voice. "Hey, pal. Is that how ya apologize? You better put more sincerity into... Geh!"

The man with the crude demeanor was in the middle of picking a fight when he noticed Subaru and froze. Simultaneously, Subaru was shocked to realize he recognized this man.

"Huh, it's Larry? You still act like a street thug even though you work for Felt now?"

"Oh, shaddap! And my name ain't Larry! The hell are you doin' here?!"

The one letting spittle fly as he complained was Lachins, who'd played the hoodlum role just the day before. According to Felt, he'd been assigned errands and was off on independent action within the city.

"Curly and Moe aren't with you? Kinda rare to see you on your own like this."

"How the hell would you know what's rare for me? We ain't known each other enough for this to feel like anythin'. Shoo, scram."

"Hey, don't be so cold. Aren't we buddies who've gone through life and death together?"

"I don't remember anythin' like that!"

Lachins shot him a disgusted look when Subaru got too chummy.

Even Subaru wasn't very sure why he had a soft spot for the guy. It was probably because Subaru's Everyman Sensor picked up that Larry, Curly, and Moe were fellow commoners. In this world, Subaru had met so many incredible people that seeing ordinary people like them once in a while came as a relief.

Though he'd been killed by them once, his fondness for them had actually grown since.

"Anyway! Don't get close to me! I'm doin' work right now!"

"For you to have work after being unemployed for so long… I'm so happy for you!!"

"Get lost!!"

As Subaru acted tearful, Lachins clicked his tongue and brushed him off, vanishing into the crowds. Subaru reflected on the fact that the cold reaction was a great relief to him for some reason.

Lately, he'd been greeted with receptions befitting his title practically everywhere he went. He was worried that he'd let it go to his head if he didn't get a reality check like this once in a while.

Of course, he belatedly realized he really had been a nuisance to Lachins, so he decided to apologize the next time he had the chance.

"Mm?"

Then, with Lachins having vanished into the throng, Subaru turned around and began to walk when he came to a halt.

—No, it wasn't just Subaru who'd stopped. Within his field of view, a great many people within the square had come to a halt as well.

"What the—? If it ain't one thing, it's another! The hell y'all lookin' at?!"

Speaking those words, Lachins pushed his way out from the frozen mass of pedestrians. Just like he had complained, everyone had stopped to stare up at a tall building overhead.

—This was a spire standing at the back of the square, extremely prominent even in such a large city.

A magic crystal clock was embedded into the upper portion of the building; it was a time tower that functioned much like a clock tower.

These towers were common in large towns and cities, and several of them were scattered around Pristella. This time tower was simply one among many.

But then that changed.

"—To all those whose conversations and busy schedules I've interrupted, I offer my apologies."

At the upper portion of the time tower, a lone figure emerged from an open window to stand precariously on the edge.

As all eyes gathered on the stranger standing before them in such a bizarre manner, the voice addressing the crowd trembled, seemingly overcome with emotion at being the center of attention.

"Please lend me but a tiny instant of your time. Thank you."

The tone of the voice that opened with an apology and a word of thanks was particular to those who were more concerned with their appearance than genuinely showing gratitude. Everyone listening was assailed by an uncomfortable sensation, as if that voice itself mercilessly clawed at their hearts.

These disturbing feelings were doubtlessly amplified by the speaker's bizarre outward appearance.

This person's head was covered in raggedly wrapped bandages that left one eye visible, gleaming mysteriously as it surveyed the world below.

For clothes, they had a black robe with long, misshapen gold-colored chains wrapped around both slender hands, ending in hooks. These were dragging across the floor as the speaker came forward one purposeful footstep at a time, hastily heading to the top of the tower.

Glancing at the audience, unable to peel their eyes from the bizarre sight, the speaker smiled—at least, the gloomy contortion of their mouth, which was hidden by bandages, made Subaru think that was a smile.

"Thank you, and sorry. I am the Archbishop of the Seven Deadly Sins, charged with Wrath—"

Voicing that terrifying preamble aloud, the eccentric offered an introduction.

"—My name is Sirius Romanée-Conti."

4

In contrast to the other Archbishops, the tone of Sirius's voice was chummy, outgoing, and even cheerful.

This strange announcement delivered by someone wrapped in bandages left everyone looking up at the tower and unable to speak.

Perhaps it was partly due to the speaker's surreal appearance, but the greater factor was almost certainly the crowd's inability to process what they just heard.

Of course, these were nothing more than secondary reasons. There was a reason more fundamental than any other.

—How could anyone take their eyes off something that threatened their very lives?

"Eh, wha—?"

"What did they say just now?"

"You're kidding, right? The Witch Cult, here..."

The realization and chaos that had been delayed by the initial turmoil began to gradually spread through the mass of people.

But not a single person there instantly adopted the best countermeasures available. Everyone listening to the contents of the message doubted their ears, and the only thing rippling through the crowd was confusion.

"Hey, what did that bastard say just now?! Did you hear that?!"

And the same went for Lachins, who noticed Subaru and came running.

Lachins kept one eye on what was happening overhead as he wove through the crowd toward Subaru, who also couldn't take his eyes off the eccentric, despite standing apart from the rest of the audience.

For some reason, he could tell that letting his attention lapse would be an irrevocable mistake. There was no need to doubt the individual's identity.

—*That* was the exact same malice Petelgeuse had.

"Plus, *Romanée-Conti*...?"

The surname the bandaged eccentric had invoked—*Romanée-Conti*, just like Petelgeuse.

Of course, as Petelgeuse had been an evil spirit, a blood relative sharing the same name was highly unlikely, but—

"Don't tell me all the Archbishops of the Seven Deadly Sins use the same family name..."

The existence of a famous Romanée-Conti family within the Witch Cult churning out Archbishops one generation after the next was a concept so twisted that even the thought of it was enough to make Subaru crinkle his nose.

Without such trivial thoughts running through his head, Subaru would have already blown his lid.

An Archbishop of the Seven Deadly Sins was right there. It wasn't the Gluttony he was pursuing, but there was an Archbishop *right there.*

"—Gotta nab 'em and make 'em spill the beans."

He'd blaze a trail to Gluttony one way or another.

With that decided, Subaru calmed his blazing heart. Simultaneously, he focused on the link with Beatrice within his chest. By calling out to her, Subaru could convey that something was wrong. This was the firm bond that tied a contractor to his contracted spirit.

In the innermost depths of his body, he'd grasp it, pulling it toward him all at once—

"—That's quite enough!"

"—?!"

But his attempt to call Beatrice was terminated, abruptly blown away by a dry, rupturing sound.

This was the sound of the bandaged eccentric clapping their hands together. Subaru's breath caught from the noise, which was so loud that it seemed to reach every corner of the city and rocked the square itself.

Then, looking down upon the multitude frozen with shock, the eccentric's exposed, lolling eye wandered around.

"It took twenty-two seconds before everyone fell silent. But I thank you for quieting down. I am sorry. I am also very happy. And..."

Speaking sarcasm along with their thanks, the eccentric—Sirius—kept both hands together as their body swayed. Sirius really did seem to be enjoying the show, but the crude-looking chains hanging from both hands continued to undermine that impression. The discordant sound of the hooks scraping against the tower's platform and the chains rubbing against the walls really grated on the ears.

"You and you over there, and you two sirs over there also, I am sorry. Do not be so cross. I offer you my heartfelt apology for taking up your valuable time. Sorry, and thank you."

"Is…!"

Sirius squirmed all around while doing their best to convey sincerity.

The only reason Subaru did not instantly shout, *Is this a joke?!* and go deliver a beatdown was precisely because he was included among those Sirius had pointed to that moment, urging them to *not be so cross.*

Subaru noticed the three others whom Sirius had pointed at—a beast man with a sword on his hip, a woman with an eye patch, and Lachins—had all gone pale. They were probably the only ones present with any fight in them.

This was without doubt a warning: Any sign of hostility, and Sirius would nail them to the floor first.

Feeling sweat beading on his brow, Subaru cursed the stalemate he had fallen into.

Allowing the Witch Cultist to take the initiative was a terrible misstep. Including Subaru, some thirty people were in the square, trapped in Sirius's field of vision—hardly a trivial number.

One false move, and there would be instant carnage.

Everyone indicated by Sirius's finger understood this, blocking them from making a move. From the expression on his bitter face, Lachins was the only one hesitant in his decision.

Lachins probably had a wild card to play—specifically *calling Reinhard over.*

If he could do so in time, there was no one who could best Reinhard. It was a certainty that he'd settle matters with a single blow—however, the sacrifices incurred in the time it took him to arrive could never be undone.

If Lachins didn't care about casualties, he could have Sirius taken care of…hence his inner turmoil.

"Yes, thank you. It would seem that everyone has calmed down a little. I understand that you are uneasy. The ring of the words *Witch Cult* never fails to leave a poor impression. That is why even I will not ask you to disregard this. I merely wished to have all of you give me this time today because there is something I sorely wish to confirm."

"And what's that…?"

"I am sorry; please do not be noisy. I am not very smart, so if everyone talks at once, I won't know what to do. And then I'll be quite sad. That's not good, is it? But if something's wrong, please let me know. I'll do my best to answer for everyone's sake."

Sirius's insistence on maintaining a pretense of friendliness and that somewhat logical manner of speaking only made the situation all the more unsettling.

Most people also found Sirius's fashion sense, which involved covering everything but their left eye and lips with bandages, predictably disturbing. And if wariness about this was keeping everyone from making a move—

"Can I take you at your word and ask a question?"

When it felt like no one wanted to take the initiative and single themselves out, Subaru Natsuki raised a hand anyway.

Even as he sensed a wave of surprise spreading around him, Subaru did not avert his eyes from Sirius, who was still standing overhead. Looking down upon Subaru, Sirius opened their purple eye wide.

"Yes! You over there, please do. Thank you. To think you were so angry before, yet now you are willing to speak with me. What a happy occasion. Ask me anything."

"I'm not sure what you want, but I have some girls waiting for me, and four of them at that. I'd like to settle this as quickly as possible and get back to them."

"My! That is terrible; I am so sorry. Surely, we are troubling these girls and causing them sadness or maybe even anguish. That is wrong so very wrong impermissible unforgivable."

"Um, excuse me?"

As they spoke, the cheer in Sirius's voice faded, their gaze began to grow ominous, and they gasped in surprise when Subaru's bewildered voice called out.

"Oh no, oh no, I was about to get emotional. I am so sorry. I really try to watch out, but I get easily excited. Thank you for your concern."

"...Nah, that's fine. I'm just grateful that we can have a nice and calm conversation."

"I am sorry you need be so considerate. Thank you. But it's all right. I am famous for being one of the doves of the Witch Cult. I am quite sorry that the others are problematic children to some extent."

Something shocking dawned on Subaru as he continued having a surprisingly coherent conversation with Sirius.

The unexpectedly gentle demeanor, the insistence on keeping the conversation going, and the sheer impact of the initial encounter had shoved this fact aside, but Sirius, the mystery person standing above on the tower, was a woman.

Judging from the way the incredibly white fabric wrapped around her head and how it poked out from the standard Cult-issue black robe, her entire body was probably covered in bandages. Even so, Subaru had noticed telltale bulges on the chest of her tall, slender body. That combined with her manner of speech convinced him that Sirius was female.

"———"

Setting aside the issue of gender, Sirius's words and actions conveyed no sense of an immediate threat for the time being.

At first, Subaru had been extremely wary, but after conversing with Sirius for a bit, he realized that she came off as more of a true human being than Priscilla did. The initial tension in everyone's expressions fell away, leaving most people more interested in Sirius's true intentions rather than worry and fear.

In spite of the hatred he supposedly harbored toward the Archbishops of the Seven Deadly Sins, Subaru was no exception.

"Thank you; I am so sorry. Truly, I had not intended to surprise everyone. But I am pleased from my heart that we have overcome this and you are now lending me your ears."

"It's not like we've accepted or forgiven you, but we'll at least hear you out first."

"I suppose that will do. Well then, I shall get to the point about the reason why I have appeared before you like this."

As she swayed her body and rubbed the chains on both of her hands together, the high-pitched sound tore at the air around them.

Now that he took a good look, her appearance was more comical than creepy. If he thought of her as some sort of clown or entertainer, he had to wonder if she was really that far removed from someone like Liliana.

Subaru's expression softened, and the guarded walls he'd raised around his heart slowly crumbled away.

There didn't seem to be a need to call over Beatrice anymore. He'd hear Sirius out and then ask her to depart quietly.

—Peaceful and proper, not making any waves whatsoever. Wasn't that a good thing?

"So what did you wanna ask?"

"Yeah, yeah, hurry up and ask already!"

"That's right, that's right. If ya don't hurry up, I'll be late for work."

When Subaru prodded her to go ahead, the people around him raised their voices, almost jeering at her.

The last man pointed at the magic time crystal over Sirius's head, an act that was enough to provoke uproarious laughter. The wave of laughter made Subaru unwittingly relax his lips.

The amicable atmosphere brought a blushy smile over Sirius as she pressed her hands to her cheeks like she wasn't sure what to do.

"Sorry, so sorry. I really am sorry. I know you all must be in a hurry. I will soon be finished, so please bear with me a little while longer."

"I told ya, hurry it up already—!"

"Yes! Well then, I shall do just that. Er, you see, there is something I wish to confirm. To come out and say it…it concerns *love*. Ohhh, I am so embarrassed."

Thanks to the bandages, he couldn't see the color of her face, but Sirius was covering it with her palms to conceal her own bashfulness. The gesture made Subaru break into spontaneous laughter. There were grins all around him as the gradually warming atmosphere infected others, making Sirius tremble in even greater embarrassment.

"I—I expected everyone to laugh, but even so, I can't seem to look you in the face. But thank you for listening. Thank you, and also, I have a request."

"A request?"

"I am so sorry. Could I ask you to put up with me while I try to confirm *love*?"

Fidgeting, Sirius rubbed the chains from both hands together as she made that request.

The pathetic sight elicited a collective *that's all?* from the audience. As a matter of fact, Subaru had no particular objection, either. His heart warmed by the sight, he politely nodded.

When he did, Sirius brightened, her eye twinkling as she clapped her hands together.

"Really?! Thank you, thank you, and also sorry. The world truly is kind. It is kind and filled with love. I am grateful I can savor the feeling like this. We are capable of permitting and yielding to one another. That is why I say not only *thank you* but *I am sorry*."

"We get it already! Sirius, what are you gonna do now?"

"Ahhh, so sorry!"

Sirius looked deeply moved when the swordswoman with the eye patch over one eye jeered at her. The voice was casual, as if she was speaking to a friend she'd known for a decade or a classmate at a girls' school, which seemed to help Sirius relax.

As if finally remembering something, Sirius walked to the time tower window from which she had emerged, reaching her arms inside the structure.

And then—

"I am so sorry to have kept you waiting. Come on—right this way."

"——!!"

Calling out with a gentle voice, Sirius pulled something from beyond the window.

Thrashing in Sirius's arms was a tiny, moaning figure—a boy still early in years, his entire body firmly bound.

The child, ten years old give or take, was wrapped in chains from his ankles to his shoulders; there were blood droplets where a chain had bit into his mouth. He was desperately moving what he could above his neck, tears coursing in some kind of muffled plea.

"I am so sorry this is so confining. But you are a boy, so you must not cry. I wished to keep that a secret between us, but you are drenched. Now everyone will know your shame."

"Nn—! Nnn!!"

"Yeah—! It's embarrassin'—!!"

"You're a boy! Don't cry, don't cry!!"

"There's only three times in a man's life that he can cry, ha-ha-ha!"

Warm voices called out to the tearful boy as the audience joined Sirius in trying to console him.

Overcoming the urge to be scared and cry from small frights was something everyone had to go through. There was no malice involved, but a number of the comments were rather lacking in delicacy.

"Yes, yes, everyone, please do not say such things. Certainly, he is cowering a little at the moment, but this is a very brave child. Isn't that so, young Lusbel?"

With his entire body bound by chains, the kid had to weigh a fair bit, but Sirius easily carried him with one arm. Gently stroking the boy's chestnut-colored hair, she turned him toward the crowd while praising his courage.

Lusbel—the boy squirming with all his might in his effort to escape from Sirius's hand. The contrast looked humorous and laughable, just begging for someone to laugh at how pathetic he seemed.

"Yes! Now then, may I have everyone's attention? This is the young Lusbel Callard. He is a native of Pristella. He is still only nine years old. My, such fine future prospects."

"Nn——! Nnn——!!!"

"His father is Muslan Callard. He is an observer for the city waterways. His mother, Ina Callard, is currently pregnant and showing at this very moment. Will Lusbel be blessed with a younger brother or a younger sister…? Quite a happy thought regardless of which is born. Young Lusbel has a childhood friend, a cute blonde with curly hair named Tina, who he gets along with very nicely. Since the pair care deeply about each other and seem to have an ideal relationship, I spent a considerable amount of time mulling over which one I should bring here. At first, I thought I'd bring Tina, but Lusbel asked me so earnestly, it struck a chord deep within me… Therefore, I yielded to young Lusbel's enthusiasm and had him cooperate with me. He is a very brave child. You all understand that now, don't you?"

For an instant, the tale of Lusbel's courage was greeted by pure silence.

But a moment later, riotous applause thundered in the square. The audience extolled Lusbel's courage, regretting the way they had laughed at his tears, for he was a true hero.

—No, that wasn't it. It was not the time to feel remorse for their thoughtlessness. It was time to praise courage.

"Lusbel, don't cry! You're the best!"

That was why Subaru raised his voice, celebrating the heroism of the tearful boy.

"That's right, don't you be cryin'! We know ya got stones, so hang in there till the end, kid!"

Beside Subaru, Lachins had tears in the corners of his eyes as he raised a crass cheer for the boy.

"That's right, you go, Lusbel! You're the pride of Pristella!"

"Lusbel! You're marvelous! I'm sure you'll become a fine man!"

As one, the audience filled the square with cheers, applause, and acclaim for their hero Lusbel.

This beautiful scene of human virtue had been made possible by the courage and dedication of a single boy. No matter how unseemly he might have looked, it was genuine courage that gave birth to true light.

"Ahhh, ahhh...thank you, thank you, thank you! Ahhh, this is so wonderful! You all understand. I believed that you would trust in young Lusbel's courage! After all, his way is the way of *love*! I thought that by knowing him, you would come to love him as well! The more you understand him, the deeper you know him—your thoughts become one, and that is *love*!"

"Thank you, Sirius! Thank you!"

Sirius hoisted Lusbel aloft with both hands, the bandages on her face drenched with tears. Seeing this, Subaru couldn't hold back the hot tears he hadn't even noticed until moments ago.

He felt a poke on his shoulder. Beside him, Lachins pointed at Subaru and laughed at his free-flowing tears. As he did so, tears trickled down his cheeks as well, and before long, everyone in the square was overcome by the same emotion.

That moment, everyone's hearts had truly become one. They were linked by an undeniable bond.

"We rifts are born because we do not know one another. Conflict arises because we do not understand one another. And when we give up because we are different from one another, bonds cannot be wrought. Everyone, how are your hearts now?"

"It's not like that at all! None of us is giving up! Our hearts are one!"

"Thank you! Thank you! Then I take it that everyone is happy right now?"

"Damn right we are! It's the first time I've felt like this! Thank you, Sirius! Lusbel!"

With sounds of admiration and applause trained toward him, Lusbel sobbed at the highest point of the time tower. Finally, heedless of the gashes at the corners of his mouth, the boy bled as he desperately raised his voice.

"Gu, gii! Aurr!! S-svv...sv—ve...mhhh...!"

"Young Lusbel, they extol your courage; they extol love! Look down. So many people admire you. Ahhh, thank you! I am so sorry, young Lusbel. This may not be what you intended. But now I know. The world is indeed a kind place!"

Embracing Lusbel, whom she held aloft, Sirius turned her head toward the heavens as she continued in a loud voice.

"Yes, there truly is *love* in this world. Everyone's hearts have become one. Their feelings of happiness are the same. No one needs tragedy. A world where people must cry is nothing but a nuisance. The greatest emotions come when people's hearts are joined together! No one needs tragedy! No one needs Wrath!"

"That's right! No one needs tragedy!"

"Ahhh, abominable Wrath that makes my heart tremble so! Anger—in other words, rage! If this is indeed one of the Seven Deadly Sins that afflicts human hearts, if it is fate that it can never truly be cut away, then one should fill the heart with tremendous joy until there is no room left! Just like how it fills everyone's hearts this very moment!"

Letting spittle fly, Sirius shared what she had learned about *love* from on high as if it were the judgment of the heavens themselves.

Then from her upraised arms, she hurled the courage that had received envy from one and all into the sky.

"May I have your applause?!"

Sirius hurled Lusbel into the sky on the greatest stage imaginable.

Watching the boy fly toward the sun, everyone clapped. Subaru brought his hands together over and over again as hard as he could.

Uproarious applause rang out, blessing Lusbel as he soared into the sky.

The tiny body spun in midair, finally reaching the zenith of the throw, then proceeding to plunge straight toward the ground. He was inverted, falling toward the stone-paved square headfirst.

The audience cleared his impending point of impact—applauded endlessly all the while, awaiting his triumphal return.

"Nnnn———!!"

Lifting his head, Lusbel glared at the approaching ground and screamed.

Though his strength should have been exhausted, he thrashed wildly, desperately struggling until the very, very end. Sensing they had caught a glimpse of a human being truly worthy of praise, the audience was moved to tears.

And then—

"—Ahhh, what a kind world!!"

—just before the impact, Sirius shouted.

Hearing that voice, the audience's applause became one, growing louder and louder as the echoes boomed.

—Then there was a sound of something hard and fragile breaking, like an egg falling onto the floor. Everyone's vision was filled with red.

Falling headfirst onto the hard surface, the entire body crumpled, and that which had once been Lusbel transformed into a pile of crimson flesh. Fat globules of blood scattered across the square in all directions as the hero spectacularly flew apart.

And then right after witnessing this—

"—Bhhh."

—like applause that refused to end, the sound of countless eggs smashing reverberated across the square.

The ground was drowned in a crimson pool of blood.

That was how it ended.

5

"After the song, we'll have a pleasant chat, so could you prepare some snacks, Master Natsuki? Do you not think that sweets will make everyone happy and bring us all closer together?"

Just after he thought he'd blinked, he saw an olive-skinned girl shoot him a clumsy wink.

"———"

As he watched the girl sticking her tongue out in a playful pose, Subaru Natsuki forgot to breathe.

When he shifted his unsteady gaze, he saw a silver-haired girl with a soft, charming smile beside him, and also standing there was a redheaded girl, arms crossed with an arrogant look on her face.

Then he noticed the presence of a little girl in a dress gently holding his hand—

"Errr, is something amiss? Ignoring? Are you ignoring me? P-please cut that out; it's very depressing… Aah, cut—cut that out… D-don't sigh after listening to my song… Don't make such a sad face; forgive meee…!"

As Subaru fell into complete silence, the girl before his eyes—Liliana—was trembling awkwardly as if she was undergoing some kind of trauma.

Subaru set his eyes upon her, and his stiff lips trembled.

"…I feel sick."

"Wha—?! H-how can this be?! How can you look at a girl's face and say something so cruel?! Liliana has never been humiliated like this before!! My goodness, on behalf of Master Natsuki's mother, I am completely embarrassed for you!! Compwetewy!! Embawwassed!!"

As Liliana faked anguished tears, her mouth bled from the impressive way she had bitten her tongue. It was a ridiculous and transparently comical sight, but Subaru couldn't bring himself to laugh even if he wanted to.

His head was heavy. His vision was flickering. Unable to stand, he sank to his knees then and there.

"Subaru?! What's wrong?"

"Wait a— What happened, I wonder?! Subaru, Subaru?"

Beatrice, who was holding his hand, and Emilia beside them peered at Subaru's face as he hugged the floor.

Then with a face so pale that the two unwittingly gasped, Subaru—

"—I feel sick."

Even more than the death loop a year prior, he was at a loss for how to process his death. His knees continued trembling as nausea welled up.

"I feel sick."

The shock was almost impossible to endure. He felt revolted by the corruption that made his insides roil. His mind and body were buffeted by raging waves of loss. Subaru Natsuki was overwhelmed by a disgust that outweighed even the horror of death.

In his memory of the moment just prior to his death, the past felt like the blink of an eye to him. He remembered how the corruption of his soul had blotted out his mind and left him unable to recognize the abnormal for what it was. And then he recalled the mysterious behavior of that disciple of abomination—

—Archbishop of Wrath, Sirius Romanée-Conti.

Without any doubt, the being was one of the Archbishops of the Seven Deadly Sins, kin to Sloth and Greed and Gluttony. They were all envoys of vice and destruction, embodiments of nightmares that by rights should not exist.

The feeling of losing himself, of ceasing to be himself only to eventually return, was a first even for him.

"I feel sick."

The horrifying experience made him shudder. Feeling a chill coming on, Subaru trembled uncontrollably.

Like an old friend celebrating their reunion, death had clawed Subaru Natsuki to pieces.

What's more, Subaru hadn't even realized it yet.

He was only tens of minutes before the scene of his death, from which he had just returned.

The time limit was approaching again, at which point he would have to rise, clench his teeth, and fight.

A maelstrom of death enveloped Subaru Natsuki once more.

And so it began. In fact, it had already begun.

—The loop to overcome the worst day in his life was set here in the Water Gate City of Pristella.

<END>

AFTERWORD

Who was it?! Who said after the last one-page afterword that there'd be no more of those?! That would be me!

So this is Tappei Nagatsuki aka Mouse-Colored Cat. Heya, this feels a bit like old times now.

Anyway, about that afterword business, it's just what it looks like! Previously, I shrank them down for the majority of Arc 4 as I reflected on the page-number issues, but sadly, I could not find a shred of repentance within me. If possible, go take a look at the afterword for Volume 15. In my defense, I did use the word *maybe*!

In any case, *Re:ZERO* has finally reached Volume 16. What a weighty number of volumes. With Arc 4 concluded, a year has passed for our cast, giving the characters a chance to spend a little time together as the curtain rises on Arc 5.

I believe that you understand this from having already read the book, but yes, this time, we have a huge ensemble of major characters! With the city of water Pristella as the stage, this will be where the tales of their amazing exploits are born. Whether they were royal-selection candidates or Witch Cultists, most were on the bench during Arc 4, so please enjoy watching these characters come roaring back as major developments unfold. It'll be the death of Subaru!

Also, as an author, I am relieved that the passing of a year within the story gave me another opportunity to depict some peaceful, quiet moments for Subaru and company. (The only other chance until now came between Arcs 2 and 3.) I had plenty of those moments that I wanted to detail, so I hope you enjoy them all!

And so the time to depart has come once again. Allow me to dive into the customary thanks!

To Editor I, the end of the arduous battles of Arc 4 offered a brief moment of relief, but the mountain of issues continues on here in Arc 5! Let's work hard on this together! Thank you very much!

To Otsuka, the illustrator, no matter how you slice it, the cover illustration has such amazing impact! I know you are all aware of this, but Otsuka really is incredible! Thank you very much!

To Kusano, the designer, the sheer power of the front cover's makeup shows the strength of your designing! To be honest, the fight the illustrations and design put up every time is quickly becoming a running theme! Thank you very much!

And to Matsuse, who dived into the climax of the comic version of Arc 3, and to Fugetsu, who went with me to eat fried banana for that author close-up, I'll be in your care for a while longer!

Besides that, to everyone at MF Bunko J publishing department, all the reviewers, the staff at every bookstore, the businesspeople, and many others, I'm indebted to every one of you! Truly, as always, thank you all so very much!

Also, this was announced on the bellyband around this volume, but a *Re:ZERO* OVA has finally been announced, so I'm forever indebted to all the anime staff, too! Please take good care of me!

Finally, to all you readers who keep cheering me on, thank you very much for sticking with me into the new arc!

So I hope to see you again next volume! Later!

March 2018
<<It heated up so suddenly, I'm not sure whether to take off the thermal wear>>

Clind & Annerose
They appeared in an illustration in Volume 15, too! See if you can spot them!
Short eyebrows, bottom lashes
Close-cut
Overview of Pristella
The View from the Front Gate
Water
Central Partition
Water
Tower
Central Park
Tower
Tower
Main Gate
Tower
Cross Section

"Everyone, it has taken time beyond counting for you to arrive at this point. But thank you for reading this far, and…sorry."

"Ahhh, ahhh, ahhhh…the unshakable dedication to the story! The approach to reading! How truly, truly, truuuly…diligent, yes!"

"This is the preview…a place for relevant information pertaining to the coming volume, is it not? My, what would I have done if I'd gotten that wrong? How embarrassing."

"It is *fine*—let us do it. I cannot help but respond to your diligence with some of my own! To do otherwise would be Sloth! Slothslothsloth!!"

"L-let's get started. The first announcement concerns the following volume… Oh my? It seems that Volume 17 is not the next to go on sale."

"Scheduled for July is *The Love Ballad of the Sword Devil*! It is the tale of Wilhelm, the diligent and valiant swordsman who featured prominently in Volume 16, and his wife in their younger years! *Love*, it simply overflows with love!"

"Unlike *The Love Song of the Sword Devil*, which was previously on sale, *The Love Ballad of the Sword Devil* concerns how two people who overcame many obstacles to be together spend their marriage thereafter…but my, my my my! What is this? Such passionate love for each other… Flames are almost leaping from my face!"

"And that is not all! There is information concerning the new episode for the *Re:ZERO* anime! It has been determined that this will be displayed in theaters, ensuring that it is revealed to a great many eyes gazing upon the silver screen! My brain is *shaking*!"

"The new OVA episode has been slated for theatrical release, and it will go by the title *Re:ZERO -Starting Life in Another World- Memory Snow*… I am not very fond of snow. After all, when your body goes cold, it freezes your very heart. To keep that from happening, you need to fan the flames of your heart and keep them hot-hot-hot!"

"Snow! That is *wonderful*! Nature's fury is wonderful! It calls into question a person's diligence! No matter how cold the snow that falls and piles high, people *always* crave the spring hidden within! The heart that leads to action in search of that is diligence! Ahhh, ahhh, ahhhh! These are works of *love*!"

"For staying with us until now, thank you, and sorry again. But the developments in *Re:ZERO* won't stop for some time to come, so we'll be together for a while…won't we?"

"Now, let us be off! Let us go on without end! To march without halting is a demonstration of *love* with the body! It is the bestowal of *love*! It is the *only* method of making amends!"

"Yes! Truly, truly… That is correct, Petelgeuse…"

"You've gone away again, Petelgeuse… *Sigh*. I wasn't able to speak to you this time, either, *sniffle*."